MAGGIE ALABASTER
JO BRADLEY

Saving Abbie

1–3

Cover by Atra Luna Designs

Edited by Lily Luchesi

Proofread by Nora Hogan

PITCH

SAVING ABBIE BOOK 1

Nothing Under My Feet
    Written by Abbie Hart

The ground is broken,
    the air is shattered,
    my world is nothing but an echo.
    You stole my heart and ripped it out.
    Now there's nothing under my feet.

I'm falling hard,
    you're not there to catch me.
    You watched me tumble to my knees,
    you broke me down,
    you tore my last breath.

Now there's nothing under my feet.
    Nothing to stop me.
    Nowhere to hide.
    Nothing under my feet.

I landed hard,
    but I got up.
    I won't let you take my everything away.
    I'll walk away from you,
    stronger than before.
    I have everything under my feet.

CHAPTER
ONE

ABBIE

"HEY. You look like you could use some company." He slipped into the chair beside me before I could respond.

I turned my face to tell him to fuck off, but the words died unsaid on my lips.

He was hot as hell.

I mean the kind of hot that makes a woman melt immediately and leave a puddle on the chair.

And he knew it.

I didn't need my arrogant fuckboi radar to tell me one when I saw him. Unfortunately for me, I had a type.

Fortunately for him, he was it. Guys who were in for a couple of hours of fun before disappearing like a ghost.

Perfect. Life was too fucking short and unpredictable for commitment. Call me a cynic or a realist, I don't give a shit.

I swivelled around on my stool and rested my elbow on the table. It was too dark in this corner of the club to see the colour of his eyes, but I saw the lust in them.

I'd be blind not to.

"Hey, you might be right." I sipped my vodka and lemonade and toasted him with the glass. "What brings you to a shithole like this?"

He leaned in and smiled, flashing perfect white teeth. "You, of course. I've been looking all night for you."

"Really?" He was so full of shit, but I kinda liked it. I cocked my head at him and pouted playfully. "You haven't been looking all your life?"

Two could play the bullshit game.

He snapped his fingers. "Shit, you're right. I have. And now I've found you."

"So you have," I drawled. "What are you going to do with me?"

He pursed his lips speculatively. "That depends. What do you *want* me to do with you?"

We could start with 'everything' and go from there, but that wasn't very specific.

My heart raced like a motherfucking freight train and my panties were definitely wet. At this point, I didn't care what he did with me, as long as he did *something*.

"Hmmm." I licked my lips slowly and watched him watch my tongue slide across my mouth. "You look like you know what to do with your hands."

He had big hands with long, firm fingers. No rings but plenty of tattoos. He had a full sleeve on one arm and almost as many on the other. I bet there were plenty more under his tight-fitting black T-shirt. Even in the dim light, I could tell he was ripped. His biceps fought to escape the fabric.

I bet his body was harder than concrete. Harder than stone.

Not just his body either, there was something hard about his face, his eyes, like he knew how to handle himself.

He smiled and one eyebrow quirked upward slightly.

"As it happens, I do," he said slowly. He didn't even look to check if anyone was watching before he slipped a hand up my skirt.

It was too dark for anyone to see much anyway, but I had enough vodka that I didn't care if they did.

He slid his hand up my leg to the gusset of my panties. There, he started to trace slow circles around the lacy black fabric.

My hand tightened on the glass. A jolt of heat went all the way through me, from my head to my curling toes.

He peeled the gusset aside and grazed his fingers across the front of my pussy.

Oh. My. God.

Without thinking, I adjusted my position on the stool to spread my thighs wider, giving him more access to my suddenly ravenous pussy.

He smiled and circled my clit with his fingertips a few times before he slid a finger inside me, deep enough to make me hungrier still.

I bit back a moan. The music in the club was loud, but not so loud I could scream and not be heard.

"Holy shit, you're so wet." He shifted his own position, twisting his hips closer to me before slipping another finger inside me. Then another. He curled his fingers to caress my g-spot, while the heel of his hand rubbed over my clit.

He was better than good with his hands. He fed my needs with practiced skill that left me panting with ragged breaths.

I half opened my eyes and glanced around, but no one was looking our way. No one would see me tip my head back, or roll my hips as I drew closer to the edge.

I bit my lip and panted through my nose, suppressing the moan that slipped out of my mouth as I came.

I bucked harder against his hand, milking the sensation for every delicious, orgasmic drop. Stars exploded across my vision. Blood raced through my ears, louder than the music which thudded through speakers in the ceiling.

Heat thundered through me for at least a minute, maybe two, before I finally came down in a quivering, whimpering puddle.

"Fuck," I said, too softly to be heard. Judging by the grin on his face, he read my lips well enough.

He slid his fingers out of me and stuck them in his mouth.

"Tasty." He grinned around his fingers and sucked them for a moment longer.

Shit, that was hot.

"You're incredible with your hands." I should probably not feed what was clearly a healthy ego already, but I had to give credit where it was due.

"You look like you're good with your mouth." He gave me another speculative look.

The suggestion might have pissed another woman off, but I smiled. He was right about that; I was.

I fixed my panties and skirt and slid down into the perfect darkness under the table.

He said something that might have been, "Holy fuck," as I unfastened the front of his jeans.

I pushed them down enough to let his thick erection spring free. I slid my hand up and down his blazing hot length, from his head to his balls, making him harder still.

Slowly, teasingly, I ran the tip of my tongue over the tip of his cock. I savoured the taste of his precum before I took the rest of him in my mouth.

He reached down to tangle his hand in my blond hair, holding me in place while I sucked hard.

I massaged his balls with my fingers until he was quivering. His hips moved, thrusting him deeper into my mouth. I took as much of him as I could.

Not wanting to hurry, I slipped my mouth off him and ran my tongue up and down his length and around his head.

His fingers tightened on my hair, almost to the point of pain. I wouldn't have minded if he hurt me a little, but I wasn't in a position to communicate that right now.

I slipped my mouth back over him and sucked harder and faster. He bucked, driving himself deeper and deeper into my throat. I grazed my nails lightly over his balls, marvelling at the heat of his skin.

He stilled and a shudder went through him.

Hot cum squirted from his tip, into my throat. I slid my mouth off his cock and swirled his juices around like it was fine wine. Instead of spitting, I slid over so the dim light could hit my face. I looked directly at him and swallowed.

I read his lips this time when he said, "Holy fuck."

He let go of my hair and helped me out from under the table, and back into my stool.

"You aren't what I expected when I walked up to you." He kept my hand in his.

"Oh? Would you have walked up to me if you knew how it would go?" I cocked my head at him.

He grinned. "I wouldn't have waited an hour to talk to you. I would have approached you the moment I laid eyes on you."

Sure he waited that long. He didn't strike me as the shy type. I resisted the urge to roll my eyes. A little bit of flattery, even if it was bullshit, was good for my ego. Honestly, I could use the boost.

"You should have. I was sitting here all by myself." Watching and waiting for someone like him to come up or catch my eye. I hadn't seen him before he sat down beside me. He probably just walked in the door. Whatever, we had fun and weren't going to see each other after tonight. A few white lies and harmless flirtation wouldn't hurt.

"A woman like you wouldn't have sat here by herself for too long," he said smoothly. "It's a miracle someone didn't beat me to it. It must be my lucky day."

"Not just lucky," I said. "I don't let any old guy stick his hand up my skirt."

I liked sex, and lots of it, but I had *some* standards.

"Of course you don't," he said like he actually knew me. "I'm surprised a girl like you would even talk to a guy like me."

I rolled my eyes playfully. As if he didn't know exactly how hot he was. He probably had women panting after him wherever he went. If there were any surprises to be had here, it's that he was talking to me, not surrounded by a crowd of horny girls, all prettier and slimmer than me.

"Like I said, I was sitting here alone." A smile tugged at the corners of my mouth.

He laughed. "Ouch." He stroked his thumb over the back of my hand. "Do you live near here?"

"I'm staying in a hotel close by." I didn't elaborate. I doubted he'd be interested that I was in Sydney for work. We didn't even have the kind of relationship that ran to sharing names, much less details like that.

"Do you want me to walk you back there?" he asked. "It's not safe for a woman by herself around here."

I tilted my chin up. "I can take care of myself, but sure. I could use the company."

I wasn't naïve. I knew he was hoping for round two. So was I. And round three after that. He looked like he had enough stamina to spare. I certainly did.

"Great. Have you finished your drink?" He nodded towards the glass on the table.

I looked at it sideways and grimaced. The ice melted. The vodka and lemonade would taste like water. Still, because I didn't like waste, I picked it up and threw the rest of it back.

"Now I have." I placed the glass back on the table and slid off my stool.

"You're wild." He held out his hand. "I like that in a woman."

"That's me." I took his hand and let him curl his fingers around mine as we walked to the door.

A couple of guys sitting at a table near ours glanced at us as we walked past. They grinned. Apparently what we did hadn't gone unnoticed after all.

I grinned back and gave them both an air kiss. I should try to be more discreet next time in case I was recognised. Whatever. Let them talk.

Could it damage my reputation any more than it already was? It was pretty fucking tarnished.

Yeah, there was still room to make it worse.

We slipped out into the steamy air of a Sydney summer night. Or was it morning by now?

"It's just down that way." I gestured. The nicer hotels were in the opposite direction. Right now, I couldn't afford to stay there. The cheap fleabag place I was in was enough of a stretch. With any luck, my meeting tomorrow would change all of that.

It had to, I was ready to be back on top.

He didn't look like he was judging me. He could get stuffed if he was. I would have let go of his hand and walked by myself. I liked his company, but I didn't need his approval.

"What's your—"

Whatever he was about to say, was interrupted by a man stepping out of a side alley.

He was dressed from head to toe in black, from his ripped jeans to the hoodie that obscured most of his face.

I took in all of that before I noticed one hand deep in the pocket in the front of his hoodie.

Shit.

He pulled out his hand, and with it, a dark-coloured pistol. The kind you see in the movies, usually in the hands of secret agents or bad guys.

Slowly, he raised the gun.

I knew nothing about guns, except the end the bullets came out of was pointed at us.

My bet was, he wasn't a secret agent.

Fuck.

I froze.

CHAPTER TWO

ABBIE

"LONG TIME NO SEE, ZEKE," the gunman said.

What the fuck.

Zeke grabbed my arm and shoved me behind him.

"Accosting innocent people on the street now, Jonah?" Zeke asked lightly. "That's a new low even for you."

I eyed the hand that held the gun. He looked like he knew how to use it. The fact he knew Zeke was no consolation whatsoever. What the crap had he dragged me into? Was this some kind of set up? I was going to be pissed if it was. If it wasn't, how could Zeke sound so calm? I was about ready to pee my panties.

Jonah shrugged one shoulder. His hand didn't even waver. "Just doing what the boss wants me to do. He has a message for you."

Zeke's grip tightened on my arm. "Save it. I don't want to hear Reuben's bullshit."

Jonah aimed the gun at Zeke's head. "Nevertheless, I'm going to say what I was sent here to say."

"There's no message you can give me that I haven't heard a million times before." It sounded like Zeke's patience was running out.

Honestly, it wasn't *his* patience I was worried about, it was the guy holding the motherfucking firearm. I had no reason to assume it wasn't locked and loaded.

"Maybe you should listen," I suggested. "I'll do whatever it takes for us all to walk away from this." Just when I thought life couldn't get any worse, it did. This was all kinds of messed up. I should have stayed in my shitty hotel room and watched reruns of some old sitcom on the tiny TV. Not even an orgasm and a blow job were worth dying for.

"You should listen to the chick," Jonah said. "Shut your mouth and open your ears for once."

Zeke bristled visibly, but fell silent. He oozed anger.

Silently, I begged him to contain it before bullets started to fly.

"The boss said your time is running out," Jonah said. "Your time and his patience. He's waited long enough while you played around. He wants you back with the family."

The breath caught in my throat. Boss? Family? What the hell was this guy into? Trust me to be attracted to someone dangerous. One of these days I would make better life choices but evidently today was not that day.

I really needed to start thinking with my brain and not my pussy.

"I'm not going back." Zeke's face was a stone wall, cold and expressionless.

"I should go and leave you two to it." I stepped back, but Zeke still held my arm.

"I could make an example out of her," Jonah said. He swivelled his upper body until the gun was aimed at my head.

The barrel looked approximately fucking huge. A bullet coming out of that would spread my brains for metres.

Holy shit, let me get out of this intact.

I tugged my arm free of Zeke and held both of my hands up. My heart raced so fast I thought it might stop dead. I've been scared before, who hasn't? But never like this.

"This has nothing to do with me," I protested. "I don't even know this guy." Just because I had his cock down my throat twenty minutes ago didn't mean I was going to die for him.

Jonah's eyes weren't on me, they were on Zeke. Apparently he didn't care if I knew him or not. This was all about trying to get Zeke to comply.

"Leave her out of it," Zeke snapped. Apparently he wasn't in a complying mood. "You've delivered your message, now fuck off. Tell Reuben I'll think about it."

"He's not gonna be satisfied with that." Jonah cocked the gun and stepped closer to me.

Shit, just when things were starting to look up, I was going to die on the street, a bullet through my skull.

Fucking wonderful. The tabloids were going to love every minute of this. I could see the headlines now.

I shook my head and took a step back. "Please—"

Sweat sprang up under my arms. Was this where I was supposed to see my life flash in front of me? All I saw was a bunch of misplaced trust and bad choices, coupled with being screwed over time and time again.

"This doesn't need to—"

Zeke threw himself at Jonah. He grabbed the arm he held the gun in and forced it down towards the ground. The gun fired, slamming a bullet towards the concrete.

I squealed and instinctively jumped back. The bullet hit hard, bounced to about the height of my knee, then clattered on the ground.

Zeke and Jonah wrestled for the gun. Just like Jonah obviously knew how to handle one, Zeke clearly knew how to fight to take one from someone else. He kept Jonah's arm at an angle where a bullet wouldn't hit his foot if it discharged again.

Unfortunately Jonah wasn't going to let the gun be taken from him that easily. In terms of size and sheer muscle, they were equally matched.

I should take the opportunity to run away. It would have been the smart thing to do. On the other hand, I had a long list of dumb choices behind me. What was another one?

Even if it might get me killed.

For some reason, I couldn't walk away and let Jonah kill Zeke. For all I knew, he'd come after me to take care of any witnesses. For self preservation alone, I had good reason to do what I did.

I stepped closer and waited for the right opportunity. Zeke jerked Jonah's arm to the side and I took my chance. I twisted my body to the side and jammed the heel of my stiletto into the top of Jonah's foot.

He shouted with rage. Zeke took the chance to grab the gun and turn it on him.

I started to exhale with relief, but almost choked on the breath.

I wasn't expecting to see the grin on Zeke's face. It was dark and cold, in spite of the upturn of his mouth. It sent shivers and jolts of heat right through me, in equal measure.

I should absolutely not find anything about this hot. What did that say about me that I did? Yeah okay, I already knew I was fucked up. This level of fucked up was slightly surprising though. Oh well, it was never too late to learn these things about yourself.

"Now whose time is running out?" Zeke asked. He actually sounded amicable for someone who was threatening another man. Even reasonable.

"I know he would have killed me." My voice shook. "But no one needs to die here. Do they?"

Jonah stood with his hands raised. He looked more pissed off than scared. "No one needs to die. But Ezequiel isn't going to kill me. Are you Zeke?"

"I'm fucking tempted," Zeke said. "Right now I'm struggling to think of a good reason why I shouldn't."

"Because murder is a bad idea," I said. Why did I get the impression neither of them thought so and both committed it in the past?

Abbie, I told myself, *you really need to learn to judge people better.*

What started out as a bit of fun had ended up a complete fucking mess. I should have told Zeke to get lost when he sat down next to me.

My still-damp panties said otherwise. I was apparently more depraved than I gave myself credit for.

"You'll also make a mess," I pointed out. "Blood and brains and all that stuff..." I took a few steps away from them. I could slip out of my stilettos and run. I was almost certain Zeke wouldn't kill a witness.

Right?

Oh God, I was so screwed.

Silence fell for a full minute before Zeke said, "Get the hell out of here, Jonah. Give Reuben my message. I'm not coming back, no matter what he does. I'm done with the family. I don't know how to make that any clearer."

"The boss is going to be pissed," Jonah said. He shrugged, turned and disappeared back into the shadows.

Zeke exhaled loudly. "Shit." He took the clip out of the gun and shoved it into his pocket. A look of distaste on his face, he held the gun by the trigger guard, as though he suddenly found it repugnant.

"I would bet anything this was used in a violent crime in a city the same time I was there. It would be easy enough to find—" He shook his head. "I'll get rid of it."

Did I even want to know how he knew how to get rid of a gun? Okay, I kind of did. At the same time, I knew better than to ask. Whatever was going on here, I was in it deep enough already. I should get the hell out before I drowned.

"Does this sort of shit happen to you often?" I asked. Did I want to know the answer to that too? Well fuck, the words are already out of my mouth anyway.

He laughed bitterly. "More times than I'd like. Reuben is stubborn and persistent."

"Is he your boss?" I asked.

"Not my boss," he said. "It's a long story. You're better off not knowing about it. I'm sorry you got dragged into this. If I knew it was gonna happen, I would have taken you the long way round."

"You still would have approached me in the club?" I asked. "Even knowing doing that might have gotten me killed?"

He tucked the gun away somewhere under his shirt and grinned. "Hell yeah I would. I don't regret a minute of that."

His expression faltered. "I was going to offer you another round, but I need to get rid of this thing and get you somewhere safe. I can't guarantee Jonah and Reuben don't have something else up their sleeves. Like I said, Reuben is persistent."

"I'm starting to dislike this Reuben guy," I said dryly. People who didn't take no for an answer were the worst, especially if they sent gunmen after people.

Zeke laughed. "He's not the most likeable guy on the planet." He reclaimed my hand and we resumed walking towards my hotel.

"Is that why you got away from him?" I asked.

"It's one reason amongst many," he agreed. "I prefer to live my life in a very different way to what he would like."

"Is Reuben your father?" I guessed.

Zeke snorted. "Hell no. He likes to think he is. He's a pain in my ass, but I'll deal with him."

"You seem like you know how to handle yourself." I stopped outside the front of the crappy hotel I was staying in. It was almost too embarrassing to be seen there, but I felt safer with him than if I ditched him a block back.

He smiled and placed his hand on the wall behind my left shoulder. "Seems like I know how to handle you pretty well too." He leaned in for a soft but lingering kiss.

"You didn't hear me complaining." For a start, the music was too loud anyway. But no, I enjoyed every second of it. If it wasn't for that asshole and his gun, I could be enjoying a few more hours of it. Instead, all I really wanted to do was get into my room and hide under the covers. Yeah, I know, blankets are no protection from bullets. Let me have my moment.

"Me either." He gave me a soft smile. "I'm sorry our night got cut short. Next time, I'll be more prepared."

We both knew there wasn't going to be a next time. Still, it was nice to hear that if there was, I might not be accosted at the end of a gun.

I knew there was a reason I hated guns. They were really good for ruining my sex life. That seemed like a good enough reason to dislike them to me. That and the whole, 'I could be dead right now,' thing. All in all, it wasn't a positive experience.

"Thank you for an interesting time," I said.

"Interesting?" He mused. "I always strive to be interesting, but I don't think this was exactly what you had in mind. It was certainly not a part of my plans."

I shrugged as though I hadn't been absolutely terrified only a few minutes earlier.

"Whatever keeps the adrenaline pumping."

"I can think of a lot of things better than that." He brushed his lips over mine again, then stepped away. "I should hurry up. It won't be long before Jonah calls the cops and I don't want to be found with a gun on me. That involves way too many questions I don't have all the answers for."

I suspected he had all the answers, he didn't want to give them. Before I could say that, he melted away into the night.

I was left alone outside the front of the fleabag hotel, under the light of a single, flickering bulb.

CHAPTER
THREE

ZEKE

I STRETCHED my legs out in front of me, leaned back and laced my hands behind my head.

No doubt I looked every bit the arrogant rock star everyone in the room expected of me.

It was a role I was happy to embrace. Would anyone expect anything less from the lead singer of Wolf Venom, the hottest band on the whole fucking planet?

"I'm sure you're wondering why I asked you to come here." Jackson Beckett crossed his arms over his chest and scanned the room. Our band's manager, he was good at throwing his weight around. We even listened to him. Sometimes.

"We might be curious," Asher DiMarco said with a shrug and indifferent smirk. The blonde drummer was at least as arrogant as me. And had as much baggage in his background.

As far as I knew, his brother never sent anyone after him with a gun, but there was a first time for everything.

I glanced past him to where Landon and Channing sat so close they were almost in each other's laps. The bass player and the band's saxophonist were inseparable.

To my knowledge, they'd never been with a woman unless they shared her with each other. They were a package deal, which seemed to work for plenty of groupies. When groupies weren't around, they could barely keep their hands off each other.

If you asked me, they were pretty fucking cute.

Much cuter than Penn, the keyboardist, who sat on the other side of them, his face a typical scowl.

Across his knuckles, the words *Fuck Life* were tattooed in black ink. That was basically his motto and approach to everything.

"You could have texted," Penn growled.

The side of Jackson's mouth twitched in annoyance, but he didn't rise to the bait Penn threw out. Not exactly.

"What I have to say needs to be done face-to-face," Jackson said coolly. "With the new album about to drop and the impending tour, the label has decided to make some changes."

"What changes?" Asher asked carefully. He eyed Jackson suspiciously.

"And by label, do you mean Levi?" I asked. He owned White Wolf Records. While other people worked under him, sometimes he liked to make sudden tweaks. And by sudden I meant heavy-handed. Whatever was going on here, it smelled of Levi Jones.

Jackson ignored my question and responded to Asher. "We'll be adding someone else to the tour."

"We already have a support act." Penn's scowl deepened. "Blazing Violet." He seemed to loathe them as much as he loathed everyone else, including himself. Okay, especially himself.

"She wouldn't be supporting you," Jackson said carefully. "More like a co-headline."

"What the fuck?" Penn set up in his chair. "No way. We don't share the stage."

I dropped my hands and sat up too. "Wait a minute. Am I being replaced?"

This went from smelling of Levi to smelling of Reuben. Getting rid of that gun was hard enough. Luckily I knew a guy, a contact from back when I worked for my brother. He owed me a couple of favours. Even then, he wasn't happy about it, but he did it anyway.

By now, the serial number and anything that might connect it to me or Reuben, or anyone else, was gone. Somebody would probably get away with murder because of it, but I had no choice.

"If Zeke is out, then I'm out," Tully said. The lead guitarist was a man of few words, but when he spoke, people listened. Particularly when he was making sense like he was right now.

Jackson raised his hands in a placating gesture. "No one is being replaced. The label signed a new singer and her reputation could use some work. Things got a little messy with her former label."

I picked up a bottle of water from the floor beside my chair and unscrewed the top.

"And by messy you mean—?"

I took a sip as the door opened and she walked inside.

I almost choked on my mouthful of water.

I recognised that blond hair, that beautiful face, her incredible figure, and of course that mouth. I almost still felt it wrapped tight around my cock. And the way her muscles contracted around my fingers when they were deep inside her. Not to mention the fact it was a public place and she didn't seem shy at all.

The memory alone was enough to make my cock strain against my jeans.

Down boy. That didn't stop my dick from throbbing.

I coughed to clear my throat and put the lid back on the bottle.

"Yeah, she's pretty fucking messy," Penn snarled.

"I see Mr Pennington is already acquainted with Abbie," Jackson said dryly.

Her eyes—they were brilliant blue—scanned the room. They opened a little wider when she saw me. His skin paled slightly.

Yeah, she might not be the only one whose face was a bit whiter.

"I'm not acquainted," Penn said. "Her last label dropped her. Why the fuck is she here?"

That was a good question. I couldn't seem to tear my eyes off her to look back at Jackson for the answer.

"Like I said," Jackson said slowly, "Abbie has signed with the label and we have work to do to rebuild her reputation."

Penn snorted. "I'll fucking say."

"I'm sorry, I must be missing something." Asher looked around at everyone, obviously confused.

Abbie slipped into a chair, chin tilted up but still clearly uncomfortable. She glanced at me.

I offered her a smile. She gave me half a one in return.

Jackson sighed. "Things were said unfairly…" He gestured towards Abbie. "Perhaps you would like to explain."

She looked like she would like to do anything *but* explain, but she sighed.

"As Jackson said, the press has been damaging to my reputation. To the point where Onyx Riot Records decided they needed to distance themselves from me."

"She was fucking the boss," Penn said. "The *married* boss."

Every eye in the room was on her. She squirmed with discomfort.

"I had a relationship with him while he and his wife weren't together. I was led to believe they were getting a divorce." She sucked in a breath. "When they reconciled, she wanted me out. And so, I was out." She looked pissed as fuck about that.

Fair enough, I would be pissed too if someone was using me like that. And then I got the blame.

"Then there was the twenty-four hour marriage," Penn said relentlessly. "Was that a publicity stunt?"

She glanced down to the floor before she looked back up again. "It was twenty-six hours. For the first two, I thought it was real."

A heavy silence followed her words.

Penn snorted. He clearly didn't believe a word of it.

Me, I wasn't sure what to believe. She seemed to live life unapologetically and that was being held against her. If that was the case, then it was bullshit.

"How come you know so much about her?" Landon asked.

"Penn likes to read about himself in the tabloids," Channing said. "He finds out about other people that way too."

Penn stuck his finger up at him, a letter F tattooed at the base of his finger. He was all class.

"As you can see," Jackson spoke loud enough to draw the attention back to him. "Abbie Hart is signed to White Wolf Records now. As you know, we take pride in taking care of our own." He ignored Penn's snort.

"So Abbie will be touring with Wolf Venom. She'll be singing between Blazing Violet and you guys. And singing a couple of songs with you." His gaze swivelled towards me.

Aware everyone was now looking at me, I shrugged one shoulder. "Sounds good to me. The more the merrier."

She looked grateful, although she must have known as well as I did we had little choice in the matter. I could have fought it and let it get ugly, but I didn't see the point. It wouldn't hurt us to share the stage with her and have her along for the ride.

If she wanted to continue what we started last night, I was more than okay with that.

Not the part where we had a gun pointed at us, but the part where I got to come down her throat. And where she looked up at me and swallowed my cum like it was ice cream.

My pulse thundered at the thought.

"This is all kinds of fucked up," Penn growled. "We don't need a woman screwing up our act."

"Your objection is noted—" Jackson started to say.

Abbie sat up in her chair, interrupting him, her hands on her hips. She glared at Penn. "What is your problem? Did I do something to you?"

He rolled his eyes at her and looked away.

"That's just Penn," I said. "He's got a chip on his shoulder the size of Sydney Harbour. He's all right when you get to know him."

"I am not," Penn said without looking back.

I shrugged at Abbie and smiled. "The rest of us are more or less harmless."

She looked sceptical, and I was almost certain she was going to bring up Jonah, but she didn't. She had no way of knowing how much the other guys knew. I appreciated her attempt at discretion.

"Are you sure about that?" Asher grinned. "I'm not sure if the word harmless describes any of us accurately."

"That's why I said more or less." I nodded my head in his direction. "She can decide for herself where we stand on the spectrum. I suspect she's going to get to know us pretty fucking well over the next few months."

Personally, I wanted to get to know her a *lot* more intimately.

Penn scowled at her like she was something he scraped off his shoe, but the rest of the guys never turned down an opportunity for a fuck. Truthfully, Penn never turned down the opportunity either, but he seemed to have taken a violent dislike to Abbie. That was his problem, not hers, and certainly not mine. Since he pretty much hated everyone, it was normal for him anyway.

"I expect you to keep an eye on her," Jackson said. "The publicity is going to be brutal, but if anyone is up to it, you guys are."

"Hell yeah we are," I agreed.

"Are we bodyguards now?" Tully asked. I couldn't tell what he thought about the arrangement. He usually just rolled with whatever happened. "I don't think there's anything in our contracts about saving Abbie from the press."

"Like I said, we look after our own," Jackson said.

"Is she fucking Levi?" Penn had looked back around and was now glaring at Abbie. "Is that what this is about?"

It was a fair question, I supposed. Levi Jones was not known for keeping his cock in his pants any more than I was. Any more than any of us was.

"No," Abbie said firmly. "We've met a few times but that was it. Believe it or not, I got my contract based on *merit*." She matched Penn's look, fury for fury until her words sank in.

"Fuck off," Penn snarled. "We're all here because we're talented and worked bloody hard."

"Right," Jackson said loudly. "You're *all* here because you're talented. Abbie and Wolf Venom. If you fight like this in public, the press is going to have a field day. Don't. Give them. A fucking. Field day. I'm sure none of you wants to be dropped."

"No we don't," I said quickly. "They'll learn to get along." I gave Penn a meaningful look. He didn't need to make this harder than it was.

He shrugged and looked away.

I sighed to myself. I had a feeling getting along was going to be easier said than done.

On the other hand, the way she stuck up for herself made my cock even harder. I would have to try to find a way to get her alone.

CHAPTER FOUR

ZEKE

"THIS IS BULLSHIT." Penn shoved open the door to the rehearsal room so hard it banged against the wall and bounced. He pushed it back and stepped inside ahead of me.

"Yeah, tell us what you really think," I said sarcastically. "There's no point bitching about it. It is what it is."

He gave me a look that suggested he'd barely even started bitching and stalked over to the coffee machine at the back of the room.

The Australian arm of White Wolf Records took pretty good care of us. They gave us the rehearsal space in the same building as the recording studio in Sydney. Everything was state of the art, of course. Levi spared no expense where we were concerned.

It wasn't exclusively ours, in theory, but we were here more than most of the other acts.

The coffee machine was an added bonus. We asked for a fully stocked beer fridge too, but they declined for some reason. Something to do with not getting drunk on the job.

Spoilsports.

"He'll get over it." Asher gave me a playful shove further into the room.

I grinned and shoved him back.

"Now, now, children." Tully spoke in a squeaky joking voice. "If you keep doing that, someone's going to get hurt."

Asher and I exchanged a glance before we both zeroed in on the guitarist with a series of air punches.

He put up his hands in mock self-defence and laughed. "You guys are idiots."

"We love you too." Asher stopped to sniff the air before heading down to the back of the room. "Hell yeah, coffee."

"Coffee, our real true love." I grabbed myself a mug and started to spoon instant granules into it.

"Speak for yourself," Landon said from the couch under the window. He was lying across the couch, his head in Channing's lap. Channing brushed strands of blue hair lightly off Landon's face.

Penn glanced over his shoulder at me. "Everyone is your true love," he said scathingly. "Until you zip your pants back up. I'm guessing that's behind your support of Abbie. You're hoping to get her into bed. Then what?"

I poured hot water into my mug and ignored his correct accusation. "I support not making waves when making them won't help anyone."

I put down the electric kettle and picked up the bottle of milk. "Don't tell me you didn't notice how cute she was." I gave him the side eye. There was no way he'd missed that. He was as big a fuckboi as the rest of us.

I didn't bother to explain that Abbie and I were already acquainted. That would raise questions I didn't feel like answering. At some point, if it came up, I'd deal with it, but I wasn't going to volunteer the information just yet.

"Cute is irrelevant," Penn said. "If she sucks, she's going to make us all look bad." He scowled at me like having her along was somehow my fault.

"She's not gonna suck." Asher sipped his coffee. "The label wouldn't have signed her if she was. And they wouldn't send her on tour with us either. Right, Zeke?"

"Exactly," I agreed.

Asher was wrong about one thing, she *did* suck. And she was very good at it. Thinking about her mouth made my balls hurt. Having her around might be harder than I thought.

Literally. Whatever, I'd deal with that too.

"You know," I said slowly, "I'm going to have to spend more time rehearsing with her than the rest of you will. If she and I are going to sing duets, then we're going to have to do it. A lot."

That didn't sound like the worst thing ever. I liked the idea of spending more time with her. And doing it. But at some point she was going to ask about the gun and Jonah. I'd have to decide what I was going to say to her. Something which would alleviate any fears she might have about me, while being as close to the truth as possible.

At least I could assure her having guns waved at me wasn't a frequent occurrence.

Usually.

"Your loss." Penn drank his coffee in about two mouthfuls, which was impressive because it must have been hot. No one ever claimed he was normal.

He set his cup down on the bench like he expected someone else to wash it, and walked over to his keyboard.

Like we often did, we leaned against walls, benches and each other, and listened to him warm up.

He played the first couple of minutes of Beethoven's "Moonlight Sonata", while chills travelled up and down my spine. Some days, he could almost bring me to tears. At times, it was hard to reconcile Beau Pennington, the musician, with Penn, the keyboard player with an attitude bigger than Australia.

For such a grumpy asshole, the music he made with his fingers was nothing short of beautiful. He would say it's no big deal, but I've never heard anyone who played keyboard the way he could. The emotion he put into his music was something you couldn't learn. You either had it or you didn't. Lucky for us, he did.

His unmistakable talent was one of the reasons he was part of Wolf Venom, in spite of his attitude. His talent was also a big part of the reason for his attitude.

Us rock stars are a complicated lot.

Penn stopped playing and looked over his shoulder. "You guys gonna stand there or are we going to rehearse?"

"Technically I'm lying down." Landon grinned and sat up.

Penn eyed him and shook his head, but for once didn't say anything.

I shook off the effect of Penn's playing and grabbed the microphone.

The moment my hand curled around it, I got that thrill of excitement. The one that reminded me I'm an actual motherfucking rock star. Not just that, but I was the lead singer of Wolf Venom, the hottest, coolest band in the world. With the coolest name to match.

I turned on the mic and waited for the guys to get themselves organised.

I stood facing them, my game face on.

"Good afternoon and welcome to rehearsal," I said into the microphone. I tried to sound like the Chief Purser on a long haul flight. Why? Because sometimes I was a dork. "Thank you all for coming here today." Without an audience, the rest of the band was the crowd. "Keep your seatbelt fastened and prepare for a shit load of turbulence." Okay, that was off script, but it got the desired response.

The guys chuckled.

"You should have been a clown," Tully teased.

I raised the mic to my lips. "Who says I'm not? I make you guys laugh."

"We're easily pleased," Asher said from behind his drums. He played *ba-dum-tish* and grinned.

"Yeah," Channing agreed. "Our bar is really low." He played a few lively notes on his saxophone.

"You know how to hurt a guy." Without waiting for further insults to be flung my way, I launched into the first song of our new set list.

"Take Me Down Lower" could be interpreted any number of ways. The lyrics worked for people in a toxic relationship, or they could relate to oral sex. I guessed it depended on your circumstances and how dirty your mind was.

Personally, I loved songs that let the listener decide what they were about. They were always the ones we got asked about the most. Especially the ones laced with the kind of innuendos that went over kids heads, but adult listeners understood and adored.

Everyone liked to assume we put some hard and fast meaning to everything, so to speak. Sometimes we did, often we didn't.

Very often, we gave a different explanation whenever we were asked. Usually more outrageous than the last one. I think the latest had something to do with a submarine.

Who knows if anyone bought that, but it was good for a laugh.

I smiled as the guys scrambled to catch up.

Thank fuck they did. They could have left me to sing by myself. That would serve me right for being a smart ass. The guys didn't usually leave me hanging though, and certainly not when it mattered.

I strutted around the rehearsal room like I was on stage. Wishing I was.

By the end of the song, we'd all fallen into our usual easy rhythm. These tracks were new, but we played them a crap load of times already. Enough to have them down pat in our sleep.

I paused for the bridge and lowered the mic. For a good ten seconds or so, I was able to appreciate the other guy's playing. If you asked me, I would say we were pretty fucking good.

I wasn't sure how Abbie would fit into the set, but we would make it work. And then, if I could fit into her, that would be even better.

Just thinking about her and her mouth, I almost forgot to bring the microphone back up and keep singing.

That wouldn't have gone unnoticed by the other guys. Especially Penn. The guy got pissy if any of us screwed up that badly.

Yeah, okay, when was he not pissy? He was a perfectionist. There was nothing wrong with that. I sure as hell didn't want to look like an idiot, especially in front of an audience.

Particularly an audience full of people with their phones in their hands, recording me making a fool of myself.

That kind of thing was difficult to get past.

We finished the first song and fell silent. Closer to the tour, we would play the full set all the way through, multiple times. At this point, we would stop and discuss any tweaks we needed to make.

"Are we throwing in some covers?" Penn asked, like he'd hate the answer, no matter what it was. "Or are we supposed to sing her songs?"

"There's a third option in there," Tully pointed out. "A few people know one or two of our songs. It's possible she might too."

Landon snorted. "Only one or two?"

"Maybe three," Tully acknowledged.

Since our last three albums went multi-platinum, it was definitely more than that, but we got his point.

"There's no reason why Abbie can't learn a couple of our songs," I said. "I'll be happy to teach her if she doesn't."

"Are you sure she isn't after your job?" Asher asked teasingly. "That might be where it starts."

I smirked at him. "No one is taking my job."

No one was going to replace Zeke Brantley, not now, not ever. My distinct vocals were the reason Wolf Venom stood out from the rest of the pack. Why we were so popular.

Asher grinned. "That's what they all say, right before they lose their job."

I flipped him off and said, "You mean how we could replace you with a drum machine?"

"Ouch." He laughed. "A drum machine can't do what I can."

"What is that?" Tully asked.

"Look hot while playing the drums." Asher did a short roll and hit a cymbal, grooving while he did it and finishing with a flourish.

"He's got you there," Landon said.

"Thank you." Asher bowed over his drums. "I live to please."

"Don't we all," I said into the microphone. That brought my mind back to Abbie.

After we left Jackson's office, she'd stayed behind to talk to him about a few things.

I was ninety-nine percent sure Penn thought he was fucking her, but I doubted it. Jackson was more professional than that. Anyway, if he was going to sleep with any of the talent, it probably wouldn't be in his office.

Maybe.

Hell, I might be way off there. I just...didn't want to think of him and her together.

Strangely enough, her and any of the other guys wouldn't bother me, but our manager was like a father to us, in a way. Them sleeping together would be weird. But their business, of course, if they chose to do that.

"I'll talk to Jackson about it," I said. "And Abbie. Rest assured you'll all know long before the tour starts. We'll have plenty of time to rehearse and make any adjustments we think need to be made."

"The only adjustment we need to make is no adjustment," Penn said. He turned his attention back to his keyboard.

I lowered the mic so my sigh wouldn't echo through the room.

It was going to be a long tour if Penn was going to hate on Abbie the entire time.

CHAPTER
FIVE

ABBIE

"THIS IS THE REHEARSAL ROOM. Zeke will take good care of you."

For some reason Jackson seemed relieved to leave me with the guys. We'd had an amicable conversation, but I suspected he thought my reputation would be insurmountable. Or at least, a lot of work.

Imagine how Rachel feel.

He opened the door just as the guys finished a song.

They all turned towards me. Some of their expressions warm, others hostile. Landon and Channing looked curious.

Thankfully one of the warmer faces was Zeke's.

"Hey," he said into the mic just because he could.

I would have been able to hear him without it. Some of us liked to hear our own voices through speakers. I was guilty of that myself.

Zeke looked even hotter here than he did at the club. It might be the light and it might be because he looked comfortable with the microphone in his hand.

I cleared my throat.

"Hello." Even without the other night between us, it was hard to tear my eyes off Zeke.

He had a magnetic presence, and clearly knew it.

I would bet anything he knew exactly what to say or do to get people to do what he wanted. Women in particular. Hell, I hadn't exactly tried to resist.

Would I have if I knew who he was? I should have known. He wasn't exactly a regular guy. A person I might meet while walking down the street. He was the lead singer of Wolf Venom. People all over the world knew him on sight.

Me, well, I didn't tend to fangirl over other singers. I listened to them, but most of the time I had no idea what they looked like. I suspected he had no idea who I was either, until Jackson and Penn explained.

What the fuck was Penn's problem anyway? Some people liked being assholes for the heck of it. If that was his thing, I would have to try to ignore him.

I suspected that might be easier said than done. Especially when we were on tour. It didn't help that he was at least as hot as Zeke. All of the guys were. If I didn't know how good they were as musicians, I might have suspected they were chosen for how attractive they were.

Some might say the same about me, though.

"I'll leave you to it," Jackson said. "Don't worry, you're in good hands."

"Of course she is," Zeke said with one of his panty melting smiles.

God, he made me want to tear off my clothes and jump his bones. Nothing good could come out of him being this hot, I was sure of it. Except a bit of fun.

Was he even up for that now we were working together?

Why was I even thinking this? I should be focusing on the tour and my future. Not to mention my reputation. All of which was based on absolute bullshit. I was used and treated like crap and when they were done with me, they threw me away. If it wasn't for Levi and White Wolf Records...

While I was thinking and staring at Zeke, I hadn't even realised he'd stepped closer to me, and Jackson left.

"Can you guys give us a minute?" Zeke asked. He waved back towards the corridor.

One of the guys made kissy noises and most of them laughed. No prizes for guessing who scowled instead. Penn looked at me like he wished the ground would open up under my feet and swallow me up.

There was definitely something wrong with me. I found the expression as sexy as hell.

I still sneered back at him and turned away.

We stepped out into the corridor and Zeke closed the door behind us.

"What is this about?" I asked. "Are you going to tell me the guys have talked and you won't work with me?" I leaned my back against the wall and closed my eyes. When was this shit going to start getting easier?

"Not at all." Zeke's voice sounded close to my ear.

When I opened my eyes I saw he pressed his hand to the wall beside my head and leaned in until his breath brushed my cheek. He was so close I could almost feel heat rolling off him in waves. Or maybe that was me.

I looked him right in his eyes. They were vivid blue, a shade or two darker than mine. I felt as if he could see right into my soul. If he could read my mind he would know I wanted him to touch me so badly it hurt.

I cleared my throat. "I can think of two other things we should probably talk about. I'm not sure the corridor is the right place for either of them."

He sighed and stepped back away from me. "You're right. There's probably a private, empty room around here somewhere."

"That sounds dangerous," I said.

He turned back and grinned. "Oh? It does? I like the sound of that. Maybe we should find somewhere." He stepped back to me and ran the back of his fingers down the side of my cheek and across my lower lip.

He must have felt me trembling.

"Or we could rehearse before they tear up my contract," I said reluctantly. "Was that all you wanted to talk about?"

"In a way." He lowered his voice. "I wanted to say that any time you want to continue what we started the other night, I'm up for it. Mostly, thought, I wanted you to know I got rid of the you-know-what. It's not going to turn back up and cause anyone to point fingers at either of us. We could have been caught on a security camera together so I figured you'd want to know."

"Great." I hadn't even thought of that, but he was right. If the police came after him, they would start looking into me too. That was the last thing I needed. "Thank you."

I cocked my head at him when he looked like he had more to say.

His hand rested lightly on my cheek. "I can't guarantee that won't happen again. Usually, when the other guys are around it doesn't, but sending Jonah after me shows how desperate Reuben is getting. Shit might escalate. I'll do what I can to keep you out of it."

"Have you thought about talking to the police?" I asked.

He looked down at the tiled floor, then back up again. "I can't. That's a conversation for another place. Somewhere we wouldn't be overheard. Let's just say it's not in their best interests to help me or act against Reuben."

"This Reuben guy sounds like a piece of work," I said.

Zeke chuckled. "You could say that, yes." He looked at me like he wanted to kiss me. His lips were only a few centimetres from mine. All I had to do was turn my face…

"Should we go back in?" I asked instead.

"Yeah we should," he said reluctantly. "If we don't, they'll start talking about us." A smile crept onto the corners of his lips. "They'll start to think we're doing naughty things out here."

I laughed softly. "We wouldn't want them to think we're doing *naughty* things."

"They'll get jealous if they think that." He traced circles around the side of my mouth and my chin with the calloused pad of his thumb. "I'm sure they all want to do naughty things with you."

That was interesting. My eyes widened. "All of them?"

"Why not all of them?" His thumb moved down to the side of my throat. If he kept doing that, we were going to *have* to find a private room.

And I'd have to change my panties.

"Because at least one of them hates my guts," I said dryly.

"One day, Penn will get over himself," Zeke assured me. "Believe me when I say his bark is worse than his bite. Although, his bite is pretty shitty."

"I'll say." I wrinkled my nose. "I'm used to guys like him. They're usually threatened by a woman in their space, or have hang ups for whatever reason. That's their problem, not mine." Although, the tour would be more fun if he checked his bullshit at the door.

"Exactly," he agreed. "Life is too short to deal with other people's shit unless you have to. We're going to have to sit down and talk about what songs you're going to sing with us. Do you want to do that over dinner?"

"Yes," I said a little too fast. "I mean, sure."

He smiled like he was absolutely certain I was going to say yes, no matter what the question.

Part of me wished I said no, just to take him down a peg or two. A guy like him wouldn't stay down for too long though. Besides, it was hard not to like him. He was attractive, charming and at least a little bit dangerous.

I might never admit this, even to myself, but when I got over being scared about the gun in my face, I found it strangely exciting. That was all kinds of wrong, I knew that, but adrenaline had a mind of its own.

"Great." He looked serious. "Are you really staying at that hotel?"

I shrugged. "It was all I could afford."

"I'll speak to Jackson about finding you somewhere better to stay," he said. "Or..." He raised an eyebrow.

"Or?" I prompted.

"You could stay with me," he finished. "I have plenty of room at my place. I even have a spare bedroom if you'd prefer to sleep in there." His brow dropped into a wiggle.

"Is it safe at your place?" I asked, ignoring his not particularly subtle suggestion. "I don't want to wake up in the middle of the night and find a gun in my face."

He leaned in and said, "Sweetheart, if you wake up in the middle of the night and find something in your face, it's not gonna be a gun."

I snorted a laugh. "I should have seen that coming a mile away."

"If you see me coming, I won't be a mile away." His smile widened. "I'll be right there beside you. Or *inside* you."

Between his proximity, the smell of him and the conversation, it was getting more and more difficult to think straight. If we were alone, I would undo his jeans and ride him here and now. I had a feeling he knew that too. Judging by the look he gave me, the feeling was entirely mutual.

"I could use somewhere to stay while I wait for the first paycheck to roll in," I admitted.

I should also hire someone to take care of my finances so I didn't end up in this position again. As soon as I had enough money, I would buy a house and never have to stay in a fleabag hotel again.

"If you're sure you don't mind me sleeping in your spare room." Any other arrangement would feel like I was moving in with the guy. Considering we'd known each other for a matter of hours, that seemed a bit premature.

I was attracted to him, but even I didn't move that fast.

He looked a little disappointed, but nodded. "Of course I don't mind." No doubt he thought the sleeping arrangement was temporary. Maybe it would be.

One thing was for sure, it was going to be difficult to share space with him and keep my hands to myself. I'd never been very good at resisting temptation. Especially in hotter than hell form.

"We should go in and rehearse." He stepped away from me. "After that, I'll help you move your stuff in and we can have a nice dinner out. You look like you could use some spoiling. I fully intend to do just that. If you'll let me."

"I wouldn't say no to being spoiled." He was right, it had been a while. "As long as you don't expect anything in return."

"I never expect anything, especially in return," he said firmly. "But I'm always hopeful." After a moment he added, "And willing."

Yeah, I figured that about him.

CHAPTER SIX

ABBIE

"DO you know Bump in the Night?" Zeke asked.

"Of course." I nodded. Did anyone *not* know that song? It was all over the radio, top of the streaming apps and featured in fuck knows how many videos on various social media apps. You'd have to live under a rock to not know it.

Zeke nodded to the guys and they started to play.

For a while, I forgot about everything and just enjoyed rehearsing with the guys. I didn't know all the lyrics to this particular song, but I knew enough to sing along with the chorus.

"Girl, you're the one I shouldn't touch,
  you're toxic to my soul.
  When your hands are all over me,
  I just can't fuckin' stop.

You make me go bump in the night.
  I want to grind you, pound you,
  you make me beg for more.
  Without your body, I'm nothing."

The guys weren't known for having subtle songs and wholesome lyrics. Neither was I, to be honest. We would all look pretty strange singing about rainbows and puppies. Unless those puppies were hell hounds and the rainbows were a way of saying we don't care who you fuck, as long as everyone consents.

I was totally here for both of those things.

"That was awesome." Zeke was grinning as a song wound up. "We can give the backing vocalists a song or two off while you sing. Rather than have their voices detract from yours."

"Maybe she could be a backing vocalist," Penn suggested. "Then she could sing on every fucking song."

He was obviously not suggesting it to be nice.

I ignored him.

"Let's take a break," Zeke suggested. He seemed to be the leader of the band as well as the lead singer. Or maybe the other guys were just ready for a break.

Either way, they put down their instruments and Channing handed around bottles of water to everyone.

"Lucky they always provide extras." He handed one to me and his fingers brushed over mine. He looked into my eyes and smiled. And then winked.

He and Landon were the youngest in the band and they were both adorable. Especially when they curled up together on the couch at the back of the room and looked at one of their phones together.

"Cute, aren't they?" Zeke placed a hand on the back of my neck, under my hair. The gesture was casual and possessive at the same time. If it bothered any of the guys, apart from Penn, they didn't give any sign. If anything, they looked curious and none were deterred from looking at my breasts.

"They are," I agreed. "They're...together?" The look Channing gave me confused me as to where they stood.

"More or less," he said. "They're both bi, but they won't sleep with a woman unless they're both involved. Personally, it wouldn't surprise me if they had a three way permanent relationship some day. Or more than three." He shrugged.

That explained the vibe I got from Channing. What would it be like to sleep with both of them? I've done a lot of things with a lot of people but rarely ever a threesome. Certainly never more than that.

"And the others?" I sipped my water and tried not to be too distracted by the way Zeke's fingers traced circles on the back of my neck.

"I believe the term is single and ready to mingle," he said. "You know what this life is like. We're always busy and we spend half the time fending off groupies."

I snorted softly. "Or not fending them off."

"That too," he said unapologetically. "One of the perks to being who we are."

That should absolutely not bother me, but for some reason it did. The thought of him sleeping with someone else sent a flutter of annoyance through me.

I had no right to think like that, or be possessive. Just because he made it clear he wanted to fuck me again, didn't mean he didn't want to fuck the next woman who walked into the room as well.

Same for all of the guys.

I slipped away from him and into one of the comfortable armchairs near the couch.

"How long have you guys been together?"

"About six years," Asher replied. He flopped into the chair to one side of me and Zeke sat in the other. "Zeke and I have known each other most of our lives. We met the other guys at Sydney Uni bar, when we were playing with some other guys."

"What were you called back then?" Tully asked.

Asher winced. "Robot Assholes from Uranus."

I laughed. "I don't know why you didn't keep that name. It's so snappy."

"And almost accurate," Zeke said with a grin. "Fun fact, Landon is an actual robot."

Landon grinned and stuck up his two middle fingers at him. "I'm very sophisticated, and for the record, the term is artificial intelligence."

"I don't know about the intelligence part," Asher teased.

Landon turned his two fingered salute on Asher. "I know you love me."

"Of course I do, dude. No one plays bass like you do." Asher crossed his legs so his ankle rested on his knee.

"You're not going to start being all mushy on each other are you?" Penn growled. "The way Zeke is staring at that slut is bad enough."

"This from the guy who fucks anything if it's still for long enough," Tully said. "Including the receptionist in the break room on the way in this morning."

"That explains why she wasn't at the desk when I arrived," Zeke said.

In the interest of not responding angrily to Penn's insult, I pulled out my phone and started doing a little digging.

When I realised all of the guys' eyes were on me, I started to read out loud. "Beauregard Pennington. That's a mouthful. Sydney Boys Grammar. Ohhh, fancy." Apparently his parents had some money.

"What are you doing?" Penn growled.

Without looking up, I said, "You looked me up. It's only fair that I return the favour." I went on reading. "Full scholarship to Sydney Conservatory of Music. Dropped out after a year. Isn't that a shame?" My eyes widened at the next sentence. "Found—"

"Abbie," Zeke said, his tone a clear warning.

I looked up at him and he shook his head.

"Don't. It's...in the past." His gorgeous blue eyes flicked towards Penn in worry, then back to me.

I turned off my phone. If Penn asked me to shut up, I wouldn't have, but for Zeke I did.

If nothing else, I owed him for saving me from getting shot in the head. Besides, what I read was pretty horrible and nothing anyone needed to relive. Not even Penn.

"Thank you," Zeke said softly. In a louder voice he said, "As you can tell, when young Penn met us, he was on a path to greatness. We dragged him there via a dirtier route. Otherwise, he would be stuck playing classical piano in front of audiences with their noses in the air."

"Fuck that," Penn muttered.

There was obviously a lot more to this story, but I sensed I wasn't going to get it today.

"So you all grew up in Sydney?" I asked.

"Zeke and I did," Asher said. "And Penn and Tully. Landon is originally from Brisbane. Channing is a Melbourne boy."

"Me too," I said. "I mean, from Melbourne. I'm not a boy." Trust me to say something so silly. I was trying to make a good impression on them and I wasn't sure it was working. One hated me and now the rest probably thought I was an idiot.

"You're definitely not a boy," Zeke agreed. The look he gave me made me want to straddle his lap and ride his cock, even though there were five other guys in the room.

They could watch if they wanted to. That idea was hotter than hell.

"What am I sensing here?" Asher asked. "Do you two know each other? There's been a vibe between you since Abbie walked into Jackson's office. At first I thought it was just Zeke being hot for Abbie, like he's hot for anyone with nipples. But the more I look at you both, the more I think something is up." He narrowed his eyes and cocked his head at us.

I didn't know how to answer that. Fortunately, Zeke saved me from having to.

"Sometimes two people connect," he said lightly. "Abbie seems lovely and, personally, I'd like to get to know her a lot better. Wouldn't all of you like the same thing?"

"Of course we would," Asher said. "And we will. We're all going to be working *very* closely together for the next few months. The best thing we can do is all get along to the satisfaction of everyone."

My eyes swivelled to him and he smiled. Yeah, I noticed the innuendos in his words. And the way his hazel eyes lingered on mine.

Where Zeke was dark, Asher was blond, with light hair and skin. Even with a tan, he was paler than Zeke. He was at least as ripped as Zeke.

What would it be like to be in the middle of the two of them? Their hands all over me. Their cocks in my pussy and mouth.

Shit, if I kept thinking like this it was going to be difficult to get *any* work done.

I reminded myself what was at stake here. The label gave me a chance to resurrect my career. I wasn't going to get a third chance. I had to make this work or I was screwed.

"Working closely together," Penn muttered. "I can't hardly fucking wait."

I was tempted to turn my phone back on and keep reading, or throw the device at his head. For Zeke's sake, and my phone's, I did neither of those things. I couldn't afford to replace my phone if I broke it anyway.

"Of course you can't," I said instead. "Sooner or later you're going to realise how awesome I am." I didn't think I was all that awesome, but there was something about him that made me want to provoke him.

He barked a laugh. "I hope this tour does motherfucking wonders for your career. Then you can piss off and leave us alone."

For a moment, I thought he was going to be nice. I should have known better. My bad.

"I'm curious about something," I said slowly. "Did you drop out of the Conservatory of Music, or were you kicked out for being an asshole?"

What? It was a legitimate question. They shouldn't have to put up with his bullshit any more than I did.

"I left because concert pianists don't have horny groupies with hungry pussies." Penn smirked. "Not as many as rock gods do anyway."

I shrugged. "That's as good a reason for dropping out as any." I wondered if Tully's suggestion that Penn would sleep with anyone who crossed his path was accurate. I suspected it was, making his suggestion that I was a slut more than a little bit hypocritical.

Whatever, I didn't care what he did with his sex life. I certainly wasn't going to apologise for enjoying sex. Especially not to him.

"I thought so," Penn said.

That was the first almost civil thing he said to me since we met. There might be hope for him after all.

"Not that I need your fucking approval," he added.

Or maybe there wasn't.

"Are we going to finish rehearsal?" Tully asked. "As *stimulating* as this conversation is…" He gave me a wink.

Yeah, I didn't miss that innuendo either. Working with Wolf Venom was either going to be a lot of fun, or a bunch of really, really long months.

CHAPTER
SEVEN

ZEKE

MOVING Abbie into my spare room didn't take long. The whole undertaking consisted of rolling two small suitcases from her hotel to my inner-city townhouse. Piece of cake, even though she winced when paying the hotel bill. I would have offered to settle it for her, but I suspected she'd refuse.

"Home, sweet home." I unlocked the door and did a quick visual sweep inside before I let her in. I saw no sign of Jonah, or any other immediate threats. They'd have to get past my security system anyway.

Good luck with that, I thought. It was the latest, best money could buy.

I rolled her case over the threshold and closed the door behind her.

"Nice place." She glanced around.

"Thanks. It's nothing fancy." It was typical for the area. Expensive, with a view of nothing in particular, but it was convenient to all the pubs, clubs and restaurants.

I bought it a couple of years ago and had it totally remodelled. Tastefully, of course. I'd leave purple walls and gold fixtures and fittings to the other guys.

I preferred light hardwood floors and neutral paint on the walls.

Nothing I couldn't look at if I was hung over.

I took the other suitcase from her and carried both up the stairs. They felt like she stashed a few bricks in there. Maybe she did. Who knew with women?

"I've thought about getting away from the city to have more space, but this place is convenient and it doesn't take my housekeeper long to clean." I grinned over my shoulder. "What the hell would I do with six or seven bedrooms anyway?"

"Is this a rhetorical question?" she asked with a laugh.

I reached the top of the stairs. "It wasn't supposed to be, but I see you've interpreted it in a different way from how I intended. At least, I think you did." I quirked an eyebrow in question. "You are implying I should put six or seven women in those bedrooms, weren't you?"

She laughed. "Them, or your bandmates."

Interesting that was where her mind went. Was that the kind of relationship she was after?

"We would need two or three housekeepers then." I put her suitcases down to the side of my spare room and shook out my arms. "It's not the biggest room in the world."

It looked smaller, still furnished with a timber framed double bed, two matching bedside tables and a small wardrobe.

"It's a lot nicer than the hotel," she said.

Yeah, she was right there. Charging people to stay in places like that should be illegal. My place wasn't huge, but it was neat and clean. Five stars compared to that dump.

"There's a bathroom on the other side of the corridor." I nodded towards it. "You have it all to yourself. Unless you don't want to."

I wanted to slip a hand under her hair, to the back of her neck, and kiss her. She smelled like an intoxicating combination of rose soap and some kind of floral shampoo. Good enough to eat. I was aching to taste her mouth. I bet she tasted divine.

Instead, I said, "There should be hangers in the wardrobe. Make yourself comfortable. There's no hurry for you to move out. You can stay until you're ready."

It wasn't until I saw her suitcases that I realised how tough things were for her right now. I suspected everything she owned in the world was inside them.

If that was the case, she *really* needed the opportunity the label gave her. I would do everything in my power to make sure it worked out the way she needed it to. Whatever it took.

I thought I saw a tear on her cheek, but she wiped away before I could be sure.

"Thank you. You've been really sweet. Sweeter than I deserve."

That was definitely a tear she wiped away the second time.

"Hey." I put my hands on her shoulders and turned her gently to face me.

"You deserve to have people be nice to you and take care of you. You're beautiful, smart and talented. Onyx Riot didn't do right by you, but White Wolf Records will. I promise. And Wolf Venom will look after you. You're one of us now."

Honestly, I wanted to find the owner of her former label and punch him in the face. And whoever the asshole was that faked a marriage to her.

Who even does shit like that?

Judging by Penn's snide comments, it wouldn't take more than a minute or two of searching on the Internet to find the answer.

I made a mental note to do that later. Not because I wanted to intrude on her privacy, but because I knew people who could beat the crap out of other people if I asked them to.

All right, I knew people that could do a lot worse than that, but a warning should be enough.

Unless they hurt her again. Then all bets were off. There wasn't anything I wouldn't do to protect the people I cared about, including the rest of the band.

Yes, even Penn. He wasn't so bad when you got to know him.

"Okay?" I said softly. "You deserve to be safe and happy."

She sniffed and nodded. "Thank you. You and the label have been so incredible. You couldn't be any different to Onyx Riot. I know they have a business to run, but they treated me like I was a commodity." She shook her head. "White Wolf feels more like a family."

I gave her a lopsided smile. "Sometimes we're dysfunctional, but I like to think of us as family. When we're on tour, we hang out with the support act and all the tour staff. No one is above or below anyone else. Unless they're fucking."

She let out a choked little laugh before her expression turned serious. "Is that the catch here? You be nice to me in return for me fucking you?"

Ouch. The suggestion stung my ego a tiny bit. Did I really seem like the kind of guy who put conditions on being nice? Or was it that she was screwed so badly over in the past it was easier to make that assumption than think anyone actually gave a shit?

I didn't want to admit it, but it made sense. She was living in my house, albeit temporarily. Some guys wouldn't do that without expecting something in return.

"There's no catch," I said firmly. "I in no way expect you to sleep with me. You needed a place to stay, I was happy to offer. That's all. Anything that happens between us, if it does, is entirely up to you. This is a no strings attached situation."

I had some rope and a pair of handcuffs if she wanted to be tied up, but those were unrelated to her staying here with me.

She looked sceptical, but nodded. "Okay. I appreciate that."

I bent to kiss her cheek and stepped back. "I'll leave you to get settled in. I'll book us in for somewhere to have dinner tonight. Is there anything you prefer to eat?"

She lowered her eyes and looked right at my groin. A slow smile crept onto her face.

"I also like most foods. The hotter, the better." Was she talking about food, my cock or both?

"I like it hot too." And now my jeans were tight at the front. I wanted to grab her, tear off her clothes and push her down on the bed. I wanted to bury myself balls deep inside her. I wanted to come in her so hard she overflowed. I wanted to taste every centimetre of her and feel her mouth all over me.

I wanted…

Fuck, after my reassurance that she wasn't obliged to sleep with me, I couldn't make the first move, not right now. No matter how badly I wanted to.

Even though my balls hurt like hell. I *had* to wait until the right time.

She raised her eyes. There was something in the depths, like she desperately wanted to believe me.

I felt like this was some kind of test. One I didn't want to fail. If I did, I may never regain her trust. I wanted—needed—her to know I was sincere.

"I should unpack." She eyed the suitcases sadly. "It shouldn't take long."

"Right." I nodded. "Take your time. I'll put on the coffee machine for some real coffee."

"I like the sound of that," she said. Her eyes were brighter now, eager. Coffee had that effect on people. "I haven't had a real coffee in ages."

I grinned. "Then you're in for a treat. I have very particular taste in beans and the best way to brew them." Which was my way of saying I was a coffee snob. I only drank the instant stuff the label provided because that was all there was.

One of these days, I was going to take my own in. On the other hand, then I would have to share it. Maybe instant wasn't so bad.

I gave her a lingering look. Even in the face of impending coffee, it was hard to tear myself away from her. She was like a gorgeous magnet, drawing me to her.

If I wasn't careful, I would find myself falling for her.

That was dangerous in so many ways. Because we worked together. Because I had a reputation for sticking my cock in every hole I could find.

A reputation that wasn't undeserved.

I liked sex. As a single guy, I had few reasons to refuse when it was offered and it was offered often. For some reason, women seemed to like fucking rock stars.

I certainly wasn't complaining. All those women kept life interesting and my cock happy.

Mostly though, falling for her would be dangerous thanks to Reuben and my past.

If that caught up to me, worse things could happen to her than a gun shoved in her face. Reuben wouldn't hesitate to use her to get to me. Reuben wouldn't hesitate to use anyone I knew to get to me. The fact he hadn't, meant he wasn't completely desperate. Not yet.

It was coming, as inevitably as the sunset. I needed to find a way to stay out of his path. Permanently.

Whatever happened, I wasn't going back. That was a dark part of my life I wanted to put behind me and forget.

"Wait," Abbie said before I stepped out of the room.

When I turned, she put a hand on my arm and stood on her toes to lightly brush her lips over mine.

When she moved away and crouched beside her suitcases, I asked, "What was that for?"

And why in hell was it hotter than a deep, passionate kiss or a blow job?

"I just wanted to," she said lightly. "That's all."

I smiled and nodded. "Well, thank you. I'll be downstairs if you need me." I hurried away before I changed my mind about leaving her by herself.

Think about coffee, I told myself. *Maybe really cold coffee.*

Fuck, having her here was going to be…interesting, to say the least.

CHAPTER
EIGHT

ZEKE

"OH MY GOD, you weren't wrong about the coffee." She closed her eyes and looked blissed out.

"Of course. I'm never wrong about coffee." I watched her face and admired the height of her cheekbones, the curve of her chin, the way her nose turned up at the end. The sprinkling of freckles around her nose might be the cutest thing I ever saw.

"I know a thing or two about wine, beer and tequila," I added. For example, I knew tequila tasted better when licked off a woman's skin than it did drunk from a glass.

Although, what didn't taste better licked off skin?

She opened her eyes and we both spoke at the same time.

"So about Reuben…"

"So about the twenty-six hour marriage…"

We both smiled, but I had to concede the point to her.

"I owe you an explanation." I sat back on the couch and rested my ankle on my opposite knee.

"You don't necessarily owe me anything," she said slowly. "I would like to know why someone was holding a gun to my head."

"Yeah, that's fair." I cleared my throat. "Reuben is my brother. He's the oldest of seven. All boys. Reuben, Caleb and Joshua are from my father's first wife. She died under circumstances which are still not clear."

According to the police that was. I didn't have much doubt about what really happened.

"My parents got married three months after she died and I was born three months later."

"So either you were premature or..." Abbie's eyes widened.

"Or my mother was already pregnant when my father's first wife died," I finished for her. "Hint, I wasn't premature."

"Oh my god," she whispered. "You think your father got her out of the way?"

"He did, or he had someone to do it for him." I grimaced. "Or maybe it was a convenient accident. Either way, my father was known for having multiple mistresses, so he wouldn't have been alone for long no matter what went down."

I took a sip of coffee. "So then I was born, then Lucas and finally the twins, Hunter and Parker."

"That's a lot of boys," she said.

"Yep, and we range from thirty-nine down to nineteen." I sat a bit below the middle of that range.

"So that's why Reuben thinks he's your father," she said. "Because he's so much older."

"That and he inherited my father's place as head of the family when he died. A fact he likes to remind us of as often as he can." I rolled my eyes.

"And by family you don't just mean a group of related people, do you?" she asked tentatively.

"No," I agreed. "Whatever assumption you want to make about what they're into, you're probably right. I won't go into detail because if, for whatever reason, the police ask questions, it's better you have no answers to give them. For your safety."

I didn't want her getting into trouble because of me or my family, and it was hard to know who might be on the payroll. My brother's reach was wide.

"Okay, but can you tell me who Jonah is?" she asked. "Is he a relative?"

"Fuck no. Jonah is just hired muscle. He does odd jobs for my brother, like threatening people."

"And killing people?" she whispered as though she was scared there was someone outside the window, listening.

"Probably." I nodded slowly.

"So if your brother told him to kill us, he would have done that?" She looked more pissed off than scared.

I could understand that. If she died just because she was in my company, I would be irritated too.

"He would have killed me," I agreed. "He would have killed you if Reuben told him to make sure there weren't any witnesses."

"So when he threatened to kill me—" She frowned.

"He would have been going off script," I said. "He would have had instructions not to kill me, but they wouldn't have extended to you. No offence, but Reuben never cared much about collateral damage."

"That might be the worst *no offence but* I've ever heard," she said dryly. "No offence, but my brother doesn't give a shit if you get murdered."

"I'm sorry if I gave you the impression my brother was anything other than an asshole," I said sarcastically. "He's a ruthless bastard who will step on anyone and everyone to get his way. Including his brothers."

"Why does he want you back so badly?" she asked.

I grunted. "Because he hates the fact I'm out here living my life. He wants me to be the dutiful brother, doing whatever he tells me to do. I'm not interested in being his hired muscle."

She looked at me for a long moment and then burst out laughing.

I frowned at her. "What?"

It took her a minute or two to compose herself so she could respond.

"I'm sorry, I was imagining what it would be like if you tried to approach someone like Jonah did. Don't get me wrong, you'd be terrifying with a gun in your hand." She shivered lightly. "But then if they recognised you, they would probably ask for an autograph or a selfie. And then later when they realised what was really going on, they would know exactly how to describe you to the police."

I flicked a finger gun in her direction. "Excellent point. I'll have to remember to tell Reuben that the next time I talk to him. I'm way too recognisable to get away with anything."

"Would he leave you alone if he realised that?" she asked.

"That wouldn't work for a minute," I admitted. "He'd probably tell me to wear a mask or grow a beard." I preferred designer scruff that made me look just messy enough, without the hassle of having to trim a beard.

"Or he'd give me a job behind the scenes. Knowing him, he'd get off on having me drive him around everywhere or some shit like that. Or collecting money from one of his brothels."

Being an asshole, he wouldn't let me touch any of the staff, even if I paid. Not that I would ever pay for sex. I hadn't needed to yet, I didn't intend to start doing it.

"That doesn't sound as glamorous as being a rock star." She said the last word and her breath fell into a sigh. "Although, that can be overrated."

She looked so sad I wanted to kiss her heartache away.

"Which brings me to my question," I said tentatively. "You don't have to talk about it if you don't want to." I hadn't looked her up. I decided against it. Whatever she wanted me to know, she could tell me and I would listen. The rest was none of my business.

Until my curiosity got the better of me.

"There's not much to say." She shrugged. "Boy meets girl. Girl falls in love with boy. Boy suggests they elope. Girl agrees. Boy admits the marriage was just to further his career. Girl gets annulment. Boy doesn't get a broken nose, although he deserved it."

She let out a longer, heavier sigh.

"It wasn't Penn, was it?" I couldn't resist asking.

She looked surprised, but then burst out laughing. "God no. Although now you mention it, there was a resemblance between them. They were both ambitious assholes."

"I'm sorry someone thought it was okay to do that to you." I thought about sneaking in a good word for Penn, because the guy had his moments, but he could stick up for himself.

And no doubt he would the next time we were all together.

"I just wish the publicity helped my career," she said. "Instead, it made me look like an idiot. And then there was the whole affair thing." She used air quotes. "Sometimes I think I shouldn't be let out unsupervised. Apparently I make really crappy choices when I'm left to my own devices."

I scooted over closer to her. "I don't know, I've only seen you make good choices so far."

I hesitated and hoped she wasn't about to stab me in the ego, when I asked, "You don't regret what we did in the club, do you?"

"Not for a minute," she said firmly. "That was…memorable. You could have been a jerk about it, but you weren't. At least, not that I've seen." She gave me a speculative look.

"If by that you mean tell the guys or spill everything to a tabloid, no. I haven't done either of those. What happened between us is just between us. Unless we agree otherwise."

"I'd prefer if the tabloids don't know." She wrinkled her nose. "I've given them more than enough ammunition over the years. The guys, well, it doesn't worry me if they know. I have nothing to be ashamed of. And honestly, it might be easier if there aren't any secrets between you and them."

That took me by surprise. Most women seemed hellbent on keeping their sex lives secret. I guessed when yours was as open as hers was in the past, there was no point in trying to pretend it didn't exist.

She frowned and changed the subject. "Do the other guys know about your family?"

"Yeah," I replied. "Especially Asher. Like I said, he and I have known each other all our lives. His family and mine are intertwined somewhat. Although, right now his is…" I searched for the right words. "In disgrace, in a manner of speaking. His father pissed off the wrong people, so all of the DiMarco family are on the outs as far as the Brantley and Bell families are concerned."

"Bell family?" she echoed. "How many families are there?"

I shrugged one shoulder. "In this country? A few, but the most powerful are the Brantleys and the Bells. And to a lesser extent, the Fiorellis. They're all bitter rivals. For the record, if you think Reuben is bad, he has nothing on the Bells. They are as ruthless and depraved as they come. Most of them would traffic their own mothers for money."

"How charming," she said sarcastically. "I'm starting to think the people at Onyx Riot were actually nice."

I smiled. "It's all relative, I guess. No pun intended."

"Are you sure?" she asked.

I knitted my brows. "Am I sure of what?"

"Are you sure you didn't intend that pun? It sounded intentional to me." The side of her mouth quirked upwards.

I laughed. "Okay, you caught me. It was a little bit intentional. If I don't laugh about my family, I might cry. Sometimes I wish I was born into a normal family, like Channing's, or even Penn's. Asher and I got the short straw there."

"I had a normal family," she said softly. "And my life still ended up fucked up. At least you have your head on straight."

"One of my heads is straight. The other slants a little to the left." I grinned.

"I remember," she said with a nod. "And it's very tasty too."

In spite of my resolve to wait, I couldn't help myself.

"You know what else is tasty?" I took a sip of coffee and leaned towards her. I slanted my mouth over hers and carefully pried her lips open with my tongue.

When she opened her mouth, I slowly squirted the coffee inside. Then kissed her lightly for good measure.

I leaned away and hoped she wasn't about to hurt me. Not that a little thing like her could do me much damage, unless she dug her knee into my groin.

To my intense relief, she smiled and swallowed.

"That *was* tasty." She licked her lips. "There might not be anything hotter than a guy who shares his coffee, especially like that."

"I can think of something hotter than that," I said. "You."

She blushed adorably.

It was too late for me to be careful. I was already falling for her.

CHAPTER
NINE

ABBIE

"CAN YOU SPEAK ITALIAN?" I was a bit uneasy on my feet after several glasses of wine.

At some point during the walk home, Zeke's hand slipped into mine. I didn't pull away.

"No," he said with a laugh. "That's another reason why I'd make a terrible mobster. Can't speak Italian."

He was at least as tipsy as I was. "Asher on the other hand. He's fluent. Or is it French?" He snapped his fingers. "Actually, I think it's both. What a show off, ay?"

I laughed softly. "If you've got it, flaunt it."

"That's always been my motto." He swung our hands between us before pulling me closer to his side.

"You've certainly got it." He let my hand go and snaked an arm around my waist. He pulled me closer still and nuzzled his face into the side of my neck.

"You smell so good." He drew me to a stop and lightly ran the tip of his tongue from just under my ear, to my throat. "Taste good too."

I couldn't hold back the moan that slipped from between my lips.

He manoeuvred me a couple of steps until my back was pressed against a slender tree. Then his hands were up the back of my shirt and my hands were up the front of his.

He kissed his way up my throat, over my chin to my mouth. When our lips met. It was like an explosion of fireworks. His stubble tickled pleasantly.

He slid his hands around to ghost over my stomach and up to cup my breasts. He palmed my nipples through the thin fabric of my bra. They rose to tight, hard peaks in response.

Blood pounded through me like thunder. I wanted to feel every part of him on and in me. Not just because he turned me on, but because I was drawn to him. Zeke the person, not Zeke Brantley the rock star. He was sweet and sexy, even with that edge of danger around him and his family.

If I had any sense, I would stay away after what he told me about his brother, but I didn't want to stay away. Not from him and not from any of the other guys either.

I wanted to get to know all of them at some point. Yeah, even Penn. I was almost certain there was a decent guy under his exterior, albeit deep down.

Zeke drew his hand out, and peeled down the front of my shirt and the cup of my bra. He leaned in to run his tongue in circles around and over my nipple.

I was already panting out my nose before he did that. My panties were ruined.

The more I was around him, the more I realised this was going to be a permanent thing.

He only had to touch me to make me hot, much less touch me like this. And we barely even started.

He suckled for a while, before peeling back the left cup and sucking on that nipple.

I reached a hand down between us and over the front of his pants. Instead of his usual jeans, he'd worn dress pants and a dark blue button down shirt. His cock was now straining to get out of the front of those pants.

I was happy to oblige.

I undid the button, slid down the zipper and slipped my hand inside. Why was I not even slightly surprised to learn he went commando tonight? Not surprised, but pleased.

I curled my fingers around his already rock hard length.

He groaned. "Sweetheart, the way you make me feel…" He looked up at me and grinned. "I want to do so many naughty things to you."

I smiled back. "I want you to do all the naughty things to me."

His eyebrows rose slightly. "*All* the naughty things? I can think of lots and lots of them. That's just off the top of my head."

"Which head?" I circled the tip of his cock with my finger.

His breath hitched. "Both of them. But you're making it hard for the head on my shoulders to think."

He worked his hands under my skirt and grabbed my ass. My G-string left my cheeks bare to his warm, calloused skin.

"That's the idea," I said, my voice husky. "Thinking is overrated." Says the woman who got in a lot of trouble from not thinking in the past.

That felt like a different lifetime and a different person. Zeke was not my ex-lover or my ex-husband, if I could even call either of them that. He was a better person than both of them combined. Hell, Penn was a better person than both of them.

That yardstick was very fucking low.

"It really is," Zeke agreed. He glanced around me. "I don't think that tree is up to me fucking you against it. I intend to pound you harder than that."

That sent a shiver through me, so hot I was almost ready to come on the spot. He was right though. It was already bending with me pressed lightly against it.

"I would prefer no flora or fauna were harmed in the making of this session," I said. "Not to mention it might piss your neighbours off."

"That's true." He cupped my cheeks a little tighter and lifted me until my legs wrapped around his waist.

I let out a little squeak of surprise and flung my arms around his neck as well.

He chuckled and carried me up the street toward his place. Or was it our place for now?

Either way, he carried me through the front gate and froze.

"Shit."

I clung on tighter when I thought he was about to drop me. "What is it?"

He stepped back out the gate and lowered me to the ground. "I don't know. Stay here." He tucked his cock back into his pants and did them up.

I pulled my bra and the front of my dress back into place and watched him step back through the gate. Of course, I followed him. Whatever was going on here, I wasn't going to stand back and wait for it to happen. If he thought it was safe enough to get closer, then surely it was safe enough for me?

He crouched down beside something which lay on the ground near the front door.

"What is that?" I asked while looking over his shoulder.

He startled and looked back at me. "I could have sworn I said to stay back."

I shrugged unapologetically. "Yeah, well, I'm here now. What is it?"

It looked like nothing more terrifying than a cardboard box. I mean, some people might find them scary but I didn't. Until I added, "Is it ticking?"

He leaned in and listened. "No. Not that I can hear."

"Is there any chance someone sent you a cake?" I asked. If they had, I was going to spread some on myself and ask him to lick it all off. And of course I was going to put a bunch of it on him as well. How else would a person eat cake?

"It wouldn't be the weirdest thing I've ever had delivered to me." He sniffed. "It doesn't smell like cake." In the glow from the nearby streetlight, he looked a little sick.

"You should probably not see this," he said.

I hesitated. "I have a feeling you might be right, but I am in it this far. If it's not going to explode, then how bad can it be?"

"Bad," he said. Grimacing, he peeled back the lid.

As soon as he did that, the smell hit my nose.

"Oh my God. Is that...hair?" My stomach twisted into a knot. It wasn't just hair, it was hair attached to a head.

"Who is that?" Did I even want to know?

Zeke reached in gingerly and turned the head until the face was visible. "Jesus Christ," he whispered.

"Is that Jonah?" I asked.

"It was," Zeke agreed. He turned the hired muscle's face away so we couldn't see it. "Not so much anymore."

"Yeah. I don't know, but it doesn't look like he's been dead for long." I'd never seen a dead person before, so what the hell did I know?

"Long enough to be cold, but not too long," Zeke agreed. He closed the lid of the box.

"Is this another message from Reuben?" The expression on Zeke's face had me worried.

He glanced up at me. "No. Reuben doesn't tend to kill his own men. At least, not like this. And he wouldn't leave it here for me to see."

"He might have left for someone else to see?" I looked back over my shoulder, but I didn't see an army of police cars converging on the area. If anyone wanted to set Zeke up, this would be one way to do it. Albeit an extreme one.

Zeke shook his head. "This isn't Reuben's style at all."

"Okay, if it isn't his, then whose is it?" Did I really want the answer to that? How many dangerous people did this guy know?

"I have absolutely no idea," he admitted. "Whoever it is, Reuben is going to be pissed. I need to deal with this and I'm going to have to talk to him before he assumes I'm behind Jonah's disappearance."

His tone sent shivers through me.

"Deal with that?" I asked. "How the fuck are you going to deal with a disembodied head?"

He pulled out his phone and tapped the screen before he shoved it back in his pocket. He picked up the box and stood. "I know a guy."

"Of course you do." I ran a hand over my hair. "First a gun and now a head. What's next? Is this just another day in the life of Zeke Brantley?"

"No. Usually it's much more interesting than this," he said sarcastically.

I snorted. I was starting to wonder if me being associated with Wolf Venom was some kind of joke. A sick joke at that. My former label might be having a good laugh at my expense. If it wasn't for the smell coming from the box, I might assume the head was fake and all of this was a practical joke. It certainly *smelled* real. I was sober now, but my dinner staying in my stomach was a fifty-fifty shot right now.

"I should get this dealt with." He nodded toward the box. "My friend is only a couple of blocks away."

"I'm coming with you," I said without thinking.

"It's late—" he started.

"I don't care," I said firmly. "I need to know it's really dealt with." And on some level, I needed to know if all of this was actually real. I glanced around for cameras, but didn't see any. Of course, I wouldn't if they were hidden.

A significant part of me wished this *was* a joke. That Zeke wasn't carrying a real head in a cardboard box in his arms. I'd handled humiliation before, I could do it again.

Unfortunately, I was almost certain this was real.

I thought about asking to take a closer look at the head, to be sure, but for once, a bit of common sense kicked in. I already couldn't unsee what I'd seen. A better view would only make those memories stick in my head for longer.

"Besides," I added, "I don't want to be here alone if someone is walking around cutting off heads and sticking them in boxes. Not to mention there might be other parts of Jonah lying around." For all I knew, the rest of him was sitting inside the townhouse on the couch. I didn't want to be alone if I saw that. I mean, I didn't want to see that at all, but certainly not by myself.

Zeke sighed. "Okay then. Let's get this over with."

CHAPTER
TEN

ABBIE

THE LAST PERSON I expected to see when we walked through the front gate of another terraced house was Asher. His expression was as grim as Zeke's.

He peeled open the box's lid and peered inside. "Ahhh, yeah. He's dead all right."

Zeke snorted. "You think? I know some people can function pretty well without having much in the way of brains, but this dude is missing a bit more than that."

Asher closed the lid and shrugged. "You didn't give me specifics in your text message. I was half expecting to turn up with an unconscious person over your shoulder."

"Is that something he does normally?" I asked.

Asher grinned. "It's Zeke, who can tell? He does some pretty wild things."

I should absolutely not find that adorable right now, but I did. I never claimed to be appropriate. I was almost certain there wasn't a right or wrong way to behave in a situation like this anyway. Some people vomit.

Others....get turned on apparently.

"So I've heard," I said dryly. I was hoping he'd assure me this was out of the ordinary.

"This gives a whole new meaning to giving head," Asher said. "Any idea who it's from?"

"Nope. Probably not Reuben but I don't know where to start on making a list of who it might actually be. The only ones who know about this are the three of us, the rest of the band and Reuben."

"Is it possible he has a traitor working for him, or something?" I asked. "Is that even a thing?"

"It's a thing," Asher agreed. "Ask my father. Actually you can't, he double crossed Zeke's father, so he's not alive to tell the story."

Was I hearing right? Zeke's father murdered Asher's father?

What in the world had I gotten myself into? I wasn't sure, but I had a feeling getting out of it was going to be harder than getting in. It would be a lot easier if these guys weren't so fucking attractive.

Yep, there I went, thinking with my clit again.

"If whoever did this is working for Reuben, they're going to end up dead," Zeke said. "Which ultimately is not my problem. My problem is the fact I'm holding a body part in a cardboard box."

"That certainly is a problem," Asher agreed. "I think Haru is in. If anyone can deal with that he can." He turned and rapped on the door with his knuckles before pushing it open.

I sighed softly to myself and followed them inside. This was not how I thought my night would end. I was hoping for more sweat, more panting and a lot more of Zeke's cock inside my pussy.

Not dealing with a severed head with a couple of guys who knew more about mobsters than it was probably healthy to know. When I first met them, I thought they were your average, arrogant rock stars. That wasn't even the start of it. Not even the tip of the proverbial iceberg.

Fucking fuck.

The townhouse was small and narrow, like Zeke's. Unlike his, it was lit entirely with candles. Either this Haru guy loved candlelight, or didn't like electricity. Maybe he didn't have electricity.

That theory was thrown out when we stepped into a back room. Several fridges hummed with energy and an electric coffee maker bubbled away. The scent of the delicious brew filled the air.

A guy of around my height—relatively short—with black hair and dark eyes looked up as we entered the room.

His body was slender to the point of being skinny. He wore black jeans and a bright purple T-shirt with the Rock Dragons logo on the front. If I remembered right, they were an American rock band, almost as popular as Wolf Venom.

"Twice in one week," he commented. His accent sounded faintly Japanese. "I'm going to start to think you're crushing on me."

Zeke chuckled. "I would totally crush on you if you were my type."

"Liar," Haru said playfully. He held out his hands and Zeke handed him the box. "Did you bring me a cake? I'm allergic to chocolate."

"Not a cake," Zeke said ruefully.

Haru opened the box and peered inside. "Definitely not a cake." He put the box over on a table. "Where's the rest of him?"

Zeke shrugged. "No idea. Could be at the bottom of the harbour for all I know. I'm hoping we don't get any more presents like this."

"Why?" Asher grinned. "Who doesn't want to get a bit of head once in a while? I know I do."

"Great," Zeke said ironically. "The next time someone drops a disembodied head off on my doorstep, I will give it to you."

"Thanks, but I'll pass," Asher said predictably. "I'll take the other kind any day though." He gave me a speculative look.

All I could do right now was smile back, although my eyes did drop to his groin.

He was obviously getting the same vibe I was. I was as attracted to him as I was to Zeke. If it was him in that club the other night, I would have been just as happy to have my lips around his cock. I had a feeling I would get the opportunity before too much longer, if he had his way.

I managed to tear my eyes away from the tent in his jeans and looked over to Haru.

"How are you going to get rid of that?" Clearly my morbid curiosity got the better of me.

"I have a few methods," he said as though he was talking about how to cook a chicken. "Acid. Hammer. Walk to the harbour and throw it in. One time, I got a ride in a helicopter and threw some evidence out the door. We were right over the middle of the Pacific Ocean. That was fucking *cool*." He dragged out the last word.

Asher and Zeke both looked like they were trying to hold back laughter.

I had no idea if Haru was being serious or not. He sounded like he was living his best life either way.

"In this case, something more subtle. We can't have this guy's head bobbing up and coming back to haunt us." He turned away and grabbed a pair of gloves.

"I hadn't thought about being haunted, but now I have. I'm scared." I didn't really believe in ghosts, but if anyone was going to have a vengeful spirit, it was going to be a guy whose remains were disposed of like he was little more than rubbish.

I almost felt sorry for the guy. Almost. A proper funeral was probably never on the cards for him anyway, with his lifestyle, but now he had no choice to redeem himself. Would he have anyway? I had no answers to that.

Zeke and Asher laughed even harder.

I looked over at them. "What?"

Zeke shook his head. "I'm sorry. It's just this whole situation. And how cute you are when you talk about ghosts." He turned to Asher. "She's cute, isn't she?"

Asher gave me a lingering, hungry look. "She certainly is." He glanced at Zeke with the same look in his eyes.

I thought he was going to say something else, but the moment was interrupted by Haru picking up the box and depositing it, cardboard, head and all into a giant oven. The kind they use for cremations. That made sense. Jonah certainly couldn't bob back up when he was just ashes.

Haru swung the oven door closed and locked it.

I felt a twinge of guilt. Sure this Jonah guy threatened to kill me, but he was dead and his family might never know what happened. Was that fair to them, or were they in this as deeply as he was?

Either way, didn't they deserve to know?

I realised there was absolutely nothing I could do about it. At this point, I was in this as much as Asher and Zeke were. If the police found out about it, I would be just as fucked as them. Like it or not, I was going to have to keep my mouth very shut.

"Are you going to tell the rest of the guys about this?" I asked softly.

Zeke nodded with no hesitation. "What you said about not keeping secrets extends to things like this. We can't rule out the possibility this isn't just aimed at me. Someone might have seen us with Jonah and decided to make some point about the band."

I felt my face pale. "It might be about me." I hadn't even thought about that but the possibility was terrifying.

It was Asher who put his arm around me. "If it is, we won't let anything bad happen to you. It's a good thing you're staying with Zeke right now. He's good at kicking asses. Almost as good as me, and I only live a street away."

That explained why he got there so quickly when Zeke texted him.

"That house with six or seven bedrooms is sounding better," Zeke said. "If we were all there, we could all keep Abbie safe. In the meantime, I'll keep an eye on her." He gave me a look like he planned to keep a whole lot of other things on me.

That was fine by me. Finding Jonah's head was like a bucket of cold water poured on us, but it hadn't completely put out the embers. Not to mention, it would be nice to have something to take my mind off all of this for a while.

I was curious about how Haru got rid of the gun, but I decided against asking. I already knew more than I wanted to as it was. My curiosity would have to remain unsatisfied for now.

"You're pretty awesome," Zeke said suddenly.

I blinked. "I am? Why?"

He smiled. "Because most women would have thrown up, run away or cried. Not you though. You're rattled, but you're not scared. You even came here with me, which shows a shit load of balls. Or to be more accurate, cast iron ovaries."

I felt my face getting hot. It got hotter still when I realised both guys were looking at me with matching expressions of admiration.

"That's pretty badass," Asher agreed. "We've had a lifetime of dealing with this shit, that's the only reason we keep it together."

"Do we keep it together?" Zeke asked.

Asher cocked his head at the lead singer. "I mean, I guess we do. More or less." He made a back and forth gesture with his hand. "We haven't quite come unravelled yet, have we?"

"I suppose not," Zeke conceded. "We might all be badasses."

"I certainly am," Haru remarked. "Now, all of this testosterone is making me twitchy." He made an 'out-out' gesture with his fingers, in the direction of the door.

I couldn't blame him, it was doing the same to me.

I gave Haru a smile and followed the guys back out onto the street.

"Well…" I said awkwardly. "It's been an interesting evening."

"It certainly has." Asher put a hand on the side of my face and leaned in to give me a slow, deep kiss that turned my knees weak. "Good night. Sweet dreams."

In a whisper he added, "Think of me when you're fucking him."

I had no idea how to respond to that. His words and the brush of his breath on my ear made me hot all over. He made it clear he wanted to be with me, but he didn't seem to mind me being with Zeke. Who even were these guys? I didn't know, but shit, I was going to have to stock up on spare panties. Enough for several changes a day.

Before I could, he turned and gave Zeke a quick bro hug.

"Thanks for coming, bro." Zeke patted him on the shoulder then stepped away from him and took my hand.

"We have some unfinished business to attend to."

CHAPTER
ELEVEN

ZEKE

I LED her up to my room and watched her beautiful face as I lay her back on my bed.

I knew she wanted this as much as I did, but the head might have freaked her out more than she was letting on.

It wasn't everyday you saw something like that. Unless you worked in a morgue or were Hals. Blo didn't seem at all fazed by it. I suspected he saw shit like that all the time. I had a funny feeling he actually liked it. He was cool, but strange.

At any rate, Abbie seemed determined to put it all behind her, at least for now. She focused her eyes on mine and started to pull my shirt up and over my head.

I shrugged out of my sleeves and tossed it aside before I started on her shirt. Her skin was incredible. The more I saw, the more I wanted to see. I wanted to know every freckle, to know the birthmark on her hip by heart. It was shaped like a distorted crescent moon.

Right above that was a tattoo of some kind of flower. I also found a tattoo on her right shoulder, this one of a cat. She also had a different kind of flower on one of her wrists and a treble clef on her ankle.

She had a scar across her abdomen. I traced it with my finger and made a mental note to ask about it later.

In the meantime, I pulled off her skirt and very damp panties and threw them over my shoulder. They landed on my hip before sliding off and onto the floor.

She helped me out of my pants, letting cool air swirl around my hot, hard cock.

I caught her mouth in a deep, searing kiss. Her lips tasted like wine and salt. She smelled of the light perfume she dotted on her neck and throat.

The scent faded into the fresh aroma of soap the further down her body I worked my mouth and hands.

She moaned and writhed as I licked and sucked her nipples in turn. She was so responsive, she turned me on so fucking hard. Harder enough to hurt, in the best way. My balls ached for her. Begged.

Her little moans and whimpers, shit, I could get used to those. My skin pebbled every time, belly clenching in anticipation.

I worked my way down lower, teasing her belly button with the tip of my tongue. I felt a small circular scar there, like she'd had a navel piercing she let grow out.

I would have to ask her about that too.

I shuffled down lower still until I dipped my head between her legs. I slid an arm under one of her thighs, lifting her ass a little and opening her wider to me.

Slowly, with featherlight touches, I started to explore her pussy with my tongue. She tasted delicious, like sweet butter. The sounds she made when I teased her were more beautiful than music. Her hips moved, trying to push her clit into the path of my touch.

I teased that too, but then moved away to kiss the insides of her thighs.

"Zeke..." she said breathlessly. "Please..."

"Can I play with this?" I ran a finger lightly over her rear hole.

"Mmmm, yeah." She panted out her nose.

"Great." I scooted up and leaned over to the table beside the bed. I opened the drawer and pulled out a narrow, blue vibrator and a tube of lube. I caught her looking at me confused, and grinned before I continued slathering lube all over the vibrator.

I scooted back over and gently bent her legs at her knees, to open her out even more.

Slowly and carefully, with my eyes on her face, I pressed the tip of the vibrator against her rear hole. She tensed and shivered at the shock of the cool toy and lube touching her warm skin.

After a moment she relaxed and looked back at me, a gratifying expression of trust on her face. She knew whatever I did, I would do my best not to hurt her. This was a delicate operation at best, after all.

I licked my lips and pressed the vibrator in a little further. When it was a couple of centimetres in, I pressed the button on the side for a light vibrate. At the same time, I slipped a couple of fingers into her pussy and lowered my mouth back to her clit.

"Oh my God," she breathed.

I smiled to myself and licked her clit and folds lightly while simultaneously pressing my fingers and the vibrator into her. Each thrust got a little deeper, but I glanced at her every few moments to make sure she was okay with all of this.

Honestly, she seemed to be better than okay. Her hips rolled lightly and her hands were tangled in the sheets.

"God, God, God, *fuck*..." She moaned loudly, before her breath turned to a series of whimpers and groans. She ground out the most guttural sound I've ever heard and her muscles tightened around my fingers.

My hand was already damp from her juices, but she wet my fingers even more when she came. And she came hard.

Her back arched and she all but screamed at the ceiling. Her hips bucked and rolled for a minute, two. Just as her body started to still, she cried out again, bucking harder still.

Her second orgasm made my hand wetter than the first. My fingers were more lubricated than the vibrator by now. And I was loving every second of it.

I kept working her in the hope of a third orgasm, but she flopped back down and panted.

I took the hint and slid the vibrator free before I turned it off. I tossed it aside and, slowly and reluctantly, slid my fingers out of her. I could happily have kept them there all day, but my balls would probably burst.

I rolled her over onto her stomach, then carefully guided her up onto all fours in front of me. I was almost a quivering mess of anticipation by now. Making her come was ninety-nine percent of the fun, but I still wanted that one percent.

She looked at me over her shoulder while I positioned my cock outside her pussy. My hands pressed against her stomach, I slid into her slowly.

Fuck. The hot, wet, velvet heat that enveloped my cock was almost enough to make me come immediately. It took a shit load of self-control to keep myself from doing just that.

Not only because I didn't want it over that quickly, but because it would be embarrassing.

What sort of rock god would I be if I couldn't last more than a minute or two? Yeah, okay, one who had a really hot, gorgeous woman around his dick. I was only human after all.

I started to thrust slowly, pulling all the way out and sliding all the way back in, balls deep. When I moved forward, I gradually slid my hands further up her body until I had one of her breasts in each of my hands. Her nipples hardened at my touch. My cock might have hardened a little more too, which I wouldn't have thought was possible.

How did this woman make me feel things no other woman ever had before? There was something about her that drove me crazy.

Crazy in the best way possible.

I couldn't get enough. I wanted to pound her hard and fast and at the same time slowly and for hours.

In the end, she chose the pace. She pushed her hips back against me in an easy, captivating rhythm. I didn't even try to fight her. I closed my eyes and enjoyed her doing her thing, her ass pressing against me every couple of seconds.

"Girl, you're amazing," I said as breathlessly as she had spoken to me earlier.

"Hell yeah I am," she said with laughter in her voice.

I chuckled. I didn't see the point of false modesty, especially when she had no need to be modest. She was sexy, smart and incredible, not to mention she felt really fucking good around my cock.

She started to move faster, driving me closer and closer to spilling myself inside her. I tried with everything in me to make it last as long as possible, but her body drove me wild. Her hips moved faster and I couldn't hold back any longer.

I grunted and gripped her breasts a little harder than I intended as I came, releasing every drop of tension and cum deep into her body. I kept on thrusting, milking myself for every little bit of pleasure. Only when there was nothing left, I sagged, sweating and panting, against her.

She lowered herself back down to the bed, taking me with her. Somehow, I managed to stay inside her for another minute or two, totally unwilling to relinquish the warm space inside her delicious body.

Eventually, I realised I was lying on her and had to slide out and roll off.

"Wow," she said after a few minutes of sleepy silence. "That was... Wow."

"Yeah." I was at least as eloquent as she was. Sometimes there weren't the right words to describe something like this. "Worth waiting for."

"Definitely." She rolled over on her side to face me and smiled softly. "That thing with the vibrator. That was new for me."

"Yeah? You seemed to like it." I gave her a questioning glance.

"I did," she agreed. "I've done anal before, but never with a vibrator and never with oral at the same time. That made me come so hard."

I leaned in and kissed her nose. "Then I look forward to doing it again. And again. And a bunch of other stuff you might not have ever done before. I'm sure there's plenty you could teach me too."

She smiled softly. "I'm not sure about that, but I'm looking forward to trying."

That was music to my ears. Almost as much as hearing her come. A small part of me half expected her to run out of the room and regret what we did.

Only a small part, though. The rest of me was sure she knew what she was doing and was happy about it as I was.

"I'm sure you're very creative," I assured her. Now I was going to have to be as well. In the meantime, I had to ask.

"Were you thinking of Asher while I was fucking you?" I smiled teasingly.

I couldn't quite make out her blushing, but I was almost sure she was.

"You heard that?" she asked.

I shrugged the shoulder that wasn't pressed against the mattress. "I think that was his intention, but yes I heard. I don't mind if you were. Your body was here with me."

"It certainly was," she said. "My soul might have left my body a couple of times, but my body was here."

"Sorry, not sorry." I grinned. I would never be sorry for making a woman feel good, particularly her.

"You absolutely don't have anything to be sorry about," she said. "I haven't felt so good in...ever."

"Ever?" I said. "That's impressive." I didn't mind being impressed with myself once in a while. Okay, I was often impressed with myself but usually it was about music. Not that I was all that humble about my skills in the bedroom either. But I wouldn't say no to the boost in my ego anyway. An ego could never be too big. Right?

"Just being honest," she said.

She snuggled into me as I pulled the covers over both of us.

"Do me a favour," I said. "Don't ever stop being honest."

"As long as you don't," she said.

"I'll do my best," I assured her. Unless I had to lie to her to keep her safe. I put an arm over her and drew her closer as sleep started to creep up on me. The last thing that crossed my mind before I let it claim me, was that she hadn't told me whether or not she was thinking about Asher.

CHAPTER
TWELVE
ABBIE

I WOKE CONFUSED BUT WARM. My whole body felt relaxed and satisfied.

It took a couple of languid minutes more to remember why and who I was lying next to.

I rolled onto my side and cracked an eye open.

Zeke was still asleep, his side of the covers half pushed off him.

I had an unimpeded view of his bare torso and chest, tattoos, firm muscles and all. Or should I say tattoo, singular? The ink formed a scene with a wolf in the centre. It stood amongst trees and was surrounded by a variety of animals and mythical creatures. Here and there were symbols I didn't recognise or know the meaning of.

The whole work must have taken hours, and a whole lot of sessions to do.

It was almost as much a work of art as his abs. Without doubt, they also took a lot of work. They were even more impressive than his ink. Maybe it was just my priorities. I loved tattoos, but not as much as muscles.

I thought about licking them, but Zeke opened his eyes and distracted me with his smile.

"Hey beautiful." He stifled a yawn with his hand. "Did you sleep well?"

"Better than I have in years," I said honestly. Usually, I was lucky to get three or four hours of sleep in a row before lying awake for an hour or two. Judging by the light from the window, I'd been out for at least six or seven hours.

"Good." He brushed a kiss over my lips. "I'll be back in a minute." He pushed the covers the rest of the way off and got up.

I admired the view of his tight ass as he headed into the bathroom.

Disposing of guns and heads was probably illegal, but his whole body was the real crime here. No one should get away with looking that good.

He glanced out the window on the way back. His whole demeanour changed instantly.

"Fuck."

"What is it?" I pushed myself up on one elbow. "Please tell me it's not another head. Or other body parts." My heart was suddenly racing.

"Oh it's a head all right," he said. "Unfortunately, it's Reuben's head and the rest of him is here too." He stepped over to the wardrobe and started pulling out clothes.

"That's bad, right?" I pushed off the covers and started to gather up my clothes.

He paused for a moment. "Potentially. We should certainly not be naked when I open the door. Although, if you were, that might soften him up a little bit." He grinned to show he was joking.

Playfully, I scooped his pants up off the floor and threw them at his face.

He caught them and laughed. "I assume that's a no." He tossed them aside onto what I assumed was a laundry pile. He pulled on a pair of boxers and dragged track pants up over the top. Not light grey ones, unfortunately.

"I'm going to have a quick shower," I said. "Tell me you're not going to kill each other while I'm in there."

"To the best of my knowledge, Reuben doesn't want me dead." Zeke pulled a Wolf Venom T-shirt over his head and tugged it down into place.

I had a sneaking suspicion he wore it to goad Reuben. Hopefully that didn't mean things were going to get ugly.

"I hope you're right." I hurried across the corridor to the bathroom.

Before I closed the door, I heard Zeke say, "I hope so too."

This was going to be a lightning quick shower, and getting dressed. I felt uneasy and vulnerable being under the same roof with someone like Reuben Brantley. If he was even half as bad as Zeke said, then I should definitely not turn my back on him, much less be naked around him.

Just in case, I locked the door. Of course, it was the kind of lock you could open with a butter knife, but it made me feel better.

I showered in about two and a half minutes flat, making sure to clean up extra well between my legs. I dried with what I hoped was a clean towel and hurried into my room to get dressed.

From the doorway, I heard male voices talking downstairs. More than two, unless I missed my guess. Who else did Reuben bring with him and what did that mean?

Trouble, presumably.

I stood in front of my wardrobe for a couple of minutes thinking what to wear and ultimately chose a floral sundress that fell to just above my knees. Hopefully it was cute without being provocative.

I dried my hair, tied it back in a ponytail, and applied a tiny splash of make-up.

I pushed my feet into a pair of low heels and, with my heart in my throat, headed down the stairs.

Zeke stood in the kitchen, putting water in the coffee machine.

Three men stood nearby. The two in jeans and plain T-shirts were identical but the resemblance to Zeke was obvious. They were both insanely good-looking in a 'too young for me anyway,' kind of way. Somehow they managed to look menacing and casual at the same time. It was the same vibe, I realised, that Zeke had.

None of them even came close to looking as menacing as the last man. I didn't need anyone to tell me I was looking at Reuben Brantley.

He wore a dark suit and a crisp white button down shirt. He had the kind of face that was handsome, but at the same time looked like he'd never smiled in his life.

As I reached the bottom of the stairs, he turned to look at me with blue eyes so piercing I felt like he stripped me naked and whittled away my soul at the same time.

I swallowed in spite of myself. I resolved not to be intimidated, but it was hard not to be in the presence of someone like him.

"Ahhh, there's Abbie," Zeke said. "Coffee is almost ready." He didn't sound anxious, but it was in his body language. He held himself stiffer than usual, tightly coiled, like he was ready to lash out in an instant.

"It sounds like I have good timing then," I said as calmly as I could. I offered Reuben a smile, which he didn't return.

The twins, on the other hand, looked me up and down and grinned.

"She is cute, bro," one of them said. He stepped over to me and held out his hand. "I'm Parker. I'm sure Zeke has told you a lot about me. It's probably all true. If you get tired of him, look me up. Twins are much more fun. Right, Hunter?"

"He's not wrong," Hunter said. He gave me a smile that might have been seductive if I didn't have his brother to compare him to.

They were adorable, but they were Zeke two-point-oh at best. A thought I would be better off keeping to myself.

"That's Reuben," Parker said helpfully. He jerked his head towards his other brother. "Before you ask, yes he was born with that cranky expression on his face. Some of us think it was tattooed on."

Reuben's expression didn't change except a narrowing of his eyes at his youngest brother.

"I'm sure having six younger brothers would make anyone cranky," I said lightly.

Now he turned his ice cold gaze onto me. I wished I hadn't spoken.

"That depends on the brothers," he said, his voice a deep rumble. "Some are easier to deal with than others." He didn't have to look at Zeke for everyone in the room to know who he was talking about.

"Ain't that the truth?" Zeke said. He shot Reuben a sarcastic smile.

Reuben looked even less impressed than he had already. "You're the one who contacted me. Have you decided to give up on playing around at being a musician?" He talked about it like he couldn't think of a less worthy profession for his brother than that. Or a less serious one.

"No," Zeke said lightly. He pulled coffee cups out of the cupboard and placed them on the bench near the coffee machine. "I thought I'd give it a go for a little while longer. I have a feeling we'll be successful any day now." He turned away to start pouring coffee.

One of the twins chuckled, but I couldn't tell if it was Parker or Hunter. Either way, they fell silent after a glance from Reuben. Presumably, they were the dutiful brothers, even though they pushed the envelope a little bit. Evidently laughing at Zeke's comment was a step too far. Or at least half a step.

"What is this about?" Reuben demanded. "I haven't come here so you could waste my time."

Parker opened his mouth to say something, but snapped it shut again. Judging by the look in his eyes, he had a smartass comment on his lips. It was probably better if he didn't provoke his brother any further.

"Jonah is dead," Zeke said over his shoulder. He turned around, cup in hand and offered it to Reuben. "Milk?"

Reuben looked at him like he'd grown a second or third head. "You killed him?"

"No," Zeke said quickly. He put the cup down near Reuben so he could get it himself, and explained about the present on the doorstep the night before.

"Did you have him killed because he didn't get me to come back into the fold?"

"No," Reuben snapped. "Suspicions on who did?"

If I thought he looked pissed when I first saw him, it was nothing to how he looked now.

It wasn't the same simmering rage Penn had. It was a cool fury that bubbled below the surface. He was contained, more than anyone I ever met.

I suspected that was part of what made him so dangerous. He was very much in control of himself and—presumably—the people around him most of the time.

Zeke shrugged and took a sip of coffee. "Not a clue. I could guess all day and not get it right. You? Any ideas?"

"If I knew, they would be dead right now," Reuben said. He glanced at me but didn't look even slightly sorry for speaking so frankly.

I wondered if he was worried I would go to the police. I quickly realised how silly that thought was.

He knew I knew about the head and I hadn't said anything. That made me an accessory. Further, if his reach was anywhere near what Zeke implied it was, I would be dead before I found a cop who would listen to me. I was in this even deeper than ever.

Oh, goody.

"Did you have to get rid of his head before we got to see it?" Hunter complained.

I raised an eyebrow at him.

He shrugged. "Just to prove it was really Jonah."

I didn't think that was it at all, but whatever. He wouldn't be the first person on the face of the planet to be bloodthirsty, and he wouldn't be the last.

I mean, someone cut off the guy's head. That was pretty fucking bloodthirsty right there.

"It was Jonah," Zeke said. "I wouldn't have you standing in my kitchen if it wasn't."

"I thought it was because you love us." Parker pouted.

Zeke snorted.

"Ouch." Parker raised his hand as though to flip Zeke off but then he glanced at Reuben and lowered his hand.

They certainly had an interesting family dynamic. Reuben had them on a leash, but not necessarily a tight one. Or maybe it wasn't as tight as he would like it to be.

Were the twins trying to rebel the way Zeke was? I'd like to think Zeke would help them if they did, but there didn't seem to be much love lost between them and him.

I wondered about his other brothers. Was he close to any of them at all, or was Wolf Venom more of a family to him then they were?

"We'll be going." Reuben nodded to the twins, gave Zeke a long, intense glare, then headed towards the door.

"Nice talk," Zeke said. He watched them leave, his body tense until the door closed behind them.

CHAPTER
THIRTEEN

ABBIE

"SO YOU MET REUBEN?" Tully looked sympathetic.

"Yeah, he seems charming," I said sarcastically. I looked across the rehearsal room to where Zeke sat talking to Asher. They spoke too softly for me to hear, but Zeke's expression was grim. It had been since his brother left the townhouse.

Tully sat down beside me, almost close enough to touch. "He's always like that just after he's seen any of his brothers. He'll bounce back in an hour or two. He always does."

I turned my head to take a good look at him. Like the other guys, he was ridiculously attractive. He and Channing seemed to be the serious ones of the group for most part.

Right now, Tully's wide mouth was turned up in a slight smile. His eyes, which looked like liquid chocolate, caught me in their gaze.

Where I felt like Reuben tried to eviscerate my soul, it seemed like Tully was trying to see into my mind and heart. I wasn't sure he would like what he found in there either, but it was hard to look away.

"You know all about his family?" I asked, to distract from the moment. "Are you okay with it?"

He pressed the pad of his thumb to his lower lip and considered that question for a moment.

"I'm not okay with them, as such, but I'm more than okay with Zeke. He's not his family. He's tried for a long time to get away from them and put their bullshit behind him. It's hard when you live your life as visibly as we do. He could have disappeared a long time ago if he was—I don't know—a plumber."

"I can't imagine him fixing toilets." I picked up a bottle of water from the floor beside my chair and opened it to take a sip.

Tully chuckled. "Neither can I. I think he was always meant to do something in the public eye."

"That must make it difficult to be a shady person," I said slowly. "People always want to know about our families for some reason. I can't imagine Reuben liking that kind of attention on him or his dealings."

"Most of the world thinks of him as a legitimate businessman," Tully explained. "Having Zeke in the spotlight has probably made him a lot of money."

"Then why not let him keep being in the spotlight?" I asked. Making more money was good motivation for a lot of people.

"Because Reuben values obedience over pretty much everything else." Tully shifted in his seat so the side of his arm touched the side of mine.

I didn't know if he did it on purpose or by accident, but that slight touch was like a charge of electricity all the way through me. I remembered what Zeke said about all the guys wanting to do naughty things with me.

I was starting to want to do naughty things with them too.

"Even money?" It was a little harder to think, but I managed to speak coherently.

"I don't know for sure, but I suspect he has so much money he doesn't need to worry about it too much." The look in Tully's eyes suggested he knew he was getting to me and that the feeling was mutual.

I hadn't anticipated any of this when the label paired me with Wolf Venom. Honestly, all I thought about was getting my career back on track. I knew who they were, I knew their music, but I hadn't thought about connecting with any of them.

It was possible they saw me as fresh meat or something like that, but I didn't think so.

Zeke, Asher and Tully at least seemed to see me as a person. I hadn't had much time to talk to Landon or Channing yet, and Penn was…Penn.

I didn't think he would ever see me as anything but a pain in his ass.

That line of thought brought me back to Zeke and the vibrator and then for some reason I was wondering where Penn would have put it on me, or in me. Thinking like that was unlikely to get me anywhere but frustrated. It wasn't like I was going to find out anyway.

Maybe.

"What about you?" I asked. "What's your family like?"

"Pretty ordinary," he said. "I grew up in the suburbs. One sister, one dog, one cat. Several goldfish. Mum was a teacher, Dad was an accountant. Pretty boring compared to some of the other guys." He nodded towards Zeke and Asher.

"That sounds nice," I said. "Sometimes boring is safer and easier."

"And sometimes it leads you to rebel and join a rock band." He grinned and his mouth looked wider still. I couldn't remember having ever seen anyone with such a big, beautiful smile. It was impossible not to smile back.

"Is that what you did?" I asked. "What do your parents think of that?"

His smile faded and for a moment I thought he was going to say they didn't approve.

Instead he said, "They love it. Apparently I'm not good at rebelling."

He spoke so deadpan I didn't realise he was joking at first. When I did, I laughed.

"What a disappointment," I said. "What could you have done that would have pissed them off?"

"I don't know," he admitted. "I could have gone into politics. Then again, they'd expect me to change the world so they wouldn't be disappointed. Until I failed."

"Was that ever on the cards?" I asked.

"Fuck no," he said firmly. "I'd sooner work for the Brantley family, although they're nuts. Zeke is the only one of them who is close to being sane and, well, that is a low bar. Same with Asher's family. And Penn's, but in a different way."

"Oh?" I was as curious about his as I was about any of the other guys' families. It sounded like Penn came from a privileged background. It figured he turned out a spoiled brat.

"Are we going to rehearse or what?" As if he knew we were talking about him, Penn stood and moved over to his keyboard.

"Yes, we are," Zeke agreed. Whatever Asher said to him, he seemed a lot happier than he'd been all morning. The two guys seem to be closer with each other than with the other guys in the band. Not as close as Landon and Channing, as far as I could tell, but good friends anyway.

"That's our cue." Tully stood and offered me his hand to stand.

I took it and rose. I wasn't even surprised when he didn't let it go until he led me over to my mic stand.

No one else looked surprised either but, predictably, Penn looked pissed.

I sincerely hoped he would get over himself at some point. I didn't know if anything more would develop with any of the guys, but he wasn't going to get rid of me as easily as he might hope. If he didn't like that, too fucking bad. I didn't want to cause trouble between him and any of his bandmates, but I wasn't going to let him stop me from living my life.

"Abbie and I talked about it and we think she should join us on 'Before I Stay' and 'Someone I'm Over'," Zeke said. "Any objections?"

"Works for me," Landon said with an easy smile.

"Yeah, all good." Channing shrugged indifferently.

"Let's do it." Asher flashed me a grin that made my pulse speed up.

Penn grunted, which everyone, including me, ignored. If he objected, he was outnumbered anyway.

"Sounds good." Tully stepped away from me and swung his guitar strap over his shoulder.

"Good." Zeke snaked an arm around my waist. "Come on then, you motherfuckers, let's make some music!"

I pulled my mic out of the stand and brought it to my lips.

"Let's make—" I lowered the microphone and turned it on before I tried again. "Let's make beautiful music."

The guys laughed but they were laughing *with* me and not *at* me. I couldn't bring myself to look at Penn, just in case.

Zeke grinned and turned on his mic. He turned to Asher and nodded.

The drummer nodded back and started the beat for the first song.

Landon, on his bass, was right there with him. The others, like a well oiled machine, slipped in effortlessly.

Zeke and I raised our mics and locked eyes on each other. I knew the song well enough to know when to come in, but my heart raced like crazy. It always did before any kind of performance, but this was different. I didn't want to screw this up. For so very many reasons, including not wanting the guys pissed at me. They needed to know that when we stepped out on stage, I wasn't going to make them look bad.

Doubt crept into my mind. What if I messed up? What if I made a complete fool of myself? I could get out there and forget all the lyrics. Or I could come in at the wrong time. Or I could fall on my face, literally. Or I could just sound bad.

Apparently Zeke could tell I was psyching myself out, big time. He gave me a reassuring smile and hugged me a little tighter.

That was all I needed. When it came time to sing, the words came out in near perfect unison with Zeke's. Getting it exactly right was going to take practice, but we sounded pretty damn good together. Our voices were the perfect blend of his deep, gravelly masculine, and my lighter tone.

By the time we finished the first chorus, I knew we chose the right song to sing. Hopefully the label and Jackson would agree. I had a feeling Zeke had a lot of sway with both of them. Certainly a shit load more than I did. I would have to go along with whatever they decided and keep smiling like I loved the idea, even if I didn't.

Curious, I turned to see what the other guys thought. I got the impression they liked it. Certainly none of them looked like they hated it.

Every one of them seemed laid-back and relaxed. In their groove. They would have played this song a billion times before, so they could do it in their sleep. Even with a new voice added to the mix. It would take more than that to throw them off.

They all made playing their instrument look easy, which I knew none of them were. Especially at their level of skill. I could play guitar and piano, but nowhere near as well as these guys.

There was something especially thrilling about singing with other professionals like this. Not just because they were hot, but because they loved what they did and they did it well. Even if you didn't like their kind of music, you would have to appreciate their ability.

Asher grinned at me without faltering for a moment. He looked like he was having the time of his life behind his drums. He probably was.

When my gaze went to Tully, he gave me a wink. I wasn't sure whether or not making the guitar cry right now was part of the song, but he did it anyway and it totally worked.

I smiled around my microphone and turned back to Zeke. Just like the others, he looked like he was having too much fun. He certainly looked a lot happier than he had an hour ago.

I totally got that. Music was the perfect place to escape to when life got rough. It was like a blanket fort full of chocolate and wine, and a pile of good books. Okay, those things were pretty good too, but music was my life. Spending the last year without being able to perform, was a special kind of hell. One I didn't want to revisit.

The idea of going back there was much scarier than Reuben, a gun or a disembodied head.

CHAPTER
FOURTEEN

ZEKE

"NO MORE HEADS TURNED UP?" Asher asked. He leaned his shoulder against the wall beside me and crossed his arms over his chest.

"Not yet," I said. "Everything is eerily quiet. No one has waved a gun at me and I haven't heard from any of my brothers."

He frowned. "You think they're up to something?"

"When are they not?" I idly ran the tip of my finger around the Wolf Venom logo on the side of one of my headphones. The label had them made especially for us. They even let us choose our own individual colours. Apart from the logo, mine were black.

"It was annoying as shit when they were threatening me and nagging me to come back to the family, but I knew what was going on. This silence is freaky as fuck."

They were planning something. They had to be. Reuben didn't leave anything alone, particularly after one of his men was killed.

In spite of me telling him I wasn't involved, I couldn't rule out the possibility he thought I was. After all, it was my doorstep. And my head Jonah waved the gun at. And Abbie's, which was even worse.

I didn't like being threatened, but the thought of anything happening to her made my blood boil. If anyone tried, I might rip their head off. Not necessarily the one on their shoulders either.

I realised I was gripping my headphones so hard my hand was white. I loosened my grip before I broke them. Levi might be pissed if he had to fork out for replacements too often.

"They might not be up to anything at all," Asher said reasonably.

I snorted and raised my eyebrows at him. "You have met these people, right? If they aren't up to something, then they're probably dead."

"That's a possibility," Asher said. "Maybe somebody went after Jonah and then went after them." He tilted his head questioningly. "According to rumours, the Fiorellis are getting restless."

"We would have heard about it by now." I hated to admit it, but a small part of me wished that was true. They were my family, and I cared about them in a dutiful brother kind of way, but they wouldn't expect me to return to the family if there wasn't a family to return to.

Reuben's enemies would rejoice if he was out of the way. Until someone came along to fill the void. And they would. It was as inevitable as dog crap. Someone was always ready to step up and take their place.

"I guess so," Asher agreed. "Probably just as well, They wouldn't stop until they got the rest of us."

"Or the rest of the Brantley family anyway," I said. "The rest would depend on whether or not they decided to take out the DiMarcos while they were there." We talked about it all so casually, but the carnage would be horrific. Without doubt, innocent people would be caught up, not just us.

Asher grimaced. "I don't know why they'd bother. It's not like we have any power or influence anymore."

"You have plenty of influence," I reminded him. "If you wear a bright green T-shirt, bright green T-shirts suddenly get really popular."

He chuckled. "Oh good, I'm a fashionista." He pretended to fluff his hair. "At least that kind of influence is mostly harmless."

"Mostly being the key word." I looked up as Jackson walked past the room. "What is taking so long?"

"You have somewhere better to be?" Asher asked.

"Better than in the studio listening to our new album to make sure it's as awesome as we want to be? Between that and taking Abbie to lunch, it's a tie."

I wanted her to be here with us today, but the label insisted on sorting out her wardrobe for the upcoming tour. Apparently her performing naked was out of the question, worse luck.

It would be very distracting for all of us if she did, but a guy could wish, right?

Asher smiled. "She's pretty amazing, isn't she?"

I raised an eyebrow at him. "If I didn't know better, I'd think you are smitten."

"Aren't you?" he countered.

I thought about denying it, but I grinned in spite of myself. "I guess you could say that. Do we have a problem here?"

"What? Do you want me to fight you for her?" He raised his fists as if he might actually try to punch me out, but he had the goofiest expression on his face.

I barked a laugh. "First of all, I would whoop your ass and you know it. Second of all, it's my house she's staying in." If I had my way, that wouldn't change.

"And third, if she wants you instead of me, then that's up to her."

"What if she wants you as *well* as me?" Asher asked. "What if she wants all of us?"

I saw her look at Tully with the same interest she showed me and Asher. I'd also seen her cast speculative looks in Landon and Channing's direction.

Penn, she regarded with a combination of curiosity and animosity.

"As long as she's happy, then I'm down with it," I said finally. We shared a buttload of other things, why not a woman? Honestly, I'd rather share her than not have her at all.

I guessed that meant I was more than smitten. If she was anyone else, that would have freaked me the fuck out. With her, I was one hundred percent here for it.

"So it won't bother you if I ask her out?" Asher asked.

"It will bother me while there's someone out there cutting off heads and putting them in boxes," I said. "I don't even like letting her out of my sight for this long. Otherwise, no, it wouldn't bother me. She's free to see whoever she wants."

"Are you?" he gave me a questioning look again.

"Am I what?" I frowned at him.

"Are you free to see anyone you like?"

I opened my mouth to say of course I was, but that wasn't what came out.

"I don't want to see anyone else." I really didn't. No other woman even came close to her. Even thinking about it felt like cheating.

God, when did this happen? Whatever, I wasn't even mad about it.

"Neither do I," Asher admitted. "She really is something else, isn't she?"

"She totally is." I looked up as Jackson stopped in the doorway and gestured towards us.

"You're up," he said.

I nodded and stood. "I feel like this should be weird," I said to Asher. "Is it weird that it isn't weird?"

"No, it just proves that we're even more awesome than we already thought we were." He grinned.

"Huh. I wouldn't have thought that was possible." I chuckled. We were pretty amazing, and none of us were particularly modest, not even me.

"I know. I am amazed." Asher stepped out the door ahead of me.

"What are you amazed by?" Landon asked. As usual, he and Channing were virtually joined at the hip.

"Our own maturity," I said. "And the fact we both like Abbie enough to share her with whoever else she wants to be with."

"Interesting," Tully said from behind them. "Does she know any of this?"

"You're all fucking insane," Penn snapped. "We've known her for all of about five minutes and we're ready to share her around like she's a pizza."

"She's better than pizza," I said. "The point is, a few of us like her and we're not going to punch each other out over it. Aren't you proud of us?"

He gave me a look like I was speaking a different language. "After the tour, none of us will ever see her again."

"First of all, I'm going to make sure that's not the case," I said slowly. "Just because you don't like her doesn't mean the rest of us can't."

"He did include himself in 'we,'" Asher pointed out.

All of us turned to look at Penn.

"He did, didn't he?" I said.

"Fuck off," Penn said. "It was a slip of the tongue. And also accurate. We—" he emphasised the word "—have known her for about five minutes. Just because I'm a part of this band doesn't mean I give a crap about her." Like usual, he scowled.

"It doesn't mean you don't," I said. "There's nothing wrong with liking someone. Especially someone as—"

He stopped mid-step, turned and got almost chest-to-chest with me. "I. Don't. Like. Her. Get the fuck over it. The sooner the better." He pushed past me and stomped off down the corridor after Jackson.

"I've heard hate fucking is good," I called out after him.

He flipped with me off with a finger over his shoulder.

I chuckled. "Does that sound like a man who isn't interested to you guys?"

"Maybe you shouldn't push it any further," Tully said softly. Always the voice of reason. "Just because we all seem to like her, doesn't mean she feels the same way. Chances are she would only choose one of us anyway. At the end of the day, this conversation is probably all for nothing."

Asher and I sighed.

"Tully is right," Asher said. "She might have chosen already. After all, she is living in Zeke's house."

While I didn't mind sharing, I also didn't mind *not* sharing.

"I'll talk to her," I said. "See where her head is at. Don't be surprised if her answer is that she's thinking about the tour."

"We should all be doing that," Channing said. "Whatever happens will happen. I for one I'm happy to roll with it. Right Landon?"

"Right." Landon nodded and leaned over to give Channing a quick kiss on the mouth. "Rolling with it works for me."

They really were way too cute together.

"If you guys don't hurry up, you don't get to have any say in how well the songs were mixed," Jackson said, sticking his head out the doorway.

"Pig's ass. As if you're going to start without us." I laughed.

He grimaced and rolled his eyes. "Maybe not," he agreed. "But we might take the cost of the time you're taking out of your royalties."

Considering we wouldn't notice the shortfall, we all laughed. We didn't even walk faster. We were Wolf Venom, or as our fans referred to us, The Venom. Our producer and manager would wait for us for as long as it took. What was the point of being a rock god if you couldn't push the envelope? At the end of the day, they worked for us. The label wasn't going to drop us anytime soon, we made them way too much money.

I stepped into the studio and pushed my earpieces in. They were connected via bluetooth to the producer's console. The studio had headsets, but I preferred my own.

My idea of sharing didn't include earwax. Sweat, cum, lube, saliva, sure, but not earwax.

I wondered what Abbie would think about the conversation we just had. There was a distinct possibility she would think we were completely crazy.

I knew she wasn't only interested in me, but did that go beyond sex? What if I talked to her and she said it didn't? It wouldn't change how I felt about her and it certainly wouldn't stop me from fucking her.

The only thing that would stop me from doing that was her.

I wasn't wrong when I said we should focus on the album and the tour. Was now a good time to complicate things further?

Yeah, okay, on some level, I was trying to talk myself out of speaking to her because I wasn't sure what she'd say. My ego wasn't fragile, but I wanted her in my life more than I wanted anything else. If things got ugly between us, it would make the tour difficult for everyone. Levi might even pull her from it, to get her out of my hair.

The solution to that was easy. I wouldn't let things get ugly. The best way I knew to do that was with food, wine and orgasms.

Lots and lots of orgasms.

CHAPTER
FIFTEEN
ABBIE

"YOU LOOK BEAUTIFUL," London said softly, his mouth near my ear.

"What he said," Channing said as he slipped up behind us.

"You too," I said without thinking. My face heated. "I mean, you both look handsome."

The three of us hung back behind the rest of Wolf Venom. Both guys seemed happy to let the others bask in the limelight.

As for me, this was *their* album launch party. I was only here at the insistence of the guys and White Wolf Records.

I tried to argue that I might detract from the real celebration, but they insisted. The label even paid for the dress I wore.

Black and glittering with sequins, the dress was high at the front but plunged almost to the top of my panties at the back. A slit in the side revealed most of my left leg. My updo and make-up were done to perfection. I couldn't remember the last time I got all dressed up like this.

I felt sexy, but self-conscious as hell.

Okay, a lot of that was down to the media with their cameras and questions. So far, they were throwing them at the guys and asking them to stop for photos. Sooner or later, someone would notice—

I hadn't even finished that thought when someone shouted, "Abbie Hart! Can you tell us how it feels to be signed with a new label?"

I wanted to ignore them and hurry past into the party. Instead, I gave them a fake smile and said, "It feels good."

I made one few steps before another shouted.

"Abbie, what do you think about Vance getting engaged after your short marriage?"

I almost tripped over nothing, but Landon grabbed my elbow and saved me from falling.

I gave him a quick smile of gratitude. This was the first I'd heard of the asshole with anyone else. If anyone deserved to be a disembodied head, it was Vance.

I flashed another fake smile. "I wish him luck and happiness." I hoped whoever they were, they treated him the same way he treated me. Or worse. Worse was good.

"Abbie, do you think you'll be successful in reviving your career after all the scandals?" That was from Poppy Newton, a tabloid journalist who seemed to have a particular dislike for me.

The feeling was mutual.

To her, I gave the nastiest smile of all.

"Of course I do, Poppy. You know what they say about there being no such thing as bad publicity."

She gave me a similar smile in return. "Are you saying those scandals were nothing but publicity stunts aimed at furthering your career?"

I wanted to remind her she made a career out of reporting this shit to a public hungry for stuff that was none of their business. If anyone was fuelling misery for people like me, it was people like her.

In the corner of my eye, I caught Penn watching the conversation. I hoped like hell he'd keep his mouth closed for once. If he made a comment like he usually did, it might make the situation a hundred times worse. And we both knew it.

I wanted to groan out loud at the idea.

A media shitstorm could make a lot of extra publicity for the tour, but it could also get me kicked off it.

It was all too ironic, considering his colourful past. Which, I noticed, no one asked him about. Maybe they were told that subject was off-limits.

Past Penn, I saw Zeke, Asher and Tully all looking irritated. The smile I gave them was sincere. This was nothing I couldn't handle. I'd spent the last couple of years fielding bullshit questions like this.

"Come on Poppy," I said smoothly. "We both know if I was going to do something for publicity, it would be much more original than getting married for a few hours. It was just one of those things. Sometimes people are impetuous and jump in before they take a good look at the water." Sometimes the water was full of sharks, or pollution.

"Are you sleeping with Zeke Brantley?" Poppy shot off the question so quickly, it was clearly designed to catch me by surprise.

That was exactly what it did. I tried to stammer out a denial, but it wouldn't come.

"I don't see what that's got to do with anything," I said finally.

"It would explain why you're going on tour with Wolf Venom," she said with barely contained delight. She obviously thought she was onto a big story here. Or at least, another opportunity to make me look like a desperate, washed up artist.

I didn't think she'd be happy until my career was over. Bitch.

"The fact that she's talented is why she is going on tour with Wolf Venom." It was Jackson who stepped in to respond to that particular accusation. "Her private life is no one's business but hers. Now, if you'll excuse us, we have a party to get to."

Poppy looked like he'd given her a lemon to suck, but she smiled insincerely and stepped back.

"Thank you," I said softly as I walked beside the band's manager to the door of the club.

Landon and Channing jostled for position on the other side of me. Both looked like they wished they'd stepped in to help me out. Honestly, it was better that they didn't. That might have created more questions I didn't want to have to answer.

"You're welcome," Jackson said. "Like I said before, you're part of the family now. I don't like a member of the family getting attacked by rabid chihuahuas like her." After a moment, he reluctantly added, "She's probably going to publish that anyway."

I sighed. "I know. People like her can't help themselves." There were a lot of worse things to talk about than whether or not I was sleeping with Zeke, so I was probably getting off lightly. A severed head would be a much bigger story and create a shit load of problems for all of us.

"I think you handled it well," Zeke said, his eyes full of approval and—was that affection? "I would have said yes and told her to piss off." He glanced back out the door in the direction of Poppy.

"Yeah, but you have no shame." Asher grinned.

Zeke managed to squeeze in beside me and take my hand. "I have nothing to be ashamed of. And neither does Abbie." He leaned in and whispered in my ear, "Do you want me to have her killed for you? Because I could."

I wasn't sure if he was joking or not, but I shook my head. "As tempting as that is, I wouldn't want you to get into trouble for me."

He nibbled my ear for a moment and said, "Okay. Let me know if you change your mind."

I shivered with the delicious sensations his touch sent through my body. "I'll bear that in mind."

"I'm happy to make the same offer," Asher said.

When I turned to look at him questioningly, he grinned. "I'm guessing he offered to have her taken care of, because I was about to do the same thing."

I shook my head at them both. For guys who said they wanted to get away from their families and the violence they were involved in, they were quick enough to offer their families' contacts to deal with a problem. I couldn't decide if that was terrifying or sexy as hell.

Maybe all of the above.

"Can we forget about it and enjoy ourselves?" Tully stepped up behind me and to my surprise, slipped his arms around my waist. "Would you like a drink? Or a dance?"

I leaned back and looked at him over my shoulder. "Both?"

"What the woman wants, the woman gets," he said. Apparently the party atmosphere brought out his flirty side. I liked it. It was nice to see him relax a little bit.

When Zeke let my hand go, Tully took it and led me over to the bar.

"Drinks are on the label tonight," he said with a smile.

"I'll drink to that." I ordered a glass of champagne and toasted Tully with it. He toasted me back with his glass of beer.

We took a few sips and moved to the dance floor.

While I grooved carefully, and tried not to spill my drink, I glanced around and tried not to gawk like a starstruck teenager.

The guest list was a who's who of the music industry. Not just in Australia; a lot of international faces were here tonight as well. Producers, artists, executives for various labels, they all turned up to rub elbows with each other.

Several famous actors were here tonight as well. I recognised one of the world's most popular Australian action heroes standing off to the side with his equally gorgeous and talented wife.

Events like this always made me feel like I was a nobody. Hell, they probably made the guys feel like they were nobodies, and this was *their* party.

"It's surreal, isn't it?" Tully asked, as if he read my mind. "Everywhere I turn, I see someone I recognise. Someone whose music I have on my playlist. Someone I'd love to work with. I'd love to try my hand at acting some day, but who knows if I'd be any good at it?" He shrugged as though he wasn't too worried either way. It wasn't like he needed to succeed at it to put food on his table.

"I'm sure you'd be amazing," I said firmly. "What are music videos if they aren't acting?"

Apart from being really uncomfortable to make. They were definitely not the highlight of my career, especially the lip synching. I'd prefer to do just about anything else. They were an evil necessity though, unfortunately.

"True," he said reflectively. "After the tour, I might look around for an opportunity. You never know, I might be the next big silver screen hero."

I smiled. "I would come and see your movies. I know the rest of the guys would too."

"They better," he growled playfully. "I know where they all live."

I laughed, drank down the rest of my champagne and handed my glass to a passing server.

"You're making threats now?" I asked. Without a drink in my hand, I was able to move closer and put my hand lightly on his shoulder.

He took my hand and put his other one on my hip. It wasn't exactly the right kind of music for a slow dance position, but whatever. Neither of us cared.

He pressed the length of his body against mine and spoke in my ear. "I don't make threats, I make promises."

We both laughed.

In the back of my mind, I wondered if maybe he was involved in the same things as Zeke and Asher and their families, but downplayed it more than they did. He said he had a quiet, suburban upbringing, but that didn't mean he wasn't in it as deep.

I knew them for only a couple of weeks, and already I saw much more than I would ever have dreamed of seeing. Tully had known them for years and was fully aware of their pasts. I could only guess at the things he might have seen and done.

What about the rest of the guys then? It wasn't too much of a stretch to think Penn was involved in things he shouldn't be. He oozed rebel bad boy, as well as asshole.

Landon and Channing—they both seemed more innocent than the rest of the guys, but I knew as well as anyone that there was no guarantee of anything. They could be cat burglars or counterfeiters for all I knew. For the thrill, of course. Neither needed the money.

Jackson, now that I thought about it, probably knew the same things the rest of the guys did. How far up the label did it go? Did Levi Jones have any idea?

I had a feeling he must. A guy like him was too savvy not to know everything that went on in his business.

Before I completely lost my mind in speculation, Tully interrupted my thoughts and leaned in to kiss me. His mouth was rough on mine, contradicting his calm, controlled exterior. It sent a spike of desire right to my pussy.

I had a feeling if we weren't in a room full of people, he would have pushed me hard up against a wall and pounded into me until I screamed with pain and pleasure.

Yeah, he conveyed all of that with one kiss.

Holy shit.

By the time we broke apart, I was panting and yet another pair of panties was ruined.

These guys.

CHAPTER
SIXTEEN

ABBIE

AFTER THAT KISS, I danced with most of the guys—not Penn—and a few other guys who asked. Most of them were people I knew or had worked with in the past. A couple I recognised but hadn't met before.

Judging by the looks they gave me and the way they tried to touch my ass on and off the dance floor, they hoped I'd go home with them at the end of the night. My reputation didn't matter to them, they just wanted a fuck.

The only person I went home with was Zeke. My mind buzzed with questions and alcohol, a potentially dangerous combination at the best of times.

He held my hand while we walked up to the townhouse. In spite of the vibe between us, that was all we did. No kissing or undressing each other in the street.

Considering we found the head the last time we came home after an evening out, a bit of caution was understandable.

"No cardboard box," he remarked when we got close enough to see the front steps.

"Fuck yeah," I said. "No random feet that aren't attached to legs either."

"No hands. But most of all, no disembodied cock or ass." He swung our hands between us.

"Thank God for that." Those might be worse than seeing a head.

Maybe.

I didn't know.

They all sounded awful.

"No Reaper waiting outside for us and glaring," he added to the growing list.

"No Poppy Newton hiding in the bushes with her camera." I glanced around to make sure. If she was hiding in the shadows, I couldn't see her.

"Shame." He grinned, teeth flashing white in the streetlight. "We could have given her a show."

He must have decided it was safe, because he pressed me against the door and slanted his mouth over mine. He kissed me, possessive and demanding. His hands wandered up my arms, to my shoulders. He tangled his fingers in the straps of my dress before tugging them to either side.

The dress slid down my legs and pooled at my feet. I stood in front of him wearing only a black G-string and sequined black stiletto heels.

"That's better. I thought you were overdressed. You looked beautiful, but I much prefer you this way." He bent forward to flick his tongue over one of my nipples. While he did that, he slid his thumbs into the sides of my panties and pushed them down until they joined my dress on the ground.

Except for my heels, I was completely naked for anyone walking past to see. And I didn't even care.

I cared even less when he knelt down in front of me and gently pried my legs apart. He bent one of my knees enough so he could slowly start to devour my pussy with his mouth and tongue.

I pressed my hands against the door and leaned my head back, eyes closed in enjoyment. He nipped at my folds and lapped at my entrance before sucking on my clit.

My hands curled into fists as desire rose. It rushed up like a tsunami, threatening to wash me away and shatter me into a million pieces.

I couldn't hold back a moan that was so loud the neighbours probably heard. Whatever. Let them hear. Hell, let them come out and watch.

I was vaguely aware of someone walking past who stopped to do just that before they hurried on. I hoped they enjoyed the show. I also hoped they didn't video it, because that bullshit would go viral and I would be fucked in more ways than one.

Luckily it was too dark in front of the door for them to see my face clearly.

"Maybe we should take this inside," I said with what little breath I had to speak. That was followed by another moan as he pressed his fingers inside me. He curled them around to massage my G spot, while not letting up on my clit for a moment.

Or I could just come out here.

I cracked my eyes open at the sound of footsteps which stopped nearby. A couple of guys stood near the gate, watching. The polite thing to do would have been to smile, but I came instead.

I gasped out loud and bucked my hips against Zeke's mouth and hand. The whole world disappeared in an explosion of stars, fireworks and maybe a rainbow or two.

Knowing people were watching made it even more intense and exciting. Finally, I came down with a whimper and a racing pulse.

The guys actually clapped.

I gave a half bow and a choking laugh before they moved on.

Zeke slipped a shining hand out of me and stood, a grin on his face. "Seems like we put on quite the performance."

"Apparently," I agreed. "Let's take this inside. I have an idea." I bent to pick up my dress and panties.

"Should I be scared?" He didn't look at all scared or even worried. That was good, he had no need to be.

"You'll be fine," I said lightly. I waited until he unlocked the door and went upstairs with him to his room. I tossed my clothes aside and helped him to get out of his.

"I assume you washed that vibrator?" I put my hand on his chest and shoved him back on the bed.

"Of course I did." He rolled over and pulled it out of the drawer along with the lube. "You want me to use it on you again?"

I took both from him. "Not exactly. I figured it might be fun to see how it feels to do that to someone else. If you're game?"

His eyes widened and for a moment he looked a little nervous. "Um."

The bed dipped as I sat down beside him. "You don't have to if you don't want to. There's plenty of other things we could do." I could have made him do it if I wanted to, but I was all about consent.

"No, I do," he said quickly. "You just took me by surprise. I expected...I dunno, anything but that."

His eyes flicked to me, more tentative than I'd seen him before, but willing. "Promise to be gentle? I haven't done anything like this before."

"Of course I will." I hadn't done it to anyone either, and I was scared of hurting him. If anything, I'd be too gentle. I'd watch him and let him guide me. And be ready to stop the second he gave any sign of discomfort.

I applied a literal load of lube to the vibrator and put the tube aside.

Eyes on his face I bent his knees and turned the vibrator on to a low hum. I curled one hand around the base of his already erect cock and licked his tip.

I teased him like that for a while before I closed my lips around him and started to suck.

He groaned and closed his eyes. "Hell yeah, your mouth is fucking incredible."

When his body started to move with me, I slid the vibrator lightly over his balls before I pressed the very tip of the into his rear hole. It wasn't more than half a centimetre for now.

I glanced up to see his eyelids flutter, but his eyes stayed closed.

Encouraged, I pushed it in a little further. I didn't want to rush this. Anal wasn't something to be jumped into too hard and fast, so to speak.

I lifted my mouth off him long enough to ask, "Is that okay?"

"Mmmm. Hell yeah. That's…different, but I like it."

"Let me know if it doesn't feel good and I'll stop." I lowered my mouth to his cock and went back to sucking. Like he had done with me, I got into a rhythm of sucking and thrusting gently.

I only put the vibrator in a centimetre or two in. Later, if he wanted to try this again, I would see how far he could take it.

I admit, I hoped I'd get to find out. It was refreshing to be with someone who was a bit more adventurous than other guys.

He bucked harder against my mouth and I had to grip the vibrator firmer to keep it from slipping out of my hand. Or from slipping out of him. I wanted to see him come with it inside his ass.

He let out a guttural, almost animalistic groan and his whole body went stiff except his hips. They moved faster and faster as he pounded himself deeper down my throat.

An even louder moan tore from his lips as he came, blasting hot, creamy cum into my mouth. Even after that, he kept on thrusting for a couple of minutes more.

Finally, his whole body flopped against the mattress and I slipped the vibrator out so he could get comfortable. I made a note to see what else he would let me use on him and how long he would keep them in there for.

"Holy shit," he whispered. "Just when I think you can't get any more amazing, you do. You blow my mind as well as my cock." He picked his head up and grinned. He really was too hot for his own good, and probably mine.

I laughed softly and dropped the vibrator onto the floor. "I try."

He pulled me up until my head rested against his chest and kissed my hair. "You do more than try. Everything you do, you kick ass. I can't imagine not having you in my life."

I tilted my head so I could look up at his face. "I can't imagine not having you in mine either." Or any of the guys, for that matter. Even Penn, as irritating as he was. If I was nice to him, maybe he would come around eventually. If not, that was his loss.

He was silent for a moment, then said, "I guess that journalist was right. We are sleeping together."

I snorted a laugh. "If that's news to you then I'm worried about your short term memory." There wasn't anything wrong with mine. I could vividly remember her accusing me of engineering publicity stunts to help my career. And then bringing up Zeke.

"How did she know anyway?" I asked. How did these people dig up all their dirt? I mean, the stuff they didn't make up.

"Lucky guess?" he suggested. "Or the fact you're living here."

I didn't miss the fact he referred to it that way and not that I was just staying here. This wasn't supposed to be a permanent arrangement, but I hadn't slept on the bed in the spare room even once. I didn't think he was planning to evict me anytime soon.

"How did she know I was living here?" I asked sleepily.

"That information could have come from any number of sources," he said. "It's not exactly a state secret."

"I guess not." I couldn't shake the uneasy feeling that crept up on me.

Amongst the people who knew were Reuben, Hunter and Parker. Hell, even Penn might have let it leak to cause trouble for me. Reuben might have thought it would embarrass me enough for me to scurry away and hide. If that's what he thought, then he would have to think again. I would stay here until either Zeke kicked me out or I decided to leave. I wouldn't be intimidated out the door. Not even by someone who probably had hitmen on speed dial.

Okay, maybe my ovaries were bigger than my common sense right now, but I wasn't going to run away again. I'd spent enough time over the last two years running from trouble and problems caused by other people. From now on, I was going to stand my ground as long as it remained more or less solid under my feet. I had several amazing guys who were very clearly ready to help me stay upright.

Figuratively speaking that was. At least three of them might have preferred me to be horizontal. At some point, I was going to have to figure that out. Was it even possible to go there with them and not jeopardise whatever this was growing between Zeke and I?

Saying the other guys in the band wanted to sleep with me was one thing, but being okay with it actually happening was another.

Zeke muttered something I couldn't quite make out.

"What did you say?" I asked. I wasn't sure if he was trying to tell me something or if he was half asleep.

"I said I'm falling for you," he said.

CHAPTER
SEVENTEEN

ABBIE

"I SAID I'm falling for you."

His words echoed through my mind for days afterward. I hadn't answered. I couldn't come up with a coherent thought, much less the right response.

The next day, he acted like he hadn't said it all, so I didn't bring it up. I *wanted* to. A couple of times I almost did, but I chickened out at the last second.

Honestly, I wasn't sure what I'd say. I was falling for him too.

At the same time, I was developing feelings for the other guys in the band. Shit, what did that say about me? I struggled to have solid relationships with one guy at a time, much less a whole band of them. Surely they deserved better than someone who couldn't make up her mind?

These guys though, there was something about them all that made me want to tangle myself up tight, whatever the consequences. Around them I felt like maybe I could belong. To them and with them.

I needed that so badly. Ached for it. How could I walk away, especially when they seemed as invested in my career as they were in their own?

When the label wanted me to spend some time in the studio working on a new album, they came to give me support. Tully and Landon even offered to play on it.

So did Channing and Asher once the drummer was done complaining that he should have thought of it first.

However it came about, it was an offer I was ecstatic to accept.

I knew better than to hope Penn would offer, but I hoped he might. I've never heard anyone play keyboard like he did. He would make the album sound phenomenal.

Okay, *more* phenomenal.

Anyone the label chose would be amazing, but a girl could hope, right?

With that thought buzzing in my brain, I hurried along the row of neat terrace houses about a block from Zeke's.

Each was about a hundred years old, but most were kept in good condition or recently renovated. One or two were for sale. I hated to think how much they'd be worth. With any luck, and a lot of hard work, I might get myself in a position where I could afford one some day. It was a nice area and convenient to everything.

Although, a small house in a leafy suburb would be nice too.

Or a harbourside mansion if I really wanted to stretch my imagination.

Even if I could afford somewhere like that, I wasn't sure if I wanted to live in a place that big. At least, not by myself. Maybe with the guys...

I was lost in that daydream when a dark car slid slowly past and pulled up by the side of the road, between a white hatchback and a red minivan.

Something about the tinted windows made my pulse spike and sweat break out under my arms.

I ducked my head and walked faster, resisting the sudden urge to run. I would have to pass it to get to Zeke's, unless I turned back and went the long way around.

Stop being fucking paranoid, I told myself. *There's a bajillion cars parked by the side of the road.* This part of Sydney had almost no off-street parking. It wasn't even the only car with tinted windows.

In spite of giving myself that pep talk, the hair on the back of my neck rose when one of the back passenger doors opened.

It's nothing, I told myself. *Just a local doing their thang. Nothing to worry about.*

I was on edge after all the things that happened recently, and the fact I was alone for the first time in weeks.

The whole band was being interviewed on the other side of town, and the label needed me in the studio. Most of the guys weren't happy about it, but I reminded them I was a big girl and could take care of myself.

In the end, work was work.

I kept an eye on the car, but kept walking, albeit on the far side of the footpath, closest to the houses. Everything in me was on high alert. Fight or flight reflex at the ready. Should I turn and run?

No, I was fine. Everything was okay. I told myself that over and over.

Until I recognised the man who got out of the car.

"It's Abbie, isn't it?"

I wasn't sure if it was Hunter or Parker Brantley, but I doubted it was a coincidence he was here, on the same street I was walking up.

"Yeah. Hi." It didn't hurt to be polite, did it? Not yet at least. I stopped a couple of metres away from him.

I felt like a deer standing naked in front of a lion.

He smiled like we were old friends. "My brother wants to talk to you."

"Really?" I asked. "Which one? From what I've heard, you have a few."

His smile didn't falter. If anything, it got wider. "I can see why Zeke likes you. You've got balls. We both know you know I mean Reuben. And yet, you happily risk poking the hornet's nest."

I shrugged one shoulder. "You know what they say, you haven't lived until you've been bitten a few times."

He threw back his head and laughed. "I haven't heard that but I like it. I might make that my motto."

"You do that." I moved to step around him.

Just as quickly, he stepped back into my path. "I have to insist."

"He really does."

I didn't see the other twin leave the car, but suddenly he was standing at my elbow. I almost jumped out of my skin.

I half turned and swallowed. I didn't want that to be a gun in his pocket, but I didn't want him to be happy to see me either. Guys like these didn't seem like they took no for an answer.

"Fucking hell," I muttered.

"Sorry, didn't mean to scare you." He didn't sound sorry at all. The opposite in fact.

I had a feeling these guys got off on scaring the shit out of people. No wonder Zeke didn't want anything to do with them.

"Sure," I said.

"Hunter, I don't think she believes you," the first guy said. Parker then.

"Fuck knows why." Hunter shrugged and waved towards the car. "In case you weren't sure, we're not asking."

"I didn't think you were," I said. "But I can give you my number if he wants to give me a call or send me a text."

Parker chuckled. "I'll take your number. But Reuben wants to see you in person." He slipped into the back seat and scooted across to the other side.

"Look how lucky you are, you get to sit between us," Hunter said. His eyebrow wiggle looked very much like Zeke's. No one could ever think they weren't related.

I swallowed. "Right. Lucky." I glanced around but no one seemed to be watching. No one was running down the street to stop them. "Is this going to take long?"

"It will take as long as it takes," Hunter said. He put a hand on my arm and pressed me towards the car. It wasn't quite a shove, but the message was clear. I could get in or he would force me in.

I thought about screaming, but if that was a gun in his hand, hidden by the fabric of his black hoodie, then things might end badly for me.

Of course, things could end badly for me if I got into the car. So I was either fucked, or I was fucked. Wonderful.

"If he wanted you dead, you would be dead," Hunter said.

I think he was trying to reassure me, but Reuben seemed like the kind of guy who could change his mind anytime he wanted to.

Since apparently I had no choice, I slid into the back of the car. Hunter climbed in next to me and closed the door.

I grabbed my seatbelt and clicked it into place. It would be really fucking stupid to get into a crash and die, especially under the circumstances.

At some unseen signal, the driver pulled away from the curb and started to weave down the street and through Sydney traffic.

"Do you often do dirty work for your brother?" I asked conversationally.

"I have a feeling you want us to say this is a one-off," Parker said. "But it's not. We do shit like this for him all the time. What else are brothers for?"

I could think of a few things. "Is this what he wants Zeke back for? Why does he need him if he has you two?" And several other brothers to do his bidding.

"That's not for us to say," Hunter said. "But there are only two of us. We're pretty fucking epic, but we can't be everywhere." How modest he was.

"Have you tried?" I don't know why I was provoking these guys, but I couldn't seem to help myself. This, right here, might be why I got myself into trouble without meaning to.

It might also get me into a shallow grave.

"We've tried to be in the same place at the same time," Parker said. "It's a tight fit, but worth the effort. We'll be happy to show you after this if you like." He grinned.

It wasn't difficult to guess what he was referring to. "You're assuming there is an *after this*," I said.

Were they successful? No, wait, I didn't want to know. Mostly.

"That wasn't a no," he pointed out. "More and more I see why Zeke likes you. There's nothing better than an adventurous woman." He gave me a lopsided smile. No doubt he'd melted many panties in his day. He wasn't going to make me ruin mine.

"You mean one who puts out," Hunter said.

"That too," Parker agreed.

I rolled my eyes at neither of them in particular. If they weren't scary dudes, they might be hot. No, that's not true. They were definitely hot. Under very different circumstances, I might let them see if they could both fit their cocks into my pussy at the same time.

I absolutely did not sneak a speculative glance at Parker's groin. No way.

"I'm not sleeping with either of you," I said firmly.

"Who said anything about sleeping?" Parker actually gave me a wink. As if he and his brother hadn't abducted me off the street. He had a strange idea about seduction.

I snorted and turned my gaze towards the front windscreen of the car. I should probably have some idea where we were headed, in case I managed to get away from them and needed to know which direction to run.

Realistically, I wasn't likely to outrun two guys who were a foot taller than me and potentially armed. Especially not in heels.

"Is it far?" For all I knew, they were taking me to Melbourne or Dubbo, or who knew where else. Sydney was a big place.

There was a real possibility I could be dead in the next couple of hours. Or worse.

The humiliation of Poppy Newton's questions didn't seem quite so bad now.

For the umpteenth time in the last couple of years, I questioned my life choices. I could have taken a taxi back to Zeke's place, or stayed at the studio until the guys met me there.

Instead, I chose to walk by myself. A choice I made a million times before, in cities all over the world. Never with a killer on the loose, and Zeke's family lurking in the shadows.

I cursed myself, but I cursed the twins and Reuben even more. A woman should be able to walk around by herself wherever she wanted and not get hustled into the back of a car.

Or attacked. Or even wolf whistled at if she didn't want that to happen.

Fuck these guys.

Not literally.

"Not far," Hunter said lightly. "We've been staying close after what happened to Jonah. Reuben wants answers, as you can imagine."

"And he thinks I have them?" I asked. "I can tell you right now, I don't have a clue. Neither does Zeke." If we did, he probably would have told Reuben all about it, if only to keep him off our backs.

Parker shrugged. "You can tell him that. We're just doing what he asked."

"Do you ever tell him no?" They didn't seem like the kind of guys who rolled over and showed their tummy at the drop of a hat. They might be hounds, but not necessarily perfectly dutiful ones.

Both of them chuckled, but neither of them answered. That did absolutely nothing to alleviate my fear. On the contrary, I was more scared than ever.

CHAPTER
EIGHTEEN

ABBIE

WE PULLED up in front of a decent sized brick home, which looked like an old farmhouse. The area was farmland not that long ago, if I remembered right.

We were in the car for about an hour, and I didn't know this part of Sydney. If I had to run, I wouldn't have a clue which way to go, or where to find help.

Okay, fine, I would have to try charm instead. I might get out of this alive.

Or be totally fucked, because my mouth ran away when I was anxious, and right now I was scared as hell.

Please don't say anything to make them kill you, I begged myself. *Keep it together. Just long enough to get through this. Fall apart later.* That was good advice. Fingers crossed I would take it.

Parker opened the door beside him and climbed out of the car.

Hunter gestured for me to follow him.

"I like the back seat of a car as much as the next person, but you can get out now," Parker said teasingly.

I rolled my eyes towards the roof of the car and slid over so I could climb out. I did my best not to flash too much breast or leg in the process. I didn't think these two needed much encouragement and they certainly didn't need an eyeful.

"Thanks," I said sarcastically.

He grinned. "You're welcome. We can always spend a bit of time there after you speak to my brother."

"Do you ever give up?" I asked.

"Never," he replied easily. "You never know when a woman will change her mind. I can be persistent."

"No shit," I muttered.

"Me too." Just like out on the street, Hunter snuck up behind me and spoke suddenly.

They both chuckled when I jumped. Could anyone blame me for being startled? I was past being on edge and into whatever came after that. Somewhere just below full blown panic.

I glanced toward the street, but there was no contingent of cop cars or anyone that looked like they were going to stop the twins from herding me into the house.

Rule number one of self defence was not letting yourself get taken to a secondary location. Having already failed that miserably, I had no choice but to walk between them to the front door of the house and inside.

"I don't know, but it doesn't seem like a good idea to leave the door unlocked to me," I remarked.

"Who said it was left unlocked?" Hunter asked.

We stepped inside and I saw a huge man with tattoos all the way up to his neck and across one side of his face. He wore a dark button down shirt and black jeans. He looked indifferently at all of us.

I presumed he was the one who unlocked the door. He must have been watching for us.

"Thanks, Terry," Parker said.

Terry grunted.

This huge, terrifying looking guy's name was Terry? For some reason, that made him seem a little less scary. Only a little. Mostly he was scary as fuck, like the twins.

"Boss is in the back." Terry jerked his head slightly toward a corridor.

Being an older home, it wasn't all open. The front door led to a small foyer tiled with terracotta coloured tiles. Doors with dark architraves lined either side of the corridor. A staircase with the same dark stain and an ornate, square newel post, led up to the second floor.

Any other time, I would admire the history of the place. Today though, I barely paid any attention to it. I just wanted this to be over with. Whatever *this* was.

"This way." Parker started down the corridor and Hunter indicated that I should follow him. Having already scared the shit out of me twice, I didn't really want Hunter behind me, but it didn't seem like he was going to give me a choice.

Sticking with my decision to try to be nice, I walked quietly between the twins.

Parker led us all the way to the back of the house, to an enormous library.

Shelves stood from floor to ceiling and every centimetre was covered with books. None lay across the top of others, so I presumed they weren't book addicts, but they had enough of them that I almost reconsidered my assumption that Reuben was a homicidal asshole.

Almost. I mean, let's not go crazy here.

Reuben sat in the kind of leather armchair you might expect to see in an English library, or a movie. If this was either of those things, he would look up from a leatherbound book and stare at me over a pair of glasses.

Instead, he was drinking a cup of coffee. At least, I presumed it was coffee, from the smell. If he wasn't completely evil, he would offer me a cup.

On the other hand, maybe it would be better not to take drinks from men like him.

He nodded at the twins and they both slipped out of the room.

I had no illusion that they would go far. Or that this man was harmless or even unarmed.

"Please, take a seat." He waved towards the armchair opposite him, as though he was doing nothing more than inviting me for a pleasant afternoon chat.

I kept half an eye on him, but moved over to perch on the edge of the chair.

"They said you wanted to talk to me." Why not get right down to it? I wasn't here for a good time.

Before he could respond, I said, "I don't know who killed Jonah. Neither does Zeke."

"I know," Reuben said simply. He took a sip of his coffee, then set it aside on the table beside his chair.

"Then why am I here?" He seemed to be a man of infuriatingly few words. If we kept up like this, I was going to be here three days before he got to the point.

"I want to talk about Zeke." He crossed his legs at his knees.

Okay, we were getting somewhere.

"What about him?" About a thousand thoughts tumbled through my head. Was this where he told me to stay away from his brother? That was up to Zeke, not Reuben. If he threatened to kill me in order to keep me away from his brother...

"I want you to convince him to leave the band," Reuben said.

I stared at him for a solid half minute.

Then I burst out laughing.

To the surprise of no one, he didn't laugh with me. He sat and looked back at me with one half raised eyebrow.

Yeah, probably a bad idea to laugh. I bit it down hard. "What makes you think he would listen to me even if I did ask him to do that? For one thing, he's under contract."

Reuben actually looked amused at that. "You of all people should know contracts can be broken."

Ouch. He knew exactly where to aim for a direct hit, didn't he? I was right, he was evil.

Or at least mean.

"In extreme circumstances they can," I agreed. "No offence, but I don't think, 'just because you say so,' would be considered extreme. No lawyer I ever met would argue that it is."

His half raised eyebrow became a three quarters raised eyebrow.

"Right, I've never met your lawyers." Of course he would have unscrupulous people on his payroll. Probably lots of them.

I tried another angle. "What about the fact he loves what he does? Doesn't that count for something?"

"He's been allowed to do what he loves for nearly a decade." He almost sounded reasonable. At least he believed what he was saying. I had to admire his conviction, even if it was horribly misguided.

"Why try to make him stop now? What's another decade or three between family?" That didn't seem like too much to ask to me. "Or better yet, let him go on living the life he loves."

I thought Reuben might get angry, and maybe he was, but he was controlled. He could have been carved from a block of ice.

"There are more important things in life than music," he said.

I snorted. "Says the man sitting in a room full of books."

There went that eyebrow again.

Since I already put my foot this far down my throat, I might as well keep going.

"How can you appreciate one art form and not another? It's not like you're sitting in a room full of classics or anything." I used that term in the traditional sense, not to insult any of the books in question. Which, at a quick glance around, were an eclectic selection, to put it mildly.

At least one shelf was taken up with romance novels. Either there was more to this man than met the eye, or this library wasn't just his. I couldn't remember if Zeke said anything about Reuben having someone in his life, nor had I asked. There was no accounting for taste.

"Reading books or listening to music are different to writing them, or making it," he said.

I squinted at him. "What would you read if authors stopped writing? If one of your other brothers came out as an author, would you want him to stop?"

"This isn't about speculation," he said.

"Then what is it about?" I thought for a little while. "This isn't about Zeke doing what he loves, is it? You just want him to do what you tell him to do."

That was good news for any of his brothers if they were authors, but continued to be dutiful minions as well.

"I am head of the family," he said coldly. "I expect to be obeyed."

Yeah, and if this was a romance novel, I would be on my knees, calling him daddy.

Meanwhile, back in the real world, I wanted to punch him in the dick.

"I can talk to Zeke, but I'm not going to make any promises," I said. "I don't suppose you've considered a compromise? He works for you once in a while and stays with the band." I knew beyond a shadow of a doubt Zeke would never agree to something like that.

Reuben knew it too, I saw it in his intense, blue eyes.

"He won't compromise, and you won't," I concluded. "What if he never gives in and stays with the band forever?" I couldn't see him walking away. No time soon anyway, if ever.

"He will." Reuben nodded with absolute certainty. He leaned forward, elbows on the armrest of his chair, the fingers of one hand folded over the top of the other. "I can be persuasive."

"Yeah, I've heard that about the guys in your family," I said. "Did your parents never teach you no means no?"

He didn't answer that. He didn't need to.

I grimaced and said, "Is this where you tell me if I don't get through to Zeke, you're going to have me killed?"

"If necessary," he said coolly. He could have been talking about how blue the sky was today, or how the city could use more rain. Or less rain. Or something equally trivial.

Okay, I was hoping for a different response. One that resulted in me living a long, happy life. Preferably with Zeke and maybe the other guys.

I was thinking a little bit ahead here, but it wasn't every day someone told you they would kill you if they felt they needed to. I had no doubt he meant it. He wouldn't even blink if he picked up his phone right now and took out a hit on me. Or called Terry in to break my neck. He'd finish his coffee like nothing happened.

I should be more scared than I was, but if he needed my help, he'd need me alive for a while longer. In theory.

"Like I said, I'll talk to him. Honestly, though, I don't think I really have the kind of influence over him you think I do. We've only known each other for a couple of weeks." It felt like I had known him for years. Lifetimes.

"Then you're not as astute as I gave you credit for," Reuben said. "I saw the way he looked at you the other day. He obviously cares for you a great deal. Maybe even more than he realises. Certainly more than you realise."

Great, now I was getting relationship advice from the big bad wolf himself.

"And you care for him," he added. "You will want what's best for him."

"What if Wolf Venom is what's best for him?" I asked.

"It isn't. He just hasn't realised it yet."

CHAPTER
NINETEEN

ZEKE

"INTERVIEWS ARE my least fucking favourite part of this job," Asher declared.

"Yeah?" I squinted as we walked around the corner and I caught the dying rays of the sun right in my eyes. "You didn't look like you were hating it."

Of course not, he wasn't the one facing a barrage of questions about Abbie and her past. And my present, including my sex life. We usually didn't have a list of safe topics to discuss or ones which were off-limits, but I started to question that policy about halfway through.

Of course, fame brings with it an unhealthy interest in people's personal lives. That comes with the job. The last couple of relationships I had were with women who were also in the public eye. They knew the kind of questions I'd be asked and how much detail I was prepared to go into. I knew the same about them.

Abbie was different. Her past seemed to have generated some sort of unhealthy dislike from certain members of the media. Like that Poppy Newton woman, for one. The minute her name was linked with mine, I became a target of speculation too.

That didn't bother me. Their attitude toward Abbie did. And the idea that if they dug down deep, they would find out more about my family than I wanted anyone else to know.

"You know me, I go with the flow," Asher said lightly. "Also referred to as, 'no one gives a shit about the drummer.' I'm just the cute guy that sits in the back playing with his sticks."

"Very modest," I said ironically. He was right though, unfortunately. Tully and I came under the most scrutiny. Mostly me. That was what I got for being a hot and talented singer.

You had to take the good with the bad.

"Maybe we should rearrange the stage for the next tour," I said. "We can stick the drums out the front and the rest of us can hide behind you. We might start a new trend."

Asher chuckled. "That wouldn't work. Penny would want his pretty face out the front where people can see him."

He was one of the few people that got away with calling Penn 'Penny'. That didn't stop the rest of us from doing it once in a while, of course. Except Channing, who occasionally called him Beauregard. That always went down well. Not.

"You're not wrong." Penn did like to be noticed. Especially by the women in the crowd.

"Fine, we'll stick Penn out the front with you. I'll get a nice comfy armchair and sit in the back. Maybe a beanbag." I rubbed my hands together. That sounded comfortable, but not me at all. I liked to move around too much. And yeah, I liked to be seen too.

Asher laughed. "You can stay home and I'll make it a solo drum concert instead."

"Good luck with that," I said with a grin. Unfortunately for him, the drums were one instrument that couldn't really stand up by themselves, compared to others. If they could, no doubt he would be a smash hit. So to speak.

"Thanks. It could catch on. You could come along and sing on a few of my tunes." He gave me a playful shove with his shoulder as we walked.

"Isn't that what we're doing already?" I shoved him back. "You play and I sing along."

"When you put it that way, yeah. That's exactly what happens." He shoved me hard enough that I staggered sideways a few steps. "When our contracts are up, I should negotiate a bigger percentage."

I laughed and shoved him so hard his shoulder bounced off the front of the building beside us.

"Fuck, bro." He rubbed his shoulder, but he hadn't stopped smiling. "Careful with the money maker."

"You started it, bro," I pointed out.

"Yeah, well, I'm finishing it. Before one of us ends up on the road under a car." He waited a beat or two before shoving me again.

"Dickhead." I narrowly missed being pushed into the tree Abbie and I almost broke making out a couple of weeks ago. That much of my weight against it would have snapped it.

"You still love me," Asher said. "Who else would put up with your bullshit?"

"That list is longer than you think." I rubbed my arm. He was right though. He was more like a brother than any of my brothers. He was closer to me than he was to his brother or sisters as well. Although, he hadn't seen either of his sisters in a long time, so that wasn't much of a stretch.

"Okay, who would put up with your bullshit and keep smiling?" He paused and frowned. "What the fuck does that say about me? Maybe my standards should be a bit higher."

"Probably, but they're not," I teased. "Your standards are in the gutter, like mine."

He chuckled. "I think you just insulted the entire band, and Abbie."

"She's the exception," I said quickly. She was definitely way, way above the gutter.

I didn't know what the hell she saw in me, but I was glad she saw something. I meant what I said when I told her I was falling for her. Honestly, it might be an understatement. I was one hundred percent all right with that. I was happy to let myself fall head over heels in love with her. She was the most incredible, beautiful woman I ever met. We made beautiful music together, in and out of the rehearsal room.

"She really is," Asher agreed.

"Are you still thinking of asking her out?" I asked carefully.

"Thinking about it, planning it. Trying not to chicken out every time I get a moment to talk to her." He threw up his hands and let them drop to his sides.

"Asher DiMarco, if I didn't know better I would think you were shy." I shot a lopsided, teasing smile in his direction.

"Only around her," he admitted. "And this whole situation."

"If it wasn't for me, would you have asked her out already?" I asked.

"Yes. No. I don't know." He shrugged. "If it wasn't for you, there would still be the other guys in the band who look at her the same way I do. And then there's the whole thing about her being, you know, her."

"Yeah," I drawled. "You would be punching above your weight." I smiled slyly, then dodged out of the way when he swung at me.

"Fuck off," he said with a smile. "She and I would be a match made in heaven."

"Because she is an angel and you are a choirboy?" I asked. He was anything but. So was I, thank fuck. I hadn't been that sweet and innocent for a long time. Worst twelve years of my life.

"Because she is hot as fuck and I am hot as fuck," Asher said. "How could that be anything but perfect?"

"No idea, bro," I said. "Do you think it's possible for a person to have more than one, I don't know, soulmate?"

"That is a deep question, bro," he said. "If you mean Abbie and I are both your soulmates, then I don't know how to answer that."

I snorted softly. "I meant her and me, and her and you, and her and any of the other guys. I know polyamory is a thing, but you think it's really possible to love several people equally?"

"I think..." he said slowly, "plenty of people seem to make it work. Parents love all of their kids equally, don't they?"

I gave him a look. "I don't know, do they?" My father had three favourites and none of them were me. He didn't mind telling us that either.

"Good point," Asher said. When his parents split, his mother took his sisters and his father took him and his brother. I remember him being absolutely convinced it was because they'd chosen their favourites. I always felt like it was as if they were dividing property, not preferring one or two children over the others.

"We love all of our songs equally, don't we?" he asked.

"I have three or four I like more than the others," I admitted.

"I guess sometimes it's hard not to have favourites," he said. "Like you love me more than any of the other guys in the band."

"That goes without saying." I looked over at him for a few beats and smiled.

He smiled back. "Love you too, bro. I know you've always got my back."

"And you've always got mine." We understood each other's crazy lives and families better than anyone else. It was just one of those cases of if you know, you know. We definitely knew. We told the other guys almost everything, but living it was a different story.

"Even when you're being a dickhead," he said lightly.

I snorted a laugh. "Luckily that only happens on rare occasions."

"But you admit to being a dickhead once in a while?" he asked.

"I even admit to being a fuckwit from time to time," I said. "Just don't tell anyone I said so."

"Your secret's safe with me." He nodded.

I stopped as we drew closer to my front door. The city was bathed in golden twilight and mid-spring warmth, but a chill travelled down my spine.

"What is it?" Asher stopped too.

I knew he trusted my instincts. If I felt like something was off, then something was off.

I shook my head and turned around slowly, eyes and ears open. "I don't know." Nothing looked like it was out of place. At least, nothing I could put my finger on.

"Let's get inside. I want to make sure Abbie is okay." It was times like this I wished I carried a gun. A Glock in my hand right now might make me feel a tad better.

I pulled out the key from my pocket and hurried up to my door.

No cardboard box. No broken lock. No sign of forced entry. No sign of anything.

And yet, the hairs on the back of my neck stuck up and tingled.

I pushed the door in and looked around before I stepped inside. Still, nothing looked out of place. The townhouse was silent and dark.

"Abbie?" I called out softly.

No reply.

"She might be asleep," Asher suggested. "Otherwise, I think she would have put some lights on."

"Right." That was a good point. "Stay down here. I'm going to check upstairs."

I walked up the timber steps as silently as I could. If she was asleep, I didn't want to wake her. If she wasn't asleep and someone else was here, they would have heard us enter the building anyway.

I slipped upstairs and peeked into the spare room. It was empty and the bed was still as neatly made as the day she moved in. We hadn't talked about it, but she spent every night in my bed.

I glanced into the open door of the bathroom. That was empty too.

The last room was my bedroom and ensuite. If she was up here, she'd be in there.

I pushed open the half closed door and winced as it creaked. I should get that oiled. On the other hand, it made a good alarm if anyone tried to sneak up on me in the middle of the night.

I peered inside. There was enough light coming in the window to see around the room.

"Fuck." It too was empty.

"Where are you?" I pulled my phone out of my back pocket and glanced at it. There was no message from her on the screen. No missed calls. Nothing.

My heart started to race. If Reuben did something to her...

I trotted back down the stairs. "She's not up there."

"Shit," Asher said softly. "Do you think..."

"If he has, I'm going to rip his fucking face off," I growled.

A car engine thrummed closer until it pulled up outside. We exchanged glances.

It got harder to breathe.

CHAPTER
TWENTY

ZEKE

SWEAT SPRANG up on my hands and under my arms.

Like a shadow, I slipped into the kitchen, crouched and silently, gingerly, opened the bottom drawer of the cabinet. I felt around for a moment before I pulled out a fully loaded Glock.

Asher dropped down beside the couch to pull out the other one. Only he and I knew where I kept my firearms. As far as the rest of the band knew, I didn't own one.

That was technically correct. I *didn't* own one, I owned *three*.

The other was upstairs in my bedroom. If anyone tried to creep up on me in my own home, they weren't getting away unscathed.

The car door opened, followed by the sound of muffled male voices.

And a female voice.

Asher and I exchanged glances.

He mouthed, "Abbie?"

I frowned and listened carefully. It sounded like her, but I couldn't tell if she was distressed or not.

If they hurt a hair on her head, I was going to blow their nuts off.

I crept toward the door.

It was still half closed from when we entered the townhouse.

I raised my foot and carefully nudged it the rest of the way open. Unlike my bedroom door, the front door didn't squeak. It moved silently on well oiled hinges.

Footsteps hurried towards the front door, but whoever it was, was obscured by the bushes out the front.

I raised my gun.

Abbie came around the corner and froze. Her eyes widened at the sight of the barrel pointed right at her face. She let out a squeak and her lips dropped apart. She raised her hands to either side and stared.

"Jesus fucking Christ." I lowered the gun. "Are you all right?"

She looked shaken, pale.

"Um. I could use a drink." Even her voice was shaking.

I put a hand on her upper arm and gently pushed around behind me. "Who's in the car?"

I took a step towards the street just as the vehicle peeled away from the curb. The tinted windows meant I couldn't see inside, but I could guess.

Motherfuckers.

"Go inside. Asher is in there. I'll make sure they've gone." I gripped my Glock tighter and gave her a reassuring nod.

"Zeke…be careful," she whispered.

"Always," I said over my shoulder. "Don't worry, I'll be fine." My relatives, on the other hand—

I stepped past the bushes and looked down the street. It was empty except for the usual cars parked along either side. The dark car that dropped her off was gone.

Lucky for them.

The street lights flickered on as if to punctuate that the assholes who took Abbie were gone now.

I hurried back inside the house, closed and locked the door behind me.

Abbie and Asher stood in the kitchen, his arm around her shoulders, a drink of what looked like bourbon in her hands.

In full view of them both, I put the Glock back in the drawer and closed it. I didn't care if Abbie also knew where it was. She might need to know someday.

I poured myself and Asher a glass of bourbon each and passed his to him. We didn't usually drink it straight, but this seemed a good time to make an exception.

"What happened?" Asher asked.

Abbie's face was still pale, but the colour slowly started to return. She took a sip of bourbon and grimaced at the taste.

"Reuben wanted a little chat," she said.

"Fucker," I spat. "What about?" I had a few suspicions.

"He wanted me to convince you to leave Wolf Venom." She half shrugged. "I told him I didn't think you would listen to me."

"On that subject, I won't listen to anyone," I growled. "He should know that by now."

He *did* know that, he just didn't know when to give up and admit defeat. Would he ever learn? I fucking hoped so. I was past done with him and his blind persistence.

"That's basically what I said." She licked bourbon from her lower lip. "He seems to think leaving the band would be the best thing for you."

I laughed bitterly. "He wouldn't have a clue what is best for me." Only, he knew well enough to take her and not one of the guys.

"Did he touch you?" I would hunt his ass down and feed it to him if he did.

"No," she said quickly. "He was almost…amicable."

"That sounds like Reuben," Asher said. "He likes to pretend he's reasonable. I'm pretty sure most of the time he's plotting to have someone pull out my pubic hairs one by one, then take my kneecaps and feed them to his pet cockatiel."

I snorted because that was specific and somewhat accurate. Except for the part about the cockatiel. Reuben wasn't much of an animal lover.

"Honestly, I was half expecting him to give me to the twins to do whatever they wanted." Her voice shook again. "Would they actually do that?"

The fear in her voice ignited my anger again.

"Parker and Hunter like to pretend they're nice guys, like Reuben," I said slowly. "But they'll just as quickly shoot you or gut you if he told them to. I wouldn't put anything past either of them."

To my knowledge, neither of my brothers ever raped a woman, but that didn't necessarily mean they hadn't. I didn't keep tabs on them twenty-four hours a day, seven days a week.

Or at all.

Maybe I should start doing that. I could afford to have a private investigator follow them around. Although, they would probably kill them and hide the body in a shallow grave, so that would be a waste of money.

And, you know, the life of the investigator.

"I'm so sorry." I took a big gulp of bourbon. I might need a lot more of it to get through the next couple of hours. "You shouldn't have been dragged into any of this."

It was Asher who responded. "It's not your fault, Zeke. You can't help who your family is any more than I can. It's their fault this happened. It's Reuben's fault he won't let you live your life. He should fuck off and leave you alone."

I sighed. She was right, but it didn't make any of this any better.

"Maybe I should leave the band when my contract is up, before someone gets killed for me." Was it stupid or selfish to put people at risk just so I could sing and entertain people?

No one deserved to die so I could keep doing that. I might take up a hobby instead. I could learn to knit. How hard could that be?

"No," they both said in unison.

"The band is your life," Abbie said.

"Unless you're sick of us." A slight smile tugged at the corners of Asher's mouth. "I can be annoying sometimes."

"You cannot," Abbie said. "At least, not as far as I've seen."

He smiled a little more and lightly kissed her mouth. "That's sweet of you to say."

Damn, why was that hot? There wasn't even a hint of jealousy there, I wanted to watch them kiss a bit more.

When we all calmed down.

"You're not that annoying," I told him. "No more than I am, and I prefer you all alive. Is making music really worth the hassle and the risk?" The idea of losing either of them made my heart squeeze almost to the point of pain. They were both my people.

"An unreserved yes," Abbie said. "Would I put up with all the gossip and humiliation if it wasn't?"

"Neither of those end in you being dead," I pointed out.

"They might as well," she said softly. "You have no idea how brutal it's been. I think I'd rather face your brothers than people like Poppy Newton."

I supposed it was all a matter of perspective, because I would much rather deal with the press. Although, I hadn't had my name dragged through the mud.

Yet.

There was still plenty of time for that to happen. Honestly, I'd be the first to admit the media treated men better than women. Chances were, I'd get off lightly compared with what Abbie went through.

"We should put that in the 'let's talk about it later' pile and order some dinner," I said. "If any of us can eat."

Otherwise, we could just get drunk instead. Who knows what might happen then?

"I could eat," Asher said. Judging by the way he glanced at Abbie, he wasn't just talking about food.

"I'm hungry too." She looked at him the same way.

Holy hell, my heart raced faster than it had when I heard the car pull up out the front.

I swallowed. "I'll grab the takeaway menus."

"Yeah," Asher agreed. "Maybe something hot."

Call me old-fashioned, but I had a bunch of paper menus in a pile in the corner of the kitchen. I would order with my phone, not because I wasn't a complete Neanderthal, but I prefer to look over the menu and scratch off anything I tried and didn't like. I didn't scratch off much.

I picked up the pile and hunted through them. "Indian? Thai?"

"There goes that myth," Abbie said. When I looked at her questioningly, she added, "I thought guys only ordered pizza when they ordered in."

"We're enlightened gentlemen," Asher said proudly, laughter in his voice.

"Yes, we are," I agreed.

I couldn't get past the vibe in the room. It was as though the adrenaline of what happened to Abbie had translated to sexual tension.

What did that say about us that we got off on bad things happening? I suppose we were all as fucked up in the head as each other.

So were the rest of the guys in the band, now I thought about it. They'd probably find this evening's events exciting. Thank goodness no one died.

Yet.

"I'll eat whatever." Asher took his eyes off Abbie long enough to give me a shrug.

"Me too." I handed Abbie the menus so she could decide. As long as she was happy, I didn't give a shit what I ate. As long as I was near her. And Asher too.

My heightened awareness of them both was probably reading things into this that weren't there.

On the other hand, I was usually very keyed in to situations like this. I met countless groupies and learned how to discern whether they were interested or just flirting. If they wanted one night or something more.

This was definitely something more and it wasn't just me and Abbie or Abbie and Asher.

What was it then? What I felt for Asher was closer than brothers but was there something else to it? Something I hadn't realised until now?

Or, I realised it but hadn't acknowledged it? I always thought he was adorable, but more than that never even crossed my mind. Had it crossed his? Should I push these thoughts back into a box and shut the lid before I did something I'd regret?

The last thing I wanted to do was fuck up our friendship. For one thing, the guy knew where I kept my guns.

Abbie's tongue darted over her lips and she looked over the menus.

"What about a Madras chicken and lamb tikka? And some rice. And beer."

"Lots of beer." I grabbed up my phone and placed the order. "It shouldn't be long."

I took the menus from Abbie's hands, put them aside and drew her closer to me.

I pressed my mouth lightly to hers. She tasted of salt and bourbon. I deepened the kiss, letting my tongue taste hers, then drew back.

Asher put a hand on her cheek, turned her face to him and kissed her. His tongue pried her lips open and explored the inside of her mouth.

She let out a soft moan which made my cock hard as a rock.

Asher broke off the kiss and drew back from her.

I thought he'd pull back to let me take another turn.

Instead, he kept one hand on her cheek and leaned over to kiss my mouth.

It was unexpected, but it sent a wash of fire through my entire body.

"Holy shit," Abbie whispered. "That's so hot."

I couldn't disagree, especially since my mouth was busy kissing him back, my tongue tracing his lips. He tasted as good as she did.

When he broke off from me, I kissed her again. My erection was almost painful. If we kept doing this, I was going to come right here in the kitchen.

"We should probably... Dinner won't be long..." Apparently Asher was having as much trouble with coherent thought as I was right now.

I glanced down at his groin. Not surprisingly, he looked as hard as I felt. What would it be like to touch him? Or watch him fuck Abbie? God, I wanted both of those things. And to fuck her myself. Was that greedy?

I decided it wasn't. What was the point of life if you couldn't live it? And enjoy as much of it as possible.

CHAPTER
TWENTY-ONE

ABBIE

I ADJUSTED my headset and got ready to sing again.

Having been in the studio for four hours, I was ready for a break. At the same time, I wanted to get this song down right.

I wrote "Nothing Under My Feet" when I was at my lowest point. I was waiting for the annulment from Vance and the press was blowing up my phone and knocking on my door for interviews. I couldn't leave my apartment without being followed, stared at and photographed. They didn't want nice photos either; they wanted candid ones of me dressed in track pants with my hair in disarray. Or better yet, in a compromising position with somebody else.

At the time, I was barely able to get out of bed, much less go out and do anything embarrassing. The stupid thing was, I never much cared if anyone caught me in a compromising position, but the press made it all so ugly and sordid.

Vance added fuel to the fire every chance he got. Asshole.

Maybe I should have made a deal with Reuben; I would speak to Zeke if he had Vance dealt with.

Okay, I wouldn't really ask anyone to do that. Probably.

That begged the question—would Reuben make a deal like that? I had a feeling he would do whatever it took to get his brother to return to the flock. Just like Zeke would do whatever it took to avoid it.

It was not a good situation to be in the middle of.

At her and Zeke were a much better place to be in the centre of. Watching them kiss the other night still sent sparks of heat all through me.

I wanted to be with both of them and it was pretty clear the feeling was mutual all around. As soon as we finished dinner, Landon and Channing turned up at the door. We ended up having a movie marathon and falling asleep curled up on the couch together. All five of us. I could very easily get used to doing things like that.

"Okay, from the top again," Candy, the producer, said from inside her booth.

I nodded. It was just me in here right now. Later, the instruments would be recorded and then the whole thing would be mixed. I would have liked to record with the instruments in here with me, but it was easier to concentrate when I only had to worry about my vocals.

I took a quick gulp of water and started to sing into the microphone on the stand in front of me.

"The ground is broken,
the air is shattered,
my world is nothing but an echo.
You stole my heart and ripped it out.
Now there's nothing under my feet.

I'm falling hard,
you're not there to catch me.
You watched me tumble to my knees,
you broke me down,
you tore my last breath.

Now there's nothing under my feet.
Nothing to stop me.
Nowhere to hide.
Nothing under my feet.

I landed hard,
but I got up.
I won't let you take my everything away.
I'll walk away from you,
stronger than before.
I have everything under my feet."

I lifted my chin as I sang the last note.

Somewhere in the middle of writing that song, I realised I couldn't let Vance win. Or the press, for that matter. I had to get back up on my own two feet and live my life the way I wanted to. That included releasing this song. It was a long time coming, but it was the public 'fuck you' he deserved.

No one would doubt who was aimed at.

Maybe I shouldn't give him another fifteen minutes of fame, but I needed to get it off my chest. I wanted everyone to know I intended to live my best life from here on out. And if they didn't like it, that was their problem.

"Great work." Candy Davis was one of the best in the business.

Of course, White Wolf Records wouldn't compromise. Levi Jones hadn't built a successful label by cutting corners. He did it by hiring and signing the best and putting them together in the studio.

"Let's take a break." Candy took off her headphones and set them aside before she stepped out of the booth. "It must feel good to get back on the horse. So to speak."

I slipped off my headphones and smiled. "God, yeah, it really does. I didn't realise how much I missed this."

"If you don't mind me saying, you sound even better than anything I heard on the radio," she said. "The time away has given your voice an emotion and richness you either didn't have before, or your previous producer didn't manage to bring out."

"I guess there is an upside to life fucking you over," I said ironically. I knew what she meant though. Nothing I did before was as personal as the stuff I was working on for the new album. I felt it all in a way I hadn't on the last two. Like everything was coming from the heart now, not just my vocal cords.

"You're easy to work with too," Candy added. "I can't say that about a lot of people." She gave me a, 'what are you going to do,' look.

"Let me guess, you thought I would be a nightmare because of my reputation?" I tucked a strand of hair behind my ear.

She wouldn't be the first or the last to make that assumption. I tried to be respectful of the people I worked with, because a good producer could help elevate my career higher than I dared to dream.

"Something like that," she agreed unapologetically. "I don't pay a whole lot of attention to gossip or tabloids or any of that shit, but people talk, whether we like it or not. I usually don't believe half of it until I've actually worked with them. Some people are way worse than rumours suggest."

I had a list of them off the top of my head, starting with Vance and ending with Penn.

"How do you go working with Penn?" I couldn't resist asking.

"He's a pain in the ass," Candy said. "He's still not the worst of them, though. I've had a couple who refused to work with a woman. You can imagine how that went down with the bosses."

"Not very well," I guessed. "Did they replace you?"

She grimaced as we stepped through the doors into the small lunchroom.

"In one case they did, or the artist would have walked. They put their foot down the other time. Giving in to stupid demands isn't a good habit to get into."

"Amen to that." I picked up a sandwich in a plastic container and filled up a cup with coffee before taking them over to a table.

It wasn't much, but I was grateful the label supplied lunch at all. Staying with Zeke saved me a lot of money, but I was starting to run out of it. Everywhere I could cut costs, I had to. That included eating prepackaged lunches and bad instant coffee. It was better than going hungry.

Candy slid into the chair next to me, her bright pink ponytail swinging. "I can't imagine working anywhere else, even if there are jerks around. Even if those jerks can't keep their hands to themselves sometimes."

"I can relate to that," I said wryly. "Some see a woman in the industry and think she's fair game."

"Especially if we're wearing a skirt." She bit into her sandwich like she was taking her frustrations out on the bread.

"Right?" I couldn't remember the last time I sat down for a friendly chat with another woman. It was nice. "I used to work with a producer who would try to stick his hand up my skirt every chance he got. I was new in the industry and he was a lot older than me. He seemed to think there was nothing wrong with it."

Candy's eyes widened. "I wish I could say I hadn't heard the same thing a thousand times before, but I have. What did you do?"

"What could I do?" I asked. "He was powerful and I was a total no one. I had no choice." I paused for a moment before I added, "I started wearing pants. I don't think he ever figured out how to handle it."

Candy laughed. "That's perfect. Of course, we shouldn't have to change our wardrobes just because of people like that."

I sipped my coffee and sighed. "No, we shouldn't. I would never refuse to work with a producer, but I like working with a woman. It's a pleasant change."

"I guarantee I will never stick my hand up your skirt," Candy said.

"That's good to know." I had a funny feeling, if anyone tried anything inappropriate with me, the guys in the band would have something to say about it. They had enough influence to get a producer fired if they wanted to. Or killed.

She tilted her head and her ponytail dropped out to the side. "You aren't what I expected at all."

"You expected a self-centred, arrogant bitch?" I suggested. "The kind of person who is only interested in fame and fortune. Who would get married just to cause a stir?"

I didn't speak with more than a hint of bitterness. I was used to people expecting that of me by now, and being surprised when it wasn't what they got.

"I don't know what I expected," she admitted. "A lot of the artists have their heads up their bums. Or they looked terrified to be here if this is their first time in the studio. You don't. You seem like you're at home here."

That was such a sweet thing for her to say, I thought I might cry.

"Everyone at the label has been amazing. When Jackson said it was one big happy family, I thought he was full of shit." Especially with Penn giving me death glares every five minutes. "But it kinda seems like everyone makes the effort to look out for each other."

The band certainly welcomed me with open arms, for the most part.

"Levi Jones figured out the best way to make a shit load of money was to keep everyone happy," Candy said. "We try to make as few waves as possible, as much as possible. The label motto should be' we make music, not waves'." She grinned.

I laughed. "That sounds about right. I wish I signed on with White Wolf to start with. That would have saved me a lot of heartache."

"Yeah, but would you sing as well if you hadn't been through all that?" she asked.

I wasn't sure how to answer that. "I don't know," I said slowly. "I'd like to think so. If not, then I guess all the drama was worth it in the end. At least something good came out of it."

"That's a good way to look at it," she said. "We can't change the past, but we can appreciate the person it moulded us into."

"That's very poetic," I said. "Are you a songwriter as well as a producer?"

"Yeah. And I sing and play a few instruments. I guess you could call me an all-rounder. There's no aspect of the music industry I don't adore. Except maybe the cheap coffee."

She sipped hers and made a face. "You know what, you should come out with me and the girls sometime. We could go out to a club, dance and all that shit."

"I'd like that," I said. I hadn't had much in the way of female friends for a while. Not that I kept in touch with anyway. As much as I loved hanging out with the guys, it would be nice to have some female company once in a while.

CHAPTER
TWENTY-TWO

ZEKE

"THANKS FOR COMING WITH ME," I said.

Asher glanced over at me from behind the steering wheel. "I could totally take that the wrong way, but I'm not going to."

I snorted. "Sure you're not." Things could have gotten awkward between us, but thank fuck, they hadn't. If anything, it felt more comfortable. Like somehow we resolved something we hadn't known was unresolved.

In truth, we hadn't really resolved anything, apart from admitting we had a mutual attraction to each other as well as Abbie.

Since I was a kid, I've known I was bi, but I never gave it much thought, much less exploration. It was just another aspect of myself, like my eye colour. I never considered finding a guy to experiment with.

Until now, it was just about looking and appreciating attractive people, regardless of their sex.

"Okay, I am," he admitted. "Do you want to talk about the other night?"

"I don't know, do you?" I put my elbow on the armrest, placed my head on my hand and looked over at him.

I always considered him an attractive guy, but that had a whole new slant now. I saw him the same way I saw Abbie. At the same time though, he was my oldest, best friend. I didn't want to screw this up. I would never forgive myself if I ruined everything between us. If nothing else, he knew exactly what having a family like ours felt. We confided in each other in ways I didn't with the other guy. Shared war stories, as it were. Or survival stories.

"I think we should," he said. "If only to make one thing clear."

Okay, here it came. This was where he told me it was the bourbon talking. That he regretted kissing me. That he felt weird around me now.

I hurt myself thinking like that. My heart squeezed in my chest.

"What's that?" I asked carefully. It might be a wise move to listen to what he had to say before I jumped to conclusions. Yeah, as if the human brain is that rational.

He cleared his throat. "What I did, kissing you. I didn't just do that so I could kiss Abbie too. Or because of the adrenaline, or the alcohol. I did it because I wanted to kiss both of you. I'm sorry if this makes it weird, but I've been wanting to do that for a long time. It seemed like the right time, the other night."

I let out a hard exhale of relief.

"It doesn't make it weird," I said fiercely. I was beyond relieved that he had no regrets. "I'm glad you did it. I liked it, and I know she did too." She looked like she flooded her panties watching us. Remembering the expression on her face made my balls ache and cock twitch.

He grinned. "That's awesome," he said, tone as relieved as mine. "And about me kissing Abbie. You didn't mind?"

"Nope," I replied lightly. "It was kinda hot to watch."

"Yeah? It was kinda hot to watch you two, too. Now I get why Landon and Channing are into sharing the way they are. I should have known these guys were onto something long ago. They must be smarter than they look." He chuckled.

"That wouldn't be too hard," I joked. Both of the guys were very smart, like all of us, but I couldn't resist making a light dig at them.

Asher laughed. "Fuck, I'm glad this didn't get strange. I was worried you would punch me in the face or something."

"Really?" I frowned at him. "I seem like the kind of guy who would do that?" Ouch.

"No, but you never know what people might do in the heat of the moment," he said. "Especially after what happened with Abbie."

"I guess so." I shrugged. "Lucky I didn't still have a gun in my hand."

"Luckyily neither did I," he retorted. "That could have ended badly for everyone."

"Right." That was one reason I wasn't the biggest fan of guns. They tended to hurt people sometimes. Strange how that went.

"So, have you ever—" Asher paused with his mouth open, searching for the right words.

I had a pretty good idea of what he was trying to ask, but I couldn't resist stirring him up a little.

"Have I ever what?" I asked with mock innocence.

"Um. Been with another guy?" he said in a rush.

"Ahhh," I said slowly. "No, I haven't. Have you?" I went from picturing him with Abbie, to picturing him with Abbie and another guy.

Was it this hot in the car when I got inside it?

"Yeah, a couple. No one you know, just people I met on tour." He stopped the car at a red traffic light.

My eyebrows twitched. You think you know a guy, and then you realise you don't know as much as you thought you knew. I was glad he felt comfortable telling me all of this though. We were usually frank about our sex lives when it came to women, and Landon and Channing talked about their time with each other as well as women, but this was new for Asher and I.

After a few moments of hesitation, I asked, "What's it like?"

It was his turn to pause. "It's like…sex. The mechanics are a little different, but the feelings are the same."

I nodded slowly. "Gotcha. That's good to know." It was. Admitting to an attraction and acting on it were two different things. Rushing in could be bad for everyone.

"Do you think you could ever…" He glanced over at me, then back at the road as the light turned green.

"I don't know," I admitted. "I think so. This is all kinda new to me."

"Of course," he said quickly. "I didn't mean to pressure you."

"You didn't," I assured him. "You know me, I can say no when I need to."

"You definitely can," he agreed. "You've been saying no to your brother all this time and you've stuck to it."

I wasn't sure how much longer that would last, but I didn't tell him that. He already knew I was considering going back. I knew there was no chance Abbie and the other guys would let me go without a fight.

At the end of the day, this had to be my choice, just like it would be my choice to fuck Asher or any other guy.

"Yeah," I said lightly. "And Reuben is scarier than you."

"You wound me," Asher said jokingly. "I'm really scary, like all us DiMarcos."

"Okay, you're right. You're the second scariest DiMarco I know. Second only to Dane."

"Fair call," Asher said. "Dane is a scary guy. One of the top three scariest, after Reuben and your other brother, Caleb."

"It's difficult to separate the three of them," I remarked. Was it bad that I liked the fact Caleb lived in Melbourne and I hardly saw him? He was as much fun to hang out with as Reuben. Joshua wasn't much better. Or the twins for that matter. Lucas was mostly harmless, ish. Funny that I ended up the nice guy of the family.

"Sometimes I wonder why we joined a rock band and didn't go into witness protection," Asher said, half jokingly.

"Because we have talent we have to share with the world," I said modestly.

"Oh yeah, that sounds about right." He nodded. "I knew there had to be a good reason. I mean, we put up with a lot of crap from them, don't we?"

"Too much," I agreed. That was what today was about. While Abbie was in the studio recording her new album, which I knew was going to be incredible, Asher and I would deal with some things. She was safe enough there and Candy knew to watch out for her.

If there was anyone outside the band I trusted with Abby's safety, it was Candy. She was a small woman, but her tiny size and bright pink hair caused many people to underestimate her. In reality, she had mad skills in more martial arts than I knew actually existed. Abbie was as safe with her as she was with me.

"How long do you think it will be before Penny realises he's as hot for her as the rest of us?" Asher asked.

"Penn is hot for us all?" I grinned.

Asher snorted. "Probably, we're us. But that wasn't what I meant."

"No shit," I teased. "I don't know. Penn is even more stubborn than I am. He'll at least spend another couple of weeks grumbling about her being around, and giving her dirty looks. And telling everyone how much he wants her to go away."

"Meanwhile, he probably has a photo of her on his phone he can masturbate to." Asher grinned.

"Are you projecting?" I asked.

Great, now I had a mental image of Asher with his phone in one hand and the other curled around his hard cock. Only in this scenario, it wasn't a photo of Abbie, it was a video call and she was naked with her hand between her legs.

It was definitely getting hotter inside the car. I wound the window down a little bit.

"I might be," Asher agreed. "I only have your word on how amazing she is."

I smiled slowly. "You do, don't you? Sucks to be you."

He groaned. "You had to mention sucking."

I groaned playfully in response. "You had to interpret my words as a blowjob."

I wasn't thinking that at all. Well, now I was.

"Yes. Yes I did," he said. "You know, some people like to go down on a guy while he's driving."

Now there was a suggestion that would make a guy hot under the collar. Or a woman too, no doubt. How would it feel to wrap my lips around his cock? The idea made my balls hurt.

I looked over. "My head wouldn't fit between your cock and the steering wheel." Also, that might come under the banner of rushing.

"I can pull over," he said.

I glanced out the window. "No you can't. Not on a road like this. Maybe you could concentrate on driving before you get us both killed."

"That might be the most sensible thing you've said all day." He exhaled loudly out his nose. "Not even a blowjob is worth getting killed for."

"Are you sure about that?" I asked. "Maybe you haven't had a good enough blowjob."

"Possibly not," he said slowly. "Are you saying you've had a blowjob worth dying for?"

"Well, I don't want to brag." I grinned. "I did tell you Abbie is amazing."

"Shit, dude, I want to be you when I grow up. Actually, no I don't. I'd be happy to be *with* you when I grow up. When you're ready, that is. If you're ready," he added quickly.

"When I'm ready, you'll be the first to know," I assured him. Of course he would. Being with another guy would feel like cheating on Asher, just like being with another woman would feel like cheating on Abbie.

When the hell had things gotten so complicated? I think it started with that night in the dark corner of the club, when a beautiful blond woman let me slip my hand up her skirt and into her pussy.

Or maybe it started a million years ago when the dust that would become us started to form. I wasn't a big believer in fate until now. What else could it be?

We all made beautiful music together, in perfect pitch.

What I wasn't sure of was where the other guys fit into this. All I knew was that I was certain they did. We were like a jigsaw puzzle with seven pieces. Abbie was the very centre piece. I was the piece that slotted in right beside her. Penn was the piece that was shaped unusually, so it didn't seem to fit at all until you found just the right spot for it. Everyone else had their own place. We just had to figure out exactly where they went to finish off the puzzle.

If only my brother and people like him didn't sweep us off the table and scatter the pieces before that could happen.

"I hope so," Asher said so softly I almost missed hearing him speak.

CHAPTER
TWENTY-THREE

ZEKE

"DUDE, your brother has eclectic taste in books," Asher pulled one out from the shelf and looked at the bare-chested football player on the cover.

"I'm sure Lizzie King is amazing, but she doesn't seem like your brother's taste." He put the book back and pulled out another.

"Aaron L. Speck," he read. "At least this one is mafia."

I snorted at the story.

Asher opened the book in the middle and started to read.

His eyes widened. "I was already horny enough. If I keep reading this, I'm going to blow my head off." He closed the book and put it back on the shelf.

"I didn't realise you were so flexible," I teased.

"You have no idea." He grinned.

I wasn't sure if the mental image of Asher sucking his own cock was arousing or disturbing. I might think about that more later, when I wasn't as anxious as I was right now.

Terry had let us into the house and told us to wait in the library.

That was at least half an hour ago. Either Reuben was too busy to see us straight away, or he was pretending he was.

It was very much like him to let us sweat, just to toy with us. Of course, if I tried to call him out on it, he would point out we turned up unannounced. Whatever I said, he would make it my fault, so I wouldn't say anything.

I'd wait patiently until he was good and fucking ready to see us.

"Lily Lindqvi, I've heard of her." Asher pulled out another book from the shelf and took it over to sit in a chair and read. He seemed a lot less anxious than I felt. "She writes about vampires, but it's still not your brother's style."

I shrugged and leaned my shoulder against the wall. "They might be Parker's books. Or Terry's."

Asher laughed.

I stifled a chuckle at the idea of the big guy reading romance books. Or any book, for that matter.

Personally, I preferred to read thrillers, and cozy mysteries, but I've read a few romances in my day, when there was nothing else to read. Okay, and because I liked them, but that was a closely guarded secret I'd never admit to.

"Your brother isn't seeing anyone, is he?" Asher asked. "He doesn't secretly have a woman stashed away around here?"

"Why, are you interested in him?" I asked jokingly.

"Hell no." Asher glanced up from his book and made a face. "It would explain these books, that's all."

"Maybe Reuben is getting soft in his old age," I said. "He might want to read about love because the only way he would find it is if he paid for it or bribed her."

The first sign I had that Reuben stepped into the library was the sound of him clearing his throat. Of course he arrived just in time to hear me say that. Figured. Whatever, I was going to piss him off one way or another.

I turned around unapologetically and resisted the strong, initial urge to punch him in the face.

He looked at me like something nasty he found on the bottom of his shoe. Something he wouldn't even bother to scrape off. He would just throw the shoe away, or burn it.

"Ezequiel, have you come to tell me you've quit your little band?" he asked.

I hated when he called me that and he knew it. It was so unfair that he didn't have a longer version of his name. He had a shorter version though, one he hated with fierce loathing.

"Ruby, no, I haven't." I gave him a smug smile and crossed my arms over my chest.

Round one was a tie.

Asher tried but failed to suppress a laugh.

Reuben turned cold, annoyed eyes on him, then back to me. "Then why are you here?"

I lowered my arms to my sides and curled my hands into fists. Turns out, the urge to punch him wasn't just initial. I still had it.

"I'm here to tell you to stay the fuck away from Abbie. In fact, you'd be better off staying the fuck away from me and anyone associated with me."

He looked unimpressed, maybe even amused. He was certainly not intimidated. I didn't expect him to be. Fuckers like him weren't easily scared. Shame, I wouldn't mind seeing some fear in his eyes once in a while.

"I'm happy to stay away from her," he said slowly. "You know what you need to do to make that happen." He spoke in an even, reasonable tone, like he was talking to a kid who didn't fully grasp the situation.

"Yes, I do." I pretended to misunderstand. "I'd prefer not to kill you, though. I don't enjoy having blood on my hands as much as you do." Although, I might make an exception if it was his. That would solve a bunch of my problems. And create new ones. My brothers would be pissed if I did it. Except Caleb, who might be happy to take his place as head of the family. Maybe I could cut a deal with him...

"Liar," Reuben scoffed. "You can deny it all you want, but it's who you are, just like it's who I am. Just like it's who he is." He inclined his head slightly in Asher's direction.

"I can find a place in the organisation for him too. And Abbie, if you insist. She has the same undercurrent of barely suppressed violence the rest of us do."

"If by that you mean she wanted to kick you in the balls, yes, she does," I agreed. "She doesn't want to join the organisation any more than I do. Neither does Asher."

"Nope, Asher doesn't," he said without glancing up from his book. "I'll leave that bullshit to Dane. Anyone else with the last name DiMarco wants to stay right out of it."

Reuben's eyes flicked towards Asher and something crossed his features. It was so brief I almost missed it. What was that about? Annoyance at Asher's declaration that he wouldn't be coming back to the fold either?

I didn't think that was it. Reuben had never cared what Asher thought before, why would he now?

Unless... Unless he thought Asher was the reason for my refusal. He was certainly a part of it. Still, I sensed something else was going on in my brother's head. Whatever it was, I was better off not trying to figure it out.

I sucked in an irritated breath.

"Would it help if I took out a sky writer?" I asked. "In the sky they could write in big, fat letters, 'I'm not coming back.' Would you get it then?"

I suspected he wouldn't get it if I wrote it on the wall with his blood. The fact that was tempting suggested maybe he had a point about the violence of this life being a part of me. Or maybe I was just fed up with his bullshit.

"You can't sing without a tongue," Reuben said simply. "And you can't have a band without the band."

"Don't threaten me," I growled.

He scoffed. "You know me better than that. I don't make threats. If you don't obey, and soon, I will make all of these things happen. You know I can and will."

"You're a motherfucker," I said coldly enough to match his tone. "You have enough people working for you. You don't need me. I'm not going to go around killing for you, so I'd be no use to you anyway."

"You would be useful in a hundred different ways," Reuben said. "Is that what you're concerned about? That you'll have nothing to do but sit around in my library and admire my books?"

"They are pretty awesome books," Asher said helpfully. "Especially this one." He held it up.

"No, I'm not worried about being bored," I said. "Or having nothing else to do but read."

Hell, that sounded enticing. Would he pay me to sit in his library and read his books? I might actually consider it if that was what was on the table.

Fuck, what was I thinking? There was no way that was all there was to this. Even if it was, I didn't want to give up my life to him.

Besides, I had enough money that I could spend the rest of my life sitting around reading if I wanted to. I didn't need Reuben's help with that.

"I love my life," I said with finality. "I don't want to stop doing what I'm doing. I don't want to work for you. I want you to stay the hell out of my life. And away from me, Abbie and the band. How can I possibly make that any clearer? Do I need to get 'stay the fuck away from me' tattooed on my forehead?"

"Can I dare you to do that?" Asher looked up from his book and grinned.

"Let's put that on the maybe pile," I told him. "At this point it's a second last resort." I'd do it if it would actually work.

On the other hand, it might send the wrong message to fans of the band. That would suck. Maybe I could get it tattooed inside my lower lip so I could pull it out and show him whenever he pissed me off. That would work for a lot of people too, not just Reuben.

"The last resort being killing me," Reuben said dryly.

"Yeah, but that's quickly moving its way up the list." I narrowed my eyes at him. If he thought I was joking, he would have to think again. I didn't want to kill him, but we couldn't keep having this argument over and over again. And I couldn't let him kill people I loved so I'd obey him.

Reuben sighed dramatically. "You repeatedly say this life isn't for you, but then you make threats like that, proving yourself wrong. Sooner or later you will come to accept that. Sooner would be better for everyone, particularly you."

I responded with an exasperated growl from deep in the back of my throat.

"Being stubborn is a great personality trait to have, but you have to know when to give up. Because I'm not going to." I can't believe I actually considered it.

Maybe if he wasn't such an asshole, I would have agreed to give up the band eventually. Since he was a world class motherfucking prick, I was more determined than ever to stick to my guns. So to speak.

Reuben looked absolutely unmoved and undeterred. "You will. Is there anything else you want? If not, I have…things to get back to."

His pause was barely perceptible, but it was there.

Things? What was I missing here? Would he even tell me if I asked? Probably not. If he did, there would be strings attached to the response. It was probably better I didn't know.

He might have someone down in the basement he was in the middle of torturing or killing. It wouldn't surprise me one bit. I even listened for screams, but didn't hear any.

What was I thinking? His basement, if he had one, it would be soundproofed. He was a dickhead, but he wasn't stupid.

"Don't let me keep you," I said coolly. "I also have things to do. Like celebrating the fact our latest song reached number one on the charts. But you wouldn't care about that, would you?" I crossed my arms and smirked.

"Not in the slightest," he agreed. If anything, he looked mildly disgusted.

At least one of us was happy for me and the guys.

"And you wonder why I don't want to come back," I said sarcastically. "Did it ever occur to you to offer your little brother some support? Maybe if you took an interest in the things I like, I would take an interest in yours." That was highly unlikely and we all knew it.

"When you do something interesting, I'll be interested," he said. "Anyone can shout into a microphone."

"That's true," I agreed. "It's much harder to *sing* into one. You should try it sometime, it's therapeutic." According to my father, Reuben was in the boys' choir before I was born.

By the sound of it, he had an amazing voice until it broke. Maybe that was why he hated what I did so much. Because he didn't get to do it himself. Honestly, that was one hundred percent his problem, not mine.

"I would pay to see that duet," Asher said. "Reuben could give up a life of crime and join the band."

We both turned and looked at him.

He shrugged. "Or maybe not."

"There's only room for one Brantley in Wolf Venom," I said. "And it's not Reuben."

Although, let's face it, if it got him off my back about working for him, I'd actually consider it. He could be a backing singer, or maybe a roadie.

As if any of that would happen.

Honestly, it would be better if it didn't. I didn't want my brother anywhere near Abbie or the other guys. Or me.

I had to figure out a way to get him to listen. Preferably one that didn't involve bloodshed. I wished I had a clue what it would take to get him to back off once and for all. Whatever it was, I'd do it.

I had a sinking feeling he wouldn't give up until I was dead, or he was.

CHAPTER
TWENTY-FOUR

ABBIE

"I BET YOU WERE AMAZING." Tully was beside me the moment I stepped out of the studio.

Landon wasn't too far behind him. For once, he wasn't in Channing's company. Everyone needed some time apart once in a while, I supposed.

Penn was nowhere to be seen. That wasn't surprising. Unless it was directly related to the band, he was usually not around. If he was, he was busy scowling and making snide remarks.

"I hope so," I said. "It felt good. Candy seemed happy. She's so great to work with."

"She is," Tully agreed. He slipped his hand into one of mine. "She's the best in the business. I think she might be a magician. After all, she makes us sound good." He grinned.

"Hey." Landon slid over to walk on the other side of me. "*We* make us sound good. She makes us sound incredible."

"Close enough," Tully said. "Zeke suggested we might walk you home and stay with you for a while."

"He and Asher aren't back yet?" I asked. I had no idea where they went, just that they had something they had to take care of. I had a feeling it involved Reuben, but I hadn't asked. When it came to him, it was probably better I didn't know. What is it they say? Ignorance is bliss.

"Not yet," Tully said lightly.

I had the distinct impression he knew exactly what was going on. He didn't seem too worried, so I would follow his lead and not be concerned. Well, not be more concerned than I already was.

I'd feel better when both guys were back from whatever it was they were doing. Hopefully it didn't involve anything illegal. And if it did, hopefully they didn't get caught. I trusted them both enough to know if they did something, they did it for good reason.

Should I be so accepting of them possibly doing something against the law? No, but it was still kinda hot. Yeah, I'm a flawed human, sue me. I felt safer with them than I ever had with anyone else. And a lot more turned on.

I turned to Landon. "Where's Channing?"

He shrugged and responded with the same light tone as Tully. "He has some stuff to take care of. It shouldn't take long, then we should all go to the pub. We have a song to celebrate."

I smiled. "I'm so proud of you guys. I'm not even slightly surprised everyone loves it as much as they do. And the whole album. It's definitely your best yet." It really was. I wouldn't have thought they could top the last one, but they had. The sound was both very them and fresh at the same time. The emotion in the lyrics, the way the instruments played off each other, the...

I could rave about it for days. Honestly, I already had.

"Hell yeah it is." Landon grinned. He was only a year or two younger than me, but he seemed so untouched by the bad in the world. It wasn't that he was innocent, just that he wasn't jaded. Compared to me, anyway. I was jaded enough for all of us.

Either way, his enthusiasm and joy for life was endearing and adorable. And his hair was such a great shade of blue. It brought out the blue in his hazel eyes, and made his tanned skin look a shade or two darker.

He had two full sleeves of tattoos, and muscles ready to burst out of the sleeves of his dark grey tee. He wore a couple of chains around his neck and a ring on his right thumb. A leather bracelet on his right wrist completed the whole rock star look.

He probably had men and women following him around everywhere.

"Yours will be too," he added. "You have a much better label now, and better support to make it exactly what you want it to be." He spoke with such confidence and sincerity, he obviously adored White Wolf Records. That confidence was infectious too.

"You know what, you're right," I said. "I have maturity and I have all of those things as well. There's no reason I can't go platinum this time."

"Multi-platinum," Tully said. "This time next year, you'll be headlining the tour and we'll be supporting you."

I let out a choking laugh. "Wolf Venom will never be supporting me. You guys are so big you'll never support anyone. Not on tour anyway."

"At least we can support you in every other way that counts," Landon said. "Can we have front row tickets when you headline?" He actually looked hopeful, as if there was a chance I'd say no.

"Absolutely. Front row, backstage, whatever you want," I said. "As long as you're there, cheering me on."

Knowing my luck, we'd both end up on tour at the same time, but travelling to different cities on opposite sides of the planet. That might be unavoidable, but it was also something I would worry about if it happened.

"We wouldn't be anywhere else," Tully said assuringly. He squeezed my hand gently, then started to trace circles over my skin with his thumb.

Should it feel strange to touch him like this after being so close to Zeke and Asher? Possibly, but it didn't. Everything about spending time with all the guys felt right.

I looked over at him and smiled. Then looked over to Landon and did the same.

Landon grinned back and took my other hand in his.

We walked past a couple of the people who worked for the label. They gave us some raised eyebrows, but that was all. It was incredibly gratifying not to feel judged by these people who invested so much in me already.

At some point, I was going to wake up from this and realise it was all a beautiful dream. If that was the case, then I hoped I would sleep for a hundred years. Or two hundred. Or forever.

There probably weren't any spinning wheels in the building, but they might be a turntable with a needle I could prick my finger on. That might ensure I stayed asleep for long enough to make this fairytale last.

We stepped out of the building into the sunshine of the late afternoon. I blinked my eyes against the sudden glare. I hadn't realised quite how long I spent in the studio until now. No regrets, but the sudden burst of daylight was jarring.

"Hey." Channing trotted over to us from the direction of the car park. He glanced at the way Landon held my hand and smiled.

When I thought Landon might let go, he didn't. He gave Channing a quick kiss when he got close enough, but kept holding on to me.

"Did you get things sorted out?" Landon asked him.

"Yep," Channing said lightly. "All good."

"Is everything all right?" I realised how little I knew about him and Landon. They might be into the same things as Zeke and Asher's families were, for all I knew. Or worse.

They looked more innocent than the other guys, but then again, so did Parker and Hunter Brantley.

Looking innocent was no real indication of actual innocence. My reflection was proof of that.

I still trusted them as much as I trusted the other guys.

"Everything is perfect," Channing said. "Just tying up some loose ends before we go on tour."

Those words sent a ripple of excitement through me. There was nothing I loved more than singing in front of a live crowd. That was why we did this. Seeing the excited faces, listening to people singing your words back to you, watching them dance to your music, knowing they'd waited anywhere up to a year for this one night.

It was everything. The biggest rush there was.

I nodded. "Great. It's good to be organised."

"Were you worried about me?" He grinned.

"There's someone running around who cut off a man's head and left it in a cardboard box," I reminded him. "Not to mention Zeke's brother, who seemed to think it was okay to abduct me off the side of the street. Of course I was worried. I'm always going to worry while one of you is off by yourself."

"That's so sweet." Channing stepped around in front of me so I had to stop walking. He cupped my cheeks with his hands and kissed my mouth. "You're so sweet."

I found myself kissing him back and there was nothing even slightly strange about doing it. Not even when Tully held one of my hands and Landon held the other.

By the time we broke apart, I was breathless, and all three of the guys were grinning. I could get used to this, being the centre of attention for all of these gorgeous men.

If they weren't careful, I might start to feel like a queen. They all made me feel more special than anyone else ever had. Individually, they were amazing. Collectively, they were mind blowing.

Before I could gather my thoughts again, Landon turned my face toward his and he kissed me too, as deep and full as Channing had.

"Definitely sweet," he said, his lips still on mine.

We barely broke apart before Tully turned my face toward his and kissed me with lips and tongue and teeth.

All of this attention was turning my knees to jelly. If we kept doing this, someone was going to have to carry me to Zeke's place. My legs would give out before too much longer.

"We should get you home," Tully said reluctantly.

"Yeah." That was probably better than fucking out here in the street, up against a car, in broad daylight, because that was where this would end up if we weren't careful.

Okay, I wouldn't be mad about that. Until a paparazzi spotted us and took photos. Fucking clit blockers.

"Come on then," Landon said. He tugged me forward with our joined hands and we all resumed walking.

"Do any of you know what Zeke and Asher were up to?" I asked reluctantly.

They all exchanged looks which gave me my answer. They knew exactly what the other guys were doing. Judging by the way they all pressed their lips together, they weren't going to tell me. Each was a brick wall of silence.

"Should I be concerned about them?" I asked. I sighed. "Of course I should. Please tell me they didn't do something stupid."

"That depends on your definition of stupid," Landon said.

"Anything which would get them killed," I said. "Or arrested. Or if they had to visit Haru to dispose of evidence. Or anything that would make the label drop them. Or anything that involves buying too many canned goods."

Okay, I don't know why my mind went there, except that it was difficult to store too many cans and Zeke's townhouse was small.

"I can one hundred percent guarantee you they are not buying too many canned goods," Tully said.

I waited.

"You can't guarantee anything else, can you?" I groaned.

No one answered.

I shook my head. Apparently all I could do was hope they turned up in one piece before too much longer. I wouldn't relax until I saw them both with my own two eyes.

"They'll be fine," Tully assured me. "They can take care of themselves."

"I hope so," I said. I fell into a worried silence while we walked, thoughts of fucking gone for now.

They were pushed further away at the sound of excited voices a block from Zeke's townhouse.

At first, I assumed it had something to do with him and Asher.

Until we rounded the corner and saw the throng of press outside his house.

"There she is," one of them shouted.

Like a swarm of ants, journalists with their microphones and cameras, or phones, in their hands started toward us.

Specifically, towards me.

I let go of the guys' hands to keep them from falling under any scrutiny. I immediately wished I hadn't, because their touch was comforting. Without it, I felt naked.

"Abbie Hart, do you have any comments to make?" A microphone was shoved in my face.

I frowned at the man who held it. "About what?" Oh God, what had happened to Zeke and Asher? My heart raced and panic started to rise.

"About the death of Vance," the journalist said.

I blinked. "I beg your pardon?" Was I hearing right?

"You didn't know?" Did he have to look so happy about breaking news like that to me? I must look like a deer in headlights.

"No." I shook my head. "That's terrible." Ish. "I'm so sorry for what his family must be going through."

"I'm sure you would agree it's particularly hard on his fiancée who found him. Or the one part of him," the journalist said.

"The one..." Oh God, please tell me this wasn't what I thought it was.

"Yes. Evidently she found his head on her front doorstep in a cardboard box."

The whole world started to spin.

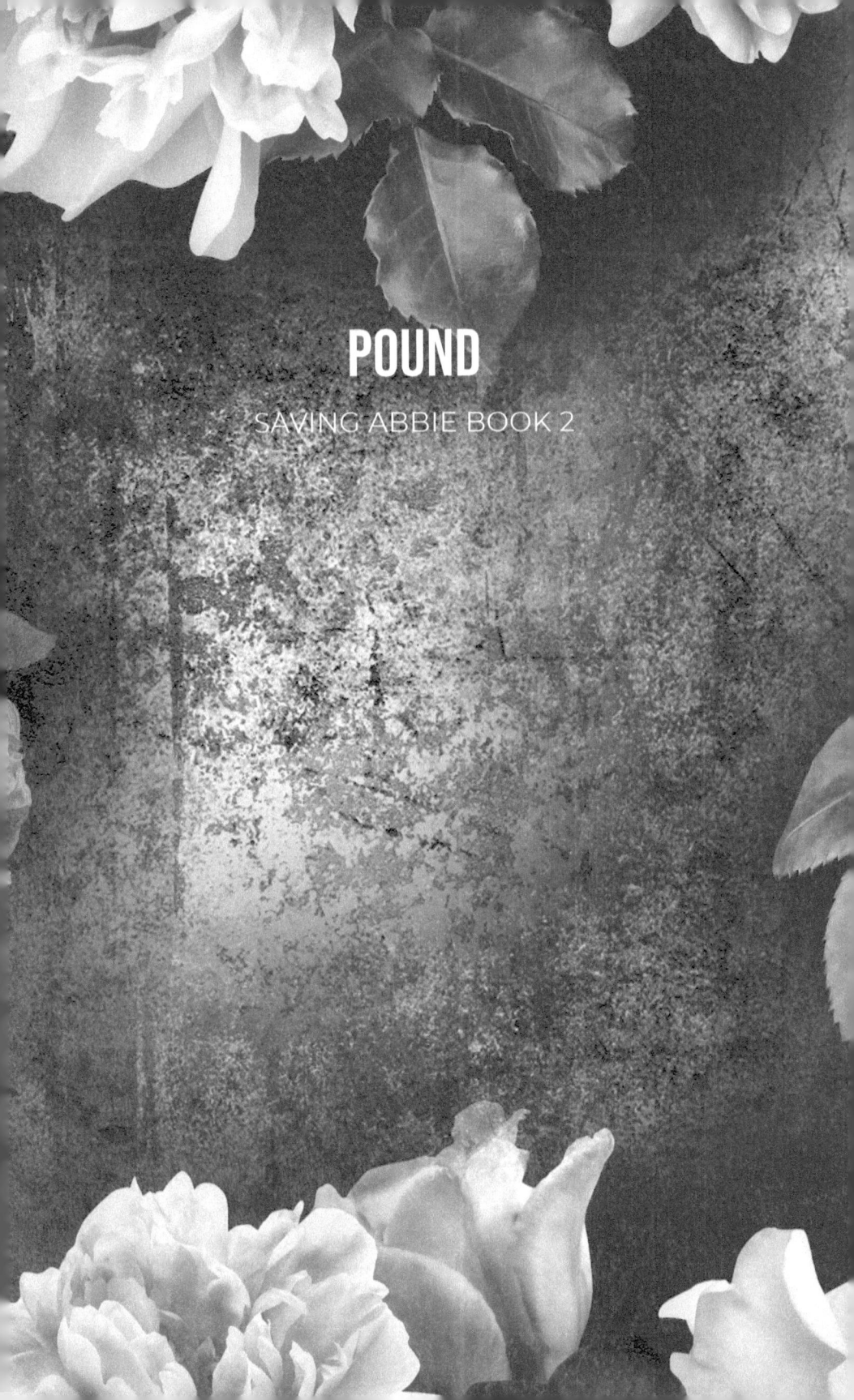

POUND

SAVING ABBIE BOOK 2

Take Me Down Lower
    Written by Zeke Brantley

You make me feel so high,
    You make me feel myself.
    Touch me there so hard,
    Take me down lower.

You're all over me,
    Before I'm over you.
    Shove me to my knees,
    Take me down lower.

I can't stand,
    But I need to run.
    Cover me with thirst,
    Take me down lower.

Take me,
    Take me down lower.
    Take me,
    Take me down lower.

CHAPTER ONE

ABBIE

"EVIDENTLY SHE FOUND *his head on her front doorstep in a cardboard box.*"

The words spun through my head over and over again like a song on repeat.

Somehow, I ended up sitting on the couch inside Zeke's inner-city Sydney townhouse, surrounded by the members of Wolf Venom, one of the hottest rock bands in the world. I didn't remember how I got there. At some point, I must have stepped inside. Everything was hazy but those words, spoken by a member of the press. Part of the pack which gathered outside on the sidewalk.

Someone pressed a cup of coffee into my hand. Judging by the smell, there was something harder in there than caffeine.

Fingers trembling, I put it to my lips for a sip. Yeah, there was a healthy dose of whiskey in there.

"Drink up, it will help to settle your nerves." That was Landon, his voice low and soothing. "Coffee and alcohol solve all problems."

I wasn't sure about that, but I took a big gulp anyway. It certainly took the edge off. The shock started to fade into acceptance. Vance was dead. Murdered. Left in a cardboard box, just like Jonah, the guy who pulled a gun on Zeke and I.

I was vaguely aware of Tully talking on the phone to someone.

"Jackson is on his way." The lead guitarist slipped his phone into his back pocket and sat in the chair opposite me. "Apparently, Vance was found a couple of hours ago. Somebody leaked the story to the press. He's going to talk to them on your behalf and will deal with them. Jackson that is, not Vance." He managed a lopsided smile.

I nodded and gave him a watery smile in return for his attempt at humour.

"Thank you. I just…" I shook my head. "I can't believe it. I mean I hated him for what he did to me, but I didn't want him dead." Not exactly. "Who would do something like this? Why?"

Someone left Jonah's head in a box on Zeke's doorstep, and now this.

"This has to be aimed at me, doesn't it?" I looked around at the guys. "It can't be a coincidence."

Would the killer come after me next? My stomach churned and I regretted drinking the laced coffee.

"It'll be okay." Channing, the band's saxophone player, put an arm around me. He smelled of soap and a hint of something I couldn't put my finger on. A cologne maybe? Whatever it was, I liked it.

I leaned my head against his muscular chest and tried not to give in to uncontrollable trembling.

Under the circumstances, it was difficult. I kept imagining Vance's head looking back at me from inside a box. In my mind, his eyes were wide open, accusing me of somehow doing this to him.

Fuck off, I told my imagination. I had absolutely nothing to do with it. I hadn't seen him in person for over a year. Thank goodness I had plenty of alibis for the entire day. I was in the studio, recording a new album.

"What the hell is going on?" Asher's voice made me jump so hard I almost spilled what was left of my coffee.

He and Zeke stepped in through the back door, identical expressions of confusion and worry etched on their gorgeous faces.

"We saw the circus out the front so we had to come around the back way." Zeke crouched down in front of me and placed his hands lightly on my knees.

"Are you okay?" he asked, his voice rough with worry.

"Yeah," I said. "Vance is dead."

He blinked in surprise, then set his mouth in a hard line. "The asshole who married you as a publicity stunt? I'm not sure if I can be persuaded to give a shit. Sounds like good riddance to me." He was uncompromising when it came to people he cared about.

People like me. I could hardly believe how close I got to him and the other guys in such a short time. Already, they meant more to me than anyone else ever had. It was becoming more and more evident the feeling was mutual all around.

"Yeah, I guess," I said. "But he was found the same way Jonah was. Just his head in a cardboard box." I swallowed to keep from throwing up. No one deserved to end up like that, no matter how shitty they were.

I didn't want to, but had to ask. "Where were you and Asher?" Did I even want the answer to that? They could have been up to something shady I was better off not knowing about.

Zeke looked surprised, then laughed, just slightly. "Not killing Vance. I can promise you. I wish I thought of it, but I didn't do it."

I wasn't sure if he was joking or not. He actually looked like he'd give the killer a high five for their trouble. That was both hot and oh-so-wrong at the same time.

I looked over at Asher. The drummer shook his head, but he too looked like he wished he was in on it.

He raised his hand. "I solemnly swear we didn't kill him."

"I believe you," I said. I really did.

Asher and Zeke exchanged glances.

"She might feel better if she knew where we were," Asher said reluctantly.

Zeke shrugged, then nodded. "I guess so." He sighed through his nose and said, "We went to see Reuben, to tell him to leave you the fuck alone."

Zeke's brother was a lot older, and the head of his family. Not just family of relatives, but criminal activity too. Mobsters, mafia, whatever you wanted to call them. Reuben was adamant Zeke would quit the band and return to the family someday. Zeke was adamant he wouldn't. Reuben tried to recruit me to convince Zeke, but that hadn't gone down very well. With me or Zeke.

"Let me guess, he didn't like that," I said. "You don't think he had anything to do with what happened to Vance, do you?"

Zeke was certain Reuben wasn't behind killing Jonah, because Jonah worked for Reuben. That didn't mean he wasn't behind Vance's death.

Zeke frowned. "It's his style, but I don't know why he would have Vance killed."

"So I would be put back under scrutiny," I suggested. "This could have a really negative impact on the tour." As in, make everything ugly as shit.

In only a couple of weeks, I was supposed to leave with Wolf Venom to tour the world. It was supposed to resurrect my career and reputation after my very brief marriage and very public affair with the owner of my former label, Onyx Riot Records.

"I might get kicked off the tour." Tears prickled in the corners of my eyes. "The label might cancel my new album."

If that was the case, I was done for. My career would be over once and for all. I would be lucky to get a job waiting tables. It was so unfair. I hadn't worked this hard just to have it all come crashing down on me for something I had nothing to do with.

Zeke put an arm around me, so I was held between him and Channing, drawing warmth and comfort from them both. "No one is kicking you off the tour. Or cancelling the album. I promise. I'm not going to let that happen to you. Or to us, because the band needs you along on this tour."

"That's debatable."

I hadn't realised Penn arrived until he spoke. Now, he stood a couple of metres away, his arms crossed over his chest, his usual pissed off expression on his face.

"What the fuck is going on?" he asked. "Jackson called and told me to get here as quickly as possible. You're all moping around here like you're at a funeral. Who died?"

"Hey Penny," Asher greeted. "Abbie's ex-husband died."

Penn's scowl deepened. "Who gives a shit?"

"He was murdered," Tully said.

Penn shook his head. "I still don't care."

"The same way Jonah was," Zeke said. "As in, there might be a serial killer running around Sydney. You might be next."

Penn dropped his arms. "Okay, *now* I care." He looked at me through narrowed eyes. "This has something to do with you? I told you guys she was trouble. Did you believe me? No. You're all too busy thinking with your cocks."

"Right, and you're not?" Asher said.

"What's that supposed to mean?" Penn demanded.

The conversation was interrupted by a knock on the door.

Asher peered through the window, toward the street. "It's Jackson." He opened the door to let the manager in, and closed it quickly before any of the press could push their way inside.

Jackson looked frazzled. Landon handed him a coffee. He gratefully took a sip.

"Abbie, I've spoken to the police and told them you were in the studio all day. They said they wanted to confirm a few things. No one thinks you had anything to do with this."

I sighed gratefully. "I hope not. It's still not a good look though, is it?" I grimaced tentatively.

He looked like he wanted to deny it, but regretfully said, "No, it's not. The timing isn't the best either. We'll make it clear you know nothing about what happened and feel terrible about him dying. We'll put together a statement for the press. They will have to be satisfied with that. Otherwise, we'll be keeping all of you under wraps until this blows over."

"How long will that take?" Penn looked at me as though this was all my fault.

Was he right? If someone was targeting me, was it fair for them to have gotten caught up in all of this too? I didn't think so, but I was grateful I wasn't alone in all of this. That was selfish of me, I knew, but it was what it was.

"You know what the press is like," Jackson said wearily. "They'll move on to something else in a day or so."

"Or Wolf Venom could distance ourselves from her right now," Penn suggested.

"Fuck off," Asher told him. "First of all, she is one of us now, whether you like it or not. Secondly the press would crucify her if we did that and you know it. She doesn't deserve that." He gave Penn a scathing look like perhaps he did.

Penn glared at him. He slumped back against the wall and crossed his arms over his chest again. It seemed he'd said his piece and was now going to see how it all unfolded.

I gave Asher a grateful smile. I didn't want the band to be at odds with each other over me, but his growling at Penn was kinda hot.

Zeke gave him a look that suggested he found it just as hot. If those two guys weren't careful, they were going to set me on fire.

I was totally here for it.

"No one is distancing themselves from anyone," Jackson said firmly. "I've spoken to Levi Jones and he agrees. If anyone is to ask, and they will, Wolf Venom is one hundred percent behind Abbie Hart. White Wolf Records is one hundred percent supportive as well. However, Levi is also glad Abbie has an airtight alibi."

"Me too," I agreed wholeheartedly. Any other day and I would have been just about anywhere in Sydney, doing fuck knows what. If anyone was trying to pin this on me, they screwed up.

I was totally here for that too. The sooner they found whoever did this, the better.

To Zeke, I said, "Do you think we slowed the police down by disposing of Jonah's head?"

He scrubbed his cheek with his hand. "No way to know. We can't undo it now. If we let the cops know we found it, we'll only get ourselves into trouble." He threw his hand up in frustration. "I wish we knew about it before the press did. We could have made it all go away by now."

"Do I want to know how?" I asked.

He grinned. "No, you don't. I'll just say I know people and leave it at that."

"I'm going to pretend I didn't hear that," Jackson said.

Zeke pointed a finger gun at him. "Good idea. You don't want to know about it either."

"I very much don't," Jackson agreed. "Everything you said needs to stay within these walls. We're all complicit if it doesn't. You don't need me to tell you what that would do to your careers." His eyes lingered on Penn in particular.

"We'd be fucked," Penn said. "That's what it would do."

His words were a relief. I half expected him to say he was going to talk to the press and throw me under the bus. Anything to get rid of me.

"Exactly." Jackson swallowed down the last of his coffee. "We've all worked too hard to throw it away now." He handed his cup to Channing. "I need to go and put out some more spot fires. Preferably before it turns into a full-blown bushfire. Stay away from the press. Either stay here or go to your homes and lock the doors. Don't answer phones. Consider this a gag order from the boss. If they have any questions, they can go through me and our lawyers."

Asher unlocked the door and let Jackson back out into the insanity of the throng outside. He quickly locked it again. "Isn't this exciting?"

"I could use a bit less excitement," I said. "Or at least a different kind of excitement."

Asher grinned.

CHAPTER
TWO

ASHER

"IT'S GOING to be a tight fit," Zeke said.

I grinned.

He rolled his eyes at me. "Dude, I wasn't talking about that."

"Sure you weren't, dude." I was. It felt like I waited a lifetime for him and Abbie.

What I wanted, more than anything, was to be transparent with them. I needed to be with both of them, in every way that mattered, but I didn't want to sneak around to do it. I wanted everyone to know who was doing what with who, and for us all to be cool with it. Otherwise, we'd fuck up what we had before it began.

"Landon and Channing can sleep in my spare room," Zeke continued, one eye on me. "Tully and Penn can crash on the couches downstairs. That leaves you, me and Abbie to squash up in my bed."

"I bags being in the middle," I said quickly. I eyed the door to the bathroom. The shower was still running. "Do you think she's okay in there?"

Zeke glanced towards the door, a frown on his brow. "Yeah. Give her a couple of minutes more. If she doesn't get out, I'll go and check on her." He opened his wardrobe and pulled out a spare pillow.

"And by check on her, you mean offer to wash her back?" I teased.

He smiled and tossed the pillow onto the bed. "If I don't, someone else will."

"You're right," I agreed. "I would absolutely offer. Since I'm a nice guy, I would offer to wash your back too. In fact, I have two hands. One for each back."

"I think you might be overestimating the size of my shower," he said dryly.

"I think it might be time to move then." The size of the shower was definitely a reason to sell a property, right? I watched enough of those home renovation shows to know party showers were a thing. We were rock stars, we had no excuse *not* to have a party shower in each of our homes.

Although, we were also new to the concept of sharing in the way we were talking about now.

"I'll think about it." Zeke pulled a pillowcase out from a drawer and started to put it on the pillow. "I could buy the place next door and blow out the walls between that and this. I could have a couple of big bathrooms and four bedrooms."

"There's that word again," I said with a happy sigh. "Blow."

He looked over at me and grinned. "It's one of my favourite words."

"Me too." I gave him a long, lingering look. He and I had been friends since we were kids, but this whole flirtation thing was new. I liked it.

My heart was in my throat, because I didn't want overstep and screw this up, I put a hand on Zeke's muscular-as-fuck bicep and gave him a light kiss on the mouth.

I thought he might stiffen in discomfort or even push me away. But like the other night, he kissed me back with an equal amount of intensity, and a little bit of tongue.

I moaned against his mouth, enjoying the way his stubble tickled my lips.

He must have dropped the pillow, because his hands were on my hips and his body was pressed up against mine. Careful not to bump my erection on his, I slid my arms around his neck.

"Holy shit." Abbie's soft voice came from the doorway.

I started to break off the kiss.

"Don't stop on my account," she said. "I'm more than happy to watch."

Fuck, that was hot.

"We'd prefer it if you joined us," I said. "Wouldn't we, Zeke?"

His face was pink and his lips were parted like he was trying to catch a breath.

"Yeah," he agreed. "But I have to get these pillows down to the guys before they bitch about not having any. Save some for me."

He grabbed the pillow and another one he'd already put the cover on and carried them to the door. He stopped to give Abbie a deep, lingering kiss on the way past.

She looked adorable in a white fluffy dressing gown and a towel wrapped around her hair. Her skin was red from the heat of the water but with no makeup on, she looked even more gorgeous than ever.

She stepped into the room and closed the door behind her. She unwound the towel from her head and let it fall to the floor. Her blond hair tumbled loose to her shoulders.

"Do you want me to brush it?" I offered. Anything to touch her.

"Sure." She crouched and pulled a hairbrush out from the soap bag inside an open suitcase on the floor. Apparently she hadn't finished unpacking it.

I knew this living arrangement was supposed to be temporary, but Zeke would happily let her stay forever.

"Sit down on the bed," I said when she stood and hesitated. "Are you feeling a bit better now?" I took the brush and started to run it gently through her hair. Every so often, I stopped to tease out a tangle. If it hurt, she gave no sign. If anything, she seemed to be enjoying the attention.

"A little bit," she agreed. "Alcohol and a hot shower solve most problems, don't they?"

"Only the ones that can't be solved with sex," I agreed.

"I dunno, sometimes I think sex creates more problems than it solves," she said with undisguised bitterness.

"Only if you're having sex with the wrong people." I finished one side of her hair and started on the other. "The right people make all the difference."

Like the rest of the guys, I had my share of partners. Mostly one night hook ups. I worried I might never be interested in anything longer lasting than that. Now, it all made sense. I was waiting for Zeke and Abbie.

Did they feel the same way? I hoped like hell they did.

"There you go, perfect." I placed the hairbrush on Zeke's chest of drawers and bent to kiss her head. Of course, now I'd do what I could to mess her hair up again.

"Thank you." She looked over her shoulder at me, her blue eyes full of promise.

"You're welcome." I slid my hands down either side of her face, down her neck. I brushed her throat with my fingers and let them dance over her skin, down the front of her dressing gown. I lightly massaged every centimetre of her, all the way down to the softness of her full breasts.

I had waited approximately a lifetime to touch her like this. Potentially several lifetimes.

"Mmm," she breathed when I ghosted the heels of my palms over her nipples. They hardened eagerly under my touch. I pinched each one between my thumb and forefinger and rolled them, savouring the way her breath hitched in response.

"Nipples are one of my favourite things." I made myself a bet that I wouldn't find any part of her I didn't want to touch over and over again.

She undid the belt on her dressing gown and let it slide down over her shoulders and off her arms. Her skin was pale except for freckles scattered here and there.

"Wow, you're gorgeous." I bent to brush my lips over her shoulder, then moved around to sit beside her, facing her.

"No, you." She wound her arms around my neck and drew me in for a searing, hot kiss. The kind that would make me see stars for days. She tugged up the hem of my T-shirt and somehow managed to get it off without breaking our lips apart for more than a second or two.

She leaned back. Her eyes raked over me.

"See, this is what I mean. You guys are like... Holy hotness. How are any of you even real?"

"Maybe we're not— Oh!" She took me by surprise when she put her hands on my chest and shoved me back onto the mattress. I wasn't complaining. No way.

I certainly wasn't complaining when she shed the rest of the dressing gown and slowly crawled up my body. She straddled my hips and lowered her mouth to mine.

The offensive fabric of my pants was the only thing between us. Everything felt too tight, like my cock was ready to break the seams to get to her. I wanted to hurry up and get out of them, but at the same time I wanted to slow down and not rush.

In the end, she was the one who undid the button and slowly worked the zipper down, as the door opened and closed. The lock clicked into place.

A moment later, Zeke was next to us, already without his shirt.

Thank you universe.

"Looks like I got back just in time," Zeke said.

"We would have waited." Although, when she grabbed the sides of my pants and slid them down my hips, then curled her hand around my erection, I realised that might have been hard. Um, difficult.

"Sure you would." Zeke's eyes were on my cock. They widened when Abbie moved down and started to run her tongue over my tip.

I reminded myself this was new to him. I had to take it slow and not scare him off.

I locked my eyes on him and placed a hand on his shoulder. Gently, giving him time to resist and move away if he wanted to, I drew him towards me. At first, it was just a light brush of lips against lips.

He lifted himself up on his elbow and deepened the kiss.

The touch of both of them was everything I hoped for and more.

I slipped my tongue inside Zeke's mouth as Abbie lowered hers over my cock and started to suck.

I groaned with the pure pleasure that pulsed all the way through me.

Slowly and carefully, I slipped my hand down to work the button on Zeke's pants loose. He lifted his hips and between us we pushed his pants down. He kicked them off the rest of the way.

"If any of this is uncomfortable, just tell me and I'll stop," I told him.

"You know it, bro," he said.

I wasn't sure if *bro* was the right word under the circumstances, but I would roll with it.

My eyes on his, I closed my fingers around his cock.

His eyes half closed and he tensed just a little bit, but he didn't pull away.

Encouraged, I started to run my hand slowly up and down his length. It didn't take long for his hips to move in rhythm with me. It was so insanely hot, I could barely handle it.

"Abbie," I managed to say over the pounding blood in my brain. "I want to be inside you. Please."

She picked up her head, gave my cock a couple more teasing swipes with her tongue, then crawled up the bed to me.

I let go of Zeke, rolled her onto her back and knelt between her legs. I took a moment to admire the view of her open thighs and already glistening pussy. Slowly at first, I explored her folds and clit with the tips of my fingers, before slipping a couple inside her to make sure she was ready for me.

"She's practically dripping," I said to Zeke.

He flashed a grin while he worked his hand up and down his cock. A bead of moisture formed on his tip, making my balls heavier than ever. I needed to touch him. I needed to bury myself in her. I needed everything, all at once.

I positioned my cock carefully outside Abbie's warm, damp pussy and slowly slid inside her glorious body.

The groan she gave was almost enough to make me come on the spot. Holy hell, she felt incredible. Even more than I could have imagined.

I reclaimed Zeke's cock, curling my hand back around him while leaning on my opposite elbow.

He lay on his side and kissed Abbie while I thrust into her and worked him at the same time. It took some concentration to get the rhythm right, especially when I was distracted by the way his hand slid over her breasts. His fingers swirled over her skin, teasing her nipples while he became more and more breathless.

He slid his hand down, over her belly and between her thighs. He must have found her clit, because he started to rub, fingers tracing circles over her. She arched her back and moaned.

Every time I thrust, I felt his calloused skin, and the crazy amazing heat of her core.

My hand tightened around his cock. I didn't know whose breathing was more ragged at this point. Maybe it was a three-way tie.

I pounded harder and harder and worked him faster and faster.

Abbie moaned loudly. "I'm going to come," she said.

"Me too," I said breathlessly.

Her eyes flickered open. "Asher... Come inside me."

Oh... Fuck. When she put it that way...

She came first, crying out. Her back arched harder and her muscles tightened around me.

I was next, a moment later, grinding hard for every drop of pleasure. For a long, wonderful moment nothing existed but orgasms and a burst of rainbow in my vision.

Zeke came shortly after, thrusting into my hand, and spilling warm, pearly cum over my fingers.

I gave a long low grunt and finally sagged, my hand curled tight around the most gorgeous man, cock still inside the most beautiful woman I ever saw.

I thought I was living before this, but now I knew I just started.

CHAPTER
THREE

ABBIE

THE FIRST THING I felt when I woke up was warmth.

I was tucked up tight between two rock hard bodies. Zeke on my left and Asher on my right. Zeke lay facing me, one arm lying over my stomach. Asher was lying on his back, one of his legs draped over one of mine.

There were worse ways to wake up than between two hot rock stars. Particularly when both of them seemed to care about me as much as I cared about them.

Zeke and I hadn't talked about his feelings since he told me he was falling for me. I sensed his hadn't changed. Mine grew the more I got to know all of the guys.

I wanted to punch Penn in the dick more often than not, but he was ridiculously hot and talented. The seven of us were becoming so embedded in each other's lives that it was hard not to include him when I thought about the collective *us*.

He might disagree, possibly strenuously, but that was how I felt.

I gradually became aware that Zeke was awake and watching me.

"Hey," he said softly.

"Good morning." I had a sneaking suspicion it was closer to afternoon than morning but whatever. Shit like that doesn't matter when you're in the middle of two guys like this. "Did you sleep well?"

"I always do when you're next to me." He pressed a kiss to my nose.

"And Asher?" I was worried Zeke might freak out about kissing and touching another guy. It was one thing to get caught up in the moment and another to have to deal with that moment afterwards.

"Him too," Zeke said after a moment. "You're not weird about this?"

"No," I said quickly. "You're the one who told me all the guys in the band wanted to do, what was it, naughty things to me? It seems like you were right."

He smiled. "Of course I was. I know the guys. For good or not so good, depending on your perspective."

I laughed softly. "It must be hard spending so much time together. Work and play and everything in between."

"It certainly is hard." He grabbed my hand and drew it down to his erect cock.

"So it is." I stroked my hand up and down his length and toyed with his balls for a minute or two.

At the same time, he reached down between my thighs and started to circle my pussy with his fingertips. He carefully stayed away from my clit until he'd touched every other part of me, including sliding his fingers through my folds and over my rear hole.

When he finally touched my clit, I was already panting.

"Are you two starting without me?" Asher asked sleepily. Apparently he woke quickly, because a moment later he was swirling his tongue around my nipple and starting to suck.

"We're just getting started," I said, breathless already.

"Oh good," Asher said around a mouthful of nipple.

Zeke slipped a couple of fingers inside me and hooked them around to massage my G spot. He leaned over and licked my other nipple.

All that attention on the three most sensitive parts of my body drove me towards the edge faster than a runaway train.

I kept my eyes half open and watched them work on me, while trying to get my head around how incredible it was to be here with both of them. A girl could definitely get used to this.

I wanted to hold on for longer, but I toppled over the cliff and into an intense orgasm that thrummed through my entire body like an electric guitar with the volume turned up to full. I cried out or maybe I screamed. All I really knew was that every bit of me was on fire in the best way possible.

I flopped, panting, onto the mattress. My head went on spinning for a minute or two.

When it was finally clear, I looked from one guy to the other.

"What?" Zeke asked. He gave me that look like he was sure I was up to something, but didn't know what.

I rolled over just far enough to open the drawer beside the bed.

"Oh." Zeke swallowed audibly.

Asher's eyes widened when I pulled out the vibrator and tube of lube. "Okay, this just got interesting."

"It wasn't interesting before?" Zeke asked. He took the vibrator and lube from me and, after a moment's pause, handed it to Asher.

"It was, but this is even more so." Asher opened the tube and applied the lube to the vibrator while Zeke rolled me onto my back and knelt between my knees.

He slowly slid his cock inside me, his eyes half closed. They closed fully and he gulped again when Asher sat beside him and held the vibrator near his ass.

"You've done this before?" Asher asked.

"Once," Zeke said, his voice strained. "Be gentle."

"Of course," Asher said lightly. "Let me know if you want me to stop."

I, for one, was glad Zeke and I played with the vibrator before. I had a feeling he wasn't quite ready to have Asher's cock in his ass or mouth. Or to have Asher suck him.

Someday, but not yet.

Zeke jerked a little, but then he let out a huffing moan that sounded like he was enjoying the way everything felt.

As much as I loved being the centre of attention for both guys, I liked that Zeke was in the centre now. Everyone deserved to feel special.

I couldn't help but wonder what the press outside would think if they knew what was going on inside the townhouse. I'd be happy if they never knew, but I wasn't ashamed of anything we were doing either.

I mean, I wasn't going to let anyone film us and put it on the internet, but I wasn't going to be embarrassed either. I've done plenty of embarrassing things in my life; having sex with two guys wasn't one of them.

"Is that okay?" Asher asked.

"Mmm-hmm," Zeke said in reply.

Of course he couldn't respond with coherent words. It was hard enough to think with his cock inside me, much less being stimulated from two angles.

Gradually, Zeke started to move, sliding out of me, then slipping slowly back in. From the look of concentration on his face, he was trying to get a rhythm of thrusts that Asher could match.

"I knew you two would be amazing," Asher said. "I didn't realise you would be *this* amazing."

"We should both come with a warning label," I managed to say.

Both guys chuckled.

"Accurate," Asher said. His voice was strained. He seemed to be very much enjoying what he was doing, but I didn't need to look to see he was also hard.

"Would you like some help?" I offered.

"Zeke?" Asher asked.

"It's okay," Zeke managed to say. "Don't want you to pop anything."

Asher chuckled. "In that case, yes please." He slipped the vibrator free, put it aside and scooted up the bed until his groin was in front of my face. I tipped my head, opened my mouth and let him slide his cock between my lips.

Almost as though they played together for so long they knew each other's rhythm, the guys started to pump into me in unison.

Filled with Zeke's cock, and with the taste of Asher on my tongue, I flowed effortlessly toward another orgasm, this one softer, but somehow more mind blowing than the first one.

I definitely screamed this time, but cut off the sound as Asher came. I clamped my lips around him as he pounded harder, grunting and grinding until hot cum spilled into my mouth.

I took a breath through my nose and swallowed as Zeke came, pounding just as hard into my pussy.

The whole world disappeared in a whirlpool of heat and sweat, grunts and moans. The slide of hot male skin on mine, tattoos and calloused hands. I could happily have stayed in this place for eternity.

We all slumped back down with sighs and pants. I was so slick with sweat by now, I was going to need another shower.

"Do we have to go on tour?" Asher asked. "Can't we stay here in bed instead?"

"Believe it or not, other places in the world have beds," Zeke said. "And get this, you don't always need a bed."

"What?" Asher said jokingly. "Are you trying to say there are other places which are perfectly acceptable for fucking?"

"I am saying that," Zeke said. "Lots of them. I'm pretty sure the three of us can find quite a few, if we put our minds to it."

"You guys," I said teasingly. "I'm certain you're both creative when it comes to finding a place."

I've been on tour enough times to know there were all sorts of nooks and crannies, even if you have to look for them, and rarely a shortage of someone happy to share them with you.

"Like a dark corner in a nightclub?" Zeke smiled slowly.

"Exactly," I agreed.

"You what now?" Asher asked.

I turned my head and watched his expression as Zeke told him how he and I met.

"Dude, where was I when this was going on?" Asher asked.

"I think you were suffering through dinner with Dane," Zeke said.

"I knew I should have missed it," Asher groaned. "For so many reasons, including that."

I rolled over and kissed his mouth. My lips were probably still red from his cock. "We'll make it up to you."

He kissed me back and then pressed his nose against mine. "You already have. Twice already. That isn't to say I'm not up for many, many more."

"I had a feeling you might be," I said.

"Can we pack the vibrator?" Asher asked Zeke.

"I would be disappointed if you didn't," Zeke replied. "As long as I get to use it on you two, too. Actually, I have a few different types in the drawer. We could take them all and play around."

"We could use one to find out what's up Penny's ass," Asher said jokingly.

"His head," I said dryly. It was either that or a stick. Whatever it was, I wished he would take it out and lighten up. Or at least stop being an asshole to me.

They both laughed.

"That makes sense," Zeke agreed. He sighed. "I suppose we should get up and see if the press is still camped out the front, waiting for blood."

I didn't want to move, but I needed to know if they were still out there too. Shit.

Could I put the blankets over my head and hide for another year or ten instead?

CHAPTER
FOUR

ABBIE

THE PRESS WERE outside the townhouse all morning but slithered away by lunchtime. No doubt they were off making someone else's life miserable.

"Just in time," Zeke said cheerfully.

"Yeah," Penn said. "We were just about to kill each other."

Apart from having to share the bathroom, all the guys got along pretty well. In spite of what the keyboard player said, no one seemed ready to murder anyone else.

"No we weren't," Zeke said. "We are going on a little excursion. The bus will be outside shortly."

Penn narrowed his eyes at him. "The fuck? Where are we going?"

"Trust me," Zeke said lightly. "You'll love it."

Penn muttered and stalked off towards the kitchen. He didn't say he wouldn't go.

That seemed pretty miraculous to me. He didn't seem like the kind of guy who liked excursions very much.

On the other hand, Zeke's idea of an excursion might be to a strip club for all I knew. Although, if that was the case, we would just all walk.

"Any idea what's going on?" I asked Asher, who sat beside me on the couch eating toast.

"No idea," Asher said. "Whatever it is, it's bound to be good. Every once in a while Zeke organises shit like this. It's always pretty sick."

"We're not going to jump out of a plane are we?" I grimaced around the lip of my coffee cup. I was game for just about everything, but that was not high on my to-do list.

Asher glanced towards the window. "I doubt it. It looks too windy out there for that. Might rain too. My guess is that it's an indoor activity." He wiggled his brows at me. "My favourite kind."

I smiled back. "Mine too."

"No shit," Penn grumbled. "You three were loud enough."

"Sorry, not sorry," Asher said without taking his eyes off me.

"I hope it's the trampoline place again," Landon said. "That was fun."

"My guess is paintball or laser tag," Channing said. He looked like he relished the idea of shooting his bandmates. With paint.

"We could be going to a movie," Tully suggested. "My guess is a private screening of the latest superhero movie."

"I could get behind that," Penn said. "Put me down for a super-sized tub of popcorn."

"I'm going to guess go-kart racing," Asher said.

"Any of that would be better than jumping out of a plane." Personally, I liked the idea of curling up in front of a movie screen. Including the popcorn. That might be the first time I agreed with anything Penn said. That was another miracle right there.

"Anything would be better than jumping out of a fucking plane again," Penn said. He gave Zeke a death stare.

Zeke shrugged unapologetically. "You didn't have to jump. For the record, you're all wrong, but if somebody wants to write all those things down, I'll plan them for another time."

"Landon," Channing said to him.

"On it." Landon pulled out his phone and started tapping at the screen. "I'm going to add bungee jumping to the list."

"Don't you fucking dare," Penn growled.

"You don't have to jump," Zeke said patiently, like he was talking to a child.

"I'm not going to get there and then not jump," Penn argued. "But I don't want to get there in the first place."

Once again, I found myself agreeing with him. I would also do it if I was there and they were egging me on, but the idea was terrifying. If I wanted a shot of adrenaline, I would get up on stage, or crawl under a table in a night-club and suck one of the guys off. For the most part, neither of those would kill me.

"Maybe Penny would prefer a visit to the museum," Asher said.

Penn flipped him off.

"I like museums," I said.

"I'll add that to the list," Landon said.

Penn gave me a look like I wasn't going to be around long enough to go on any excursions to the museum with the band.

I was determined to prove him wrong. He didn't have to like me. Whatever his opinion was, that was his problem, not mine. While I was hanging out with the rest of the band, he would have to put up with me. It would be nice if he would shut up as well, but he was who he was.

"The bus is here," Zeke said. "Everyone on board, boys and girls." He opened the door and peered outside. "If any of the press are still lurking around, I can't see them."

We all piled cups and plates into the kitchen sink and stepped outside into the sunshine.

The bus was small, the kind designed to fit about fifteen to twenty people comfortably. I had half hoped it was one of those big tour buses with a king-size bed at the back, but it was still exciting to be going somewhere interesting with the band.

"Where are we going?" Asher asked the driver as he led me onto the bus, my hand in his.

"Good try," Zeke said as he put his hand on my ass and pushed me up the steps. "She's not gonna tell you anything."

"Nope," the driver agreed. Her head was shaved except for a millimetre or two of hair, and she had more piercings than I'd ever seen on one person. She also had the kind of huge smile that made me like her immediately.

"I got paid extra to keep my mouth shut."

"Ren has worked for the label for a long time," Zeke explained. "She drives the tour bus and helps set up the stage."

Ren snorted. "Helps, my ass. I do most of the heavy lifting the boys can't handle."

"She's not joking," Asher said. "She's a certified badass."

"Shit yeah, I am," Ren agreed. She gave me a warm smile. "It's nice to meet you. Word to the wise though. At least half of the stuff that comes out of these guys' mouths is bullshit."

"Hey," Asher protested. "We're not that bad."

I grinned back at Ren and let the guys herd me to the back seat of the bus. It was the only place where three people could sit next to each other. I sat in the middle with Zeke on one side and Asher on the other.

Channing and Landon sat together in front of us. Tully sat on the opposite side of them.

Penn sat by himself at the front of the bus, sideways with his feet on the seat. He pulled out his phone and started to tap on the screen, the usual scowl on his face the entire time.

"So we're not allowed to know where we're going," I said slowly. "Are we allowed to know how long it will take us to get there?"

"That depends on traffic," Zeke said.

"This is Sydney, everything depends on the traffic," Asher pointed out.

"I should have asked, on a good day how long will it take us to get there?" I clicked my seatbelt into place.

"On a good day, maybe fifteen minutes," Zeke said. "But because this is Sydney, probably three hours." He grinned.

I snorted softly. Even on a bad day, it wasn't usually that bad. Unless a vehicle broke down on the Harbour Bridge or something. Then three hours might be a conservative estimate.

"With Ren's driving, we'll get there in ten minutes," Asher said. As if to keep me from falling off the seat in case of an emergency, he placed his hand on my thigh.

Zeke did the same to my other leg.

I felt much safer now if an accident occurred. And I hadn't seen any sign of the press.

Bonus.

The police stopped by shortly after we got out of bed, but they had little to say, or ask. They'd already been to the studio and clarified my whereabouts that day. According to them, I wasn't considered a suspect.

No doubt they'd keep me in mind if they turned up any evidence that pointed to me.

The jilted ex would always come under suspicion until they found the real killer. I wasn't naïve enough to think otherwise. All I could do was hope they were found quickly, before they struck again. And if they did kill someone else, it could be dealt with before the press found out. Or the police, for that matter.

What was I thinking? Would I happily hide a murder to save myself the inconvenience? Maybe. It would raise so many questions I didn't have answers for and cast suspicion on the guys as well. If the police started to dig into their pasts, who knows what they would find? Just a wild guess here, but probably things better left buried.

The bus pulled away from the curb and navigated the narrow streets and parked cars before pulling out onto a busier road. Judging by the traffic, we wouldn't be getting to our destination quickly. Whatever.

I was curious to see where we were going, but it was nice to hang out like this for a while.

"Do we get a hint?" Tully sat around and rested his arms on the back of the chair.

"Nope," Zeke said. "Did you bring your passports?"

"We need passports?" Asher frowned.

For a moment, I started to panic. Where was mine? I certainly didn't have it on me.

Zeke grinned. "No. Just figured I would shit stir you all up."

Asher leaned past me to punch Zeke on the arm. "Asshole. Lucky we're not skydiving. I might be tempted to shove you out of the plane without a parachute."

"You would never do that," Zeke said. "You love me too much."

"Depends on how much you piss me off," Asher said, his voice a mock growl. "Penn would help me. Wouldn't you, Penny?"

Penn looked up from his screen. "Huh? Whatever shit you're on about, leave me out of it." He looked back down at his phone.

"Looks like you're on your own there, Ash," Zeke said. "Lucky for me, everyone else in the band loves me."

"Most of the time," Tully said.

"Ouch." Zeke pretended to be hurt, but I doubted the tease caused him any more pain than Asher's punch, which hadn't even made him flinch. "It might be time to think about going solo. Or Abbie and I could form a duo." He gave me a speculative look.

"You'll need a drummer," Asher said. "At least for when you go on tour. I'm in."

"And a lead guitarist," Tully said.

"And bass guitar and saxophone," Channing said.

"You know that defeats the purpose of going solo, right?" Zeke said dryly.

Asher grinned. "It looks like you're stuck with us then."

I noticed Penn hadn't volunteered to join us if we took on this new venture. Fortunately for everyone, it wasn't going to happen. Everyone, that was, but me. Being a part of a band permanently would solve so many problems. On the other hand, it would probably create a few as well.

"That might be the shortest breakup in music history," Zeke said. His expression was reflective but a smile tugged at the corners of his mouth.

"Should we start referring to Abbie as Yoko?" Penn didn't glance up from his screen.

He might have meant that as a joke and he might not, but it stung. The last thing I wanted was to come between the guys. If Wolf Venom broke up someday, I didn't want it to be because of me.

"We're not breaking up," Zeke said. His voice was tight and his expression at least as pissed off as I felt. Evidently he didn't like the comparison either.

His expression and tone lightened when he spoke again. "If we break up over anything, it will be because of the way the tour bus smells after taco Tuesday. In that case, it will be everyone's fault."

"Except mine," Asher said. "Only pretty smells come out of my ass."

We all broke up laughing, but Penn's accusation lingered in my mind for a long time afterwards.

CHAPTER
FIVE

ASHER

"I SHOULD HAVE KNOWN." I thought we were up for a fun day out, or at least a few hours of fun. In retrospect, that was kinda naïve of me. Given the events of the last few days, I really should have guessed what Zeke had in mind. More than that, I should have thought of it first.

Ren pulled the bus up in front of the shooting range and the door groaned open.

Zeke shrugged unapologetically. "We could all use the practice. Whatever is coming for us in the next while, I want us all to be prepared for it." He glanced at Abbie. "Do you know how to shoot a gun?"

She shook her head. "No. I've never even held one."

"We'll teach you," I said. "Zeke is right, we should all be ready. You never know when you might need to shoot Reuben in the cock. Besides, it's fun. Not *jumping up and down on the trampoline in your socks* fun, but still fun."

She didn't look convinced, but she got off the bus and held my hand as we walked into the range. It almost felt like we were boyfriend and girlfriend. Or boyfriends and girlfriend.

As far as I knew, only Zeke and I fucked Abbie, but I knew the rest of them wanted to.

Even Penn, although he wasn't ready to admit it. Even to himself.

Was it weird that none of that bothered me? Often, life goes along the lines of boy meets girl, or boy meets boy, or girl meets girl, or some combination like that. Then they either live happily ever after or they don't.

How often does it go girl meets six guys and they all live happily ever after? Maybe it was more common than I knew. Now I thought about it, I understood why a lot of people would go for it. There was always someone around when you needed to talk, or fuck, or whatever.

Could a relationship like that happen for us? I couldn't see why not. It wasn't even weird that, in the middle of that, Zeke and I had a thing going on, and Landon and Channing had a thing going on. And all of us still wanted a thing going on with Abbie.

I wondered if Penn and Tully might get it on with each other too. I doubted it. I was almost certain they were straight. Shame, they'd be cute together.

The range was pretty quiet at this time of day. Only a couple of staff were in attendance. They hurried to hand out .22 calibre handguns after most of us pulled out our licenses and flashed them.

The fact none of the staff even glanced at Abbie, much less asked for a license, suggested Zeke called and paid in advance. Probably double or maybe triple the usual fee. That or his brother owned the place, because letting someone in without a firearms license was highly illegal.

Whatever, I'd never tell.

Zeke handed Abbie a Pardini SP pistol and showed her how to use it. The rest of the guys, apart from me, dispersed into their own bays and started to practice.

"We'll try with a twenty-five metre bay." He and I could easily shoot the target at fifty metres, but this was Abbie's first time, so we'd take it easy on her.

"Oh, they have paper targets like in the movies," she said.

I grinned. "It's much more fun if it looks like you're shooting someone."

She raised her eyebrows at me.

"What? I meant it's more fun than shooting at a circle, or a can. Although, shooting cans is fun."

"Only if you're drunk," Zeke said. "Otherwise, it's not much of a challenge."

"You two do this a lot?" She looked slightly alarmed. "Shoot things, I mean."

"Just for practice," I assured her. "We don't go around shooting people."

"If we did, we would be back in our family businesses," Zeke said. "Like Asher said, we do this for practice. The other night, when my brother dropped you off at my place after he abducted you, I could have shot you by accident if I didn't know exactly what I was doing. Handling guns isn't just about hurting people, it's also about making sure you don't hurt people."

"That makes sense," she said. "If I ever picked one up to defend myself, I would probably end up shooting myself in the foot."

"It happens more often than you think," I said dryly.

She cocked a head at me. "Have you shot yourself in the foot?"

I laughed. "No, but I've been tempted to shoot Zeke in the foot every once in a while." I hadn't, but whatever it took to lighten the mood.

"Ironic, I've been tempted to shoot Asher in the cock." Zeke grinned and his eyes dropped lower.

"Because you're jealous of how much bigger I am than you," I teased. "You wouldn't really do that. We'd both regret it if you did." I gave him an intense, heated look.

Using that vibrator on him turned me on so hard I could hardly think at the time. My balls got so heavy they hurt. I badly wanted to use my cock on him, specifically *in* him, but I wouldn't rush. Besides, Abbie's mouth was just as incredible as I knew his ass would be.

Remembering coming down her throat was enough to make my cock twitch.

"I would regret it too," Abbie said. "How about you two make a deal to never shoot each other? Except with water pistols."

I had no intention of shooting Zeke with an actual gun. Likewise, he had no intention of shooting me.

I hoped.

"That should go on the list for summer," I said. "A band water fight. Complete with water balloons. And white T-shirts."

"And no bras," Zeke said.

"Yes, Zeke should definitely not wear a bra," I said jokingly. I swatted his hand away when he went to sock me. "I'm starting to think you're not responsible enough to handle a gun."

"I totally am." Zeke stepped up and took aim at the paper target. "I'll even show you how it's done."

He gave the paper person two new eyes and a hole through their paper heart.

"Is it wrong that I found that hot?" Abbie said.

"I definitely found it hot, and I've seen him do that hundreds of times," I said. "It might be the only thing I will admit that he does better than I do."

"What about singing?" Zeke asked.

I shrugged. "You might be better than me, but I'm not going to admit it." I wasn't a bad singer, but I wasn't anywhere near as good as Zeke and we all knew it. I was okay with that. I was a lot better on the drums than he was. And in the bedroom, if I said so myself.

Give me time, I would teach him all my tricks. And Abbie too.

"Dude, I think you just did." Zeke handed me the gun. "Let's see if you can do better than me." He gave me a lopsided smile like he didn't think I stood a chance. Dude knew me better than that. I would at least give him a run for his money.

"Challenge accepted." I waited until the paper target was changed out for a new one, and aimed. The poor paper person got three in the chest. I was aiming for a triangle pattern, but didn't quite pull it off. Close enough. If the paper person was real they'd be dead now.

"Not bad," Zeke conceded. "Let's see how well Abbie can do."

Here was where we could get into an argument over who was going to stand behind her and steady her arm. Instead, I leaned against the Perspex between the bays and crossed my arms over my chest.

At some point, if she wanted to learn, I would teach her to play drums. When it came to shooting, Zeke was the better instructor.

Besides, this way I got to stand back and watch.

I won't lie, I would have liked to see him bend her over then and there and slide his cock into her. The thought of the noises she'd make was enough to set my pulse on fire.

Remembering how her mouth and her pussy felt around my cock made my balls throb like I hadn't come in days, not hours. The memory of Zeke's mouth on mine was no less compelling. Between them both, they were going to drive me absolutely wild.

I was at least one million percent here for it.

While Zeke went through the basics of how to aim and fire and deal with the recoil, I pictured the logistics of bending them both over. There were so many interesting combinations we could try. Throw the other guys into the mix and the combinations were endless.

Penn was not only unfair when he suggested Abbie would be the one to break up the band, he was also wrong. If anything, she'd brought us closer together. I doubted I would have been able to act on my feelings for Zeke if it wasn't for her. Even more, I doubted Zeke would have responded the way he did. At least, not as quickly and relatively easy.

Things made more sense with her around.

"Okay, squeeze the trigger gently. Watch out for the recoil. She will bounce back at you faster than a flicked cock," Zeke said.

I held back a chuckle at his analogy. I didn't want to distract Abbie, especially when she had a weapon in her hand. Surprised people do dangerous things when they're holding a gun.

Abbie squeezed and let out a squeal. "Whoa. I didn't expect it to feel like that."

"That's what I said the first time," I said with a grin.

They both snorted a laugh.

"I was talking about shooting," she said.

My grin widened. "So was I." I couldn't resist putting a hand on my groin.

Both of them followed my hand and swallowed. Yep, the three of us had a vibe going on.

"Try again," Zeke said to Abbie. "It'll be easier now you know what to expect."

She fired again and didn't squeal, which was disappointing because the sound was kinda cute. On the other hand, her knowing how not to shoot me in the head by accident was also cute.

Priorities.

"Good," Zeke said. "Now let's see if you can hit the target." He spoke in soothing, patient tones. More patient than I would be. More patient than any of the guys.

To a greater extent than any of us, he saw what guns could do in the wrong hands. I'd seen enough. At the end of the day, we both wanted the same thing; for Abbie to be safe.

She aimed again and managed to nick the side of the target's arm.

In the corner of my eye, I watched someone approach. Penn, his hands in his back pockets, a sardonic expression on his face.

I gave him a warning look to discourage him from saying anything nasty. Typically, he ignored it. He was never particularly big on being told what to do, even if it wasn't verbally.

Abbie glanced at Penn over her shoulder.

"Try again," Zeke said. "You need to learn how to shoot even with distractions."

She nodded and aimed again. This time, she nicked the target in the leg.

Penn snorted.

She turned again to give him a dirty look, but he said, "Pretend it's me."

That must have helped, because her next shot got the target right between his legs. If it was a guy, she would have shot his balls off. He would probably bleed out in a few hours.

Poor guy.

"Thinking about my cock," Penn said dryly. "That doesn't surprise me." He turned and walked away.

She didn't deny it.

CHAPTER SIX

ABBIE

"YOU DID PRETTY WELL for your first time," Asher told me over the rim of his coffee cup.

"Thanks." I eyed the open packet of chocolate covered biscuits on the table and debated whether or not I should have another one. "At least I know which way to point it so I don't shoot myself in the face."

He laughed softly. "I'm sure you already knew that. And now you know how to shoot Penn in the dick. Who knows when that skill might come in handy?"

He was so strikingly cute and hot at the same time. He was muscular enough that he could be intimidating if he wanted to be. He also had that dangerous edge Zeke had; that undercurrent of violence in everything he did.

"It might be sooner than you think," I said dryly. "Unless he loosens up before the tour starts."

"I don't think Penn knows the meaning of the phrase loosen up," Asher said. "He's wound tighter than one of Tully's guitar strings."

"I've noticed that about him." I gave in and reached for another biscuit. "So, your family is like Zeke's?"

I'd been wanting to ask him about them, but the chance hadn't arisen until now. The press hadn't bothered us for a couple of days, so the guys had gone back to their places or to the gym down the street to work out. I opted to stay in Zeke's townhouse and Asher stayed with me. It was the first time he and I had been alone together.

"Crazy?" Asher asked. "Pretty much. We just have more girls in the family."

"How many siblings do you have?" I bit into the chocolate biscuit.

"There's four of us," Asher said. "Two older than me and one younger. Dane is the oldest. He teaches history at Brutham Academy. He is the wannabe Reuben Brantley of the clan. He's only teaching history until he can regain the family's fortune and favour. Needless to say, I think he'll be teaching for a long time." He shrugged.

"Rose likes to pretend she stays the hell away from all the bullshit. That she's all about the quiet life." He put his empty cup aside and reached for a chocolate covered biscuit.

"But she's involved too?" I asked.

"Up to her eyeballs." He bit into his biscuit and chewed. "She's not open about it. I guess you could say she's the smart one."

"You're smart," I told him.

He grinned. "Thanks, I like to be away from all the bullshit, so I could be the smartest one." He took another bite.

"The DiMarco family was only ever on the edge of things, trying to keep from being caught between the Brantleys and the Bell family. Mostly, we did a crap job of it, but it worked out pretty well for this generation. So far anyway. Except Dane, but that's his problem." He shrugged and bit off a corner of the biscuit.

"And then there's you, and you have another sibling?" I dipped the corner of my biscuit into my coffee and nibbled on it.

Asher sighed and a look of sadness crossed his angular face. "Yeah. My younger sister Mina. I guess she wanted to stay away from the bullshit too. She got married at eighteen and shut the rest of us out. She sends us a text message to wish us a merry Christmas every year, but that's all the contact we have with her."

I curled my fingers over his hand. "I'm sorry. Do you miss her?"

"Growing up, she and I were the closest," he said. "In age and, you know, we got on with each other the best. Her nickname when she was a kid was Mina Sunshine, because she was always smiling and laughing. She was sweeter than the rest of us. I guess that's why she shut us out. She's probably living in the suburbs with a bunch of kids by now." He blew out a breath, puffing out his lips.

"Have you tried to contact her?" My heart ached for him.

"Yeah, a bunch of times," he said. "I guess she doesn't want to be found. Zeke has offered to use his family's contacts to look for her. They'd probably find her in an hour, but if she wanted to talk to us she would, you know? She has our numbers and I'm pretty easy to find."

"You miss her but you respect her privacy," I said slowly. "I understand that. I'm not sure I'd be so restrained." Of course, I spent a lot of my time jumping in feet first and then looking, so it stood to reason, if I needed to find a family member by any means, I would do it. And then regret it later.

Asher shrugged. "She's better off living her life away from the family anyway. Her kids will grow up not knowing what their grandparents were involved in."

"They might also grow up not knowing their uncle is a bad ass rock star," I said.

"That is the downside," he agreed. "But their safety is nearly as important as finding out how cool I am." He grinned.

"Nearly," I agreed jokingly.

"What about your family? Are they into anything dubious?" He finished his chocolate covered biscuit and started to lick his fingers clean.

"Probably," I said. "Nothing illegal though." That I knew of. "My parents are retired. I have an older brother, Nathan. He lives in London and works at a bank. And I have a younger sister, Breanna. She's also a singer, but she works as a mechanic during the day."

"Women in greasy overalls," Asher said slowly. "That sounds hot to me."

"Don't tell her that," I said. "She'll either hit you with a tire jack or make you work for her until you beg her to let you stop."

Bree was an independent woman who hated sexist comments about women in the trades more than anything. I didn't blame her; she dealt with that from the first day of her apprenticeship. It was probably old after the first hour. Still, she stuck it out and proved them all wrong. She was a tougher woman than I would ever be. And an amazing singer.

"I'll be nice," he promised. "I have to think of my hands." He held them up and scrutinised them.

"Wouldn't want those getting dirty," I teased.

"Hell no," he agreed. "Although, it depends on what I get them dirty with." He peered into my cup and found it empty. He took it out of my hands and placed it on the table beside his.

"Does it now?" I watched his every move carefully.

"Yes it does." He took my hand and drew me closer to him.

"Like what?" I asked.

"Like this." He slid his tongue across my lower lip, then back across my top lip. He captured my mouth in a kiss so hot it made my toes curl.

I've always been a big fan of sex, but the more I was with these guys, the more I wanted them. One kiss and I was already wet and weak-kneed.

"You're so beautiful," he said against my lips.

"No, you," I laughed into his mouth. He was, though. His body was like a statue carved to striking perfection. I would never get tired of looking at him or any of the guys. Every single one of them was a work of art.

"Tasty too." He pulled back and looked at me like he was up to something. Before I could ask, he gently pushed me back on the couch and hooked his fingers in the waistband of my shorts.

I lifted my hips to help him pull them off, and my panties with them.

"See, beautiful." He ran his hands lightly up my legs, to the insides of my thighs. His fingers caressed all around my pussy without sliding in or touching my clit. He looked as though he'd never seen a pussy before and was fascinated by it. Or maybe just that he never got tired of looking at them. Or at mine. I got that, I was never tired of looking at and touching cocks.

"You make me feel beautiful," I said. That was something I could get used to feeling. Not just from him but the other guys too. I felt not only desired, but appreciated. Cared for. Maybe even loved.

"Is that all I make you feel?" He kept on teasing me, almost but not quite touching me where I wanted him to.

"No, that's not all." My hips moved as if they had a mind of their own, seeking his fingers, which continued to evade me.

"What are you feeling now?" He leaned to kiss the inside of my knee.

"Frustration," I said with a throaty laugh. "If you don't touch me soon, I might implode."

"What if I don't touch you?" he asked. "What if this touches you?"

He reached for a chocolate covered biscuit and held it up in front of his face, a sly smile on his lips.

"Asher what are you—"

He put a finger to his lips, then moved it to my knee and slowly spread my legs wider apart. With one hand resting lightly on my belly, he slowly inserted the biscuit into my pussy.

Apart from a slight flash of initial cold, it didn't feel unpleasant. It felt more like he was putting a small vibrator inside me. Without the vibration.

Carefully and with a look of fascinated concentration on his face, he slid the biscuit all the way in, to his fingers. Then back out again. With increasing speed, he started fucking me with the chocolate covered snack. He moved his hand from my belly down to my clit and started tracing circles around and over it. Finally, he fastened two fingers on my clit and started to rub harder and faster.

"You like that?" he asked.

I liked it so much I couldn't respond with words, just with a moan and the bucking of my hips.

"I thought you might," he said. "I want to see you come."

I was already close, but his words pushed me to the edge. I dangled on the precipice for an enticingly long time before I finally tumbled over, muscles clenching around his hand and the biscuit. My back arched and I cried out with pleasure. Stars danced a beautiful ballet show in front of my eyes for a minute, maybe two. I started to come down when another orgasm hit me, this one sweeter and more beautiful than the first.

I cried out again, longer this time, bucking hard against his fingers, needing the sensation to last as long as possible. It could have been a couple of minutes or it could have been an eternity.

Either way, I finally came down and sagged against the fabric of the couch.

His eyes on me, Asher slid the glistening biscuit out of my pussy and took a bite. "It's even tastier like that. I should send a proposition to the people who make them. We could both make a fortune." He grinned.

I shook my head at him while he happily munched on the chocolate covered with my juices. At least life with him would never be boring.

"Would you like some?" He held out the half eaten biscuit.

"No thank you," I replied. If it had his cum on it I might, but not mine. I had a feeling that could be arranged without too much trouble.

"I can think of something else I'd like," I said.

"Yeah?" He raised a speculative eyebrow at me. "What's that?"

"As much fun as a biscuit is, it's not as good as a cock," I said. It was close though, especially when chocolate was involved.

"I was hoping you'd say that." He helped me out of the rest of my clothes and I returned the favour.

When we were both naked, he stretched out over me on the couch and slid his thick cock deep and hard into me.

Yep, definitely better than a biscuit.

CHAPTER
SEVEN

ASHER

"SHIT."

I frowned at my phone. I wanted to ignore the text from my brother, but he would send another one, I knew. Or worse, call me.

"What is it?"

I looked from my phone to Abbie's worried face. She really was wildly beautiful. I was certain she didn't realise how gorgeous she was. That was part of her charm. She was not conceited or arrogant. She left that to us guys.

"My brother wants to see me. He suggested meeting up for dinner." I tossed my phone onto the coffee table.

"Is this one of those, 'you have no choice' things?" she asked.

"He has a choice," Zeke said from where he sat opposite us, his eyes on his own phone. "He can go to dinner with his brother, or his brother will keep on insisting. Unlike my brother, who would send a car and one of his employees with a gun."

"Dane doesn't like to be ignored," I said. "It's easier to get it over with." After a moment I added, "I'm not sure he wouldn't send a car and a guy with a gun too. I just tend to give in more easily."

I was lucky in that I didn't hate my family the way Zeke hated his. We didn't always get along, but without the kind of power and influence the Brantley family had, there wasn't a lot Dane could do to me.

That didn't mean he wouldn't try if he could get away with it.

"So you're going?" Abbie asked.

"He's going, and so am I," Zeke still didn't look up from his phone. "Neither of us should deal with our families by ourselves. Tell him you'll meet him tonight or tomorrow night. If he wants to hang out with you, it will have to be before the tour starts."

I grabbed my phone and typed a message back to Dane. It didn't take him long to respond.

"Tonight it is," I said. "A couple of hours from now."

Zeke finally lowered his phone. "The three of us should get ready then."

"You want me to come too?" Abbie looked from me to him in surprise, laced with a dose of caution.

I gave her a slow grin. "Love, if I had my way, you'd come all day, every day." I would never get tired of hearing her moan, and watching her hips roll when I touched her.

Likewise with Zeke. I'd be happy to spend the rest of my life curled up in bed with both of them. As long as I could take an hour or two away to perform on stage. That was a whole other rush I wasn't ready to live without.

"We're not leaving you here by yourself," Zeke said. "Dane has no partic-ular reason to see you as a threat. You should be safe enough."

It was the, 'should be' part that worried me, but Zeke was right, we weren't going to leave her here by herself.

Since the night the press camped outside, I'd basically been living here too. My place was just around the corner, so I popped back whenever I needed a change of clothes, but spending time with both of them here felt natural and normal.

"Okay," Abbie said.

She didn't seem even slightly scared about meeting my brother, even after what I told her about him. While Reuben was inclined to use people or try to make them do what he wanted, Dane was friendly, in the hope it would be to his advantage some day.

That was the problem with my brother. He was like a snake in the grass. You didn't see him until you tripped over him and face planted onto the ground. Or until he bit you.

"Stay on your guard around him," I advised. "You might make the most innocent comment and find later on he uses it against you in some way. He's always looking for an angle or an advantage."

"Why doesn't he work for Reuben?" Abbie asked. "You said he's trying to find ways to get the family back in with the Brantleys, or at least to be more powerful?"

"Reuben doesn't trust him," Zeke said.

"Reuben doesn't trust anyone," I pointed out. "Except for a couple of the men he has working for him." To Abbie I said, "Damon and Gianni are as bad as Reuben."

"If anything, Gianni is worse," Zeke said. "He's not just happy to kill for

Reuben, he *likes* doing it. The slower the better. Reuben only kills to get rid of people."

Abbie shuddered. "He sounds charming. What about this—Damon? Does he get a kick out of murder as well?"

Zeke and I exchanged glances.

"Damon is like the best friend you never wanted," Zeke said finally. "He's smooth and slick. Where Reuben thrives on being an asshole, Damon likes to pretend he's nice. Then you let down your guard, just a little bit, and he'll stick a knife between your ribs."

"They both make Reuben sound like a saint," she remarked.

I snorted a laugh. "They do, don't they?"

"They're all as bad as each other," Zeke said. "The evil twins, Hunter and Parker, as well. Those two also thrive on pretending they're nice."

"How do we know you're as nice as you seem?" I asked teasingly.

"Because if I stab either of you with something, it won't be a knife." Zeke grinned.

Those were words guaranteed to make me as hot as hell. Any time he wanted to stab me with his cock, he was welcome to. I knew he knew that. I hoped he would feel comfortable enough to do that sometime soon. Approximately before the anticipation killed me.

"Promises, promises," I muttered.

He gave me a heated look, but changed the subject. "Can you believe the tour starts in three days?"

Abbie suddenly looked nervous. Funny how talking about people killing other people and stabbing was less terrifying than the idea of performing.

Okay, I got it, really. All the shit with our families took place in the shadows. The tour would take place within full view of the entire world. There was absolutely nowhere to hide. Especially for her.

Me—I could sit at the back of the stage and drum, and more or less avoid scrutiny. The press wasn't likely to forget her past or the death of her ex anytime soon. No doubt they would be following her around, waiting for her to do something embarrassing so they could tell everyone how she tripped up. Bloodsucking assholes. I didn't know how they slept at night. Hopefully alone and miserable.

"Part of me wishes it would hurry up, and part of me wishes it was another six months away," Abbie admitted. "I mean, we're ready, after all the rehearsal but..."

"But the press have been assholes to you and you're worried they're going to keep doing it," Zeke said.

"Not just them," she said. "Audiences too. After everything they've heard about me, what if they hate me?" She chewed on her thumbnail with obvious nerves.

"Not a chance," I said with absolute confidence. "They're going to fall head over heels with you the way we have."

"They might turn up with preconceived ideas about me and not even give me a chance," she pointed out. She lowered her hand to her lap and sighed.

I reached over and pulled her to me until she fit neatly under my arm, her head to my chest. "If that's the kind of people they are, we don't want them at our concerts. Believe me when I say our fans are very open and supportive. And you know what, if they don't like you when they walk into the venue, they'll *love* you when they walk out." How could anyone not love her? She was incredible.

"Asher is right, sweetheart," Zeke said.

"Can I get you on video saying that?" I asked teasingly.

He flipped me off. "You're right *this time*." To Abbie, he said, "Anyway, I'll be here standing beside you, telling the audience how amazing you are. Which won't be necessary, because the moment you sing, they'll forget every single dumbass word the press ever made up about you."

"You make it sound so easy," she said. She nestled in tighter to my chest, like she was trying to absorb my confidence in her. She could have it. I had plenty to spare.

"It is easy, love," I assured her. "You have the full support of the band, the label and even the support act. Violet heard you sing the other day and told me she's jealous you're not singing with Blazing Violet instead of us."

She looked sceptical but Zeke nodded.

"She said exactly that," he said. "I heard all of it. Blaise even agreed with her, and he rarely agrees with anything she says."

"That's true," I agreed. The lead singer and lead guitarist seemed to despise each other, but somehow they worked perfectly well together on stage and in the recording studio. They were like two versions of Penn, difficult as shit but talented as fuck.

"It's too late to arrange that," Zeke said regretfully. "Maybe we could organise something for IslandFest."

Abbie gave him a funny look. "IslandFest?"

"Yeah," I said. "It's a week-long music festival out on an island in the Caribbean. We're booked to play there after the tour is over. We one hundred percent expect you to be there."

"Damn right we do," Zeke said. "What could be better than a week in a tropical resort with a bunch of other bands and all the shenanigans that go down at events like this?" He wiggled his eyebrows.

Yeah, sex on the beach wasn't just a cocktail at events like that. It was just another night.

"If the label still wants me around after the tour is over, I'd love to go." Abbie looked excited.

Hell yeah, I'd like some sex on the beach with her, please and thank you.

"Even if the label doesn't want you around, we do," Zeke said firmly. "But they will. I guarantee it. Levi Jones has never been wrong about an act yet. He has the uncanny ability to pick, well, a winner. Look at Wolf Venom for example. We were a scrappy bunch of guys with a bit of talent and a lot of attitude. We were ambitious but he saw more in us than we saw in ourselves. He put his faith in us and we didn't want to disappoint him. So we didn't."

"You definitely didn't," she agreed. "But I'm pretty sure you would have killed it no matter who you signed with. You guys were always destined for big things."

I squeezed her shoulders. "So were you. You just met some of the wrong people along the way. But you're with us now, and we are going to help you shine the way you deserve to."

I thought about my words for a moment.

"Is that a new song coming on?" Zeke asked.

"Yes, probably," I said lightly. For both of us, and the rest of the band, who all wrote songs as well, there was always a new song coming on. Inspiration was pretty much everywhere, especially lately.

"You deserve to shine," I sang under my breath. I hummed a few bars.

Zeke and Abbie exchanged amused glances. As if they weren't just as bad as I was at catching a tune at a random moment.

"You laugh now, but it's a guaranteed number one hit," I said.

"You have to write it first, dude," Zeke said.

"A mere formality, dude," I retorted. "After all this time, I would have thought you would've believed in me a bit more." I pretended to pout.

"I do believe in you," he said. "I also know how many unfinished songs you have lying around." To Abbie, he said, "It's lucky he doesn't write novels. If he did, there would be a million different chapter ones and no chapter twos."

"Why are you attacking me like that?" I said, trying to hold back a grin.

Unfortunately, he wasn't wrong. Every time I started to write a song, another three or four popped into my head. Every single one of them demanded to be written right now, so none of them ever got finished. Except the handful that did. One of these days, I would figure out how to focus better. In the meantime, I would comfort myself with the knowledge that the ones I did finish were all really good.

"We should start getting ready to go out for dinner," I said reluctantly. I would have preferred to stay here and let Zeke attack me a bit more. Maybe with his tongue.

CHAPTER
EIGHT

ASHER

"HE'S LATE." I glanced around the restaurant but Dane was nowhere to be seen. Of course not. Leave it to him to make plans and then turn up when he felt like it. Although, he might be lurking in the shadows, waiting to jump out at us, like a tiger hunting its prey.

"Nice place though," Abbie said. She was dressed in a cute little black dress and heels. Her hair was tied back in a simple ponytail and she wore only a touch of make-up.

Her hand brushed mine and I resisted the urge to grab it and never let it go. I didn't, it would be the first thing Dane noticed. We'd already discussed before we got here that we would all play it cool, just in case.

"At least he wasn't early," Zeke said. "If you kept him waiting, he would bitch about it."

"True, true," I said. "I guess that means I get to bitch at him for keeping us waiting." I wouldn't though, because it wasn't worth it. It would only give him the shits and would come back to bite me some day. Dane had a good memory.

I smiled at the server who greeted us with obvious recognition.

She had smiles for Zeke and I, and narrowed eyes for Abbie. Lucky for her, she didn't say anything, just led us to our table and moved away while we got seated.

"I guess she's not a fan," Abbie muttered.

"Don't let it ruin your night," Zeke said.

I grinned. "No, leave that pleasure to Dane."

"You're making him sound like a massive pain in the ass," Abbie said.

"I can neither confirm nor deny that he is a pain in the ass," I said. "You get to make your mind up if he bothers to show."

"He bothered," a voice said behind me. Dane slipped into the chair next to me before I could even turn around.

Anyone seeing us together for the first time could tell we were related. He was slender where I was muscular, but we had the same blue eyes and face shape. He had dark hair like my father and Mina, where I was blond like my mother and Rose. Several people have commented that we both have the same intense stare and resting bitch face.

Dane's gaze swept around the table, taking in all three of us. He gave Zeke a friendly nod, but his eyes lingered longer on Abbie.

I couldn't tell if he recognised her or not, but he clearly admired her. There was no reason why he shouldn't, she was a beautiful woman.

He held out his hand and she shook it.

I did a quick introduction and then jumped right into things.

"Was there something you wanted to talk about?" I didn't see a point in waiting until the end of dinner to get whatever he wanted to get off his chest.

"Can't I want to have dinner with my baby brother?" He gave us all a dazzling smile. If I didn't know him so well, I would have bought it. Who knows, maybe he'd lightened up recently. Stranger things have happened, right?

I gave him a level look. "Maybe, but you look like you have something to say, so you might as well get it over with."

"Were you always so cynical?" Dane asked. He was still smiling, but a hint of irritation crept into his voice.

"Yes," I said. "I was born cynical. It probably came from overhearing conversations before I was born."

Dane laughed. "I would think you were joking if I wasn't born to the same family. A lot of shit went down back in the day."

"That's an understatement," Zeke said. He looked relaxed and friendly, but none of us were going to forget his father had Dane's and my father killed. There was always going to be a certain level of awkwardness between the two families. Or at least between Dane and Zeke.

Dane had to blame someone and Zeke was often right there in front of his face. He would probably bear the same animosity towards anyone with the last name Brantley.

Ironically, he would also roll over and show his belly if Reuben gave him the chance. He would hold a grudge right up to the moment where it was in his best interest not to.

Dane's eyes flickered over to Abbie.

"She knows everything," I said.

Dane laughed. "Probably not everything. There's a metric shit ton of blood-filled water under the bridge." He stopped talking when a server handed around menus.

I opened mine and skimmed it while I waited for the server to move away.

"She knows enough," I said when it was safe.

"Enough is a dangerous amount," Dane said.

"Better than not enough," Zeke said. "Do you know who Abbie is?"

"In spite of what my brother might think, I don't live under a rock," Dane said. He gave Abbie a warm smile. "Of course I know who Abbie Hart is. I'm a big fan."

"Thank you." She blushed slightly.

Yeah, my brother could be charming when he wanted to be.

"What's your point?" Dane asked. "That I shouldn't know who is going on tour with my little brother?"

I might give him ten points for knowing about that, but he always made it his business to know shit like that.

"We've had a little trouble with some parcels being left on doorsteps," Zeke said.

"Parcels, plural?" Dane asked. "I heard about one of them. Does Abbie have a crazed fan?"

"Is that what this is about?" I asked. "You're worried about me going on tour with someone who might have a stalker?"

Dane chuckled. "You can take care of yourself, can't you?"

"Thanks for the concern," I said sarcastically. "For your information, yes, we can take care of ourselves. I think what Zeke would like to know is, are you responsible? The other head belonged to Jonah, one of Reuben's henchmen."

"No doubt he deserved it, but I had nothing to do with it," Dane said. He looked indifferent, almost bored, like we were discussing the weather.

I believed him when he said he wasn't involved. Unfortunately. It might have been easier if he was.

The server returned to take our orders, so we fell silent again for a few minutes.

"I assume you want me to keep an ear out for who is responsible?" Dane said once the server moved away. "I'm more than happy to do that. My network has been growing nicely over the last couple of years. You might be surprised the kind of information that comes my way."

I had a feeling this was why we were here.

"Like what?" I asked carefully.

"Like the fact the Bell twins, Chloe and Lila, are competing with each other to see who will take over the Bell family someday," he said slowly.

I grimaced. "That won't be pretty. How old are they?"

"Eighteen," he replied.

There was something more to his response, but I had a feeling he wouldn't tell me what it was if I asked.

"What has that got to do with us?" Zeke asked.

Dane leaned forward and leaned on his elbows. "I've taken sides."

"Good for you," I said. "I still don't want anything to do with any of this."

"I think we should hear him out," Zeke said softly.

Dane nodded at him. "I've always thought you were the smart one."

"He is," I said. "I'm the hot one."

"We're both hot," Zeke said. He leaned forward towards Dane. "Whose side have you taken and why does it matter to us?"

"I've taken Chloe's," Dane said. "She is the older of the twins. And, I believe, the most capable. Why does it matter?" He cocked his head. "Because your brothers have taken Lila's side."

"I have a lot of brothers," Zeke said. "But I'm going to assume you're refer- ring to Hunter and Parker, since they go to Brutham and so do the Bell twins."

I blinked a few times.

"I'm sorry," Abbie said. "I don't know what any of this means."

"It means there's going to be a shit storm," Zeke said. "The rivalry between siblings is bad enough, but when you put the Brantley family on one side and the DiMarco family on the other..." He shook his head. "What the fuck were they thinking? I understand you taking sides." He nodded to Dane.

"If you can't get in with the Brantleys, you might as well get in with the Bells," I said.

Dane shrugged unapologetically. "By whatever means necessary."

"My brothers should stay out of any shit involving the Bell family," Zeke said. "We could only end up causing trouble for everyone."

"Because the Brantley family and the Bells hate each other?" Abbie said.

"Exactly," I said. "Let me guess, Reuben is going to be pissed." After a moment I added, "Unless it was his idea?"

Zeke snorted. "Unlikely. I'd bet anything he doesn't know about it."

"He wouldn't ask your brothers to seduce this girl for his own gain?" Abbie asked.

All three of us guys exchanged a glance.

"If she was anyone but a Bell," Zeke said. "Even more than wanting me back in the family, he wants every single one of them dead."

"He's not gonna be impressed with you aligning yourself with Chloe Bell," I told Dane.

He shrugged. "Like you said, if I can't get in with the Brantleys, then I might as well have the Bells at my back."

My brother always did like living dangerously.

"You asked me to come out tonight to warn me?" I said.

Dane shrugged again. "I figured if the shit hit the fan, you'd want to know about it in advance. Especially because of your close association with Zeke."

"That's touching," I said. "You could have stuck to teaching. That would be safer for all of us, especially you." I stared at him for a moment. "Wait a minute, is Chloe your student?" I waved a hand. "Wait another minute, are you sleeping with her? Hold on, don't answer that. She's how much younger than you?" I grimaced.

He chuckled. "Either you want to know or you don't. The fact is, it's none of your business."

"Sounds like a yes to me," Zeke said. "Frankly, I don't give a fuck about your love life. Or your sex life. We appreciate the warning. We'll do our best to stay out of whatever shit the rest of you create."

Zeke massaged his forehead with his fingertips. He looked like he was starting to get a headache. If Dane wasn't there, I would have offered to kiss it better. Right now, that would muddy the waters even more than they already were.

I locked my eyes on Abbie's. She must have thought we were all completely crazy. Maybe we were. Who would be a part of a feuding, mobster family and not run away and hide somewhere far away from them all? Why would Zeke and I chase fame when it brought us into a whole different kind of limelight?

Those were valid questions and I didn't know the answers to them either. I guessed it was that we wanted to live our lives our way and hoped that, at some point, our families would settle down and stop being murderous assholes. That didn't seem like too much to ask, did it?

I didn't think so. I offered her a smile, but it probably looked more like a grimace. I wished we hadn't dragged her into any of this shit to begin with.

"Is this where you say you think I should tell Reuben what Hunter and Parker are up to?" Zeke asked.

"He's going to find out sooner or later," Dane said.

"Either we can tell him," I said slowly, "or we can go on tour and pretend we had no idea. And hope like fuck everything blows over while we're away." I knew which option I preferred.

Zeke sighed heavily. "It seems like we have some talking to do."

CHAPTER
NINE

ABBIE

"WHAT ARE YOU GOING TO DO?" I leaned back on the swing.

We walked home from the restaurant. About half way back, we stopped in a park to enjoy the warm evening.

After the pre-dinner conversation, we only chatted about mundane things and made small talk until the meal was over. Dane didn't seem as bad as Asher made him out to be, but I knew better than to take him at face value. I've met way too many people like him.

"I don't know." Zeke sat on the swing beside me and kicked off the ground.

Asher sat on the other side but seemed content to rock back and forth gently. "Why do they keep dragging us into their bullshit?"

"I wish I knew the answer to that," Zeke said. "All I have is because they suck."

Asher laughed bitterly. "Yeah, well, I already guessed that much."

"What do you think is going to happen?" I asked. "I mean, they talk about gang wars on the news all the time. People ending up dead and all that. Gun battles in the middle of the street. Innocent people having their houses and cars shot up. Is that where this is leading to?"

"Our families are a little more civilised than that," Zeke said. "It's more likely to lead to poisonings, disappearances or people being shot while they sleep. Those kinds of things. They move around in the shadows, I guess you could say. Like vampires."

"I'm not sure if I call that civilised," I pointed out. "If people end up dead, it's pretty fucking horrible." Depending on the person.

I still couldn't quite bring myself to feel bad about what happened to

Vance. If that made me a terrible person, then so be it. At least I wasn't the one wielding... Whatever they used to separate his head from the rest of him.

"It's more civilised because it's less likely to result in collateral damage," Asher said. "Or having the police identify the family as some sort of organised criminal entity. What they talk about on the news is usually a bunch of street thugs."

I wasn't quite sure I saw a difference, but I didn't bother to say so.

I leaned back and swung a little higher. "I haven't done this in so long." I hadn't stepped foot in a park, much less sat on a swing. It was definitely something I should do more often. It was... liberating. Like I was back in my childhood when I had no cares about anything.

For a little while, I was able to forget about worrying about much of anything.

"I have," Asher said. "But it wasn't this kind of swing."

I caught sight of his grinning face and laughed as I flew past him. "Yeah, well. When you put it that way..."

"I knew I was missing something when I decorated my place," Zeke said. "I'll have to order one when we get back from the tour."

"Hell yeah," Asher said. "Every house should have a sex swing. Or two. And maybe a whole room dedicated to pleasure."

"Isn't that what bedrooms are for?" Zeke asked. "And kitchens. And bathrooms. And living rooms. And..."

"True," Asher said. "But I meant something more specific. I have a funny feeling you knew that."

Zeke chuckled. "I did know that. You want a dungeon like Tully has."

I almost lost my grip on the chains of the swing. "Dungeon?"

"It's not exactly a dungeon," Zeke said. "Just a room with paddles, feathers, blindfolds and shit like that. It's kinda his thing."

Holy shit, that sounded hot.

I slowed the swing down a little. "Is this a place you go to often?"

"We've been there once or twice," Asher said. "I'm sure he'll be happy to show you around if you ask nicely."

"He'll like it even better if you insist," Zeke said. "Or better yet, let him insist."

"That won't bother you guys?" I asked. Because holy shit, that sounded all kinds of delicious.

"Not at all, sweetheart," Zeke said lightly. "If you're having your needs met, then I'm happy."

"Same here," Asher said. "Paddling and smacking aren't really my thing, but I don't want you to miss out on something you might like."

For the millionth time I wondered who these guys even were and how I got so lucky to meet them. And why, of all women on the face of the planet, they wanted me.

"If I spend time with one of the guys, what will you do?" I asked carefully.

"Are you asking if we'll find other women to fuck?" Zeke asked. "Personally, no. I meant it when I said I was falling for you. Both of you. You two are all I need."

"What he said," Asher agreed. "I'm good with you having a relationship with all of the guys, but I only want to sleep with you two. Not that the other guys aren't hot and all, but the heart wants what the heart wants and all that shit."

"Yeah, it does," Zeke said. "The other guys are like brothers, but that's all they will ever be. Brothers who share my girlfriend."

Girlfriend. I liked the sound of that. It made my heart flutter. That and the idea of having six boyfriends. Was that how this would end up? Hell, it might.

Of course, that included Penn, and I had no real idea where I stood with him. He seemed to like the possibility I was thinking of his cock at the shooting range. There might be some hope for us some day.

"Brothers and boyfriend who share your girlfriend," Asher said. He sounded tentative, like he wasn't quite sure that was a step too far for Zeke.

"Yes, that," Zeke said. "My girlfriend Abbie, my boyfriend Asher, and me. That sounds pretty fucking awesome to me." He nodded firmly as I swung past.

"To me too," I agreed. I leaned back and looked towards the sky, letting the swing move back and forth slowly. Even though I couldn't see the stars past the city lights, it was still the perfect night. A nice dinner, two incredible guys and a relaxing swing in the park. What else could a girl want?

"How many times has that car gone past?" Asher asked.

Of course it couldn't last.

"At least three," Zeke said. "Don't stop swinging," he added quickly as I went to put my feet on the ground to stop myself. "It could be nothing, but if it isn't we need to play it cool."

"What do you think it is?" I tried not to panic. It could be anything from a lost driver, to someone ready to shoot us as they drove past, or even the press lurking around us. I couldn't rule out that it might be the killer searching for another head.

"I don't know," he said. "We'll give it a few minutes, then leave as though that was exactly what we were planning all along. Let the swing slow down by itself."

"Okay." I stuck my legs out in front of me and let the momentum gradually die away.

My heart was racing and my palms were so slick it was hard to cling onto the chain. Flying off and landing on my ass on the rubber under the swing would definitely not be the definition of playing it cool.

"All right, they've gone around a corner," Zeke said. "As casually as you can, get off the swings. Talk, laugh, just act naturally."

I lowered my feet and ran a few steps before I was able to bring the swing to a full stop.

"That was fun," I said more loudly than I probably should have. "We should do that another time."

"We should." Zeke drew me to him and tucked me under his arm.

"I'm trying to think of a joke, but nothing is coming to mind," Asher said. He walked close to the other side of me, so our hands brushed against each other every so often.

"We could talk about how our cocks are so much bigger than everyone else's," Zeke said.

Asher grinned. "That's not a joke, it's true."

"We all know that, but talking about it will make us look like we're not suspicious about strange, dark cars gliding past in the middle of the night," Zeke said.

"True," Asher agreed. "We could talk about getting some chocolate sauce and dribbling it all over Abbie. And then licking it all off."

"I like that conversation," I said. "We could also dribble it on one of you and the other two could lick it off." The downside to being covered in chocolate sauce myself was that I wouldn't get to taste it.

"We could have a bath in chocolate," Asher said. "Or champagne."

"I don't know, wouldn't that be sticky?" I said.

He shrugged. "I don't know. It would be fun to find out."

"Any sign of it?" I asked. A white van and a light-coloured hatchback passed by, but neither slowed.

Asher grabbed my hand to stop me from walking, turned and kissed me. When he pulled back, he glanced over my shoulder.

"Don't look back, but it's parked by the side of the road. I can't get a good enough look to see if anyone's in it. If they are, the doors are closed. If they're coming for us, they're not doing it yet."

We went on walking.

"It could be Reuben has sent someone to intimidate us," Zeke said.

"I hate to say it, but it's working." I was trying hard not to freak the fuck out. "It would look really bad if we started running, wouldn't it?"

"Absolutely," Zeke agreed. "Not only would they know we know they're there, they would also know they have us worried."

"Only worried?" I asked. "I think I'm going to pee my panties." Ruining them was one thing, this was something else completely different and definitely not welcome.

"Yeah, that's really not how we want you wet," Asher said.

"If they wanted us dead, we'd be dead," Zeke said. "And if they were planning to abduct us, they would have done that too. They might be people going about their lives."

"Do you believe that?" I asked. I hoped he'd say yes, but I knew he wasn't going to.

"Not really." He shrugged. "But I'm not gonna let myself be intimidated either. If that's what Reuben thinks, he can go to hell."

It was difficult to resist the urge to look back, but I managed to control myself. If Zeke was right and this was an attempt to scare us, then I had to try not to look scared. Easier said than done. I couldn't forget the way the evil twins bundled me into the back of a car so Reuben could have a conversation with me.

"Is this his last chance to try to get to you before the tour?" I asked.

Zeke snorted softly, which wasn't the response I was hoping for. "He won't let up just because we're out of Sydney. He likes to remind me he has a long reach."

"I'm starting to wish I'd kicked him in the dick when I had the chance." I huffed.

Both guys chuckled.

"Please don't do that unless I'm there to see it," Asher said.

"Me too," Zeke agreed. "And if you do that, you better be ready to run like hell. Otherwise he'll come after you or send one of his men. You don't want to get on the wrong side of Damon or Gianni."

"I'll bear that in mind," I said. They certainly didn't sound like people I wanted to meet, much less cross. Hunter and Parker were bad enough.

I startled at the sound of a car engine approaching slowly.

"Don't look back," Zeke urged.

I had been just about to do just that.

My heart raced harder. I had the sinking feeling I was about to die here on a Sydney street in the middle of the night. That was not how I wanted to die.

The car drew even with us and stayed there for a good ten or twenty heartbeats.

A moment before I gave in to panic, it slipped past us and roared away into the night.

CHAPTER
TEN

ABBIE

"THIS NEVER GETS OLD." I stood at the edge of the stage in the biggest stadium in Sydney and looked out at the floor and chairs which were currently empty. The place looked like it would fit at least a billion people.

In reality, it fit about eighty thousand, which was pretty close to a billion, as far as I was concerned.

"It really doesn't," Tully agreed. He stood a couple of metres away, his guitar on a strap around his neck. "Everything else we do leads up to concert nights. At least, that's how I see it. Making albums, all the interviews and shit, it's all so we can get to this."

"I agree," I said. "Nothing compares to performing. Although, sex comes pretty close."

I couldn't help thinking about what the guys told me about Tully and his room. There was no time to ask about it now, or insist. This morning's sound check was the official start of the tour. I was excited as fuck, and not at all sad to leave Sydney behind for a while.

He gave me a lopsided smile. "If you think performing is better than sex, then you might be having sex with the wrong people."

"I heard that," Asher called out from the back of the stage.

"Me too," Zeke said from the side.

Penn looked over his shoulder at them from where he stood in front of his keyboard. He grimaced, then looked away. Surprisingly, for once, he had no smart ass comment to make. Or maybe he'd kindly save it until later.

Tully grinned. "Did I hit a nerve? Sorry, not sorry."

Something clattered to the ground at his feet. It took me a moment to realise Asher had thrown one of his drumsticks at him.

Tully crouched and snatched it up before throwing it back.

Asher managed to catch it before it hit him in the face. "Hell yeah, I have mad catching skills."

"Makes up for the fact you can't throw for shit," Landon teased.

Asher waved the drumstick at the bassist. "Don't make me get up, come over there and whip your ass with this."

"As if you could, old man," Landon scoffed playfully.

"Who are you calling old man?" Asher asked. "You're only a couple of years younger than me."

"And yet I'm so much wiser than you are." Landon swung his bass guitar strap over his head and settled the bright purple instrument into place.

"In your dreams," Asher retorted.

"You guys are all full of shit," Penn said.

"See, Penn is the wise one," Channing said. "He is well aware how full of shit you all are."

"Who says I wasn't including you in that?" Penn asked.

"I do," Channing said. "Wait, you think I'm full of shit too? I'm hurt." He put his saxophone to his lips and played a sad tune.

"You'll get over it," Penn said.

"Says you," Channing said. "I think I might be scarred for life."

Penn rolled his eyes at him and turned back to his keyboard.

I caught Zeke's grin and smiled back before I stepped away from the edge of the stage. He pulled his microphone out of the stand and turned it on.

"Anyone not in the band should get off the stage for soundcheck." Penn had looked back up from his keyboard and was now looking right at me. He had so much disdain on his face, I almost backed up a step.

"I'll wait in the wings," I murmured. I felt a bit like a kicked dog. Lucky for him I didn't turn around and bite him.

He looked like anywhere in the stadium would be too close, but he turned away. Evidently he knew getting me off the stage was as good as he was going to get.

All of the guys looked like they wanted to tell me to stay, but in the end, Penn was right. I wasn't a member of Wolf Venom. This was their soundcheck, not mine. I would get my time on stage before them and with them, but not now.

Zeke gave my hand a quick squeeze as I walked past him. "Let us know if we suck."

"You could never suck. Not your music anyway." I managed a small smile, slipped my hand out of his and hurried down the steps to the space behind the stage.

From there, I could walk around to where the audience would stand, or slip into a seat. It wasn't every day a girl got a private concert from one of the biggest bands in the world, even though it was only a soundcheck. Honestly, I would take what I could get.

They started up playing and I moved to get out of the way of a couple of the tour staff.

They gave me a smile and nod, and hurried on with what they were doing. At least they were friendly. And professional.

"They're pretty awesome, aren't they?" Violet Fletcher-Jones and Blaise Turner appeared from down the corridor.

She wore skin tight black jeans and an equally tight black T-shirt. Her hair was coloured to match her name, and she wore boots with heels so high she was almost as tall as Blaise. Without the extra height, she would be lucky to come up much past his shoulder. What she lacked in height she made up for in personality.

"Yeah, they're pretty good," I agreed. More than pretty good, but I didn't want to overdo it.

Blaise snorted. "Pretty good? Jesus Christ." He gave me a look that reminded me of Penn, but with a lot less dislike. He seemed to save that expression for Violet.

"I don't want to sound like a fangirl," I said. Or a groupie. I was officially dating two of them, so I should be well beyond either of those things.

"You don't," Violet said. "Just ignore him. He got out of bed on the wrong side about twenty years ago and never changed."

Blaise rolled his eyes. He looked like he would have told her to fuck off if I wasn't there. He had more restraint than Penn at least.

"You must be excited about tonight," she continued. She looked as though she was barely able to stand still.

"I really am," I agreed. "I'm sure you guys are too." I glanced around but couldn't see the other band members. No doubt they wouldn't be too far away.

"I'd be more excited if we were headlining like we should be." Blaise gave Violet a glance like it was her fault somehow.

If there was more to that story, I was probably better off not knowing. It might be something private between them. Or between them and the rest of the band.

"We will be," she told him, her tone terse. "This tour is the biggest thing we've ever done. It's going to be an amazing learning experience for all of us."

He grunted. "We know enough."

She shrugged. To me she said, "If you ever want to go out and get a drink, just us girls, let me know. Sometimes it's nice to get away from all the testosterone, if you know what I mean." She gave Blaise a sarcastic smile.

He responded with a matching one that Penn would have been proud of.

"Yes, I do," I agreed. While I adored the guys, it was nice to talk to another woman once in a while. Candy and I had started to text each other regularly, and made plans to hang out when the tour was over, but it would be nice to have a female friend during the tour.

Although, my blond hair was boring in comparison to their bright pink and bright purple. Maybe I should colour mine blue or something.

"That would be great," I said sincerely. "Hopefully we can fit in some sight-seeing here and there too." I knew there wouldn't be much time for that, except out the window of a bus, car or van. Or a plane. But what time I could find, I would try to take it.

Violet grinned. "I want to make sure we see the Eiffel Tower and some American football. Maybe some soccer when we're in England."

"It's also called football," Blaise said. "If you call it soccer in England, they will crucify you."

She shrugged. "Whatever. Kicking a ball around on the grass." She waved a hand in dismissal.

I got the distinct impression she was trying to bait him. Judging by the expression on his face, it was working. Even in the dim light down here, his face looked a little pink.

"All of those things sound like fun," I said. "Maybe we can see a hockey game while we're in Canada. I have a couple of friends who live on the eastern side. I know one will be happy to take us. She pretty much lives to go to hockey games."

"I like that idea," Violet said. "What could be better than hitting a ball with a stick?" Her perfectly shaped eyebrows wiggled up and down a couple of times.

Blaise grunted with disgust. "In case you hadn't guessed, Violet knows nothing about sports. She likes to go and watch it to see the men running around and getting sweaty."

We both looked at him like we couldn't work out what the problem was.

He looked from one of us to the other and back again, then shook his head. "You fucking women are all the same."

"Awesome?" Violet asked. She smiled sweetly.

"That sounds accurate to me," I said. "For the record though, I like to go to sporting events for the atmosphere. The sweaty men part is a bonus." Admittedly, it was a pretty good bonus.

Speaking of sweaty men, I glanced back up the stairs for a glimpse of the guys. Zeke moved around the front of the stage, singing as though he had a whole audience to perform to.

When I thought about it, he probably did. People already started lining up outside in the middle of the night, in the hope of getting a front row spot. No doubt they were listening from the outside and getting excited. Singing along, dancing and enjoying the whole pre-concert experience.

I'd done exactly that more times than I could count. Being on the inside was more exciting, but being out there was a shit load of fun.

"I can't wait to get out there," Violet said. "I'm so full of adrenaline right now, I could run around the whole arena and it would barely take the edge off."

"Why don't you then?" Blaise asked. "I'll take over as lead singer. I'm sure no one would notice."

She rolled her eyes at him. "They would notice when they heard a voice that sounded like a cat having its tail pulled."

"Fuck off," he retorted. "I sound better than that."

"Yeah, a little bit," she agreed.

I wondered how long it would be before they slept together. It was pretty obvious, at least to me, they had it bad for each other. Did Penn and I come across that way? I'm sure myself and all the other guys did at least. If these two got it together, they might set the world ablaze. Pun totally intended.

I turned my attention to listen to the guys, with my professional ear. The sound in the stadium was amazing, of course. They were built to have perfect acoustics as well as the space to get lots of bums on seats and feet on the ground.

A shiver of excitement passed through me. Tonight, I'd either start to put my career back on track, or I would spectacularly fall flat on my face.

I hoped to hell it was the first.

CHAPTER
ELEVEN

ASHER

"THANK YOU, Sydney! We're Blazing Violet. You guys were fucking fantastic!"

Violet gave a last wave to the crowd, put the microphone back in the stand and headed off the stage with the rest of her band.

She gave us all high-fives as she passed us by. Everyone except for Abbie, who she hugged.

When did that happen? I didn't realise they were friends. That was awesome. Maybe I was biased, but I wanted everyone to like Abbie as much as I did. She deserved it. And it made everyone's lives easier if we all got along.

Speaking of getting along... I looked over to Penn.

His face was turned towards the stage. For once, he wasn't scowling. He wasn't smiling either. He looked lost in his thoughts.

In spite of what people thought, there was a decent guy deep down. Not even that deep, to be honest. He'd been through a lot, and put up stone walls around himself. Once in a while, he'd open up and show the real him. That hadn't happened recently. He was shut down tighter before a tour. Hell, we all were. None of us wanted to fall on our faces. Even now, the fear of failure hung heavy over us. Impostor syndrome happened even to the best of us.

He must have sensed I was watching; he turned and looked at me. The sides of his mouth drew back slightly before he turned and looked away.

The last few weeks were hectic to say the least. I got caught up in releasing the album, preparing for the tour and getting to know Abbie. I hadn't had the time to make sure the rest of the guys were okay.

We were usually good at looking out for each other. I made a mental note to try to do better.

"You're up," Zeke said to Abbie. "Don't worry, you're going to be amazing."

"Break a leg," Penn said with an ironic smile.

She looked like she wanted to flip him off. Instead she smiled sweetly. "You too, when it's *your* turn on stage."

He narrowed his eyes at her like he was angry, but there was an underlying current there. Like all he really wanted to do was drag her off to bed.

Honestly, she had the same expression on her face.

"Phew, it's hot in here." Landon fanned his face with his hand. Evidently he was catching the same vibe. It was hard not to catch it, it was electric.

"You'll be incredible," I told Abbie, if only to change the subject. "They're going to love you."

She flashed me a nervous smile and then hurried up the steps towards the stage.

The keyboardist and guitarist the label booked to play with her were already in place, waiting for her. I would have liked to play with her, but we'd get our chance.

Besides, having all women on the stage was cool. Jewel Ruby and Macquarie Tanaka were some of the best the label had. Of course. They didn't have anyone who wasn't incredible.

Okay, I might be biased about that too.

Abbie grabbed the microphone out of the stand and checked it was on. She looked anxious but excited.

I hoped to hell the audience would accept her. Eighty thousand asses was a lot to kick if we needed to.

"Good evening, Sydney," she said into the microphone. "I'm new in town. I'm sure you've never heard of me, but I hope we can be friends."

The applause and cheers that met her words weren't as enthusiastic as those that followed Blazing Violet off the stage, but I didn't hear any boos or jeers.

It was a start, right?

She gave Jewel and Macquarie a smile and a nod and they started to play. After a moment, she lifted the mic to her lips and started to sing. It took her a bar or two, but she quickly found her groove and started to have fun.

By the end of the song, the audience was joining in, singing and clapping. It wasn't quite with the same warmth and fervour they showed when we performed, but it could have gone a lot worse.

She finished her last song and gave the audience a wave.

"Thank you, Sydney. Are you looking forward to seeing Wolf Venom?" She turned her ear towards the audience. "What? I can't hear you. *Are you looking forward to seeing Wolf Venom?*"

The crowd went wild cheering, clapping and stomping their feet.

I grinned. It was impossible not to get caught up in the excitement, in spite of the flutter of nerves. That always happened before the start of the tour; the combination of anticipation and terror.

By the end, I'd be too tired to be nervous.

"Should we bring them out?" Abbie asked.

Again, the audience cheered and roared.

She grinned. "They might need a bit more encouragement. They're all super shy."

She laughed into the microphone and the audience laughed with her. Everyone in the room knew we were far from shy.

"Tell them to come on out," she told the crowd.

Eighty thousand people shouted simultaneously, *"Come on out!"*

"I guess we better go out there." Zeke shook his head and laughed. He started up the steps and the rest of us followed.

The audience went absolutely crazy.

Zeke pulled out the microphone from the other stand and slipped an arm around Abbie's waist. "Abbie Hart, ladies and gentlemen. Isn't she something fucking else?"

His words were met with a bigger cheer than most of hers, but she smiled in response.

"Wolf Venom is something fucking else," Abbie said into her own mic. "Blazing Violet and I were just keeping them warm for you."

"That's nice of you." Zeke walked over to the side of the stage, grabbed a bottle of water and took a gulp. "What do you say we give them a little something special?"

The glance she gave him sent my mind plunging straight my cock.

"Oh yeah?" she said. "You have something in mind?"

"Yeah, do you know the words to 'Take Me Down Lower'?" He put the bottle down and stepped back to the middle of the stage.

"I think I've heard of it," she said as if they hadn't practiced the song a hundred times before.

"I'll start, see if you can catch up." He grinned.

That was our cue to start playing.

Zeke sang to the first chorus before Abbie joined in.

The audience was a lot more receptive to her by now and cheered when she sang.

She was a lot more relaxed as well. When the song ended and she put her microphone back on the stand, she looked disappointed. She would come back near the end for her second song, but until then, she would be watching from backstage.

She flashed me a smile before she disappeared down the steps.

My eyes weren't the only ones which followed her off the stage. All of the guys did except for Penn, whose back was to her.

She was replaced by Isaac, one of the guys from the label.

Phone in his hand, Isaac started to move around the stage, recording us to share on social media. Fans got a kick out of watching sneak peeks of our concerts from different places all over the world. It was the closest thing to being there we could offer them. Plus, some of us secretly got a kick out of watching the footage back. Like me.

I grinned at the phone as Isaac pointed it at me, and added a bit more grooving to my playing. I didn't want the audience to think I only played the drums, I wanted them to think I looked cool doing it.

People often commented that I made it look easy. After so many years of playing, it was second nature. Especially with the songs we'd played for years. I could have played them in my sleep.

Isaac moved past me and focused on Landon, who of course *had* to arch his back and raise his bass guitar to show off his skills. He pursed his lips as he played, adding another layer of cool to his performance.

There was, after all, more to being a part of a rock band than just the ability to make music. You had to be willing and able to perform, even when under pressure. Some may say *particularly* when under pressure. Eighty thousand people were watching us right now. If the idea freaked any of us out too much, we were in the wrong profession.

I looked out at the audience. Most looked around my age, but a few were younger and a few were older. Most wore T-shirts with the Wolf Venom logo on it—a wolf's head with glowing green eyes and protruding tongue. White liquid trickled and dripped off the end of the tongue.

Because we're mature, we joked that it could be cum, beer or whiskey, but it was supposed to be venom. Either way, it looked pretty fucking awesome to me.

One of the guys in the audience was wearing a banana costume, which was pretty fucking awesome too. When Isaac reached him, he held the phone toward him for a couple of seconds. Banana-guy was going to get a big kick out of watching that back later on.

Hell, I was gonna get a kick out of watching it back later on. It wasn't every day you saw a guy in a banana costume. It must be hot as fuck under there.

Isaac followed Zeke around the stage for a while, before he stepped down the side of the stage to film the audience.

"Are you having fun, Sydney?" Zeke shouted into his mic.

They roared in response.

"Great. We have a little surprise for you. Don't go anywhere." He slipped his microphone into the stand. We all put down our instruments and headed towards the steps.

Everyone except for Penn.

"What's going on?" Abbie asked when we stepped down toward her. She looked worried. Evidently this was a surprise for her too.

Zeke grinned and removed off his sweat drenched T-shirt. "Just a little something we added since the last tour."

She looked confused but mostly distracted by the sight of Zeke's sweaty torso before he pulled on the dry tee a staff member handed him.

Understandable, the view was pretty fucking awesome.

I managed to tear my eyes off him and changed my shirt before I slipped an arm around her and tucked her close to my side.

"You'll love it," I told her. I hoped the crowd did. This was a risk, like adding Abbie to the lineup. It could be the best choice ever, or a major fuck up. I knew which one I was voting for.

Penn sat in front of his keyboard and waited until the audience was silent. Okay, as silent as eighty thousand people could be.

Isaac climbed back onto the stage to film him.

My heart raced with anticipation. For Penn's sake, I hoped this went down well. If it didn't, he'd be angrier than a drop bear all tour. Only real, because drop bears are an urban myth to scare tourists.

Penn placed his hands on the keys and leaned towards the microphone.

With the attention of everyone in the stadium, he started to sing Hallelujah, just him and his keyboard.

"I didn't know he could sing," Abbie whispered.

"If it's music related, he can do it," I whispered back. And he did it well.

The audience was quiet through the whole thing, enraptured by the moment he created.

There was no doubt in the mind of anyone there that he was born to perform. He captured everyone's attention from the first note to the very last.

If I was ever jealous of anyone, it was him and his innate musical ability. The band was fucking lucky to have him, and he knew it.

When he was finished, the crowd burst into their wildest applause yet.

"Wow," Abbie breathed. "That was…"

"Hot?" I suggested. I turned and locked eyes on her.

"I was going to say awesome, but hot works too," she agreed.

I smiled and gave her a quick kiss before I hurried back onto the stage.

After all, we couldn't let Penn have all the limelight, right?

CHAPTER
TWELVE
ABBIE

"THAT WAS FUCKING FANTASTIC." Violet toasted all of us with a shot of vodka, then tossed it back.

After the concert we were all ushered into limousines and driven to Zodiac Underground, the club owned by a guy named Will Holding.

According to Zeke, Will was Bev's best friend. He assured me we would be well taken care of and the label would pick up the bill later.

They had free alcohol.

"Most valuable player of the concert has to go to Mr Beauregard Pennington," Landon declared. "We would all take our hats off to you if we were wearing hats." He threw back a shot of tequila.

Penn shrugged and almost looked pleased at the praise. Almost. "Just doing my job," he said with a grunt.

"You kicked ass," Channing said. He was sipping on a beer with more restraint than his boyfriend.

"You really did, my friend." Zeke tapped him on the shoulder. "I better be careful or the label will give my job to you. Or worse, you'll leave the band and go solo."

"Fuck that," Penn muttered. "Too much pressure. If I wanted that I would have stuck with the Conservatory of Music."

"Nah," Asher said. "Your talent would have been wasted there."

I would have agreed, but I suspected if I said anything, it would bring down Penn's mood. This was his moment. I didn't want to take it away from him.

In the end, the choice was taken out of my hands when Asher said, "Let's give a special mention to Abbie, who also kicked ass." He held up his whiskey and cola to toast me. "That should shut the press up now."

He looked so adorably proud my heart skipped a beat or two.

"Both of their performances should," Zeke said quietly, but equally proud.

I knew what he was referring to, we all did. In the past, the press had been as shitty to Penn as they were to me. Although, I was an innocent bystander in the shit that happened to me. The things he did...

I pushed it out of my mind. It didn't matter now. The past was the past. No one wanted to live there. I certainly didn't.

"When did you guys plan Penn's solo?" I asked Zeke, who sat beside me at the large table. Technically, it was several tables pushed together, but whatever. "No one mentioned it at rehearsal." I wondered if I should be mad at them for keeping that a secret, but decided against it. It was a wonderful surprise, and at the end of the day, the band's secret to keep. I didn't need to know everything they did, all the time.

He shrugged. "It's something we've had in the works for a while now. It's a good chance for me to get a toilet break." He grinned.

Penn flipped him off. "Yeah, that's the only reason I'm doing it," he said sarcastically. "So you can think of me while you're holding your dick."

"Do you *want* us to be thinking about you?" A smile tugged at the corners of Asher's lips.

"I'm fucking unforgettable," Penn said. "I wouldn't blame you if you did."

I tried not to snort too loudly. He wasn't wrong. He was one of the more memorable people I knew.

He turned, narrowed eyes on me. "Who got the bigger applause? Me or her?"

I opened my mouth to retort, but Zeke put his hand on my arm.

"Let's not fight, okay? It's going to be a really long tour if we start on the first night."

I sat back and closed my mouth.

Penn smirked and turned away.

Asshole.

Zeke took his hand off my arm and rested it lightly on the back of my neck instead. He looked thoughtful.

"Should I be worried?" I asked.

His brow creased. "Worried about what, sweetheart?"

"The expression on your face. You look like you're up to something." I picked up my glass of wine and took a sip. I wasn't in the mood to get plastered tonight. A light buzz was enough, especially after a big concert. That was all the lift I needed.

"Do I?" He gave me a smile like he was definitely planning something.

"Don't worry, it won't be anything bad." He paused for a beat, then added, "I don't think it's bad. Other people might disagree." His brows twitched.

"What are you plotting?" Asher asked from the other side of me.

"World domination," Zeke said lightly. "What else?"

"That's not your world domination face," Asher said. "That's your, 'I'm going to run something by the label and it's going to be epic,' face."

He chuckled. "I have different faces for those two things?"

"Yes," Asher said. "They're two of my favourite faces." He grinned. "You can guess what my first favourite face is."

"The one I have when I'm about to hand you a fresh cup of coffee?" Zeke asked.

"That's definitely in my top four," Asher said.

"Orgasms!" Violet suddenly shouted. "That's your favourite face, isn't it?"

Everyone turned to her and laughed. She was going to have one hell of a hangover in the morning, but she was clearly enjoying herself.

"She's right," Asher said. "That's my favourite expression on anyone's face, especially mine."

"That gives a whole new meaning to the expression 'cum face'," Tully said.

"Cum face is an expression?" Landon asked. "Is that like cockhead?" He blinked like his intoxicated brain was trying to make sense of what Tully said, but couldn't quite manage.

"No," Tully said. "It's more like, 'oops, I missed coming in your mouth and got it all over your face instead.'"

"Oh." Landon nodded. "That makes sense." He still looked confused.

I watched Tully while he spoke and thought again about the room the guys mentioned. Only now, my imagination extended to Tully squirting cum over my cheeks and chin. The idea made me feel all warm inside.

"How do you miss coming in someone's mouth?" Asher asked. "You must have really shit aim." He was also showing signs of how much he'd had to drink.

Tully picked up a slice of cheese from a bowl in the middle of the table and threw it at Asher. It landed squarely in the drummer's drink with a plop.

"What the fuck, Tull?" Asher pulled out the cheese and flicked it back at Tully. It flew past the lead guitarist and landed somewhere on the floor.

"Who has shit aim?" Tully laughed.

"Still you, cockhead," Asher retorted playfully.

Zeke shook his head at them. "Some day they'll grow up, but today is not that day."

"I've heard a rumour," Asher said, suddenly serious. "Apparently, growing up is overrated. I plan on never finding out." He nodded so firmly he might have fallen off his chair if there wasn't a table in front of him.

Zeke shot an arm out to steady him and pressed him against the back of his seat.

"Thanks, babe," Asher muttered.

"Ash, dude, that is the smartest thing I've ever heard you say," Landon said. "I'm not gonna grow up either."

"Me three," Channing agreed.

"Yeah, leave all the adult shit to Penn, Tully and I," Zeke said. "And Abbie." He gave me a speculative look.

"Fuck nope," I said. "So far, growing up is overrated as fuck. Hard pass."

I wouldn't go back to my childhood either. Could I choose a point where I was more innocent than right now, but old enough to do things for myself? That sounded like bliss to me.

"I don't want to be an adult either," Tully declared. "I'm happy to defer to you and Penn. As long as you don't try to impose an early bedtime, or stop me eating cake for dinner."

"When have you ever eaten cake for dinner?" Zeke laughed.

"Never," Tully said with a nod. "But I want to be able to, if I feel like it."

"Noted," Zeke said. "Tully can hereby eat cake for dinner whenever he wants."

"Can I eat it off Abbie?" Tully asked.

That question took me by surprise and actually made me blush.

"What flavour?" Yeah, that was the important thing here wasn't it? I resisted the urge to slap my hand across my eyes.

Tully cocked his head at me. "I'm pretty sure you would taste good with any flavour, but maybe something with lemon in it."

Penn grunted something that sounded like disapproval, but he was ignored by everyone else at the table. Presumably he didn't like lemon flavour. Yeah, that was it.

"That sounds accurate," Zeke said. "Wouldn't you say, Asher?"

"Lemon or chocolate," Asher agreed. "But she tastes pretty good without any flavouring as well."

A month ago, I would have been embarrassed to have people talk about me like that. No, maybe embarrassed wasn't the right word. I would have felt uncomfortable, and thought they were just trying to be nice.

Now, I felt a lot more confident and knew they were describing me the way they saw me. Or tasted me. I actually liked hearing it now.

A girl could get a healthy ego at this rate.

"Talented and delicious," Zeke said. "That's one hell of a combination."

"That description fits you too," Asher told him. He gave Zeke the most adoring look.

They were just so fucking cute together. The three of us together made one hell of a combination.

"And you," I said before anyone thought this conversation was making me uneasy. "Both of you."

"I think I'm going to be sick," Violet declared. She clapped a hand over her mouth, stood and ran from the table towards the toilets.

"What she said," Penn said with a grunt. "I have *not* had enough alcohol for this conversation."

"And Violet had too much," Blaise said, speaking up for the first time in an hour or two. "Whereas I've had just enough." He toasted me with what I thought was bourbon, and a grin.

I knew he wasn't interested in me in that way, but all the talk about taste and cake was pretty interesting.

I grinned back at him. "I have a feeling this tour isn't going to be boring." Absolutely bat shit crazy maybe, but not boring.

Luckily, I liked a bit of bat shit crazy in my life.

"That is for fucking sure," Asher said. "It's going to be one hell of a ride and I'm here for every second of it." He put his hand up to Tully and they high-fived each other.

"Me too, babe." Zeke grinned.

I wondered if he'd decided to talk to Reuben about the evil twins and their relationship with Lila Bell.

Every now and again I caught him with a frown on his face. He was obviously thinking about it, and troubled. It didn't seem fair to have a heavy burden on his mind when he should be thinking about, and enjoying, the tour. I wished there was something I could do to help, but short of trying to find Reuben Brantley's phone number and contacting him myself, all I could do was be here for Zeke when he needed me.

"Are you okay?" I asked him softly.

"Yeah," he replied.

He shook his head and his dark expression lifted. "If I haven't mentioned it recently, you were mind blowing tonight. Fans are going to be talking about that concert for the next fifty years at least. Grandchildren will be impressed their grandparents were there."

I snorted a laugh. "You make it sound like the moon landing."

He grinned. "It's way bigger than the moon landing. And it actually happened."

"I didn't take you for a conspiracy theorist." I finished the last of my wine.

He shrugged one shoulder. "I'm not, I just know we were out of this world."

I groaned at his pun. "Is that why you're the adult here? Because of the dad jokes?"

He rubbed the back of his head. "I'm practising."

"For being a dad?" The idea made my heart jump a little bit. I hadn't thought where children might fit into this arrangement, or even if they could. It would certainly complicate things a lot more.

He grinned slowly. "Or a daddy."

That was a whole other conversation.

CHAPTER
THIRTEEN

ABBIE

"THERE'S SOMETHING ABOUT MELBOURNE," I sipped my coffee and enjoyed the view of the Yarra River out the window.

"It's one of my favourite places to hang out," Asher said. "One of our first concerts was here. They've always been super supportive of us. They have great taste." He smiled over the top of his mug. "And good coffee."

"They like to claim the whole band is from here," Zeke said. "So does Sydney. If one of us is from somewhere, the whole place will try to claim all of us. It's funny as fuck."

That was normal. Australia was often trying to claim people from New Zealand as ours too. Vice versa, probably.

"Whatever it is, they were really great last night," I said.

Either the people in Melbourne didn't read tabloids, or they were just nicer to me than the Sydney crowd. That wasn't to say I hadn't encountered my share of the press here too. A contingent waited outside the venue for us to go past and several threw questions at me. One or two were related to my singing. The rest were about Vance and my affair with Pete.

I ignored all of them, lifted my chin and stepped into the venue surrounded by six hulking rock stars. It was the best, 'fuck you,' I could give them without words.

The photos of us which later showed up online were a hot-blooded woman's fantasy right there. If only they knew how much of that fantasy I was really living. On the other hand, fuck them. They didn't need to know how lucky I was.

"They'll be really great tonight too," Zeke said. "The fans who went last night have been raving on social media all day. Tonight's crowd will be even more psyched up."

"Especially the ones who went last night as well," Asher said. "And the other night in Sydney. There are whole social media pages of people who follow us all around the country whenever we tour. I can't decide if it's cool or if they're stalkers."

"I think it's cool," I said. It was pretty fucking awesome to have fans that dedicated.

"Stalkers wouldn't pay for tickets, would they?" I grimaced. "Wait a minute, I don't want to know." They'd probably do whatever it took to get close to the object of their affection. No one ever said they acted rationally.

Honestly, I didn't want to think about it too much. I had enough trouble without throwing stalkers into the mix.

"I think it depends on the stalker," Asher said. "I mean, if I was going to stalk me I would spend my money on tickets."

"Me too," Tully said. "We might have enough tickets on ourselves as it is, though."

"Speak for yourself," Asher retorted. "I'm humble."

"No offence, dude, but you just said you would spend a lot of money buying tickets to see yourself," Zeke said. "That doesn't sound very humble to me. It sounds pretty fucking awesome though. I'd buy tickets to see you too."

"I'd buy tickets to see U2," Tully said. "They're my second favourite band after us. Is there a better song than 'I Still Haven't Found What I'm Looking For'? When I was younger, I dreamt of playing with Bono."

"Who didn't, bro?" Asher asked.

"I didn't," Penn said.

Everyone turned to look at him.

"You didn't?" Tully asked.

Penn shrugged. "I wanted to be successful because of my own talent and hard work, not because I was riding on someone else's coattails. Or fucking them." Of course he couldn't resist giving me the side eye.

"Piss off," I growled. Just because I wasn't quite as skilled at the keyboard as him...

"All of us are successful because of our talent and hard work," Zeke said, speaking over Penn's response. "Even me." Of course he couldn't resist a dig at himself to lighten the mood.

I tilted my head at him. Even joking, I hated hearing people put themselves down. Especially someone as awesome as Zeke.

"No one could ever accuse you of not being talented," I said firmly. "For some reason, it seems to be easier to accept that a man can be successful without having to suck anyone off." I glared at Penn. His words got under my skin much more than I should have let them.

I pushed my empty coffee cup aside and got to my feet. "Excuse me, I need some air."

I waved Zeke and Asher back down when they both started to stand. "I'm fine. I just need a moment."

Neither of them looked happy about it. Nor did Tully for that matter, but they all stayed in their seats while I slipped out the door and into the street.

Not wanting to see three worried faces, and Penn's smug one, in the window, I turned and headed off in the other direction.

Channing and Landon went to do some sightseeing and shopping, so I kept an eye out for them just in case. In my current mood, I didn't want to answer any more questions and no doubt they would have them.

I pulled a pair of sunglasses out of my bag and slipped them on my face. I should have a hat so I didn't get sunburnt, but in my experience that was the easiest way to draw attention to myself.

Something about the combination of hat and sunglasses screamed, 'I'm trying to hide my identity.' If I wanted to keep from being noticed, I had to act casually. I was just another person going about their day in the city.

That illusion lasted for all of about five minutes, before a young woman glanced at me, looked away, then looked back. She whispered to her friends, who all started to stare.

"It is, isn't it?" one whispered loudly.

"It looks like her," another said. "She *is* on tour with Wolf Venom."

Fuck.

I gave them a smile and hoped they would keep on walking.

Of course, they didn't. All four of them hurried up to me, phones in their hands.

"Abbie Hart?" one asked tentatively. She had bright red hair and more freckles than I could count.

"Guilty," I said, trying not to sigh. "Hello there."

A woman with dark hair in a mess of curls squealed. "I told you guys!"

The redhead winced. "Amber! I'm pretty sure they heard you in Tasmania."

Amber looked unapologetic. "Can we get a selfie?"

"Sure." Even before everything turned to shit, I never said no to a fan who wanted a selfie or an autograph. What was a couple of minutes out of my day to make their day better?

She posed beside me and held up her phone.

I slipped off my sunglasses and smiled. "Say cheese."

She took a picture of us smiling and one of us laughing at the absurdity of saying cheese.

"Can I have one too?" the redhead asked.

I posed with all four of them in turn and then with the five of us together. They all took turns in taking a photo of us as a group.

"Thank you so much," Amber gushed. "You've been so sweet. We've all been fans since your first album, haven't we girls?"

"Yes we have," the redhead said. "We can't wait for the show tonight."

I had a funny feeling they were big fans of Wolf Venom, but were aware of my music from before I signed with White Wolf Records. At any rate, they were being nice, so the least I could do was be nice in return.

"You're going to have the time of your life," I assured them. "Blazing Violet and Wolf Venom are both on fire right now." If only they knew at least four of the guys were a couple of hundred metres away. They would absolutely lose their minds.

They all looked like they were ready to jump up and down with excitement.

"We should let you go," the redhead said finally. "No doubt you have a shit load of things to do before tonight. We do. We came in to get our nails done and buy new outfits."

"I'm sure you'll look amazing," I said. "I'll keep an eye out for you."

"We'll be waving like crazy," Amber said.

"I'll wave back," I assured her. The four of them would probably make it up near the front somehow. "Enjoy the rest of your day."

"You too." To my surprise, each of them gave me a quick hug before they hurried on, talking excitedly.

It was a refreshing change from Penn's accusation that I was riding on the band's coattails. I hurt my own feelings by remembering his comment. Mostly, it stung because it was in the back of my mind from the moment I signed with White Wolf Records.

When Jackson suggested I go on tour with the guys, I almost said no because of it. I wanted to stand on my own two feet. I still did.

As for the press, I could just imagine what they would say if they knew about my growing relationship with the guys. They wouldn't pull any punches. They would say any success I had from here on out was because of who I was fucking.

The question was, how did I get past that? I didn't want to stop being with the guys and I didn't want to flush my career back down the toilet just when it was starting to climb back out.

How in the hell was I going to have everything I wanted and needed without looking like an idiot?

I slipped my sunglasses back on and ignored the looks from a few people who sat at tables at a nearby café. They must have witnessed the exchange with the four other women and all the fuss they made over me. At a quick glance, I didn't think any of them knew who I was. Not to look at me anyway. My name tended to be more recognisable than my face these days.

Again, I wondered if I should colour my hair bright blue. Fewer people would recognise me that way. Until they saw me at a concert with bright blue hair, then I would stand out like dog's balls. Okay, that might be a bad idea.

In the past, when things were at their worst, I'd taken to wearing a brunette wig. It only fooled the press for a little while and led to rumours that I wasn't a natural blond.

It was strange the things they decided to focus on and target me for. As if anyone really cared what my natural hair colour was. Well, unless they want to be an Abbie Hart lookalike. That actually happened more often than you might think.

"Hey, wait up," a voice called out behind me.

I didn't need to turn around to know it was Asher.

He and the other three guys caught up to me, and Asher slid his hand into mine.

"Are you doing okay?" Zeke asked. "Penn can be a dickhead sometimes, but his bark is worse than his bite. Right, Penn?"

"My bite is fucking awesome," Penn said. "Zeke wants me to say sorry, but I'm calling it how I see it. How plenty of other people see it. It is what it is."

I tried to stop myself, but I couldn't help it. I rounded on him so fast he took a step back.

"You don't think I fucking realise that?" I snarled. "I know what people are thinking and saying, because I'm thinking it myself. This was your tour and I should have said no to coming along. This whole fucking thing was a giant mistake."

I threw up my hands and glared through a haze of tears. "People are paying to see *you*. Not me. I should be back in Sydney working on my new album and planning my own fucking tour. Are you happy now? Or would you prefer I just packed up and went home?"

"As a matter of fact—" he started.

"Abbie, no," Asher said. "Penn, what the fuck?"

"No one's going home," Zeke said.

Without meaning to, I snapped at him, "Maybe they are."

I turned and stalked away in the direction of our hotel. The small glimmer of happiness I got from meeting those fans was shattered into a thousand pieces already. All I wanted to do was be as far away from here as possible. From Melbourne, from the guys, especially from Penn.

Until I saw the cardboard box sitting outside the door to my hotel room.

CHAPTER
FOURTEEN

ASHER

I GAVE Penn a dirty look and hurried off after Abbie.

It didn't help that he was right, to some extent. Not about Abbie going home. Not when he said she didn't have a place on the tour. No, he was right about people talking, and saying the shitty things he said. He didn't have to regurgitate them, especially the way he had.

There was home truth and then there was being a motherfucker. He definitely crossed that line.

"Abbie, wait," I called after her a couple of times. She didn't wait or even slow, until I skidded to a stop behind her, a couple of metres from the door to the hotel room.

"Fuck. Is that what I think it is?"

She shook her head. "I don't know. It looks like the one Jonah's head was in. I can't bring myself to look."

She flinched when I put a hand on her shoulder.

"We shouldn't stand out here. Someone might come." I stepped around her and crouched beside the box.

"What the fuck? Not another one." Zeke stopped behind Abbie and placed his hands protectively on her shoulders.

Tully pulled up a couple of seconds later. "What is it—shit."

"Fucking great, more drama," Penn said. "What the fuck next?" He threw up his hands.

"Be glad you're not inside there," I growled. I scooped up the box and waited for someone to pull out a keycard.

"What the shit is that supposed to mean?" Penn demanded.

I ignored him and stepped inside when Zeke unlocked the door.

"Come in or stay out there, but either way close the door," I said to Penn. I placed the box on the table and looked at it for a long moment. "Do we want to guess who is inside this?"

"Yeah," Zeke said sarcastically. "Whoever gets it right gets a hundred bucks." He exhaled loudly. "Just open the fucking thing. Or I will."

"Be my guest." I waved my hand at the box and took a step back.

To be honest, I was really hoping this time there would be a cake inside there. I mean, a guy could hope, right?

Zeke took his hands from Abbie's shoulders and stepped over to the box. He slipped open the lid and peered inside.

"The bad news is it's not a cake. I also have no idea who it is."

"But it is a who?" I asked tentatively.

"It's definitely a who," he agreed.

Abbie groaned.

Tully placed a hand lightly on her lower back and started to lead her over to the couch. "Come and sit for a—"

"Wait," Zeke said. "Abbie, you need to look and see if you know who this was." He looked pained, like the last thing he wanted was Abbie anywhere near the box. "Shit, I'm sorry."

She nodded and reluctantly walked the few steps back to glance inside the box.

"Fucking hell," she said softly.

"You know who it is?" I asked as gently as I could, considering we were talking about another disembodied head.

"Yeah, she was Pete's wife," she said in a tiny voice.

"The woman who wanted you kicked off your label when she got back together with him?" Zeke asked.

Abbie nodded and leaned into Tully. "I hated her guts, but I didn't want this to happen to her." After a moment, her eyes snapped up to Zeke's face. "What are we going to do? Should we tell the police?" She looked terrified.

"Fuck no," he said. "We'll deal with this." He looked over at me and I nodded.

"I'll contact my sister. She'll know someone." I pulled out my phone and tapped an innocent looking message into the screen before pressing send.

"You have a brother who lives in Melbourne, don't you?" Abbie asked Zeke.

"Yeah, I do, but he would go straight to Reuben about this." Zeke closed the lid on the box. "The last thing we need to do is give him more ammunition. If they pin this on any of us, the tour and the band are fucked. Even if the allegation doesn't stick, which it wouldn't, we'd be in enough trouble for our careers to be over."

I smiled.

"What?" Penn snapped.

"You've met my sister, Rose," I said. "If anyone can find a way to pin this woman's disappearance on her husband, it will be her."

Zeke smiled. "I like that idea. Get us out of the shit and get some revenge for Abbie in the meantime." We exchanged high-fives.

"You guys are completely insane," Penn said. He sighed dramatically out his nose. "You're going to make me take part in this, aren't you?"

"Sorry, Penny, you're already in this as deep as the rest of us are," I said without even a hint of apology. He deserved it after being an asshole. "If it was you in trouble, we would help you out, and you know it. We have in the past."

He hated discussing that time in his life, but I couldn't help bringing it up right now. I was pissed off at him for what he said to Abbie. I still hadn't ruled out the idea of punching him in the cock, or the face. Maybe when this was dealt with.

He crossed his arms over his chest and scowled. "Fine. If only to make sure it's dealt with."

"Tully?" I asked.

"I'm in," he said immediately.

"We're in too," Landon said as he and Channing stepped through the door. "What are we in— oh. Is that another one of those gifts?"

They both had arms full of bags, Landon maybe double as many as Channing. They set them down beside the door. It looked like they had a successful shopping trip.

"If you want to call it that," Zeke said.

My phone pinged. I pulled it out and looked at the screen.

"Rose says to head on over. We'll have to borrow one of the tour vans. It's going to be a squeeze." I went to pick up the box.

"Wait a minute, you fucking idiot," Penn said. "If that's the same kind of box the others were found in, don't you think someone is going to notice?"

I hesitated, my hands a few centimetres from the box. "You're right. We need something a rock band would carry around without looking strange."

Zeke nodded. "Tully and I will go to the venue and grab a box out of the rig truck. There must be hundreds they used to carry around our equipment. The rest of you stay here and don't answer the door to any police or press."

I nodded, locked the door behind them, and walked over to the bench in the corner of the room. I flicked on the kettle that sat in the middle of a tray, and started to make us all coffee.

We weren't far from the venue, but it was still going to take some time. Time in which none of us was going to relax. It wasn't too much of a stretch to think whoever left the head might have informed someone about its existence.

The longer the minutes ticked past, the more nervous I got.

Abbie looked even more anxious than I felt. I wanted to hold her and tell her this was all going to be okay, but was it?

If anyone was going to be screwed over in this, it was her. I was going to do everything I could to make sure that didn't happen.

Hell, I was going to find a way to make whoever the fuck was doing this, pay.

I was only ready to admit this to myself for now, but I was in love with Abbie. I was not going to let anything bad happen to her. I was sure as hell not going to let anyone pin the blame for this on her.

I jumped at a tap on the door and cold coffee splashed over my hand.

I hadn't realised I'd stood there lost in thought for over half an hour. None of us had said a word since Tully and Zeke left. I hadn't even taken a sip of my drink.

I put my cup aside, shook my hand to dry it, and stepped over to the door.

"Who is it?" I called out. *God, don't let it be the police. Or anyone from the label. Or a roadie. Or a fan. Or…*

"It's Tull and I. Let us in," Zeke said.

I exhaled in relief and unlocked the door. I opened it a crack and peered out to make sure it was only Zeke and Tully, then opened the door and stepped back. Between them they carried a box big enough for one of Channing's saxophones.

Tully kicked the door closed behind him and they opened the box.

"Bring that over here." Zeke waved at the cardboard box.

We all looked at it, but I was the one who moved to pick it up and place it inside the other box.

I wasn't sure if it started to smell or if I was imagining it, but I moved quickly with it anyway. I wasn't squeamish, and I'd seen dead people before, but the whole situation was different. Nastier somehow.

"If anyone asks, we're taking an instrument to be fixed," Zeke said. "The mouthpiece got broken. Channing got too rough with it, or something."

"Wouldn't happen," Channing said. He didn't look too worried about the false accusation though. It was for a good cause after all.

"Maybe you hit Penn with it," I said dryly.

Penn flipped me off. "Maybe he tried to beat some sense into Asher."

"Okay, quit it," Zeke snapped. He and Tully closed the saxophone box and he hefted it into his arms. "Asher, in my pocket are keys to the van."

"Is that all that's in your pocket?" I reached inside and pulled out the keys.

Zeke chuckled. "No, that's not all. But that's all that matters right now. All of you stay close to me and Abbie. But… try to look like we're not up to something."

That was going to be a stretch since we were *definitely* up to something.

I opened the door and held it while Zeke carried the box out. The rest of us did as he asked and stayed close to Abbie. I slipped my arm around her waist and pulled her hip to mine, but she looked pale and scared.

"We've got this," I assured her. "This isn't the first time we've dealt with shit like this. It's probably not even the tenth."

"But is it the last?" she asked. "Or is this the third in a long line of shit like this? What if it never ends?"

"I hate to say it," Penn said slowly, "but even you are going to run out of people who hate you sooner or later. This bitch and that Vance asshole were the two worst, weren't they? Who else is there? And don't say me, because no one is cutting off my head."

Abbie shrugged. "Pete. Poppy Newton. I'm not sure either of them hate me, they just made my life difficult. Honestly, I don't think Vance and Calista hated me either, so you're probably safe." She gave him a sarcastic half smile.

He sneered at her in return.

Yep, in spite of all the words and dirty looks, they were still hot for each other. It was only a matter of time before they gave in. It was probably even less time before she and Tully became more involved. He was quickly becoming a fourth wheel in this arrangement. In a good way.

We followed Zeke to the van and piled inside, the box safely in the back.

I took the driver's seat with Zeke beside me. The others took the two rows of passenger seats in the back.

"I hope Rose knows what you're getting her into," Zeke said.

"Nothing she can't handle," I said. She was one of the toughest women I knew. She and Abbie would get along.

I hoped.

Rose had a tendency to make snap judgements and stick to them for life.

I started the engine and we headed out to the suburbs.

With any luck, we'd be back before anyone noticed we weren't around. Not to mention back in time for tonight's concert. Missing that would get us into more trouble than being found with a severed head.

Well, almost.

CHAPTER
FIFTEEN
ASHER

"HOW NICE OF you to drop by with a present," Rose said dryly.

She lived in an unassuming townhouse in Carlton. It reminded me of Zeke's place, but bigger, and decorated with a lot more pastels colours and floral patterns. We always joked that she had taken her name and ran with it.

I guessed you could say that about most of the family.

Dane was like a Great Dane, growling and snarling while trying to protect us. Me, I was trying to set the world on fire, figuratively speaking. The only one who deviated was Mina. She didn't have a mean bone in her body. At least she didn't compared to the rest of us.

I grinned. "You know me, always dropping by with something fun."

Rose peered into the box. "Friend of yours?"

"Yes, I always like to cut the heads of my friends. It stops them from running away." While she rolled her eyes at me, I told her the real story.

She looked over at Abbie with curious eyes. "I heard about you from Dane. He seemed to like you."

Abbie gave her a watery smile. She didn't seem in much of a mood for small talk. "Thanks. He seems nice. Can you deal with that for us?"

"Blunt," Rose said approvingly. "I can, but I might need something in return some day."

"Whatever we can do," I said. "Within reason."

I brushed hair back from Abbie's cheek and stroked the back of my finger along her jaw.

Her skin was still pale from the shock of seeing another disembodied head. It wasn't something anyone should get used to seeing. As chill as I was about it, my stomach still turned being in the same room with it. The whole situation was all kinds of fucked up.

"Yeah, as long as it doesn't involve us getting in the middle of shit between my family and the Bells," Zeke said. "Or the Fiorellis, for that matter."

"I make no promises," Rose said. "Dane has put us in a precarious position. Men and their cocks." She looked at Abbie and rolled her eyes.

Abbie responded with a half smile. "Men and their ambition."

"I feel attacked," I said dryly.

"Me too," Zeke said. "Sounds pretty accurate though."

"Well... Yeah." I shrugged.

"Can we get this over with?" Penn said.

"Still got the stick up his ass I see," Rose remarked. Before he could respond, she added, "I will deal with the head. You mentioned you wanted the finger pointed at this Pete guy, if possible? Was that Vance person with his label too?"

"Yes, he was," Abbie said. "Why?"

"Two people turned up dead and they're connected to the same person," Rose said slowly. "Is it possible Pete is actually involved?"

Abbie sucked in a breath. "I hadn't even thought of that. I don't think so, but... I mean, maybe."

"Are you suggesting he killed all these people and is trying to pin it on Abbie?" Tully asked. "What an asshole."

"I'm only saying it's possible." Rose tapped the tips of her long, bright red fingernails against her cheek. "The question is, what would be less disruptive, if this head turned up on his doorstep, or if she disappeared entirely? This could turn up in six months time. Twelve months. Or never. Any idea where the rest of her is?"

I shook my head. "None. That could be a problem, couldn't it? Bits of her might start to turn up sooner or later."

"Yeah, but there's nothing we can do about that," Rose said.

"If her head turns up in the next day or two, people are going to ask Abbie questions," Zeke said. "People are going to notice because she is connected to this woman and Vance as well. Even if we can prove where Abbie was when Calista was killed, it's still going to cause a stir. Personally, I'd prefer to avoid a stir of this kind."

"Me too," Abbie said. "If it interferes with the tour—"

"You could always drop out," Penn said.

"Give it a fucking rest," I snarled. "If nothing else, she is under contract, and Levi isn't going to tear it up. Get the fuck over it."

Penn rolled his eyes and stalked away toward the townhouse's pretty courtyard.

"So, disappearing this for a while," Rose concluded. "We wouldn't want anything like a mere murder to get in the way of your careers." Her tone was somewhere between amused and ironic.

"We really wouldn't," I agreed. "You're the best, sis."

"Of course I am," she said. "I'm wondering if I should make Dane disappear as well, before we all end up in trouble."

I laughed. At least, I thought she was joking.

She raised an eyebrow at me.

My smile faded. "Anyway, we appreciate this. I know it's not the best present I've ever brought along with me."

"It's not the worst either," she said. "There was that cake that time."

I sighed. "How many times do I have to say sorry? I had no idea there were nuts in it. Lucky you keep an EpiPen handy."

"That's not by luck," she said dryly. "It's because I don't want to die by being poisoned by my baby brother."

I clapped a hand to my forehead. "Well at least a head in a cardboard box can't poison you. Unless you eat it." I lowered my hand slowly. "You're not going to eat it, are you?"

She might have a particularly unorthodox way of disposing of remains that I didn't know about. I made a note not to eat any meat products she offered me ever again.

She socked me hard on the arm. "No, I'm not going to eat it, you fucking idiot. Did you hit your head with the drumsticks a few times too many?"

I stuck my tongue out at her. "You *were* my favourite sister."

"Only because Mina doesn't talk to you anymore." A shadow passed across her eyes.

"I miss her too," I said softly.

Abbie leaned against me and gave me a squeeze. "She sounds a special person."

"She was," I said. "She *is*. I respect her need to cut the rest of us out of her life, but it still sucks."

"At least I'm still talking to you," Rose said. "In spite of the dubious gifts you bring me. How about some books next time? Or a voucher for one of those nice gardening places. Or home decor places. Or even a nice bottle of expensive wine."

"Well I'm sorted for the next five birthdays and Christmases," I said lightly. "I won't need to ask you what you want."

"You should still ask," she said. "I might have changed my mind by then."

I groaned. "So is there anything you want us to do? Turn on the barbecue? Dig a hole? To get rid of the head I mean."

She shook her head. "No, I'll deal with it. The less you know about it the better. If people start asking questions, you don't want to have the answers to them."

"We've had a lot of practice in lying," I said. "But you're right, it's a lot easier if we don't know anything."

"I'm always right," Rose said. "One day you'll remember that." She wagged a finger at me.

I swatted it away playfully. Yeah, I'd much rather deal with my relatives than Zeke's.

"We're sorry to get you involved in this," Abbie said softly. "I don't know what I would have done if I had to deal with it by myself."

"You would have figured something out," I said confidently.

Chances were, her career would have been over the moment Jonah's head turned up.

Or worse. Without Zeke to stop her, she would have gone straight to the police. If she told them about Jonah and the gun, Reuben would have had her killed. She wouldn't have walked out of the police station alive. Or if she had, she wouldn't be alive long after that.

Sometimes knowing dubious people like us was an advantage.

"I would have been fucked and you know it," Abbie said.

I grinned.

She smacked me on the chest. "I didn't mean that kind of fucked."

"I know, I couldn't resist." I rubbed my chest. If I wasn't careful, these women were going to leave bruises.

"Try harder," Rose said. "I don't need to know about your sex life."

"Right back at you, sis," I said. Honestly, I had no idea if she even had one. Most men seemed to be scared of her for some reason. Oh, it might be because her baby brother was a big, badass rock god. That would do it, right?

Yeah, okay, maybe it was because she was scary. She took no bullshit from anyone, and was smart enough to figure out a way to pin this on Pete without causing Abbie and the rest of us too much drama.

"Are you expecting a guest?" Channing said from the front of the townhouse. He and Landon were assigned to keep watch, just in case someone spotted us.

"No," Rose said. "Just you clowns."

"Well, a black SUV just pulled up outside the front. I can't see inside, but I have a feeling they're watching this place." Channing shrugged.

"Fuck," Zeke said under his breath. "If you can take care of this, I'll go and see who it is."

"Go for it." Rose picked up the box and carried it to the back of the house.

I had no idea exactly what she'd do with it, but if the police arrived and searched the place, I was sure they wouldn't find it. She was way too smart for that.

I followed Zeke to the front of the house, my arm still around Abbie. I leaned around the curtain and looked out the window.

The SUV was just as Channing described. It reminded me of the one that followed us around that night in Sydney.

"This is just a wild guess here, but I would say Reuben is probably involved," I said.

"I'd say you're right," Zeke said. "Tully, Channing, Landon: keep an eye on Abbie. Asher, you and I are going to go and talk to them."

"Are you sure that's a good idea?" I glanced around to see Penn come in from the courtyard.

"Who's doing something stupid now?" he asked.

"Wanna come and find out?" I asked him.

He shrugged. "Sure. It could only get me killed, right?"

I patted him on the shoulder. "That's the spirit."

He jerked his shoulder away, but followed Zeke and I out the front door and across the footpath.

Zeke walked around to the driver's side window and tapped on it.

At first, I thought whoever was inside was going to ignore us.

Slowly, the window started to slide down.

"I'm not gonna lie, I was hoping it would be someone cool," I said. "Like Levi Jones or the lead singer of the Rock Dragons, what is his name? Strike West? Yeah, that's it."

Stuart 'Strike' West was a legend.

Zeke grinned. "That would be cool."

"Their keyboard player is cooler," Penn said.

"You always think the keyboard player is cooler," I remarked.

"That's because they are." He looked through the car window. "What the fuck is this about?"

The man who sat in the driver's seat looked at us with narrowed eyes. "When you're done with your comedy act, I have a message for you. Specifically for Zeke."

Zeke sighed. "Let me guess, Caleb wishes us well for our coming tour. Tell him we said thank you very much, it's going nicely so far."

"He wants to see you," the man said.

"Of course he does," Zeke said. "Tell him we're busy. If he wants to talk to me, he's going to have to come to the stadium tonight."

Penn snorted. "Good luck getting past security."

I jerked a thumb toward him. "What he said."

"How did he know we're here?" Zeke asked.

That was a very good fucking question.

The man didn't answer. Instead, he said, "Caleb will see you at the venue before the concert. Have security informed so there's no trouble." The window slid back up and he drove away.

"That's fucking great," Zeke growled. He looked ready to punch someone. Or something. "When will my motherfucking family learn how to use text messages?"

I didn't know the answer to that.

Mine knew how to text, but they still pulled shit like this.

CHAPTER
SIXTEEN

ABBIE

I NIBBLED on the corner of a sandwich.

I hadn't had much of an appetite since seeing Calista's head in the box. Every time I closed my eyes, all I saw was her hair, damp with her own blood. Thankfully, her eyes and mouth were closed.

However she'd died, she looked peaceful. As peaceful as she could be under the circumstances.

I hadn't wanted her dead, but I certainly didn't want her to suffer. I didn't want anyone to suffer, not even Vance. Not even Penn when he was being a dickhead. Not even the guys' families when they were making life more difficult.

"What do you think Zeke's brother wants to talk about?" I asked Tully and Asher.

Ever since we arrived at Rod Laver Arena to get ready for the concert, at least two of the guys had been with me. First it was Zeke and Penn, but they'd swapped out about half an hour ago. Before those two, Landon and Channing had taken a turn.

I felt as though I was walking around with a contingent of bodyguards. Hot, tattooed, talented bodyguards. None of them seemed to mind the duty, even Penn, surprisingly enough. I had a feeling he wanted to fuck with Zeke's brothers. That made a pleasant change from him trying to mess with me.

"Who knows?" Asher said. "Probably the same shit as Reuben. Caleb is funny though, because he always has a different angle. Funny weird, I mean. Not funny ha-ha."

"What do you mean?" I couldn't imagine any of Zeke's relatives being humorous. Okay, maybe the twins, but not Reuben and not Caleb from what

I'd heard about him. Zeke must be the only truly funny one in the family. Luckily, he more than made up for the rest of them.

"Like he'll suggest Zeke might help out here and there, and make it like it's no big deal, but every little thing turns into something much bigger. We can get a lot of things past customs as part of the tour, for example. He'll suggest we carry one little case of diamonds, but it ends up being a huge case full of guns or something. There's only so much Jackson can turn a blind eye to. You know?"

"So don't offer to carry anything for any of Zeke's brothers," I said. "Got it." That was a pretty good general rule about anyone's brothers, even mine.

"Speaking of brothers," Tully said softly.

I looked over to the door as Zeke walked in with an older man who looked like a slender version of him. With a lot fewer tattoos, as far as I could see.

"I don't know what's more shocking," Zeke was saying. "The fact you're at a rock concert or the fact you're actually dressed for it. I didn't know you owned a pair of jeans."

They were black jeans at that, paired with a dark button down shirt. I would have called Caleb hot if I hadn't seen Zeke first.

Like the rest of the family, he had that air of danger about him. That wasn't from just having learned he ran guns and smuggled diamonds either. He looked as though he'd be more comfortable telling someone to kill someone else than he would ordering a fast food meal. Or attending a rock concert for that matter.

"I own several pairs," Caleb said evenly. "I even listen to music once in a while."

"You're shitting me?" Zeke said sardonically. "Next you'll be telling me you smile once in a while."

Caleb did smile. He even laughed, which sounded sexier than it probably should. "I'm not Reuben. I know how to have a good time once in a while."

"Yeah?" Zeke asked. "When? When you're rocking out in the front row of a Wolf Venom concert? Or when you're trying to set me up to get in the shit?"

"Both of those are fun," Caleb said. "Would you believe I'm just here to say hello to my younger brother?"

Zeke responded to that with a flat stare. "No."

Caleb shrugged. "Suit yourself." He seemed to notice the rest of us standing on the other side of the room for the first time. He gave nods to Tully and Asher, which weren't quite warm, but also weren't as chilly as the look Reuben would have given them. His eyes lingered on me, curious and admiring.

In about three seconds flat, he had me mentally naked and standing in front of him. Or kneeling, since his eyes settled on my mouth.

I swear I saw his cock twitch in his pants.

"This is—" Zeke raised his arm to gesture towards me.

"I know who she is," Caleb interrupted. "Abbie Hart. You're quite an interesting woman from what I've heard."

If he was trying to intimidate me, it wasn't going to work.

"I absolutely am," I said with no hint of modesty. "I'd hate to be boring. Where would the fun be in that?" I smiled sweetly.

"I have no idea," he replied. "Personally, I try not to be boring as well." He licked his lips like a hungry wolf.

Zeke cleared his throat. "Why don't you tell us why you're really here, so then we won't waste any more of your time?" He looked like he was about ready to pick up Caleb and throw him through the nearest window. Was he big enough to do that? He looked angry enough.

"You can also tell us how you knew we were at my sister's place," Asher said.

"Lucky guess," Caleb shot back.

"Bullshit," Zeke snapped. "Someone in the crew is working for you. Who is it?"

Caleb turned towards him slowly. "If they were, why would I tell you? That would be fucking stupid. Exactly how long would it take before you had them fired?"

"About two seconds," Zeke said. "I don't appreciate having people watch me and spy on me for you or for Reuben. I'm not a twelve-year-old. If you won't tell me, I'll find out for myself." His eyes snapped with anger.

"For the record, no one is working for me." Caleb was completely unruffled. "I can't guarantee they aren't working for Reuben and feeding me information."

"It's the same. Fucking. Thing," Zeke snarled.

"How closely are they watching?" I didn't know I was going to speak until the words were out, but there they were. I couldn't take them back.

"Close enough that I know you, my brother and Asher are having a relationship with each other." What Caleb thought of that, I couldn't tell.

I would do as well playing poker against him as I would against Reuben. Badly. I made a note never to play strip poker with any of them.

"Close enough to see anyone delivering any presents to any of us?" Asher asked.

"Zeke, your brother is—" Landon skidded to a stop at the doorway. Channing was right behind him, and almost ran into his back.

"I see he found you," Landon said as he ducked aside to avoid getting bowled over.

"I told you Caleb would find him." Penn appeared half a minute behind the other two. "I don't know if he's got a radar or if he's one of those dogs that sniffs out shit."

Apparently he had no filter when it came to Caleb either.

"If I was the kind of dog that sniffed out drugs—" Caleb started.

Penn's face turned pink and his lip curled.

"Can you tell us what you're fucking here for?" Zeke snapped.

I had a feeling if Caleb didn't hurry up, Penn was going to pick up something heavy and use it on him. That wouldn't end well for any of us, especially Caleb.

"I'm here looking out for one of the family's assets," Caleb said as if that couldn't be construed as offensive at all.

Zeke gave him a hard stare. "Are you talking about me? I am not a motherfucking *asset.*"

"That was what I tried to tell Reuben," Caleb said. "But if you're not an asset, then you're a liability. You know what happens to liabilities."

Zeke growled low in the back of his throat and lunged at Caleb. He grabbed the collar of his shirt, drove him back and pinned him to the wall.

"*Don't fucking come here and threaten me.* You might have contacts but so do I. If you don't leave me, my band and Abbie alone, I will fucking *end you.* Do you hear me?"

He shoved Caleb a little harder. Any more pressure and he'd put his brother through the wall.

"Get your hands off me," Caleb said coldly. He sounded a lot more composed than I would be if I was in his shoes.

Zeke held him there for a good minute or two more, then stepped back.

"Get the fuck out of here before I have security throw you out on your ass."

I had no doubt he could and would do just that. Honestly, I wouldn't blame him. Coming here to threaten him took some balls, but it was a dick move on Caleb's part.

I had a funny feeling he wouldn't care very much about my opinion.

Caleb straightened his shirt and stepped away from the wall. His gaze swung around to me. "When you get tired of playing with boys, look me up. I'll show you how real men fuck."

"Um, thanks." What else was I supposed to say to an offer like that? He seemed to be completely sincere in the offer as well. Of course, he was out of his tree if he thought I would actually take him up on it. He wasn't even in the ballpark when it came to being as hot as any of the Wolf Venom guys.

He nodded and strolled out the door as though completely un-worried and unhurried.

"Well, he's a fucker," Penn remarked. "To be honest, I've always thought so."

"I've never known you to be anything other than honest," Zeke told him. "You're a hundred percent right, he is a fucker."

"I see what you mean," I told Asher. "He seemed like he was trying to be nice and then, bam." I could hardly believe he'd blatantly threatened Zeke the way he had. Maybe I shouldn't be surprised, given the kind of people these were.

"Yeah, his family doesn't really do nice," Asher said. "They do pretend nice and then they threaten to kill you."

I stepped over to Zeke and wound my arms around his neck. He was so tense and stiff with anger. I wanted to soothe it away if I could.

"Would they really do that?" I asked softly. "Try to kill you?"

He put his arms around me and rested his head on my shoulder. "They might if they realised I'm never going to give in and go back. They can try though, but they're not gonna succeed. I meant what I said to him. I also have contacts. We're talking last resort shit here, but I'll do what I have to do to keep myself and all of you safe."

Asher stepped to the side of us and put his arms around us both. "I'll do whatever I have to do too."

Tully slipped over to the other side and also embraced us. "Me too."

"I'm always up for a group hug," Landon said.

"I am too," Channing agreed.

They both surrounded us and gave us all a big squeeze.

On some unseen signal, we all turned and looked over to Penn.

"What?" He sighed through his nose. "Fine. Whatever happens, I'm in too."

He squashed in between Asher and Landon and somehow we all managed one big hug.

Let them throw things at us. We had each other's backs and nothing was going to tear us apart.

CHAPTER
SEVENTEEN

ASHER

"IS it wrong that seeing you pin Caleb to the wall was hot?" I grinned over my shoulder at Zeke and stepped into the hotel room.

"It was hot." Abbie kicked off her shoes and pulled the tie out of her hair. She shook her head until it fell to her shoulders, smooth except the kink her tie left behind.

Zeke shrugged and closed the door behind us. "He gave me the shits. He's lucky I didn't shove him through the wall. I was fucking tempted."

"We're rock stars, aren't we supposed to trash rooms?" I asked jokingly.

"Only hotel rooms," Zeke said with a laugh.

"Have you ever trashed a hotel room?" Abbie sat down on the edge of the bed and started to rub her feet.

"No. That would piss the label off," Zeke said. He pulled off his shirt and threw it over into the corner.

I sat beside Abbie and admired all of his muscles and tattoos. He really was a work of art. They both were.

I turned to her, pushed her back gently and caught one of her feet in my hands. "Let me do that."

She placed her hands behind her head and let out a soft, relaxed sigh. "I'm not going to argue with you. I feel like I've been standing for a week."

"At least the concert went well." Zeke sat beside us wearing only his boxers. He grabbed Abbie's other foot and started to massage her toes.

"When is it not?" She rolled her head to the side to look at him. "Serious question, you guys must have played a bad gig at some point in your lives?"

"The high school talent show was pretty bad." I pressed my thumbs into the arch of her foot. "We played with a bunch of guys who..." I stopped to choose my words carefully. "Let's just say they're not playing music anymore. We were pretty terrible."

"We didn't get chased off the stage." Zeke grinned, looking like a seventeen year kid again.

I chuckled. "That's true. Remember—what was his name? Orlando? He was trying to juggle and kept dropping the balls everywhere."

Zeke cocked his head at me. "I thought that was the act. He was supposed to drop them and look funny."

I frowned. "Now you mention it, you might be right. I hadn't thought about that."

I rubbed Abbie's toes one by one, then moved up her foot and onto her ankle and calf.

"That feels so good," she groaned.

I grinned and worked my way up higher until I slid my hands up her short skirt and massaged her thigh. Zeke was only a few centimetres behind me.

She raised her hips to undo her skirt and pushed it down. Zeke and I both grabbed the waistband and tugged it down her legs and off over her feet.

She pulled off her own shirt until she lay between us wearing panties and a white, lace bra so sheer, a hint of nipple blushed though.

"If I saw that before the concert, I wouldn't have been able to focus," Zeke said.

"Same here." I kissed the inside of her knee, and slowly licked my way up higher.

Halfway up her thigh, I stopped to pull off my shirt and threw it aside.

I was pleasantly surprised when Zeke unfastened my jeans and helped me out of them.

He must be feeling bolder now. How bold might he get?

I kept on kissing my way up the inside of Abbie's leg, until I was able to run the tip of my tongue over the gusset of her panties.

She shivered deliciously.

I hooked my fingers under the waistband of her panties and slid them down her hips.

"Thank you." Zeke lowered his face between her thighs and teased her pussy with his tongue.

"Any time." I dropped her panties to the floor and scooted up to her side. She twisted her upper body so I could get my hands behind her and unhook her bra. I pulled it down her arms and tossed it over my shoulder.

Then, because fair's fair, I scooted down to help Zeke out of his boxers. His cock was already so hard, I couldn't help but run my tongue over his tip. I watched his face for his reaction. Was it too much, too quickly?

He lifted his glistening mouth off Abbie's pussy and gave me a heated glance.

Not too much then. Shit yeah.

I lowered my mouth onto him, taking as much of his length as I could fit. I had only done this once before, with a guy whose name I couldn't remember now. I'd thought about doing it to Zeke approximately a bajillion times.

His cock did not disappoint.

Neither did the way he rolled his hips as I sucked and lightly massaged his balls with my fingers. Curious—they felt like mine, but different at the same time. His might be a little longer but mine were wider.

Either way, they felt amazing.

Abbie groaned as Zeke slurped at her pussy. Every sound made my own cock harder and harder, begging to be touched. I could fondle myself, but I waited.

Seeing them both enjoying themselves was even more of a turn on than being touched.

Abbie's hips rolled harder as she cried out as she came.

Was there a more beautiful sound than someone you loved having an orgasm? I couldn't think of one.

Zeke lifted his face and smiled. He was obviously thinking the same thing I was.

"You're overdressed," he told me.

I took my mouth off him and glanced down at my boxers. "So I am." I went back to sucking.

"I hate to interrupt," Abbie said with a laugh. "But I'd like it if one of you would fuck me."

"Asher has a spare cock," Zeke said.

I took my mouth off him again before I choked on a laugh. "You make it sound like I have two of them. I mean, what I have is big enough for two."

Neither of them disagreed with me.

Sweet.

I wriggled out of my underpants and threw them aside.

Zeke gave me a speculative look.

"Whatever you're thinking, the answer is yes," I said immediately.

"You don't know what I'm thinking." He cocked his head and raised an eyebrow. He was so stinking cute.

"I bet I do." I glanced in the direction of the lube which lay on the table beside the bed.

Before he could respond, I straddled Abbie's hips and lowered my mouth to hers in a deep, intense kiss.

"I heard a rumour," I said between kisses, "that you need to be fucked." My cock certainly needed to do some fucking.

"You heard right," she said breathlessly.

"You've come to the right place." I gently pried her knees apart with mine and pressed my cock into the mouth of her pussy. Even that tiny touch of wet heat was like throwing alcohol onto a raging fire.

With a grunt, I pushed deep into her.

Her back arched. "Yes, fuck, yes, just like that."

She let out a moan so heady she drove me straight to the edge of the cliff. I had to take a moment and pull myself back before I came too soon. I wanted to savour every second of this. Make it last as close to forever as I could.

Finally, I couldn't hold myself back any longer, I started to pound into her with firm, smooth strokes. "Fuck, you feel good."

In the corner of my eye, I saw Zeke reach for the lube. My heart raced even harder.

It was getting more and more difficult to keep from coming.

It was even more difficult when Zeke placed a tentative, lubricated finger on my rear hole. Lightly, gradually getting more confident, he spread the lube around.

He tossed the tube aside and swallowed audibly.

"Are you sure?" he whispered.

I didn't know if he was checking in with me, himself, or both.

"I'm sure if you are," I told him. "Take your time." I wanted everything he had to give, but only if he was ready to give it.

"Okay." His voice was rough with desire, laced with a touch of nerves.

Slowly and carefully, he pressed the tip of his finger inside me.

"Is that all right?" He sounded like he would pull it right out at the first sign of my discomfort.

Funny how he could be violent and hot, and then a few hours later sweet, considerate and hot.

I glanced over my shoulder. "It's more than okay, babe. I want...all of you, if you're ready to give it."

I wanted nothing more in the world than to have my cock inside the woman I loved while the man I loved had his cock inside me.

He didn't say anything, but he put his hands on my hips and pressed something hard against my ass. I knew it wasn't any of his fingers, because they were gripping me and trembling slightly.

His cock pressed a little harder, until the tip slid inside me.

I tensed a little and stopped still to let my muscles get used to having him there. Bit by bit, they stretched and relaxed, allowing his thick heat to slip in further.

I thrust into Abbie, then pulled back out and slowly pushed myself onto him. My muscles stretched more, taking him deeper and deeper.

The sensation of having him inside me, while being seated inside her was like nothing I ever felt before. My balls might explode with how good it felt. It was... The most all encompassing sensation I ever had.

He groaned. "Holy fuck."

Those would have been my words if I was capable of speaking right now. I wasn't, at least not with words. My whole world was all about sliding my cock in and out of Abbie, and feeling Zeke's cock filling me more and more. Finally, he sank all the way into me and started to thrust slowly.

Holy gods. I was ready to see stars a few universes over already.

Leaned forward as I was, I brushed my chest over Abbie's nipples with each stroke. They quickly became hardened peaks, all perky and cute.

I fucking loved her nipples. Hell, I fucking loved all of her.

And all of him.

"You two are killing me," I said. "In the best way possible."

"You're pretty epic yourself," Zeke said. "And so fucking tight."

That sent a shiver of pleasure and delight through me, and made my balls hurt like they might burst.

I was almost certain he'd done anal with plenty of women, so it was nice to know I could hold my own against them. Of course I could, I was me. Or something like that anyway.

I gritted my teeth.

I tried not to come, but when Abbie groaned and came, she forced the orgasm right out of me. I couldn't hold it back any longer.

Almost in harmony we grunted and groaned, driving each other to heights that stole coherent thought and oxygen from my body.

Just when I thought it couldn't get better, Zeke came too, filling my ass with white hot cum.

The grunt of pleasure he gave would have made me come if I wasn't in the middle of an orgasm already. As it was, it lasted longer and ran deeper than ever before.

Almost as one, we sagged and flopped down onto the mattress, cocks sliding out of holes, air sucked back into lungs.

I ended up in the middle of the two most gorgeous people in the face of the planet.

"Are you both good?" I asked once I managed to remember how to speak.

"I am," Abbie said. She stretched her arms above her head.

"Yeah," Zeke said.

He sounded a little... I don't know, off? Not bad, just not quite himself.

I rolled my head to face him. "Are you sure? If that was too soon for you—"

He looked back at me, contemplative rather than upset, thank fuck.

"It wasn't. I just need a minute to get my head around it. I've never screwed another guy before."

I smiled softly, trying to mask the concern I'd pushed him away by moving too fast.

"I'm honoured to be your first."

"I'm glad it was you," he said. "I don't have any regrets, in case that's why you look so worried."

"That obvious, huh?" I should have known he'd see straight through me. He always did.

"I'm glad you don't. I don't either. In fact, I can highly recommend fucking your girlfriend and your boyfriend at the same time."

He grinned. "Hashtag relationship goals."

I grinned back. He might need to work up to doing that, but he seemed willing to try. There were a whole bunch of things I would like to try with both of them, if we could work up to it.

"You know what else is awesome?" Abbie said.

"I turned to face her. "What?"

"If both of your boyfriends fuck you at the same time. But first, I need a shower. Who's with me?"

CHAPTER
EIGHTEEN
ABBIE

"YOU'LL BE FINE," Zeke assured me.

I resisted the urge to either look down at my feet or run away.

I might still do both. I hadn't decided yet.

"What if I'm not fine?" I said. "This is a huge deal. If I do this the wrong way, I could end up getting hurt."

Yeah, what was new? These days, I was living my whole life on a knife's edge, a step away from either the end, or something amazing.

"What if Levi Jones wants to see me so he can break the contract?" I asked.

"You've met him before," Asher said. "You know he's a huge fan of yours. The tour has been going perfectly. There is absolutely no reason to think he's going to break anything. If anything, he is probably planning to bring forward the release date of your new album. Strike while the iron is hot and all that."

I groaned. "Don't say that. That fills me with even more anxiety and pressure. It's nowhere near ready. It's going to take months. I'll probably have to rerecord a lot of it."

Zeke put his hands to either side of my face and turned me to look me in the eye.

"That's bullshit and you know it," he said. "You've made albums before. You could probably do it in your sleep. You know Levi, he would never bring the date forward, or even think about doing it, unless everyone involved was absolutely convinced it was ready. That includes Candy, and I know she's a big fan of yours too. Now, are you going to jump?"

"Yeah, jump. Or get out of the way," Penn said.

I looked down at the water about twenty metres below the rock we stood on. "Are you sure this is a good idea?"

"Of course we do," he said. "We come here every time we're in Queensland. Apart from the concerts, it's the highlight of the tour. This part of it anyway. Would we bring you up here if it wasn't safe?"

"Maybe," I said doubtfully.

All of the guys laughed. Even Penn. To my surprise, he hadn't suggested pushing me off the rock. Yet.

"Okay, but you have to go down with me," I said.

As Zeke grinned. "I'm always happy to go down with you and *on* you." He slipped his hand into mine.

I felt someone take my other hand and turned to see Tully beside me.

"I could use some support too," he said. "I'm scared of heights."

"Really?" I asked. "Big, bad rock god like you?"

He shrugged one shoulder. "Really. We're all afraid of something. Landon is scared of spiders."

Landon shuddered. "Because they're horrible. All those legs wiggling and shit." He wiggled his fingers in the air.

"I don't like small spaces," Channing said.

Asher sighed. "I don't like centipedes. Same thing about wiggly legs. I don't think Zeke is scared of anything."

"I'm scared of accidentally ripping Reuben's head off and living in peace once and for all, but I don't think you'd call it a phobia. More like a fantasy."

I snorted a laugh and glanced sidelong at Penn. I didn't think he would tell me what he was scared of, if he was scared of anything.

He grunted and said, "I fucking hate clowns."

"Yeah, I think that's pretty universal," I said. "They are horrifying."

"Sure are," he said. "Are you gonna jump?"

I sucked in a breath. "Okay, on the count of three?" Zeke and Tully nodded.

"One."

"Two."

"Three."

They both squeezed my hands and we jumped. It felt as though we fell for days, before we plunged through the top of the water and down into the blue depths.

I managed to keep hold of both guys' hands until we bobbed up, laughing and gasping for air.

"That was fun!" I shouted.

"Look out!" Asher shouted. He tucked his arms around his knees as he jumped and landed like a bomb a few metres away.

Water washed over us and I let out a squeal.

"Asshole," I told him when his head appeared above the water.

He grinned. "You know you love me."

He was right, I did. One of these days I would find the right chance to tell him that. Not yet though. I still needed to figure out where I stood with all the other guys and where they stood with each other. Until then, I would be careful not to break their hearts or my own.

I wanted to be absolutely certain about the present, much less the future, before I took any more plunges into deep water.

I adjusted my bikini top, which had somehow managed to stay on even after the jump, and blew him a kiss. He would have to be content with that for now.

I turned and started to swim back towards the beach. Before I got more than about fifty metres, I stopped to watch Penn and then Channing and Landon jump. The bassist and the saxophonist jumped hand in hand, but Penn did a perfect, smooth swan dive.

Of course he had to do it better than everyone else. He always seemed like he had something to prove.

It seemed right to applaud him when he came back up for air.

He gave me a glance, but I couldn't tell if he was pleased or annoyed at the attention.

Rather than stick around and wait for him to scowl at me, I swam back to the beach. I stepped out onto the sand and picked up my towel to wind around myself.

"What is it with Penn?" I asked Tully who had followed me out of the water. The others seemed content to stay in and splash each other, or body surf.

"He always seems to... I don't know, try to be better than everyone else. Like he feels as if he has to try really hard."

Tully picked up his own towel and started to dry his hair. "Uptight upbringing," he said. "His parents had certain expectations. I think he puts those expectations on himself. Or he just wants to be the best version of himself he can be."

"There's nothing wrong with that, I suppose." I sat in the sand, pushed my hat onto my head and pulled out my sunblock. "He could try being a nicer version of himself."

Tully laughed. "There's nothing with trying to be better, unless you drive yourself crazy doing it. You want me to do your back?" He held out his hand and I handed him the sunblock.

I leaned forward while he rubbed it all over my back and shoulders. "Thank you. I'll do yours when you're finished."

Like the rest of the guys, he was tanned, but you can still get badly burnt even with a tan. I wouldn't be much of a girlfriend or even a friend if I didn't do what I could to stop him from being in pain. Plus, I'd get to touch him with slippery lotion.

Win-win.

"So what are you scared of?" he asked. "Up there on the rock, we all shared our fears. What's yours?" He quickly added, "You don't have to tell me if you don't want to."

"I don't mind," I said. "It's pretty obvious I'm scared of failure, but I don't think that counts. That's kind of an artificial fear brought about by past assholes."

"Totally understandable," he said. "I would also understand a newfound fear of cardboard boxes."

"That too," I winced. "Especially with body parts inside them." I took the bottle from him and scooted around behind him to apply the lotion to his back.

"I'm scared of needles," I said finally. "I know they're necessary at times, but they freak me the fuck out."

"Don't want to sleep for a hundred years?" he asked teasingly.

I snorted. My hand made a wet slapping sound when I lightly socked his back.

"I meant medical needles. I'm also not very fond of knitting needles, because I have absolutely no finesse for creating things like that. Before you say it, I also don't like pins and needles."

He chuckled. "Who does? Where do you stand on pine needles?"

"I don't mind them, as long as I have shoes on," I said. "Why do I always end up having weird, silly conversations with you guys?"

"Because we're weird and silly?" Tully suggested. "Isn't that what you like about us, or am I stretching here?"

"It's one of the things I like about you," I said. "There are lots of other things too."

"Such as?" he asked.

He was fishing for compliments but I decided to take the bait and let him reel me in.

"I've never felt so included before," I admitted. "I've never felt as much a part of something as I do with you guys. Not just *something*, but something *special*. Also you guys are funny, talented, hot and when I'm around you I feel like a goddess." I couldn't be much more honest than that.

"You are a goddess," he said softly. "I know for a fact we would have found you one way or another. The universe decided it, probably a million years ago. And here you are. That probably sounds even weirder than talking about needles, but I believe we all have a place in the universe and the universe just had to help us find it. Even if it takes a million years."

That was an intense concept. A million years of dust ending up right here on this beach.

"Those are some long-term goals right there," I said. "But I like it. I love the idea that the universe always intended me to find you guys."

"Even Penn?" he asked teasingly. "I shouldn't joke. He is definitely part of the universe's plan for all of us. No one could be given as much talent as he has for no reason. We might not know the reason, maybe ever, but there is one."

"I didn't realise you were so spiritual." I finished his back and put the cap back on the bottle of sunblock.

"I have a variety of interests," he said. "Mostly I'm a big believer in understanding the universe and ourselves. Listening to our bodies, paying attention to what our senses tell us, things like that."

That made sense. We all had times in our lives where we ignored ourselves, whether it was our bodies telling us to slow down, or our instincts telling us not to jump into things.

"Zeke and Asher mentioned you were into..." How did I even put this? "Blindfolds and things like that," I finished tentatively.

He moved around to sit cross-legged on his towel in front of me. "I'm into increasing what the senses feel, to better appreciate stimuli. Sometimes that includes blindfolds. Sometimes it includes feathers and paddles. It helps to move past the day-to-day and appreciate everything our bodies have to offer us."

He sounded like a meditation guru, but his tone was so casual he could have been talking about last week's cricket match. I'd seen him watching one, so I knew he enjoyed the sport.

After a moment of reflective silence, he added, "Sometimes that also means understanding that pain can bring pleasure. And so can giving pain. Does that scare you?"

"Not nearly as much as needles do," I said. If anything, I was intrigued. Okay, more intrigued than I already was.

"Would you show me some time?" I asked.

He grinned. "Of course I will. I know a place in Perth. I'll take you when we get there, if you like. But I should warn you, it can be a very mind opening experience. Everything might seem boring afterwards."

He wiggled his brows and I got the feeling that was his way of saying he was going to ruin me for all the other guys.

I doubted that, but he was certainly welcome to try.

CHAPTER
NINETEEN

ABBIE

"HEY, I hear things are going good." Levi Jones looked every bit the modern businessman. Long hair tied back in a manbun, worn out jeans and an old T-shirt. He wasn't much older than me but the success of White Wolf Records meant he had a lot more money than I did.

He had a lot more money than all of us. No one could argue he hadn't worked for every cent of it.

"So far," I agreed. The vibe at the weekend long TideFest music event, where Wolf Venom were playing on the Saturday night, was a little strange though. Maybe it was the heat of far North Queensland, or maybe it was my imagination. The crowds seemed a little on edge.

Nothing out of the ordinary happened so far, just the occasional fight and underage drinking. Security had those in hand before they escalated.

Apart from that, the audience was receptive to Friday night's acts, which had gone on late into the night. When they'd stopped singing, the crowds hadn't. They danced and sang and had a good time until the last of them finally crawled into their tents around dawn.

For the most part, I'd stayed behind the scenes with the guys, hanging out with the other bands and solo acts. I was still fangirling over meeting the legendary Rock Dragons, who had come all the way from the east coast of the United States just for the event.

All of them were so nice and even took selfies with me. Yeah, I felt like a total groupie except without throwing myself at any of them. From what I could tell, they all had wives or girlfriends anyway, even if I wasn't busy with my guys. If they were the kind to cheat, they weren't my type anyway.

"Thank you for believing in me, Mr Jones," I said sincerely. "I appreciate it so much. I don't even think I can express it."

He grimaced and took a sip of beer straight out of the bottle. "You can start by calling me Levi. Mr Jones makes me sound like I'm sixty years old or something." He smiled to show he wasn't actually offended.

"Levi," I corrected myself. I could relate. I didn't like being called Ms Hart, or Abigail all that much. Both were too formal for me. Better than *washed up bitch*, but still…

"Candy tells me good things about your upcoming record." He waved me toward a couple of camp chairs which were recently vacated by members of Blazing Violet.

I sat and tried not to smile at the quaint way some people in the industry still referred to them as records. Although, lots of albums were still being produced in vinyl record form, the same way some books were produced in hardback. People always liked their collectible forms of art. There was nothing wrong with that.

"I'm pretty sure she could make a singing potato sound good," I said. "Thank you for the vote of confidence though. With her, it's super easy to want to do even better, you know? She gave me a couple of pointers, which made a huge difference."

"If anyone could make a singing potato sound good, it would be her," Levi agreed. "I wish I could find a singing potato. I have a feeling that would make me a rich man." He laughed.

I joined in with him. "I have a feeling you're right. I wonder if they would sing the theme song to MASH."

He laughed even harder. "They probably would, and they'd be good fun at a roast."

I groaned. That was a dad joke worthy of Zeke.

"They'd probably wear skinny jeans and spend all day hashing things out instead of getting boiling mad," he continued. "The only other potato-related pun I can think of is chip, and I can't think how to put that in sentence."

"You could always *not* put it in a sentence," I said with a laugh. "Sometimes you just have to give up when the chips are down."

He put up his hand and I gave him a high five.

"You win that pun-off," he said.

I took a sip from my water bottle. "If I'd known we were having a competition, I would have tried harder."

He looked at me like he was trying to work in another pun, but I was out too, unless I could figure out how to add fry into the conversation.

"Anyway, so far everyone at the label is impressed with you." He leaned back in the chair and crossed his legs like he was sitting in an executive meeting and not in a makeshift backstage area. He looked like he would have been at home just about anywhere.

I envied him that. Would I ever feel that comfortable in my own skin? The guys were certainly going a long way to getting me there, but I still had a long way to go.

"I'm impressed with everyone at the label," I said. "You've brought together such a good team. Everyone is so professional and friendly."

He seemed pleased at the observation. "That was what I was going for. Somewhere relaxed and comfortable, where people are happy to turn up to work each day and work ridiculously long hours. Personally, I can't think of a more rewarding career than working in music. I'm privileged to have had the opportunity to work with people like you and Wolf Venom, the Rock Dragons, and Blazing Violet. The insane amount of talent blows my mind on an hourly basis. You all put your faith in me as much as I put it in you. I am truly honoured and humbled. I know that probably sounds a bunch of bullshit, but it's true."

"It doesn't sound like bullshit to me," I said. "You're right. A good, solid working relationship goes both ways. If you signed the wrong people, your business wouldn't be so successful."

"Exactly," he said. "I've heard some singers who practice a song so much they sound incredible, but if you throw something different at them they sound like a turtle being strangled."

I almost choked on a sip of water. "I hope I don't sound like that."

He grinned. "You wouldn't be here if you did. Unless of course the listening audience wanted that sound. Stranger things have happened." He spread his hands to either side.

"That's true," I said with a laugh. I would never judge anyone for their taste in music, but plenty of it wasn't my thing. Fortunately, most of it was, or I could at least appreciate it for its artistry.

"So, how are the boys treating you?" he asked. "I realised it might have been a big ask to send you on tour with them. They can be a handful. So can their groupies. They tend to gather wherever the guys go." He didn't seem to be concerned or passing judgment, just stating a fact.

"The boys are certainly a handful at times," I agreed.

As for groupies, I noticed them hanging around, especially outside the stage door after concerts. None of the guys seemed remotely interested in any of them. Not even Penn, who had no real reason to turn them down. I had no strings tied to him, even though I wanted to.

"Nothing I haven't been able to handle." I watched his face, trying to gauge his response to my comment. Did he know about my relationships with the guys? Or Zeke and Asher's relationship? Would he care? As long as it didn't interfere with the band, then I couldn't see why he would have a problem with it.

On the other hand, people often had unexpected ideas about things. Levi Jones might be chill, but he was also a businessman. If he thought something would interfere with the label, then he would have something to say about it.

"Good," he said with a nod. "They're an interesting group of boys. Maybe more so than any of my other bands. They've certainly been through a lot."

"So I've heard," I said carefully. "I think everything has brought them closer together. I don't know that I've met another band that got along as well as they do. I mean, they have their moments, like everyone else, but they come together at the end of the day." Sometimes literally.

"What doesn't kill you makes you stronger," Levi said. "You're also proof of that."

"Unfortunately, that's also true," I said. "You heard about what happened to Vance?"

So far, I hadn't heard anything about Calista. At some point, that was going to drop like a bomb. I wasn't looking forward to it. I hoped like fuck Rose would give Asher some warning before it happened so we could brace ourselves. Otherwise, we would just have to weather the storm when it came.

"I did," Levi said. "It couldn't have happened to a bigger piece of shit."

I blinked in surprise. I agreed with him but I hadn't expected him to say that.

"Um. I mean..." I stammered. "It was all very tragic..."

He snorted with absolutely no mercy whatsoever. "I'm sorry for what his family is going through, but if you have to use a talented, beautiful artist because you aren't talented enough to make it on your own, then you're a stone cold asshole. Okay, maybe he didn't deserve to be murdered, but he deserved an ass whipping."

"I can't argue with that," I said with a sigh. "The thing was, he was talented. He was just impatient to get further along in his career."

Levi leaned forward. "If anyone on my label did what he did, I wouldn't just tear up their contract. I would make sure they ended up back where I found them. I have no time for people who step on other people to get their way. This industry is a bitch, and it is difficult to get ahead, I acknowledge that. But if you're going to be a shit person, then you have no business being successful as far as I'm concerned."

He sat back. "I'm sorry, that came off as forceful. I'm a big believer in nurturing talent and letting people grow into their own."

"Some people are saying that sending me on tour with Wolf Venom is a fast track," I said, again speaking carefully. I hoped I wasn't shooting myself in the foot by being so candid.

"That is also bullshit," he said firmly. "You were already on track, you didn't need a shortcut. I wanted you to join this tour to spice things up a bit. Which is exactly what it did. Okay, sure, it give you additional exposure, which is good for you and the label. But no one stepped on anyone else on the way. In fact, it's been good exposure for Wolf Venom as well. And Blazing Violet. I prefer to think of it as a mutually beneficial arrangement."

"I hadn't thought of it that way," I admitted. Now he mentioned it, the extra publicity wouldn't have hurt the guys, it would have helped them. And Violet and her band too.

"That's why I'm the boss," he said with a grin. "It's my job to think of shit like this. Me and my executives. So you guys can make the music and wow the ticket-buying audiences, and we think up ways to get them to part with more and more of their money. It seems to be working pretty well for everyone, I think."

"I think so too," I agreed. "Thank you. I don't mean to sound like an artist with a fragile ego, but it's nice to have some validation once in a while." Not just from the audience, but from someone who put his reputation on the line by signing me after all the shit I had gone through. "You don't regret signing me?"

He looked surprised, but then chuckled. "Not for a second. Not yet anyway. Why? You're not planning to jump ship are you?"

I snorted. "No fucking way. You're stuck with me. Unless I start to sound like a turtle being strangled. Or a singing potato."

"Good, because White Wolf has no plans to let you go any time soon. Even if you're not an actual singing potato." He grinned.

CHAPTER
TWENTY

ABBIE

"THE CROWD IS TWITCHY," Blaise said as he and the rest of Blazing Violet stepped off the stage. "I don't think they're here to hear us."

In fact, thousands of people who attended the festival, were standing in front of the stage chanting, "Venom! Venom! Venom!"

I peered out through the flats that made up the wings of the stage. "Maybe I shouldn't go out there. It's you guys they want."

Honestly, it sounded like they were ready to tear the place down if they didn't see the guys shortly. *Really* shortly.

Zeke put his hands on my shoulders and started to massage them. "You'll be fine. Go out there, do your thing and they'll settle down."

"They fucking better," Penn growled. "I'm not going out there if they don't. Fuck that."

"Scared of the audience?" Asher asked, teasing lightly.

"Not usually," Penn said. His eyes flicked toward the stage uneasily. "I just don't want to be out there if they start shit."

Neither did I, but when the MC announced me, I sucked in a breath and nodded to myself. I had performed at plenty of events like these before. All I had to do was step out on the stage and sing. Nothing I hadn't done a thousand times before.

"Here goes nothing," I took a step forward, but Asher stopped me. He gave me a quick but searing kiss on the mouth.

"That's for luck. Not that you need it. Go out there and slay them." He patted me on the ass, then gave me a gentle shove out onto the stage.

I turned back long enough to shake my finger at him, then headed over to the microphone. I didn't even get that far before the audience started to boo.

Okay, I was hoping for a warmer reception than that, but I could deal with it. Like Zeke said, I needed to start singing and I would be fine.

I took the microphone out of the stand.

"Get off!" someone shouted.

"Homewrecking bitch!" someone else shouted.

"We want Venom. We want Venom. We want Venom!"

Someone even shouted, "Murderer!"

Fuck. I'd had tough crowds before but this one—

I didn't see anyone throw anything until a sharp pain blossomed through the side of my face and my vision went dim.

"Fuck, get her off the stage!" someone in the crew shouted.

Something warm trickled down my face and someone put an arm around me, but it was all a blur amidst a rain of cans and plastic bottles landing on the stage.

"It's okay, we've got you." That sounded like Zeke's voice. He scooped me up off my feet and carried me off stage to the sound of the audience jeering and shouting insults.

"Fucking hell," Asher said. He crouched beside me as Zeke lowered me to the floor.

I was vaguely aware of him pulling off his shirt and pressing it to the side of my face.

"Someone get the ambos," Zeke said. "And some ice."

"I'm okay," I murmured. I realised that was blood running down my cheek. Someone threw a motherfucking can at my face. A full one, by the feel of it.

"No you're not," Zeke insisted. "I'm no doctor, but you're bleeding."

"Yeah, it looked nasty to me," Asher said.

"I'm not going out on that fucking stage," Penn declared.

"Usually I would suggest you think about someone other than yourself, but in this case I agree with you," Zeke told him. "Is security onto whoever threw that? And the rest of them? Until they've hauled their asses out of here, none of us are going out on stage."

People were talking and running around, but the pain was slowly starting to fade.

"Abbie?" Tully sat beside me and stroked my hair. "You're going to be fine. Think about our date in Perth. We're going to have an amazing time."

"I'm not going to die," I muttered. "It fucking hurts though."

"I know it does," he said soothingly.

"They grabbed the guy," Channing said. He flopped down beside me. "They're dragging him out right now. And a bunch of other people."

"Yeah," Landon agreed. He knelt beside Channing. "It's getting ugly out there. Some people are trying to stop security from dragging them away. They're talking about cancelling the rest of the festival."

"Why do a handful of people have to ruin it for everybody else?" Asher complained. "Most of the crowd was great, it was a handful of people stirring everyone else up."

"Oh my God, what happened?" Violet sounded breathless, as though she'd run back from wherever she and the rest of her band went after their set.

"Assholes started throwing cans and bottles," Zeke growled.

"Fucking hell," that was Levi Jones. He sounded even angrier than Zeke. "Where the fuck are the organisers? I'm going to rip off some heads and—" He stomped away.

I almost felt sorry for the organisers, but if people were out there making trouble, they should have removed them the day before. Honestly, they shouldn't have let me go out on stage if there was that much animosity. I should have listened to my instincts and stayed offstage. If I had, everyone would be rocking out to Wolf Venom right now.

"The ambos are here," Channing said.

"About fucking time," Zeke growled under his breath, although only a couple of minutes had passed. The organisers would have had an ambulance on-site for emergencies and injuries like mine.

The guys, except for Asher—his hand was still on his shirt pressed against my cheek—moved aside to let the ambulance officer crouch down beside me.

"Hi, I'm Dave, what's your name?" He sounded cheerful, like he had done this a million times before. He probably had.

"Abbie," I replied "It's a Saturday. We are at TideFest."

"No concussion then," Dave said. "I'm gonna take a look at your face. Okay?"

He peeled off the shirt and I winced.

"You have a nasty gash, but I've seen worse." He poked around a little bit. "No need for stitches but I'm going to put a bandage on there to contain the blood and help the skin to knit." He reached around in his bag before cleaning the gash and placing gauze and an adhesive bandage over the top of it.

"Is that going to leave a scar?" Landon asked.

"Are you hoping it will or hoping it won't?" Asher asked.

I was wondering the same thing.

"I dunno," Landon said. "On one hand, scars are cool. On the other hand, Abbie might not want a scar on her face."

I didn't, but I could have had much worse if the can hit a little higher. I could have been knocked unconscious, or worse. Thank fuck they banned glass bottles from events like this. One of those would have hurt like a bitch.

"There you go," Dave said. "Just so you know, I was looking forward to hearing you sing. Big fan. Now, I hate to love you and leave you, but if things get messy out there, I'm going to be needed."

Asher helped me sit up, but I leaned against him because my head spun a little and ached.

"Thank you," I told Dave before he left.

He nodded, rose and hurried away.

Levi reappeared a couple of minutes later. "The organisers are confident they weeded out all of the troublemakers, but they're going to put extra security in the crowd for the rest of the event. It was that or cancel the rest of it." He sucked in a loud, furious breath.

"I refused to let any of you go out there without some sort of measures in place. It's bullshit that it's come to this. People come to these events to enjoy themselves, that includes the fucking acts."

He shook his head in frustration, then crouched beside me. "Are you okay? I'm just about ready to sue the organisers over this. No one should get out there on stage and be the target of projectiles."

"I'm fine," I said quickly. "No need to sue anyone."

He glanced up at Zeke. "They're lucky they didn't throw a bottle at you. They'll be arrested and charged with assault, but at least they'll get out of it alive."

I was wondering if he knew about Zeke and Asher's families, but that comment confirmed it.

"If they threw it at me, I would have picked it up and smashed them over the head with it," Zeke said bluntly. "If I was on stage and saw who did it to Abbie, I would shove it up their ass until it came out their throat."

"You'd have to get in line." Asher said. "I haven't ruled out finding out who they are and doing exactly that."

"Only if you want your contracts torn up," Levi growled. "In this case, let the law deal with it. I'll make sure they get everything that's coming to them."

"It sounds like you guys need to get ready to go out on stage," I said. The audience was gearing up again, albeit a bit more subdued now.

"Are you up to joining them?" Levi asked.

I blinked in surprise, then winced when it hurt. My face would probably be a mess of bruises for a week or two. Thank God for makeup.

"I'm not sure the audience wants me out there." I sure as hell didn't want to be the target of things being thrown at me, whether they were bottles or insults. As it was, videos of me being struck in the face were undoubtedly going viral already.

The press were going to love every minute of this.

Fuck.

"A few assholes didn't," he agreed. "But me and the boys want you out there. And so does the majority of the audience. It's your choice, but if I were you I would show them you're not going to let a few dickheads hold you back. You haven't let them stop you yet, have you?"

"For the record," I said slowly, "offering me a challenge like that is totally unfair."

He grinned. "Good. Then get up and go out there and give them hell."

I sighed and let Asher and Zeke pull me to my feet. "Are you sure this is a good idea?"

"This is a great idea," Zeke said. "We'll be right beside you the whole time. If anyone tries anything, they'll have to go through us first."

"They might do that," I muttered. "I need to change my shirt." Mine was covered in my blood. I ran a hand over the side of my hair. I would need to rinse that as well. Some of it was matted together.

"I need a shirt," Asher said. His was also covered in my blood.

"Do you?" Zeke asked him. "Do you really?" He managed to grin.

Asher grinned back. "Technically, no, but it wouldn't be fair to the other men in the audience to have my body on display like that. Just think how busy the ambos would be with fainting women."

"You have a point," Zeke said. "We wouldn't want anyone getting hurt because of your hotness."

We both gave Asher long, heated looks. Personally, I wouldn't mind seeing him play all shirtless and sweaty. People would probably pay good money to see that. And he would be worth every dollar.

Penn snorted.

"Send someone down to get a couple of band tees from the merch stand," Levi said to one of the festival volunteers. They nodded and turned to run off.

Only when they were out of sight, did Levi swear under his breath. "I should have specified Wolf Venom T-shirts. Hopefully they'll figure it out."

I laughed softly and winced. Singing with a bandage on my cheek was going to be interesting, to say the least. I hoped this wasn't a bad omen for the rest of the tour.

In the back of my mind, I hoped even more that this had nothing to do with Zeke's family, somehow causing trouble this far away from Sydney. If they got desperate, they might try anything. Including injuring me to cause trouble for Zeke. Or to serve as a warning for us all.

CHAPTER
TWENTY-ONE

ABBIE

IN THE END, I only sang one song with the guys before bowing out.

In spite of maybe but probably not having a concussion, my head was still spinning and I needed to hunt down something for the pain.

At least Asher looked cute in a bright purple Wolf Venom T-shirt. Mine was an interesting shade of green.

The audience was much nicer the second time around too. They gave me a resounding applause when I stepped back out on the stage, and clapped when I left.

I found the first aid station easily enough. After they made a fuss and checked my already bruised face, they gave me some pills for the pain. I snagged a water bottle and flopped down in a camp chair backstage.

From here, I could sit back and enjoy watching the guys perform. They and the audience were having the time of their lives now. Considering all the drama, that was just as well. They came so close to missing out entirely. That would have been a shame for everyone.

Levi grabbed up another camp chair and sat down beside me. "Are you sure you're okay?" he asked over the music. "I can have someone drive you to your hotel if you want?"

"I'm fine." I took a swig of water and swallowed the second pain pill. "It's mostly my ego that's bruised. I'm used to people throwing accusations, but not cans. I don't know which is worse."

"Neither is okay." He still looked furious it happened at all. "I want to apologise. I should have liaised with the organisers better. What happened out there was completely preventable. No one— No one should step on that stage with any risk to their personal safety."

"Every time we step out there, we're risking something," I said with a shrug. "We all have bad days."

"In theory." He sucked in a breath and visibly forced himself to relax. He turned toward the stage and took a few moments.

Without looking back at me, he said, "I don't think I've ever heard these guys have a bad day. Not on stage anyway. I heard about Jonah."

He didn't even change his tone before he added that last bit. Because of that, it took a moment for his words to sink in.

"Oh?" I asked slowly. How much did he know? My heart started to race like crazy. Was I about to get in a shit load of trouble?

He turned to give me a look like he was suppressing an eye roll at me for trying to play dumb. "He waved a gun at you and Zeke and ended up in a cardboard box."

"Ah." Apparently he knew everything. Perhaps that shouldn't surprise me, but it did. "How did you—"

"Jackson told me." He jerked his head in the general direction of the band's manager, who stood a few metres away, talking on his phone. "Nothing goes on within my label that I don't hear about sooner or later."

"So… you know there are similarities between that and what happened to Vance," I said. Sweat sprang up on my palms. "I had nothing to do with either of them."

If he didn't believe me, I was screwed. A sliver of panic wormed its way into my mind. Had he sat with me to tell me he was breaking my contract? Or calling the police? Or—

To my relief, he said, "I know you didn't." He crossed his legs at his knees. "You need to be careful. If someone is targeting you, we don't know if or when they might escalate."

I sat around the chair. "You think they might come after me?" I hadn't thought of that. I'd assumed they were trying to scare me. I hadn't considered I might be the target of a killer. Now I thought about it, I wished I hadn't.

"I would suggest that a person who leaves heads in cardboard boxes is probably not entirely sane," he said. "That being the case, you don't know when and where they might become more unhinged. Jackson said the guys have been making sure you're not left alone. I think it would be a good idea to keep doing that until we figure out who's behind this."

"Yeah, I guess so," I agreed reluctantly. I didn't want to be a burden to anyone, but the guys didn't seem to mind acting as my bodyguards. They all looked good doing it.

"I know you're an independent woman." He must have guessed at the reason for my reluctance. "But your safety is important to me. To the boys too, from what I've seen." He gave me a knowing look.

Yeah, I wasn't even slightly surprised he knew about that too.

"Is that a problem?" I asked. Some bosses didn't like their employees getting involved with each other, but this was a different situation to working in an office. The average label didn't have much say over their acts' personal lives. That didn't mean he didn't have an opinion.

"Not at all," he said lightly. "As long as it doesn't create drama. I like my label drama free."

"Good idea," I said dryly. I wished Onyx Riot had the same philosophy.

"Of course it is." He smiled smugly. "I'm happy to take credit for it."

I laughed. "You have plenty of good ideas you can take credit for. Like signing the boys." My gaze went back to them just as Channing began a saxophone solo.

"That's certainly one of my better ideas," Levi agreed. "Jackson tells me—"

Whatever he was going to say was interrupted by a loud voice speaking behind us.

"Of course Abbie will want to talk to me, we're old friends," Poppy Newton was saying.

I groaned.

"Fuck," Levi growled. He pushed himself up from the chair and he and Jackson both stepped towards the journalist.

"Who let her in here?" Jackson demanded.

"You took the words right out of my mouth," Levi said. "Security—"

Poppy smiled ingratiatingly at them both. "I won't take long. I just thought Abbie would like to address what happened on stage earlier."

"Are you following me?" I narrowed my eyes at her. "Shouldn't you be in Sydney annoying people?"

She clicked her tongue. "Don't be like that."

If there was a more annoying phrase, I couldn't think of it. I could be however I wanted to be. Right now that was pissed off.

"Someone threw something at me and got arrested. I'm fine. The end." I shrugged.

"You also got booed and had accusations thrown at you," she said smoothly. "Would you like to comment on those accusations?"

"No she wouldn't," Jackson snapped. "One of those is ancient history and the other is an ongoing police investigation. They've already ruled out her involvement, as you would be well aware if you've done your homework. Now, I suggest you leave before security removes you by force."

"Now," Levi added, if Jackson's words didn't have enough impact on the woman.

Poppy smiled over at me sweetly. "Which of these men are you sleeping with?"

If she thought she would take me by surprise, she was mistaken.

I laughed.

"Neither of them." I knew she was also referring to the band, but my answer was technically correct. Levi and Jackson were both attractive guys, but my hands were full enough as it was. Besides, neither had shown that kind of interest in me. They were both more like big brothers than potential lovers.

I thought about asking who she seduced to get in here in the first place, but I decided not to lower myself to her level. Let her deal in sleaze, I would get on with my life.

A couple of security people stepped to either side of her and one gestured toward the doorway. "This way please."

"Until next time," she said over her shoulder before she was herded away.

Jackson scrubbed his face with his hand. "That woman is a fucking menace. Her and people like her. And people who read the shit she prints."

"She is a fucking vulture," Levi agreed. "The organisers are going to need to lift their game for next year if any of my bands are going to take part. No one should be coming backstage to harass any of the acts." He pulled a cigarette out of his pocket that looked like more than tobacco. "Excuse me, I need a smoke after all that."

He held out the joint towards me. "Do you want to join me?"

"No thank you." I waved a hand in refusal. "I've never been much of a fan. I'll have a few drinks later on, when the guys are finished playing." And if I was lucky, a few orgasms as well. Both of those things would go a long way to relieving my tension.

"Jax, keep an eye on her." Levi nodded towards me, then headed outside, in the opposite direction from which security took Poppy.

Jackson nodded and sat in the camp chair Levi had vacated.

"Jax?" I hadn't heard anyone call him that before.

He shrugged. "Levi and I go way back. He's the only one who gets away with calling me that."

I raised my hands in surrender. "I wasn't going to do it. I think it's cute he has a nickname for you. People who've known me for a long time call me Abs." Ironic since now I seemed to be surrounded by guys with lots of abs.

"I'm sure they do," Jackson said. He looked like he had something else to say, but was trying to figure out how to approach the subject.

Finally, he said, "Tully told me what happened in Melbourne." He looked towards the floor, then back at me. "I'd like you to know you can come to me and tell me these things too. At some point, somebody is going to ask a question about something I don't know anything about. I need to know what's going on so I'm not caught off guard."

"Like Poppy Newton?" I asked.

"Exactly," he said. "I understand it's a difficult thing to talk about."

"Yeah, it is." How would I even start that conversation? Hey, Jackson, we found another head. Don't worry, we dealt with it with the help of Asher's sister. It's all good now.

I had a feeling he was suggesting I say just that.

"This doesn't bother you?" I asked. "I mean..." What did I mean? "People around me keep turning up dead. That's got to be disconcerting." I told him what Levi said about the killer possibly coming after me.

"It's a scary as fuck," he agreed. "That's why we're all keeping an eye on you and each other. We only get through this if we work together. Okay?"

I felt like he was telling me off, but he was right. If someone was after me, then I needed to trust the people who were trying to keep me safe. Likewise, they needed to trust me to keep them safe. I might not have big muscles, but I could punch and kick if I had to.

Plus I knew which way to point a gun now. That might come in useful someday.

"I'm sorry I didn't come to you and tell you," I said. "The next time I find a head..." I groaned. "What am I saying? I hope there *isn't* a next time. They might be finished making whatever point it was they were trying to make. Or maybe they got all that murder out of their system."

A girl could hope, right?

"I hope there isn't a next time too," Jackson said. "But we can't make any assumptions. We shouldn't relax until they catch whoever is doing this."

He rubbed his hands over his face. Managing a band and me was enough work without this thrown in on top of it. This must all be above his pay grade.

Hell, it was above mine.

"That could be hard when the police only know about Vance," I said.

"That's true," he said, "but his murder should give them enough clues to figure out who did it. Unless..."

"Unless what?" I didn't like the sound of that.

"Unless they're a professional," he finished.

"You mean hired by Zeke's family?" I suggested. "Zeke already ruled out Reuben's involvement, since Jonah worked for him."

"There's also Asher's family," he said.

"His sister helped us," I argued. Why would Asher's family come after me anyway? Unless this wasn't about me. If that was the case, then what was it about?

"That doesn't mean she isn't involved. Or that Dane isn't. I'm not necessarily saying they are, just that we can't rule out anything right now. With any luck, we won't see anything from them ever again."

"You don't believe that?" I asked.

He hesitated for a moment, then shook his head. "No, I don't. Just be careful and if you see anything weird, tell me. Okay?"

"Okay," I agreed. If I wasn't on edge before, I sure as fuck was now.

CHAPTER
TWENTY-TWO

ASHER

"IS THERE a chance your family is involved with whoever is killing those people?" Abbie asked.

"Did Poppy actually turn up backstage?" I asked at the same time.

We both snort-laughed.

"You go first." I sat back in my seat and crossed my arms over my chest. It was going to be a long bus drive back to Brisbane, for the flight over to Perth. We might as well get comfortable.

"Jackson suggested the possibility of a professional leaving those... gifts," she said. "Zeke said it wasn't his family. I'm wondering if it might be yours. I don't know why they might come after me, but I don't know them like you do."

I scratched my forehead. "Me either. Dane and Rose like you. I can't think of anyone else who might be involved, unless they're trying to fuck with Zeke. Who the fuck knows why these people do what they do?"

"Not me, that's for sure." She sighed. "I don't suppose there's any chance I pissed off the Bell family somehow?"

"Shit like this is definitely their style," I agreed. "I can't see it though. Hunter and Parker might have put Lila up to getting herself and her family involved, but I doubt it. They wouldn't risk pissing off Reuben by killing Jonah or going behind his back. If the family went after the Brantleys, they would go after Reuben, not hang around on the fringes trying to annoy Zeke. My money is on someone who isn't a professional. It's too sloppy for that."

"Sloppy?" she echoed.

"Yeah." I shrugged. "Anyone could have found them. Vance wasn't anywhere near the others. It's inconsistent. Not that I'm a detective or anything. I've just watched them on TV a few times."

She shook her head and smiled. "I'm sure that makes you an expert."

"Absolutely," I agreed. "In that case, I'm an expert on a shit load of things. Especially sex."

"Is that your way of telling me you watch a lot of porn?" She raised a perfectly shaped eyebrow at me.

"I wouldn't say a lot," I replied. Enough, but not recently. Why watch it when you can be doing it instead?

"You didn't answer my question about Poppy. How did she get backstage?"

"I have no idea." She stopped and frowned in thought. "Maybe she's the one doing it."

It took me a moment to realise what she was getting at. "You think she might be the one leaving those *gifts?*"

"She turned up here, a long way from home," Abbie said. "For all I know, she's getting paid to stalk me." She sighed out her nose. "I don't know, maybe I'm paranoid."

I hoped so, at least where Poppy Newton was concerned. If she was involved, then she wasn't working alone. She wasn't big enough to wrestle Jonah or Vance, much less cut their heads off. The killer had to be a man, or be working with a man.

I didn't tell her any of this; she was freaked out enough as it was.

"I think Poppy is out for money," I said slowly. "She might go a long way to get a story, but killing is extreme. Her career would be over if she was caught."

"Not just her career," Abbie said. "What if she was trying to pin it on me and get the scoop on it? Breaking a story like that would *make* her career."

"If that's the case, then I hope she gets the mental health care she clearly needs," I said. "Because that would be all kinds of fucked up."

"It really would," she agreed. "I suppose talking about it isn't going to get us anywhere, is it?"

"It's better than keeping your thoughts bottled up," I said. "I get you're scared."

I slipped an arm over her shoulders and pulled her to me as best I could with the seatbelts getting in the way. "I wish I knew who was doing this so I could end them."

She leaned her head against my chest. "You mean that literally? You would personally kill them?"

I couldn't tell if she was scared or turned on by that idea. Hopefully turned on.

"If I have to," I admitted. "There's nothing I wouldn't do to keep you safe and happy. There's nothing any of us wouldn't do." I waved a hand around the bus and the guys nodded. Most of them.

"I have a limit or two," Penn said.

"What a shock," Abbie said sarcastically. She waved a hand at him before he could retort. "I don't expect you to do anything because of me. Any of you. I certainly don't expect you to do anything illegal."

"You might not expect it, but that doesn't mean it wouldn't happen." I grinned. We all lived our professional lives totally above board, but our personal lives toed the line once in a while.

She shook her head at me. "I don't want you to get arrested doing anything to keep me safe."

"I won't," I said. "They'd have to catch me first. I'm sure you noticed, some of us have families who know exactly how to get us out of the shit before things get too far. "

"But at what price?" she asked. "Zeke going back to his family? You going back to yours?"

"Whatever the price has to be," I said firmly. "We're not losing you. Whatever happens, we'll deal with it. Together. Okay?"

She sighed. "Okay. I just... I hope you don't regret anything. That's all. I feel like I've turned all of your lives upside down."

Penn turned his face, but for once kept his mouth shut.

"Yes, you have," I told her. "In the best way possible. Firstly, we got to meet you, and you are incredibly special. Secondly, Zeke and I would be best buddies until the end of time if you hadn't helped us to open our eyes to each other."

I looked across the aisle at Zeke and smiled at him. I could hardly believe we made that step. I'd have to write a song about how I felt, because I couldn't put it into words or even coherent thought. Everything changed and it was all for the better.

He smiled back. "What Asher said. Being best buddies wouldn't be so bad, but I like this more." He reached across the aisle to put his hand over mine.

"Me too," I said.

Channing and Landon gave a shout. I jumped and I looked back over my shoulder. They were both leaning over, looking out the window.

I sat forward and tried to figure out what they were looking at.

"Smartass." Beside us, in a bright red Porsche, with the top all the way down, was Levi Jones. He wore a leather jacket and sunglasses and probably looked cooler than I did right now. Honestly, he looked cooler than any of us did right now.

He waved over at us and revved the engine. He had the biggest smile on his face.

"Is he trying to race the bus?" Abbie asked with a laugh.

"It certainly looks like it." As bosses went, Levi was a long way from the suit wearing, stick up the ass kind, that was for sure. We all smelled weed on him more than once, and apparently now he wanted us to take part in an illegal race on the highway.

The man was a fucking legend. He probably had a woman with her face in his lap as well, because why not? If anyone could get away with it, it would be him.

The bus driver revved the engine in response, but the old girl wasn't up to going much faster than she already was. She was certainly not going to contend with a Porsche, no matter how much we wished it would.

"He totally makes the rest of us make sense, doesn't he?" I asked. "I mean, he's obviously insane and so are we."

Tully, Landon and Channing were all standing up and waving their arms out the window at Levi. It was like being on the school bus back in high school or something.

Abbie shook her head. "Insane might just be the right word, yes. At least everyone is having a good time doing it."

I looked from the window to her. She'd taken the bandage off her face already, revealing a hell of a bruise. The mark from the can was starting to heal. I didn't think it would leave a scar.

At this point, I didn't know who was luckier, her or the idiot who threw the can. If she was badly hurt, I would have hunted him down and badly hurt *him*.

What sort of prick throws things at someone on stage, especially a woman?

If you want to throw things, take up a sport, or at least throw things at people who deserve it. Like that Poppy Newton bitch. I wished I was there backstage when she appeared. I would have given her a one way ticket out of the venue, on the end of my foot.

"Awww," the other guys groaned in disappointment.

Levi accelerated and pulled his Porsche away from the bus. In a minute or two, he was completely out of sight.

Ironically, he'd likely only get back to Brisbane a couple of minutes before us, but he had to do it in style.

"I'm starting to think you guys are just overgrown boys," Abbie said.

I raised my eyebrows at her. "Oh? You hadn't realised that already?" A slow grin crept onto my face. "I thought that was what you liked about us." I pouted playfully.

"It is," she said. "You guys know how to have fun, no matter what you do. I hope you never stop doing that."

"If we do, you have my permission to smack my ass and remind me to keep having fun," I said. "Actually, you can smack my ass anytime." I looked over to Zeke. "That goes for you too."

"I might just take you up on that." He gave me a speculative look and a slight eyebrow wiggle. Fuck, he was so hot, that look made my cock hard.

Of course, now my mind was racing in about fifty different directions, all of them to do with being sweaty and naked with Zeke and Abbie.

When she was lying on the ground with blood on her face, I heard Tully mention plans for a date in Perth.

I knew exactly what that meant and I was all for it, but I wondered how that would change our dynamic.

Hopefully for the better. I was here for it.

CHAPTER
TWENTY-THREE

ABBIE

"WE'VE GOT to go to Gate Twelve," Zeke said.

We arrived at the airport just in time to catch our flight to Adelaide.

A lot of acts, especially international ones, never made it to South Australia, or Western Australia.

Personally, Perth and Adelaide were two of my favourite places to perform. Maybe because concertgoers appreciated actually getting to see someone for a change.

With any luck, they'd build a large venue in Canberra, so we could perform there as well. The capital of Australia missed out on a lot of acts, but there wasn't anywhere big enough for an act like Wolf Venom.

What they had was fine for someone like me, but the guys needed a bigger capacity. Otherwise they'd play every night for a year to fit everyone in.

"For once, I'm glad to have interviewers waiting for us," Landon said. "It's a long fucking drive from Brisbane to Adelaide. We've done it a few times before."

Honestly, under any other circumstances, I would have travelled with the cars and vans, but the guys weren't going to let me out of their sight. When they had to fly, so did I.

Was I arguing with that? Hell no.

"At least we don't get to miss the joy of driving over the Nullarbor plain from Adelaide to Perth," Asher said with a grimace. "Kilometre after kilometre of absolutely nothing."

"It's a good chance to catch up on naps," Channing said.

"You mean it's a good chance for us to listen to you snore for hours on end," Penn told him.

Channing grinned. "It doesn't bother me."

Penn snorted. "Of course it wouldn't? You're asleep at the time, dumbass."

In spite of his words, a hint of a smile on the corners of his mouth showed he was teasing.

If he wasn't, Channing wouldn't give a crap anyway. He knew Penn well enough not to take anything he said too personally.

I shook my head and smiled as they bickered with each other. They wouldn't be them without razzing each other every chance they got.

Zeke slipped his hand into mine. That earned us some curious and even jealous looks from people who passed us by and recognised the guys.

If they only knew the half of it.

"I haven't had a chance to talk to you properly since the festival," he said. "I've been trying to think what to say."

He paused for a moment, looking regretful and angry. "I should have been on stage with you. Or closer than I was before any fucking cans started to fly. I'm pissed off at myself. I screwed up. I'm sorry for letting you down."

I looked up at him as we walked. "Zeke Brantley, none of that was in any way your fault. You're not my babysitter, or my bodyguard, and you can't stand right next to me on stage every time I step out there, in case something happens." I wouldn't put it past him to try.

"If you're going to do that, I might as well not step out there at all. Or I'll have the staff erect a Perspex shield so I can stand behind that while I perform." That wouldn't be weird *at all*. Yeah, fuck that.

"That might be a good idea." He looked thoughtful.

I poked him in the chest. "I'm not performing behind a wall. I'd prefer not to perform at all. I could take a flight back to Sydney right now." I turned and took half a step in the opposite direction.

He pulled me back to his side and tucked me firmly against his hip. "You're not going back without me, and I'm under contract so I can't go back. You're coming with me if I have to tie you up and carry you over my shoulder. Actually, that's a good idea."

He stopped walking and pretended to lower his shoulder to lift me up onto it.

I took a real step back. "Don't you fucking dare." I pointed at him with a finger of my spare hand, then shook it a few times under his nose.

"Fine, I won't, but don't pretend you're not coming with us." He tugged me towards the gate.

"Of course I'm coming with you," I said. "But stop blaming yourself for what happened. It's not your fault. It's the fault of a handful of assholes who will probably be banned from events like that for life." They wouldn't get any sympathy from me. Whatever they got, they deserved it.

"Whether or not it's my fault, I'm gonna keep being salty about it for a while," he said.

"Zeke is good at taking things to heart," Asher said. "It's one of the things we love about him. He's broody and intense, and protective. And ready to belt the shit out of anyone who crosses us."

"I've noticed that about him." I smiled up at Zeke. "It's definitely part of his charm."

"Only a small part," Zeke said modestly. He gave us both a lopsided smile.

"Yeah, that's what Zeke needs," Penn said sarcastically. "A bigger mother-fucking ego. You know they can't take the top of the plane off to fit your head in it if it gets any bigger."

Zeke grinned. "If it can fit your ego, it can fit mine."

Penn groaned while the rest of us laughed.

Asher patted him on the shoulder. "You walked right into that, Penny."

"Fuck off," Penn told him. Again, he looked like he was trying hard not to smile.

I wondered if his face would crack if he actually did. It might, or he might look even more attractive than when he scowled. Would I ever get to find out? I hoped so.

"We probably need a bigger plane for all of our egos," Tully said. "They're pretty healthy."

No one argued with that.

We stopped at Gate Twelve as they started to board everyone onto the plane.

The attendant paid more attention to our boarding passes than they did to any of us. Hundreds and hundreds of people walked past them every day. Plenty of them more famous than any of us.

At least, more famous than me.

We were waved through the bridge and onto the plane. Predictably, the guys herded me into the middle seat of the side with three seats. Asher sat on the window and Zeke sat on the aisle. Channing and Landon sat behind us and Tully and Penn sat in front.

"You know they're going to want to interview you too, right?" Zeke asked.

"What?" I blinked at him. "Jackson said they wanted to interview you guys."

He shrugged one shoulder. "They're still going to want to talk to you."

"And you're telling me this now because the door to the plane closed and I can't get up and run away?" I raised one eyebrow at him.

He grinned. "Do I seem that devious to you?"

I raised the other eyebrow at him.

"Ouch, you wound me, woman." He pressed a hand to his chest over his heart.

"I'm just getting started," I growled playfully.

"I'm sure you are." He lowered his hand. "For the record, I thought of it as we sat down. You would have come to the same conclusion in a hot minute. We're touring together and people are curious about you after all the things they've heard. Without doubt they'll want to ask about the festival. If they didn't know who you were before, they will now. Who wouldn't be interested in someone who tried to catch a can with their face?"

While he smiled, I socked him in the chest.

"If I tried to catch it, I would have done a better job of it than that," I told him. "Even with my face."

I lightly touched my cheek. It only hurt a little bit now. The concealer I applied this morning covered the bruising so no one would know it was there, even if they looked close. Keeping myself from flinching at anything heading toward my face, that instinct would last a while longer.

"As much as I would like to see you catch a can with your face, I won't suggest we try that," he said. "Unless you want to introduce it as part of your act. In which case—"

I turned to Asher. "Do you think they would let us throw him out at a hundred thousand feet?"

Asher looked thoughtful, but his blue eyes shone with mischief. "I don't know, we could ask. Do we want the parachute included in this special offer or just a shove?"

"Ha fucking ha," Zeke said sarcastically. "Neither of you would push me out of a plane. You both love me too much." He gave us both an intense look that spoke volumes about the way he felt.

"We certainly wouldn't push you out of a plane," I agreed. I was going to add something nice, maybe even admit that I did love him.

Asher spoke before I could.

"No, we wouldn't, because if they opened the door it would depressurise the plane and we would all die."

"At least I would take you with me," Zeke said.

"How about you fucking don't," Penn said over his shoulder. "I'm too young and hot to die." And he said Zeke had an ego. His was certainly equally robust. With good reason, admittedly.

"Yes you are," Asher told him. "So am I."

"We all are," Landon called out from behind us.

The plane jolted and started to taxi towards the runway.

A little flutter of nerves passed through me. Partly at the prospect of another city and more concerts, partly at the idea of interviews. And partly at the idea of getting closer to Perth and my date with Tully. Added to that the idea of talking about the festival and the worry of whoever was stalking me might be following right behind us.

The list of reasons to have nerves seem to get longer and longer every day.

To think, a few weeks ago the only thing I was worried about was going on tour and getting my career back on track. Now everything seemed so much more complicated. Some things, like my growing relationships with the guys, were amazing, but the constant need to look over my shoulder sucked hairy donkey balls.

Would I have embarked on this journey if I'd known what I was getting myself into?

I thought about that for a moment and realised the answer was easy. It was a resounding yes, with a nice long chorus and an even longer bridge. Even with the shadow of a killer hanging over us, I wouldn't have missed any of this for the world.

Like Tully said, we were always meant to find each other. I believed that with my whole heart. One way or another, we would have met up and connected.

I didn't know why we were set on such a difficult path, but we would travel it together and we would come out the other end stronger than ever.

In the back of my mind was the lingering thought that we had to survive it all first. When I looked to my left and my right, in front of me and behind, I was surrounded by six muscular, intelligent, protective guys. I couldn't be safer.

I may not sing behind a wall, but I was surrounded by one. A big, badass wall of smoking hot muscle. If the universe put me through all that shit so I could end up here with them, then maybe the universe was looking out for me after all.

I really was one lucky fucking girl. Wasn't I?

CHAPTER
TWENTY-FOUR

ABBIE

THE PLANE LEVELLED off and the *fasten seatbelt* light went out. Because I didn't want to formulate to fuck with me again, I left mine on just in case. The guys all unbuckled theirs and reclined their seats as far as they would go.

Except for Asher. He looked over at me with a smile on his face.

"What?" I knew that look and I should probably know better than to ask.

He leaned over closer to me and whispered in my ear. "Have you joined the mile high club?"

Heat crept up my neck and onto my face that was less a blush than a pulse of excitement.

"No," I said. "Have you?" Wait, did I really want an answer to that? I didn't care about their past sex lives, but I didn't necessarily need specifics.

Instead of answering, he asked another question. "Do you want to?" He put a hand on the top of my thigh.

I looked around. "I don't know. Would we get in trouble?" They couldn't throw us off the plane, but they could turn it around and leave us back in Brisbane.

He grinned. "Nah, it'll be fine. Come on."

I glanced back at Zeke.

He also grinned. "Go on, have fun. There's not enough room in there for three anyway."

I leaned over to kiss him lightly on the mouth. "You're the best."

"Fuck yeah, I am." He slipped on the headphones provided by the airline and started to groove to whatever music was playing through the system. Probably Wolf Venom.

I undid my seatbelt and followed Asher through the aisle of the plane, to the tiny toilet. I didn't dare to look back over my shoulder to see if anyone was watching us. If there was, there would be no doubt as to what we were up to.

It crossed my mind that someone might take a photo and that would be the next thing about me to go viral, but I couldn't bring myself to give a shit anymore. It might be a welcome distraction from people talking about throwing cans, and stray heads.

"This is definitely a tight fit." Asher pressed me back against the sink and slid his hands up my shirt and across my stomach.

"Yeah, they really could make these a bit more spacious," I said. "With room for a shower and a bath. Maybe a king-size bed."

He chuckled. "I'll be sure to insist on a private jet and not a commercial flight next time."

"You do that." I ran my hands over the front of his pants and felt his cock harden under my touch.

He had more influence with the label than I did. On the other hand, sure Levi Jones drove a Porsche, but he wasn't made of money. Not yet.

I undid the front of his pants and worked them down far enough to free his erection. I curled my fingers around his cock and stroked him a few times.

"Mmmm." He pushed himself deeper into my hand and rucked up my skirt. He pulled the front of my panties aside and slid the tips of a couple of fingers down my seam and over my clit. His other hand went down my leg until he gripped my thigh and pulled up my knee to open me out to him.

We worked each other for a couple of minutes until we were both breathless and I was as wet as fuck.

"I need you inside me," I whispered. Between his touch and the vibration of the plane, I was feeling wobbly at the knees. I leaned back between the sink and what little wall there was and let him hold me in place while he positioned his cock outside my pussy.

"Abbie," he said softly. "Fuck, you are amazing." With almost teasing slowness, he slid his full length into me.

I groaned in pleasure at how full he made me feel. I forgot the close surroundings and lost myself in the moment.

While his hands were busy holding me in place, I reached up with one of mine to massage my own nipple through the fabric of my shirt and bra. Then the other one.

"That is fucking hot," he said. "Would you rub your clit for me?"

His words were almost enough to make me come on the spot, but I slipped my hand down between my legs and started to trace slow circles around my clit.

"That's my girl," he whispered. He thrust in and out of me slowly, his stomach nudging my hand every time he drove in deep.

"This was a good idea of yours," I said.

"Hell yeah, I agree." He was already panting and his voice was ragged.

I wanted to tell him I loved him, but the time wasn't right. I didn't know why but it wasn't. When the time came, I'd shout it from the rooftops.

Instead, I said, "I'm going to come."

"Mmm, please do. I'll be right behind you." He thrust a little harder.

"How about you come at the same time as me?" My breath was just as ragged.

"Like, on the count of three?" He grinned.

"I don't think I'm that disciplined," I said breathlessly. "That might be something we can work on."

"Absolutely." He looked at me through half closed eyes. "I want to teach you to come on command. That will be fun when you're out on the stage."

I started to laugh, but it came out as a moan.

"Don't you dare." That would be...interesting. If no one knew it was happening, it could be fun. I put that into the 'maybe' pile to think about later.

I closed my eyes and rubbed myself a little harder, while I bucked my hips in unison to him. I gripped his upper arm with my spare hand and dug my nails into his skin as I came.

He came at the same time, thrusting harder and breathing heavily.

Holy shit, there was something particularly hot about hearing someone orgasm while you're in the throes of one yourself. It made me come again, just as I was coming down from the first one. The second one was deeper, more intense and possibly involved fireworks, rainbows and a meteor shower or two.

When I came down fully, I was a panting, weak kneed mess of deep satisfaction and a whole lot of wet, sticky cum.

"Oh yeah." Asher leaned his head against the wall for a minute or two before he slid out of me and let my leg back down. "Welcome to the club, baby."

"You too," I said, since he hadn't answered the question about it earlier.

He smiled and kissed my mouth, brushing his tongue over my lips and teeth.

I kissed him back, then reluctantly pulled back and said, "I need to get cleaned up."

That began a couple of minutes of awkward shuffling around the tiny space, but we finally got sorted out and unlocked the door.

I hoped to sneak out without anyone paying much attention to us, but the minute we stepped out the door, the plane erupted into applause.

I clapped a hand over my face, which was burning hot and probably fire engine red, and hurried back to slip into my seat.

I didn't even peek out from between my fingers to see if anyone was videoing us. They probably were. Wasn't that the point of phones? To video people doing things and sharing it with the world later? People could get away with anything these days. That was both a blessing and a curse.

Oh well, I would deal with it if it went viral. I had, after all, made my bed by going in there with him in the first place.

Asher, being Asher, grinned and raised his hands to accept every piece of attention. He slipped back into his seat looking like the cat that got the cream.

People definitely took photos and videos of him doing his walk of fame. It wouldn't do his reputation any harm.

I shook my head and resisted the urge to grab a blanket and put it over my face for the rest of the flight. I should have realised we'd be noticed, and maybe even overheard. I wished I dared to own it the way he did. Maybe someday.

"That was some wild turbulence." Zeke looked happy Asher and I got to have that time alone. Giving his blessing and being okay with it could have been very different things.

Lucky for me, both of them were so accepting and open. There didn't seem to be a drop of jealousy between them. Not even when it came to the other guys. What did I fucking do to deserve to even meet these beautiful boys? Whatever it was, it must have been really good.

Really, really good.

I frowned at Zeke. "There wasn't—" I realised he was teasing. I slapped him lightly on the chest. "You're such a brat."

He laughed. "I'm sorry, I couldn't resist."

"You don't sound sorry at all." I looked at him through narrowed, but playful eyes.

He just went on grinning and looked over the top of the chairs. "Looks like you came just in time for lunch. That was lucky. There would be nothing worse than going hungry while getting your fill."

I decided to ignore his puns. "Good, I'm hungry." There was nothing like sex to work up an appetite. I couldn't argue with his turn of phrase either. I did get my fill. Asher had an impressively thick cock.

"Me too," Zeke said. "And this is an almost three-hour flight. There's plenty of time for an extra snack later, if you're feeling up to it."

"It wouldn't go unnoticed if I went in there with two different guys on the same flight," I remarked.

"That's true," he agreed. "If people are going to talk, we might as well give them something interesting to talk about."

"Maybe," I said slowly.

Who was it that said fame is a bitch? If we were absolute nobodies, no one would care what we got up to.

No, I wasn't that naïve. Either way, it would end up on social media and people would talk. I could imagine the names I'd get called, whereas the guys would be thought of as heroes.

Fucking double standard.

"Let's eat first and think about the rest of it later." I wasn't going to lie, the idea of screwing Zeke on board the plane was very appealing, even without the king-sized bed.

Okay, the idea of fucking him anywhere was hot. I couldn't get enough of him or Asher. I was looking forward to figuring out a few things with Tully too. And the other three guys.

Was I turning into some kind of sex fiend or something? I was thinking about it a lot more than I ever had before. The more I got, the more I wanted.

I was one hundred percent here for every bit of it.

In the back of my mind, I was scared about what the future would hold. Not just worrying about killers and people throwing cans, but what would happen when the tour was over? Would we be forced to go our separate ways? Would the guys all forget about me and move on to other people?

The idea was like a wrench around my heart, twisting it almost to breaking point.

I didn't want to live my life separately from the guys and I didn't want to move on with anyone else. Somehow, I was going to have to find a way to broach the conversation with each of them. I needed to know what they wanted and what they needed.

I hoped to hell what they wanted and needed was me.

CHAPTER
TWENTY-FIVE

ABBIE

"THAT JOURNALIST WAS NICER than Poppy Newton," Tully remarked as we walked out of the studio together.

"That wouldn't be hard," I said dryly. He was right though. Xander Riley was much nicer than Poppy and a shit load more respectful. He wanted to talk to me, but he only asked about the can and if I was okay. He seemed genuinely concerned that someone would throw things at a performer on the stage.

He asked what my thoughts were on preventing future incidents like that.

All I could say was to suggest security remove any troublemakers as soon as they could, and provide lots of bins for empty cans. What else could they do? They could ban cans, cups and bottles altogether, but people would go thirsty and go home.

As much as I'd like to prevent anyone else from getting hurt, greater measures would only ruin the fun for those who were there to have a good time.

I told him that as well. The last thing I wanted to do was rain on anyone's parade.

He nodded at that and turned his attention to the guys, and I got to sit back and relax.

He didn't ask any hard-hitting questions, but it was nice to listen to the guys answer the ones he did ask. Mostly they were about their favourite songs, the process of writing songs and any highlights of the present tour or past tours.

There wasn't one question about anyone's personal life or their sex life. If anyone noticed Asher and me coming out of the plane toilet, it wasn't mentioned.

So far, nothing surfaced. With any luck, it wouldn't.

"Did Jackson give him a list of questions to ask?" I walked between the guys as we headed to our hotel. It was a nice day and only about ten minutes away.

Spending time being normal like this was a refreshing change to the crazy pace we had the last couple of weeks. And the crazy pace we would have after the Perth concerts. Once we left Australia, it would be go, go, go for the next couple of months.

I was looking forward to it, but I'd also appreciate this downtime. I mean, any chance I got to be with the guys was a bonus as far as I was concerned.

"Probably," Asher said. "But Xavier doesn't deal in sleaze and bullshit anyway. His angle is the light, fluffy stuff. His job is to make us look good so we'll talk to him again. It's a mutually beneficial arrangement."

"That makes sense," I said. "I would be happy to talk to him again. That was much less stressful than I thought it would be." I wished all journalists were like him. Light and fluffy was something I could get behind all day every day.

Zeke hung an arm over my shoulders. "See, you have nothing to worry about. And if you did, we would have kicked his ass."

"I appreciate that," I said. "But I don't think that would have gone down very well."

"Not as well as you and I on that flight," he agreed.

I grinned. I still couldn't work out exactly how we'd managed that, but we had. We even got another round of applause afterwards. I might have even given a small bow to the plane full of people. Honestly, a few of the women look at me like I was a hero. That was a refreshing change. I much preferred that to being treated like a slut.

"It's a shame we're driving over to Perth," Asher said.

Zeke hung an arm over his shoulders as well. "Luckily rest stops are a thing."

We were all smiling and laughing as we walked through the front doors into the hotel.

We managed to make it up to the sixth floor in the elevator without anyone fucking anyone else, and stepped out into the corridor that led to our rooms.

"Who brought the extra suitcase?" Asher asked.

"The what?" I looked questioningly at him, and then down the corridor.

Sure enough, a small suitcase with the handle slightly raised, was parked outside the door to the room I would share with Zeke, Asher and Tully.

I stopped mid-step. "Please tell me suitcases aren't the new cardboard box."

Zeke approached it carefully. "There's no tag on it, so it didn't come on the flight with us. It's possible one of the roadies left it here, thinking it was ours."

It certainly looked like one of the suitcases the tour staff travelled with, but they weren't any different to the average suitcase you could buy from just about anywhere.

"Is it ticking?" Asher asked.

"Not that I can hear," Zeke said. "We should take it in and have a look."

I didn't like that idea, but the alternative was worse. Mostly, that meant leaving it there for someone else to find.

"It's probably got someone's spare underwear inside." Asher pulled out his key card and unlocked the door.

Zeke picked up the case by its handle and carried it carefully inside. We all piled into the room before Asher closed the door behind us.

Zeke crouched beside the suitcase and, with a look of fierce concentration on his face, gripped the zip and wound it around so the case opened.

"That was what I was afraid of," he said.

"What?" I asked.

He opened it all the way.

My stomach turned at the sight of Poppy Newton staring back at me. Even dead, she seemed to be accusing me of something.

"Fucking hell."

Asher slipped an arm around me. "That must have come here via the rest of the tour luggage. So whoever did that stashed it with the rest of the equipment—"

"Or the killer is a part of the tour," I finished for him.

SESSION

SAVING ABBIE BOOK 3

Holding On
Written by Tully Cole

And any way you spin the words,
    You can't help hearing yes.
    But there is never long enough,
    To tell me all the rest.

I'm holding on,
    Barely holding on.
    Saving time, for you.
    I'm holding on,
    Hardly holding on,
    To the one I never knew.

Time is an illusion,
    You know it never ends.
    But the start is no beginning,
    The healing never mends.

I'm holding on,
    Barely holding on.
    Saving time, for you.
    I'm holding on,
    Hardly holding on,
    To the one I never knew.

The choices you told me,
    The race to the lie,
    It will never be over,
    For you and him and I.

I'm holding on,
    Barely holding on.
    Saving time, for you.
    I'm holding on,
    Hardly holding on,
    To the one I'll never know.

CHAPTER ONE

ABBIE

"ON THE UP SIDE, she's quiet this way," Asher remarked. "She can't ask any stupid questions."

"Yeah, that's the takeaway here," I said.

The band and I were sitting in a hotel room in Adelaide, nearly at the end of the Australian leg of the tour, looking at the disembodied head of tabloid journalist Poppy Mawson. The last time I saw her, she managed to get back-stage at the festival in far North Queensland, just after I got hit in the face with a can. The band's manager, Jackson Beckett, and the owner of the label, Levi Jones, had security remove her.

Things got a little heated, but not so out of hand that I expected to see her like this.

Asher shrugged. "I'm not wrong."

"Can we stop Asher from making stupid comments?" Penn asked from where he stood near the window.

I didn't know if he was standing guard or trying to keep apart from the rest of us. Maybe both. Of all the guys, he was by far the touchiest.

I ignored Penn's comment and looked over at Zeke. "Please tell me you know a guy."

His family was basically Australian mafia. If anyone could clean up this shit, it would be them. Same with Asher's family.

Zeke shook his head slowly. "Not in this city, no," he said regretfully. "We'll figure something out."

A knock at the door made me jump so hard I wouldn't have been surprised if I hit my head on the roof.

"Jesus fucking Christ," I said under my breath.

"Landon, see who it is," Zeke said to the rhythm guitarist.

The younger guy nodded and bent to look through the peephole. "It's Jackson."

Zeke only hesitated for a moment. "Let him in. He should know about this."

Landon unlocked the door and eased it open.

Jackson looked at him funny. "Anyone would think you guys are up to something." He stepped inside.

Landon closed and locked the door behind him. "When have we ever done anything wrong?" he asked sweetly.

Jackson raised his eyebrows at him. "Now I know you're up to something. What is it?"

"This," said Tully, the lead guitarist. He waved towards the suitcase with Poppy's head inside it.

Jackson stepped over and peered inside. His brow creased heavily. "Fuck." His face paled, then he looked a little green.

Hands to either side, he took a few steps back. "Where the hell—" He shook his head, turned and staggered into the small bathroom. He thudded to his knees in front of the toilet, retched a couple of times before being loudly, violently sick.

"I guess we can rule out his involvement," Asher said lightly.

"I'll make sure he's okay." Channing slipped into the bathroom.

"What are we going to do with her?" I perched on the edge of a chair to the side of the room. "People are going to notice her disappearance. It's been almost twenty-four hours already, if I had to guess. I mean, that's about how long it's been since I saw her."

"Same here." Jackson emerged from the bathroom, his face wet where he must have rinsed it. Channing had a hand on his shoulder. "As far as I know, security escorted her out, and she left the festival. I have no idea where she went after that."

Jackson rubbed a hand over his damp forehead. "If I knew she was going to end up like this, I would have kept tabs on her."

"Did anyone see her after she was kicked out?" Zeke asked.

"You guys were on stage at the time," I pointed out. "She was long gone before you were finished."

"That's right," Jackson said. He looked thoughtful, his eyes everywhere but on the head. "Asher, if we can repackage her and I can get a courier to take her to Melbourne, can you have your sister Rose deal with her?"

"Absolutely," Asher agreed. "I'll talk to her now. How do you guys feel about the last person she spoke to being the guy who threw the can at Abbie?"

I touched the mark on the side of my face left by the can. It could have been worse, but that asshole triggered a bunch of other people to throw cans and bottles onto the stage too. Monkey see, monkey fucking do.

In spite of that, I said, "I don't want anyone to get in trouble for a murder they didn't commit." In particular, I didn't want *us* to get blamed for a murder *we* didn't commit.

Jackson shook his head. "It wouldn't have worked. Security showed him out, but the police dealt with him shortly after. It's unlikely he would have had the chance to kill Poppy. It would be better if Rose can make it look like a nasty accident. That way, we won't have to answer any questions."

"One nasty accident on a lonely highway from far North Queensland to Sydney, coming up," Asher said cheerfully. He stepped away and started to tap at the screen on his phone.

Jackson sat on the chair beside me and cradled his face in his hands. "You realise this shit is above my pay grade, right? The average band manager doesn't deal with dead bodies. As far as I'm aware, anyway."

"You never know," Tully said. "Just because we don't hear about it doesn't mean it doesn't happen."

Jackson cocked his head at him, then shook it. "I hope it doesn't. This is all sorts of fucked up. Do we have any real idea who is doing this?"

"None," Zeke said simply. "No one's seen any of these special deliveries. They turn up when none of us are around." He looked very much like he took that personally for some reason. "It's possible one of the tour staff left this without knowing what was inside."

Jackson grimaced, but nodded. "I'll ask around, but everyone's so busy, and there's a shit ton of luggage to account for."

"And they aren't going to admit to being responsible if they are," Asher pointed out.

"That too," Jackson agreed.

"I wish they would stop," I groaned. "What's next? They kill one of you guys? If this is about me, maybe I need to drop out of the tour." How could I even consider continuing if there was a chance it will put their lives at risk? If any one of them even got a bruise because of the killer, I'd never forgive myself.

Penn opened his mouth, but closed it at a sharp look from Zeke.

"It might not be about you," Jackson said.

I did a double-take and looked at him in confusion. "What do you mean?"

"Jonah's killing might have been an attempt to get to Zeke," Jackson reasoned.

"Vance pissed off Levi because of what he did to you. So did Calista. And Poppy, for that matter. Whoever is doing this might be targeting the label in general, trying to discredit us. You might just be collateral damage in a war that has nothing to do with you. So no, you don't get off the tour that easily." He managed a half smile.

I looked from him to Zeke. "Are you sure Reuben isn't behind all of this? Maybe he had Jonah killed to throw us off the scent?"

Zeke's mouth twisted to the side. It took him a while to respond. When he did, it came with a half shrug. "At this point, I wouldn't rule out anything or anyone. Except myself."

"It's not Levi is it?" I asked carefully. Jackson said it himself when he said people pissed Levi off. Waving a gun and threatening the lead singer of one of his more lucrative bands would not make Jonah popular with the man.

"I've known Levi Jones for the better part of a decade," Jackson said. "He would do pretty much everything for his label and his artists, but he wouldn't kill. Besides, he was with me for most of that day and night. We had dinner together before we oversaw the packing of all the equipment."

In spite of his words, there was still a sliver of doubt in the back of my mind. Someone was doing this and Levi had as good a reason as Reuben. Levi wanted to protect his label the same way Reuben wanted to destroy it, or at least force Zeke out of it.

"Any chance you and Levi are working together?" Penn asked.

My brain hadn't even reached that possibility, but as soon as he asked it, I understood why. If Jackson was Levi's alibi and Levi was involved, then so was Jackson. That was a disturbing possibility.

"No," Jackson said, immediately and firmly. "I can't handle dead animals, much less people. Also, dealing with that," he jerked his head towards the suitcase containing Poppy's head, "is going to cause a shitload of hassle. Have I ever been known to cause myself unnecessary hassle?"

"You usually leave the creation of unnecessary hassle to us," Asher said.

Jackson pointed a finger gun at him. "Exactly. I didn't do this or any of the others. I can promise you that. But I will help you to deal with it. If only because we're all fucked at this point if I don't."

"We appreciate that," I said as sincerely as I could. He was taking care of us, but covering his own ass too. That was a wise move. I was a big fan of self preservation.

"It doesn't seem like we're any closer to answers than we were before." If anything, we had more and more questions piling up on top of each other. It wasn't the kind of pile-on I liked.

I believed Jackson when he said he wasn't involved. His reaction to seeing Poppy said it all. He was genuinely surprised and horrified. And grossed out. Honestly, I couldn't see Levi doing this either, but until I was one hundred percent sure, I'd be on guard around him.

"I'll take the suitcase and get it sorted out." Jackson looked at it in disgust.

"Maybe you should discuss a pay raise with Levi?" Asher suggested. "If this keeps going on the way it is, we all should."

"You're a multimillionaire, is that not enough for you?" Penn asked, his eyes narrowed at the drummer.

Asher shrugged. "You never know when there's a rainy day coming."

"How rainy would a day have to be before you would end up broke?" Penn scoffed.

I cleared my throat. "Shit happens." Not that I was ever a millionaire, much less a multimillionaire, but it was easier to have your life go down the toilet than some people think.

Penn, of all people, should understand that.

"Unless you're going to spend your money on solid gold toilets, or private jets with hookers on them, then I think you'll do okay," Penn said to Asher. He gave me a glance like he wasn't surprised I got myself into trouble.

I resisted the urge to flip him off and said, "I can't see Asher buying solid gold toilets."

"And he doesn't need a jet with hookers on it," Zeke said.

"I might need a jet," Asher said. "Sorry to disappoint the hookers of the world, but they will have to stay at home."

"What would you need a jet for?" Tully asked.

Asher looked at me and grinned. "Because fucking Abbie in a king-size bed would be more comfortable than the plane toilet."

While I blushed, Jackson looked from him to me and back again. "Please tell me you didn't," he groaned.

I looked towards the ceiling. "Ummm."

"Me too," Zeke said smugly.

"This brings me right back to the way you guys make more hassle for me," Jackson said.

"I'm sorry?" I ventured. We couldn't go back and undo it now even if we wanted to. Which, honestly, I didn't. We didn't do anything wrong. I was over being made to feel like having emotions, and acting on them, was a bad thing.

"Yeah, well, we'll worry about that if it goes viral," Jackson said. "I would rather deal with that than this. On a scale of one to a hundred, scandals are a lot easier to deal with than murder."

"You have a lot of experience dealing with murder?" Asher asked teasingly.

Jackson fixed him with a look. "Not yet."

Asher frowned. "Hey. Are you threatening me?" He obviously knew Jackson didn't mean anything serious by it.

The guys all knew each other well enough to joke around and not to take each other too seriously. It was refreshing after the way my last label was.

Onyx Riot Records was a hot mess at best. Not just when it came to me. Everyone there was in it for themselves. They would climb over each other to succeed.

Vance, my husband for twenty-six hours, was a good example of exactly that. I thought he cared about me until after we got married and he admitted he'd done it for publicity.

I should have seen it coming, but love is too fucking blind sometimes.

"I don't threaten," Jackson said lightly. "I promise." A smile tugged at the corners of his mouth. He would no more hurt Asher than I would. Unless that was what Asher was into.

"Now, don't make me threaten you with what might happen if you're late for tonight's concert." He got to his feet and waited for Zeke to zip the suitcase before he gripped the handle and rolled it towards the door.

"Will it be a public whipping?" Asher asked.

"Don't threaten us with a good time," Tully said with a grin.

Jackson snorted before he let himself out of the hotel room.

CHAPTER TWO

I WATCHED Abbie's face while all of this went down. One minute, we were having a nice afternoon, and the next everything went to shit.

Again.

While part of me wished I was responsible for—how do I put this—delivering the head of her... ex-mjie to her door, literally, I hated seeing what this was doing to her. She'd been through enough rough shit in the last year or so without body parts turning up unexpectedly.

Okay, if they turned up expectedly, that would also be bad.

I believed Jackson when he said he hadn't done it. I've known him for long enough to know he's like a protective bulldog when it came to his acts, but not a murderer.

Out of him and Levi, Levi made more sense. Even then, I didn't see it.

Zeke's family made more sense. Or Asher's. Reluctantly, I added mine to the list.

I told Abbie I had an ordinary upbringing. Some day I'd have to tell her the rest. If—when—I got past my fears about how she'd react. I owed her the whole truth. She needed to know before things went deeper between us. Would she still want to, if she knew? Like so many things lately, I had no answers for that either.

"We should try to eat something and get ready for tonight's concert," Zeke said reluctantly.

I couldn't even tell you when he started to be the leader of the group, as well as the lead singer of the band, but none of us questioned it. We didn't always do what he told us to, but we usually followed along. It was easier than arguing, and he was often right. Just don't tell him that. His ego is big enough.

I lowered myself in the chair beside Abbie, took her hand and gently pulled her onto my lap. She looked surprised but didn't protest. Instead, she nestled into me and let me tuck my arms around her.

I liked holding her like this. I felt as if I'd waited forever to be with her the way Asher and Zeke had, but I needed to wait a bit longer. Until our date in Perth. Then I would introduce her to all the things I liked and let her explore and find what she liked.

Until then, I'd rely on my imagination. That went to some wild places I hoped she'd go for real. In particular, the thought of her blindfolded and tethered to a bed made my heart race and my cock get a little harder.

Judging by the flicker of her eyelids, she felt it poke into her thigh. She smiled and wriggled her ass a little bit.

"If you keep doing that, we're going to miss the concert," I whispered in her ear.

"The audience might not notice if I'm not there," she said bitterly. "But I'm pretty sure they'll notice if you aren't."

"They *will* notice if you miss it," I said. "You're right though. The absence of the lead guitarist would cause a stir." Shame, I could think of a few fun things we could do instead of getting up on stage and performing.

"We could always ask Blaise to play with us," Zeke offered, a trace of a sly smile on his lips.

Smart ass.

I rolled my eyes at him. "As good as Blaise is, I don't think he knows our songs as well as I do."

The lead guitarist of Blazing Violet, our support act, was amazing. I'd love the opportunity to play with him sometime, but I wasn't ready to have him replace me quite yet.

"Which is Tully's way of saying fuck off," Asher said.

"I knew that." Zeke nodded.

"Hey, I'm also capable of telling Zeke to fuck off," I said to Asher. I looked straight at Zeke and said, "Fuck off."

Zeke chuckled. "Right back at you, dude." He grabbed his phone. "What does everyone feel like?"

I wanted to taste Abbie's pussy, but instead I said, "I could go for a burger."

"Burger sounds good," Penn said.

"Something vegetarian," Abbie said. "I've seen enough meat for one day."

Zeke and Asher grinned.

I chuckled.

Penn rolled his eyes.

"I was talking about the human head," Abbie said, looking slightly sick. "The kind that goes on shoulders. I never get tired of seeing the other kind."

"That's good," Zeke said. "For a minute there I thought I traumatised you with my cock."

"If anyone's cock would traumatise you, it would be Zeke's," Penn said.

"That's because it's so big it's shocking," Zeke said.

Penn snorted. "You wish."

"We could spend the rest of the afternoon talking about Zeke's cock, or we could get some food," Landon said.

"Or we could do both," Channing suggested.

The pair never made any secret of their bisexuality. They had a reasonably solid relationship and only slept with women when they were both involved. Sooner or later, that would extend to Abbie. We all knew that, it was just a matter of when.

She was taking her time getting to know each of us, and we were getting to know her. As far as all of us were concerned, there was no rush.

In the meantime, there were no other women in our lives, romantically or sexually. That was another thing that just…happened, but it felt right. With her in my arms like she was right now, I didn't want to touch anyone else.

"I vote for both," Asher said.

He and Zeke had a thing the way Channing and Landon did, but theirs was new. It seemed to me they only just admitted their bisexuality to themselves. The pair had been friends since they were kids, but lovers only recently. They also put Abbie in the centre of everything they did. I wasn't sure if they had, or even would, be with each other without her present.

That was one hundred percent their decision and I respected it.

Someday, I would like to share her with them, but first I would like to have her to myself. We had a lot to explore and learn about each other. I was looking forward to every single moment of it.

"Okay burgers with meat for the guys. Burger with vegetarian shit for Abbie. Talking about my cock, optional," Zeke said. "I'll order all the side salads and crap as well."

"You make it sound so appetising," Penn said sarcastically.

Zeke didn't glance up from his screen. "You don't have to have any, Penny. You can always watch us eat."

"Fuck off," Penn told him.

"I thought you'd feel that way," Zeke said. "Okay, it should be here in about twenty minutes."

"One of the best things about going on tour is not having to cook," Asher remarked.

"Since when did you cook?" I asked him.

He shrugged. "I don't, but when I'm on tour I don't have to feel bad about it."

"I'll make a note to ask Jackson to pack a portable kitchen for you," Zeke said teasingly.

"Go for it, but I'm not gonna use it," Asher said. "A portable incinerator might come in useful."

"Is that even a thing? Landon asked.

"If it isn't, then it should be," Asher said. "It would make it much easier for people to dispose of their enemies."

"I think, on average, most people don't have enough enemies to justify buying something like that," I pointed out.

"Certainly not after buying it," Asher agreed. "You're right though. I don't have any enemies that I know of. Unless Jackson was right about the killer targeting the label in general. The enemy of my label is my enemy."

"You should get that on a T-shirt," Zeke said. "I'll take one in every colour."

"Thanks, babe." Asher gave him a quick kiss on the mouth. "You'd look cute in a purple one."

"Of course I would." Zeke pretended to fluff his hair. "I look good in everything." He grinned and kissed Asher back.

Penn snorted. "Says you."

"Says me too," Asher said.

"Me three," Abbie said. "But you all do."

"Even me?" Penn asked.

"Even you," she agreed. "You're pretty on the outside, even if you're an asshole on the inside." She said it in the same teasing banter we all used with each other.

"Funny, I was thinking the same about you," Penn retorted.

His icy attitude towards her was slowly melting. Very slowly, but it was happening. Some day he might even relax his attitude towards himself.

Yeah, that might be a bigger ask.

"At least you admit I'm pretty," Abbie said.

"I never said you weren't. Doesn't mean you're not a pain in the ass." Penn shrugged.

A couple of weeks ago, we would have rounded on him for saying things like that to her. Now, there was no real malice behind his words.

Besides, she could stick up for herself.

"According to the tracker, our food will be here in a minute," Zeke said. He didn't seem concerned that the conversation had turned away from his cock. There was always the possibility we could change back to that topic at any moment. We were nothing if not unpredictable.

"Let's wait outside for it," Landon said to Channing.

"Make sure no one else drops off a head before the food comes," Asher said.

Landon flashed him a grin. "I make no promises."

Abbie groaned. "With any luck, that will be the last one."

"Aren't you out of enemies yet?" Penn asked.

"I wouldn't have thought of any of them as enemies," she said slowly. "As far as I know, the only one left I had any trouble with, apart from you, is Pete. We've already established that you wouldn't let anyone cut off your head, so that leaves Pete."

"Should we warn him?" Asher asked.

"And say what?" Zeke asked. "He's already had his wife's disappearance pinned on him, and the police are looking into him in relation to Vance's death. We can't warn him that someone might come after him and avoid him going to the police to clear his name. It's already too fucking messy as it is."

"I suppose so." Asher shrugged. "There's no loss if he ends up dead, is there Abbie?"

Her body went stiff in my arms. "I don't want him dead, but when I said his wife wanted me kicked off the label after our fling, I might not have told you everything."

I brushed hair back off her cheek. "What is there?" I asked gently.

She sighed. "Pete comforted me after what Vance did. We only slept together a couple of times, as a spur of the moment thing when I was... At my lowest."

I instantly wanted to punch this Pete guy in the cock.

"What an asshole," Asher said. "I'm almost starting to look forward to seeing his head in a box."

Abbie wrinkled her nose. "Don't say that. He took advantage, but so did I. He was estranged from his wife, he was as vulnerable as I was. Maybe my head deserves to be in a box."

"Never," Zeke growled.

"There's more?" I pressed lightly.

She nodded. "When he and Calista got back together, he admitted what he did with me. She insisted he kick me off the label and made him choose between that and her. What choice did he have?"

"But?" I prompted. She clearly had more she wanted to share, but it hurt her to do it.

Seeing her in this kind of discomfort made my heart hurt.

She sighed and her tongue darted across her lower lip. She took another couple of moments to compose herself, or her thoughts.

"In order to terminate the contract, he used the unbecoming behaviour clause in my contract," she finished.

We all took a moment to absorb that.

"Fuck." Apparently Zeke absorbed it faster than the rest of us. "You sleeping with him was inappropriate behaviour for someone signed to his label?"

"Motherfucker." Asher looked like he was about ready to put his fist through the wall. "What a fucking hypocrite."

I held Abbie closer and stroked her hair. "That's a bullshit thing to do."

She shrugged. "He told everyone I had an affair with a co-worker, and that was it. I was gone. I thought about suing him, but after everything I'd been through… It was too much."

"Do you want me to take a hit out on him?" Zeke asked. He didn't seem to be joking.

"Tempting, but no," she said reluctantly. "It is what it is now. If he hadn't done what he did, I wouldn't have signed with White Wolf and I wouldn't have met you guys the way I did."

I smiled. It seemed she'd gotten on board with my philosophy that we were meant to be together, no matter what. I firmly believed we would have found each other somehow. If not in this life, then in the next.

"Remind me to thank him if I meet him," I said. "Before I kick his ass."

"Food is here," Landon said as he and Channing stepped back inside.

That ended the conversation, but not the anger that lingered in the back of my mind.

CHAPTER
THREE

TULLY

"HELLO ADELAIDE!" Zeke said into the microphone.

The crowd roared.

They responded enthusiastically to Blazing Violet, and to Abbie.

It was her first performance since the festival; she was anxious. We were all anxious for her. Even while there, before she went on, I thought she might turn and run away.

Fortunately, she didn't. Or unfortunately, since there was still the potential threat of a public whipping for missing the concert. Or maybe a private whipping, just for me and her.

With that thought in my mind and suddenly heavy balls, I stepped out on stage and swung the strap of my black and gold guitar over my head.

Ever since I held my first guitar at the age of eight, it felt comfortable in my hands. Like I was made for the instrument and it was made for me.

I'd like to say I was a prodigy like Penn and immediately knew how to play, but that would be a flat out lie. I had lessons from a guy down the street, who needed the money because his band hadn't taken off yet. Like anyone obsessed with playing an instrument, I practised every chance I got.

When I got my first electric guitar at age thirteen, I was up half the night practising, with headphones plugged into my amp. I don't think my parents realised how little sleep I got, but no regrets from me. I didn't fail at school, so no harm, right?

"Let me introduce us," Zeke said. "We're Wolf Venom."

The crowd roared and started to chant. "Venom! Venom! Venom!"

We launched into our first song for the night, 'Holding On'. The crowd screamed so loud I didn't know if they could hear us or not.

They soon settled down and danced and sang along with us.

While I played, my gaze skimmed along the row of people who stood at the front. A lot of them had Wolf Venom T-shirts in every colour they came in.

Unfortunately, I couldn't see anyone dressed as fruit. Not even an animal costume. Maybe I should get myself a carrot costume to wear on stage. Jackson would love that.

Not.

Zeke danced past me, microphone in one hand, the other raised to encourage the audience to clap along. Many of them did, but most people had a phone in their hand, filming us.

I knew some musicians hated when audiences did that. More than one tried to ban phones from their concerts altogether. Personally, it didn't worry me. As long as people were enjoying themselves, then there was nothing wrong with having a memento to watch later. In a year or two, when they'd forgotten who we were, they'd probably delete the footage from their phones anyway.

Unless one of us did something super embarrassing, like falling over, or tumbling off the side of the stage. That shit would follow us around forever.

I turned at movement in the corner of my eye.

Abbie stepped back on stage to sing with Zeke.

Not long ago, Penn violently and loudly objected to her singing on stage with us.

Now, he looked up from his keyboard and watched her walking too. He probably thought no one was paying attention to him, but I saw the hunger in his eyes.

I didn't blame him. She was a beautiful woman with the most incredible, lush body I ever saw. She wasn't afraid of her sexuality, or the connection she was developing with all of us. Other women might run away from the prospect of becoming involved with six, somewhat crazy, guys. But not Abbie. She seemed to love every minute of it.

She pulled the other microphone out of the stand and stepped over to Zeke on her long, shapely legs. Even in heels, she was shorter than the lead singer. Than any of us. She was small but perfectly formed.

She straightened the hem of her skirt which fell halfway down her delicious thighs, and raised the microphone to her luscious lips.

"Hey," she said to Zeke as if she wasn't standing on stage in front of thousands of people.

"Hey." He turned to her. "Fancy meeting you here. Do you *come* here often?" No one in the arena missed the inflection.

The audience laughed.

"Not yet," she replied with a laugh. "I figured you could use some help on a couple of songs."

The audience cheered.

"Yeah?" Zeke asked. He turned to look at the crowd and stretched out his hand. "I would appreciate a hand." He grinned.

The audience snickered. More than one woman shouted out her willingness to give him one. Or a mouth.

I didn't doubt they meant it too. Zeke had that impact on women. And men.

Channing played a short, seductive tune on his saxophone.

Zeke chuckled and he and Abbie started singing, 'In Deeper', which fit perfectly with the suggestive introduction. Of course, that was the point. To get the audience going before the sexy lyrics. The crowd didn't even seem to mind that Zeke and Abbie were clearly singing to each other. If I was the jealous kind, I would be envious of the obvious connection.

I wasn't though; Abbie and I had a connection of our own.

They finished their two songs and we all put down, or stepped away from, our instruments, except Penn. The rest of us hurried off stage to let him do his solo and to have a quick toilet break, and change out of our sweat-drenched tees.

Abbie and I stopped and stood at the bottom of the steps to the backstage area to listen to what song he chose that night. Every night it was different. He claimed he didn't know what song he was going to play and sing until he actually began.

I had no reason not to believe him. Sometimes all we could do was go where the music took us. And the mood of the audience. He always nailed that too, giving them what they probably didn't know they wanted.

He placed his fingers on his keyboard, leaned forward to the microphone and started to sing 'Imagine', of all things.

"How does he do that?" Abbie asked. "He can be such a dickhead, but then he plays and sings so beautifully, I want to cry."

I slipped an arm around her waist and fitted her in against my hip. "He's a complicated guy." No one would argue he was insanely talented as well. He could easily go out by himself as a solo artist. It was a good thing he didn't, since the band was better for having him as a part of it.

We were a dysfunctional family at times, okay, a lot of the time, but we had each other's backs. That was one of the reasons he stuck with us. And why we put up with him when he was being a grumpy pain in the ass.

I stood on my toes and peered up the steps towards the audience. All I could see was thousands and thousands of phone lights waving slowly back and forth, like a sky full of dancing stars.

I lowered myself back down as Jackson joined us. He placed a hand on the wall beside him and watched, a thoughtful look on his face.

"What?" I asked him.

He turned his face towards me and cocked his head. "What?"

"You look like you're thinking something," I said. "Should we be scared? Or is the public whipping coming up next?"

He rolled his eyes towards the ceiling and smiled. "No public whipping. At least not today. I think there are laws against shit like that."

"Hey, as long as everyone is consenting…" I grinned. "So what are you actually thinking? You didn't tell me if I should be scared or not."

"You shouldn't be," he said. "It doesn't involve you. And anyway, it's just a thought at the moment. I'll have to run it past Levi or one of the executives."

"Are you going to put his keyboard on a platform that lifts up off the stage?" Abbie asked.

Jackson quirked an eyebrow at her. "I wasn't going to, but that's not a bad idea. Maybe for the next tour."

"You could elevate Asher too," I said, grinning. "They could sit up in the back and look down at us all."

"I see you like to spend the label's money," Jackson said dryly. "Too much of that would get expensive and difficult. Not to mention how much that would cost to insure. And the risk of broken bones."

In spite of his words, he didn't look as though he hated the idea. On the other hand, we were always trying to come up with ways to make each tour different and special. I had a feeling this idea wouldn't fly, so to speak, for all the reasons he mentioned. We'd have to come up with something else.

Which begged the question, what was Jackson thinking? He obviously wasn't going to tell us until he was ready, which sucked. One way or another, I'd find out.

"You're welcome," I said. We made a ton of money for the label, why shouldn't we have some say in how to spend it? Honestly, I suspected Asher would hate being elevated like that anyway. He preferred to sit back behind his drums and make an impact with his beat, not with showy theatrics.

Jackson smirked and we all turned back to listen to Penn.

Penn kept the audience captivated until the very last note died away.

Just in time, the other guys trotted back from the toilet, each dressed in clean, dry shirts.

I gave Abbie a quick kiss on the mouth, as did Asher and Zeke, then we headed back onto the stage to a rousing applause.

Zeke grabbed his microphone back out of the stand. "Beau Pennington, ladies and gentlemen." He waved towards Penn, who gave the audience a seated bow as they cheered and clapped.

"I don't know if I can follow that," Zeke told the fifty-three thousand strong crowd in confidence.

They cheered.

"Probably not," Penn said into his mic. He didn't smile but he looked smug.

It was a miracle his ego wasn't bigger than it already was. Plenty of guys as talented as him were absolute nightmares. I knew one who wouldn't even share his hotel room with anyone else in the band or on the tour. And that was before he got big enough to afford a separate room.

Penn was arrogant, but he was also realistic. Some of the time anyway.

The audience laughed.

Zeke turned and pretended to wave to someone off stage. "Can we get his microphone turned off please?"

Again, the audience laughed, and many shouted, "No!"

Penn shrugged. "Thanks everyone. I'll send you all your fifty dollars each after the concert." He sat back and laced his hands behind his head as though he was done for the night.

It wasn't often he joked around. Abbie must have made a good impact on him if he was doing it now. By the time she was done, he might even smile once in a while.

Predictably, the audience roared louder than ever. Who wouldn't like fifty dollars just for getting behind Penn? Hell, I'd take it.

Zeke laughed and nodded. That was our cue to launch into the next song.

CHAPTER FOUR

ABBIE

IT WASN'T until after the concert and before the meet and greet that I got a chance to catch up with Jackson.

"Did you deal with it?" I asked, deliberately vague in case anyone overheard.

"Yep," he said simply. "As long as Asher dealt with his side, then it's sorted."

"Do you really think it's not about me?" I asked tentatively. I wanted to believe that, I really did, but if they were going after the label, surely they would go after people like Candy, Jackson or even Levi himself? On the other hand, if they did that, the target would be obvious. Wouldn't it?

Hell, I didn't even know any more.

He rubbed his chin. It looked like he hadn't shaved in a few days. That was understandable given how busy tours were.

"I don't know," he admitted. "Unless whomever is doing this leaves a note or is caught, we may never know the real reason. It might be over now, for all we know."

"I hope so," I said. "There's enough pressure on all of us without…that."

"You're not fucking wrong there," he said. "Just in case, keep an eye out at the meet and greet. Let me know if anyone looks familiar. I know of a few instances where enthusiastic fans turne up at these kinds of things. Often repeatedly. Sometimes they're just enthusiastic fans. Other times they're more."

"Stalkers?" I had heard of the same thing happening, but I couldn't recall seeing the same faces over at Lover again at past meet and greets. Was I looking? No, not really. Faces blurred together eventually.

"Possibly," he agreed. "If they have a chance to get close to the object of their obsession, they will. Meets and greets are a good way to do it. Where else but a place you can get near and blend in at the same time? It's twisted as shit but people aren't always reasonable."

I snorted. "Really? What a shocker." I patted his shoulder. "Sorry to be sarcastic but that might be the understatement of the century."

He smiled.

He had become like a big brother to me. That was what I needed during this crazy ride. Several boyfriends and a big brother. A girl would have to be safe with all of them around, wouldn't she?

"Just slightly," he agreed. "Fortunately we're surrounded by the members of two bands who are *always* reasonable." He made a face.

I laughed. "So what were you thinking while Penn was playing?" I asked, hoping to catch him off guard. I knew Tully wanted to know, and I certainly did.

"Don't tell me they're rubbing off on you," he said with a groan. "I can't talk about it just now. When I can, you'll be one of the first to know."

"Okay, now I'm scared," I said, my eyes wide. "You're not gonna put me on a platform are you?"

He chuckled. "I would, since it was your idea in the first place, but the insurance would still be ridiculously expensive. Cables would be safer." He looked thoughtful, but he hadn't quite stopped smiling.

"The guys are rubbing off on *who* now?" I teased.

"Maybe I rubbed off on them?" he suggested.

"If that's the case, then you only have yourself to blame," I said dryly.

"Huh. In that case, they are rubbing off on me. Don't worry, it doesn't involve cables, platforms or anything particularly dangerous."

"Particularly dangerous?" I echoed. "So it's dangerous?" I wasn't sure I liked the sound of that.

"Not physically dangerous." He gave me a cagey look.

"I know it's not going to jeopardise my career," I said. "After everything that's happened, you wouldn't do that to me."

I hoped.

"Absolutely not," he said. "Exactly the opposite."

"Are you really going to get me this intrigued and then not tell me?" I complained.

He smiled. "Yes."

"That is pure evil," I told him. "I thought you were nice too."

He laughed. "I am nice. Trust me, it will be one hundred percent worth the wait."

At this point, the only thing I could think of was a plan for a solo tour. I liked that idea, but I didn't know why he wouldn't just come out and say that. Unless he had to run it past Levi first. That made sense, I suppose.

"What happens if it isn't?" I asked.

Before I could even mention it, he said, "No public whippings."

I sighed dramatically. "Oh bugger, I was looking forward to that."

"Too much information." He grimaced.

"Does that bother you that I'm in a relationship with Zeke and Asher?" I asked. "And that Tully and I are going on a date when we get to Perth?"

"And that Penn, Channing and Landon all look at you the way the other three do?" he said. "It was unexpected, but not entirely surprising. I mean, I didn't see it coming before you met the guys, but if any group of men was going to share a woman, it would be them. Okay, and the guys of Blazing Violet, with Violet, even if they don't see it yet."

"You don't think that's weird at all?" I asked.

"Should I?" he asked. "I've been around for a while and I've seen all sorts of different things and different relationships. What you're doing is, I think, more normal than other people realise."

"Would you do it?" I asked.

He looked surprised at the question, but then thoughtful. "I might if the right situation came along. I'm away so much of the time, would it be fair to ask a woman to wait at home alone? At least this way, she would always have other people around when she needed them."

I tilted my head. "That's very enlightened of you. A lot of guys would just go away and not worry about what the woman thought or felt."

He shrugged one shoulder. "It's not the seventeen hundreds anymore." He gave me a long look before adding, "Have you thought about what happens after the tour?"

I straightened my head and shook it. "I've stressed about it, but we haven't talked about it or anything. I mean, things are new. I don't want to make any assumptions about the way anyone else is feeling or what they're thinking."

"I can make a few," he said. "But I can also understand your reluctance to plan for the rest of your life right now. Especially with all the—" He cleared his throat.

"Yes, all *the*," I agreed. "It looks like the meet and greet is about to start. I don't suppose anyone is waiting to meet me." Except maybe potential stalkers. They could wait forever.

"Several," he said. "You're more popular than you think. I'll stay close by all night, until the meet and greet is over, just in case anyone tries anything funny. This is one time when the guys have to do their own thing, rather than watching over you. I don't want to give security too much information, for obvious reasons. After the can throwing incident, they know to keep an eye out for you or anyone behaving strangely. That has put everyone on edge. How are you feeling after that?" He peered at my cheek.

"I'm okay," I said lightly. "Going out on stage tonight was daunting, but once I was out there I was fine. Plus, people can't bring cans or bottles into the venue." That went a long way to settling my nerves a couple of hours ago.

"Good, I'm glad you bounced back so quickly," he said approvingly. "I know plenty of singers who would have refused to go out on another stage again after that."

"My career wouldn't last very long if I ran away every time shit like that happened," I said dryly. Fuck knows I had plenty of excuses to quit, but I hadn't taken any of them.

If anything, I was more determined. I wasn't going to let a little tin can, or aluminium can, ruin the rest of my life.

Disembodied heads, that was a different story.

"That's why the most successful people are the ones who have stuck it out," he said. "The guys have had plenty of chances and reasons for quitting, but they haven't. Actually, I'm not sure they would let each other quit."

"Yeah, they would give each other hell if anyone suggested it," I agreed. "They're a pretty amazing team."

"They are," he agreed. "And you are a pretty amazing addition to it. Levi knew what he was doing. Obviously. He's gotten rich knowing what he was doing."

I blushed at his words. "I'm not sure Levi knew entirely what he was doing. I mean, he wouldn't have guessed I might end up in a relationship with the guys."

Jackson leaned his shoulder against the wall and crossed his arms over his chest. "I wouldn't underestimate what Levi Jones would or wouldn't have guessed. He knows all of the guys pretty well. I wouldn't be surprised if he has a bet with someone that you would get together with at least one of the guys."

I matched his pose by crossing my arms. "Have you got a bet with him?"

He smiled slightly. "I might. I might not. It wouldn't be professional of me if I did, would it? It certainly wouldn't be professional of me to admit it."

I surprise myself by feeling comfortable enough with him to poke my finger into his chest. "You really are as bad as the guys, aren't you?"

He grinned. "There's a reason Levi chose me as their manager and not someone else. Who else would put up with them but someone as batshit crazy as they are?"

"I think you just called me crazy, in a roundabout way," I said slowly. I squinted at him. "But I'm not sure."

"I think I'll leave it up to you to interpret it however you want." He straightened up. "Okay, security is letting people in. Remember, I won't be far away. I'll be watching the whole time."

I nodded. Nerves that hadn't been there a moment ago fluttered through my belly.

"I appreciate it." I meant that. It was good to have someone looking out for me when the guys were busy with their fans. I trusted Jackson as much as I trusted any of them. Maybe more so, because I wasn't clouded with lust when it came to him. I liked him, but I would never look at him that way.

Would I?

I stood awkwardly while security herded people in my direction. The smiles on their faces were gratifying. After the festival and not just the cans but also the words, it was nice to be greeted by people who were actually happy to see me.

"Hey," I greeted the first in line, two women about the same age as me. They both looked about ready to jump up and down with excitement.

"Oh my God, I can't believe we get to meet you," the taller one with short, dark hair gushed.

"I keep thinking we're dreaming," the shorter one, with long blond hair, agreed. Her blue eyes were huge with genuine joy.

Meeting people like this made doing my job more worthwhile than anything else. It made me realise I was actually touching people by just opening my mouth and singing.

What could be more rewarding than that?

"If you're dreaming, than I am too," I said. "Should I pinch myself and see if we wake up?"

"No!" The brunette waved her hand at me. "I don't want to wake up. Can we get a selfie?"

"Of course." While I got into place beside them, I scanned the line of people waiting to meet me. No one looked familiar, strange, or out of place, but I wouldn't relax fully until this was over. After all, what did a stalker look like anyway? Probably just a regular person. One you would never suspect of stalking and killing people.

I smiled when both women held up their phones and took photos. I didn't stop smiling for another hour or two after that.

My face was going to hurt tomorrow, but I loved every minute of it.

CHAPTER FIVE

ABBIE

"I ALWAYS FORGET how pretty Perth is." I looked out at the Swan River, which meandered past the restaurant. "This is nice."

"It is nice," Tully agreed. "It's nice to have you to myself. The other guys are adorable and all that, but I've been looking forward to having time alone."

"Me too." I turned to give him a soft smile. "I keep thinking I'm going to look over my shoulder and see the rest of the guys watching over us or something."

"I do too," he admitted. "They're probably hiding out somewhere we can't see them." He pointed at a building across the river. "Like in there, with binoculars on us. Just in case—" He flipped off the building.

I laughed. "Would they be that far away? They're more likely to be hiding behind a bush or around a corner." I waved in no particular direction. "Except Penn. I can't imagine him bothering to hide."

"He's probably in the hotel bar, drinking," Tully agreed. "That's more his speed."

"That sounds accurate," I said. That was where they all were when we left. According to Asher, they were going to have a couple of drinks and then head to dinner.

"Can I ask you a question?" I slowly turned my wineglass around, my fingers on the stem.

"Of course," he said without hesitation.

"Just like that?" I asked. "What if I ask you something you don't want to answer?"

He took a sip of his beer. "Then I'll tell you I won't answer it. But most things are an open book as far as I'm concerned."

"Now I'm thinking I should ask you something more personal," I said. "I was just going to ask about groupies. I've seen a few hanging around since we arrived."

"Yeah." He put down his beer and picked up his fork. "Is this where you ask what the other guys might get up to when you're not looking? Are you worried they're all hooking up with different people as we speak?"

"I probably sound paranoid." I grimaced. "They've given me no reason to think they would, especially Zeke and Asher, but they are rock gods. If you guys share me, what right do I have to expect them not to do what they want, with whoever they want?"

I hated the idea of sharing them with anyone apart from each other, but here I was, sitting with Tully. Was I a hypocrite?

"This might come as a shock, especially coming from a guy," he said slowly, "but there's more to life than sex. We all care about you, a lot, and none of us want to lose you. This arrangement, this sharing thing, is something new and different for us. But..." He wrinkled his brow in thought.

"We each give each other different things," he said finally. "We're friends as well as bandmates. We're brothers, if you like. We play together and we don't go and play with other bands, generally speaking. You give each of us something different too. Like Zeke and Asher give each other something different. Like Landon and Channing do." He paused for a moment.

"It's like how a song is made up of a bunch of notes. Those notes appear in a lot of different songs, but when you put them together in a certain way, they make something special and unique."

"Musical notes aren't known for being exclusive," I pointed out.

"No, but certain combinations of them are, or people get sued," Tully said. "Trust that the guys care about you enough to be a part of this song instead of running off after a new one. Speaking for myself, I haven't been interested in another tune since I met you. I feel—I don't know—whole somehow. Like we had the song but we were lacking the right tempo."

I blushed at that, but I knew what he meant. All my life I was missing something and now I knew what it was. I just didn't expect it to be six guys.

Was that greedy of me? Or was it just that when the right tune was made, all we could do was roll with it?

"Can I be the tranquillo?" I asked. I would happily set the tempo to tranquil and peaceful, rather than the wild, frenetic pace of the last year or so.

"That would suit you," he agreed. "Or maybe something a little faster. Not too fast, but fast enough that we have to work hard to keep up with you. You wouldn't want to make it too easy on us." He grinned and stabbed his fork into his ravioli.

"No, not too easy." I wound spaghetti around my fork and managed to get it into my mouth without dropping it everywhere.

Bonus.

"So you had an ordinary childhood compared to Asher and Zeke?" I asked once I swallowed.

He hesitated.

"You don't have to talk about it if you don't want to," I said quickly.

Childhoods were a touchy subject with these guys. With good reason. Zeke and Asher's family were into some bad shit and from what I knew, Penn's family had expectations of him he struggled to meet. I had no idea about any of the other guys.

"It's okay," he said slowly. "I told you I had an ordinary childhood, but that wasn't the whole story. I was taken from my family when I was about six and raised by the people I think of as my parents. My biological parents were associates of the Brantley family."

Why did that not surprise me? They seemed to have their fingers in a shit-load of pies, and lives.

"I'm guessing things didn't go well?" I asked as gently as I could. "What happened?"

"My mother was the second best assassin in Melbourne," Tully said.

"Second-best?" I echoed. Wait, did he say *assassin?* Yes, he had.

Shit.

"Someone hired her to take out a hit on one of the Bell family. They took that as well as you might expect. In return, they hired the first best assassin to take her out."

"That sounds like a movie," I muttered.

He smiled and his eyebrows jerked upward quickly. "It does." He took a gulp of beer. "My father lost it after that. Started drinking, getting into all sorts of shit he shouldn't get into. He pissed off a lot of people. One night, he got into a fight he couldn't win and ended up dead on the side of the road."

"Oh God," I breathed. "That's terrible." No wonder he was reluctant to talk about it.

Tully shrugged. "No loss. He was getting violent at home. Nothing I couldn't handle, but it was getting more and more out of hand. I was going to go and live with my aunt, but Zeke's father stepped in and pulled some strings to have me placed with the family that adopted me. My aunt was almost as bad as my father."

"That's the first time I've heard of anyone with the last name Brantley, other than Zeke, doing something nice," I said.

He shrugged again. "I was the same age as Zeke. Apparently he had a soft spot for me, because of my mother. He wasn't too happy she was killed."

"I'm sure you weren't either," I said.

"No, but I hardly remember her." He took another gulp of beer. "She was often away. I had no idea why at the time. I would never have guessed if I tried. I mean, what kid guesses his mother is a hitwoman?"

"I think superhero is usually about as outrageous as it gets," I said. "Or aliens from another planet. I always hoped mine came from Saturn. Until I was about seven, I waited for a spaceship to come and collect us." I rolled my eyes at my own silly childhood fantasy.

"And then you became a singer instead," he said. "That's a childhood fantasy that doesn't come true for most people. But for you it did."

"I often wonder why," I admitted. "Why me and not a billion other talented girls? Plenty of them work as hard as I do and are just as good, if not better than me. Tons are prettier and have better bodies than I do, which shouldn't be a requirement, but it often is."

I hated that aspect of the industry. Being talented and wanting to put in the work, that should be enough.

"That's easy," Tully said. "There's something about you. Something that makes people sit up and take notice. It's not just that you're beautiful and have a smoking hot body, which you do. People want to watch you and be around you. The things that happened to you in the past, was all because other people are jealous of that magnetism you have."

"And my ability to make dumb choices," I said dryly.

He leaned forward and put his hand on mine. He looked me straight in the eyes. "People took advantage of your sweet nature, but I promise you there was a lot of jealousy involved. Vance wanted what you had. Calista too. And Poppy. If I dig down deep, I'll probably find that Poppy Newton was a frustrated singer who couldn't make it. Or an actor maybe. Something you are and she could never be."

"Possibly." I wanted to believe that. Not that people were jealous of me, but that things didn't happen because I was a complete dumbass.

"Definitely," he said firmly.

"What about Jonah then?" I asked. "Was he jealous of Zeke?"

"Probably," Tully said. "Who would want to be a street thug when you can be a rock star?"

"Reuben?" I asked.

Tully laughed. "I'd love to see you call Reuben a street thug to his face. But don't do it if you value your life. He likes to think he's a long way above all of that shit. Above street gangs and above the law. He's the king of the castle and we're the dirty rascals."

"I would have thought of him as king of the dirty rascals," I said dryly.

"That sounds about right," Tully agreed. "But his family looked out for me when my family didn't. You might say I owe them. Sooner or later, Reuben is going to remember that and come calling for a favour."

"He hasn't already? He asked me to try to talk Zeke out of leaving the band.

He didn't want you to do the same thing?" I swallowed the last gulp of wine and mopped up my sauce with a piece of garlic bread.

"Reuben is smart enough to know I wouldn't do that, and Zeke wouldn't listen to me if I did," Tully said. "It's not in my best interest to try to convince him to walk away. Whereas with you, you could make a future with Zeke away from the band. You might even have considered that once the tour is over."

"I hadn't. Not yet anyway," I said. That made a twisted kind of sense though. Reuben was trying to get to Zeke through me and vice versa. "At some point, we might have to think about life after music, but not for a while. Not while Wolf Venom is selling out stadiums all over the world. Why doesn't Reuben just wait until that happens?

"Firstly, it's not going to happen," Tully said with a confident smile. "We're going to be selling out everywhere until we're too old to stand. And even if we didn't, Zeke doesn't want anything to do with that lifestyle. None of us do." He paused for a moment then added, "There's something else. Something you should know. I..." He rubbed the back of his head. "I hope this doesn't scare you off."

"After everything that's happened already, I'm not sure what you could possibly say that *would* scare me off," I said.

It would have to be pretty fucking bad. I was almost certain he wasn't about to admit he was the one leaving all those heads lying around. What could be scarier than that?

"You haven't heard what I have to say yet," he pointed out.

He sat forward and rested his chin in his hands. "When my adopted family took me in, they started to train me in my mother's profession."

It took me a solid minute to even begin to process what he was trying to say.

"Whoa." I sat back in my chair but had the presence of mind to speak softly. "You trained as an assassin?"

He glanced down at the table, then back up again. "Yeah. It's not a craft I practice now, and it's not something I'm proud of, but yes. They trained me in... all aspects of the job."

I felt the blood drain out of my face. "Have you ever—" Fuck did I even want to know the answer to that?

He looked back down at the table and for the longest time I didn't think he was going to respond. When he looked back up, I saw the answer in his eyes.

"So, yes?" Holy shit.

"Once, and like I said, it's not something I'm proud of. The job made me enough money to buy the kind of guitar I needed to join Wolf Venom when they were starting out. I know that's no excuse for what I did, but that was why I did it. For what it's worth, the guy was a powerful man who was using his position to get away with raping women and young girls. If I hadn't done it, someone else would have. And if they hadn't, he would have kept doing what he was doing."

I felt like I should have been horrified, but for some reason, I wasn't. Tully was a good guy, and I could see that killing, even someone evil, weighed heavily on his mind.

But I had to ask. "The heads?"

He shook his head. "Not me. From what I saw of Poppy and Calista, it's not someone trained to have any finesse. Those two, at least, weren't professional hits. I doubt the other ones were either."

I wasn't sure if I had enough wine for this conversation. I wasn't sure if enough wine existed.

"So you have no interest in going back to that life?" I asked tentatively, even though I was sure of the answer.

"None," he said firmly. "That's in the past, much to my parents' disappointment."

"Good, because I can't imagine you as a hitman," I said. "You make a much better guitarist." That would explain why Brantley senior placed Tully where he did. He must have had a plan for him.

There was something wrong with me, because I found him hotter than ever, knowing he was a trained assassin. I mean, you don't meet people like that every day, much less go on dates with them. Knowing he had skills made me feel safer than ever.

"Ain't that the truth," he said lightly. "I'm not bothered by death, but I don't want to kill people for a living. Or even by accident. The previous generation must be shaking their heads at us."

"Yes, it's disappointing that you don't want to follow in their criminal footsteps," I said ironically. "Young people these days."

He grinned. "Right? With such delinquents. Imagine raising rock stars instead of thugs."

"Maybe there's hope for the world yet," I said.

CHAPTER SIX

ABBIE

"OKAY," I said slowly, "this wasn't what I was expecting."

"What were you expecting?" Tully pressed his hand lightly to the small of my back. "Whips and chains hanging from the walls? A line of St Andrews crosses? A few sex chairs and a swing?"

"Ummm…"

I'd been to places like this before so yeah, that was pretty much what I thought I'd see here.

In reality, the club—Desdemona's—was plush and high-end. I suspected they catered to whatever their clients wanted. Including discretion.

The floors were white marble, the walls a soft blue. Dark blue couches lined the walls, broken up by deep armchairs and mahogany tables.

If I didn't know better, I'd assume we were in an expensive lawyer's office. That was probably the idea. If anyone walked past, they'd assume nothing interesting went on here. Unless you're the kind of person who finds legal stuff fun.

I mean, whatever floats your boat.

Tully chuckled. "I know a few places like that too, but Desdemona likes to make things more personal. When I booked, I gave her a list of what and how I wanted things for tonight."

I glanced at him in surprise. "You had to book?"

"Hell yeah, weeks in advance," he said. "Some people wait *months* to get in here."

"It helps to be a rock god." My gaze skimmed over several tasteful paintings on the walls. They were all landscapes, but not of anywhere I knew.

"Sometimes," he said unapologetically. "I don't usually throw my name around but how else am I going to impress you?"

"By being you?" I suggested.

Don't get me wrong, I liked that he was willing to make the effort to introduce me to his world and do it in a way I'd feel comfortable. And okay, I kinda didn't mind him throwing a little bit of weight around. He wasn't the kind of guy who would do it often, and not without good cause. He was no Vance or even Penn.

"I'm awesome," he said with a grin, "but I'd like to be awesome on the next level tonight. Fuck knows how long it'll be until I have you to myself again. If I make this memorable enough, it might be sooner."

"You make it sound like you need to fight the other guys for a chance to be with me," I said. That wouldn't end well for anyone.

"Whatever I have to do," he said in a light, teasing tone. "Hey, Desdemona." He greeted the woman who appeared through a side door.

She was absolutely stunning. Tall, almost as tall as Tully, and more curvaceous than me. Her skin was the darkest brown I ever saw. She held herself like a woman who knew exactly how gorgeous she was. She owned every centimetre of it, from her long legs to the cleavage that pressed up from the front of her bright red dress.

"Mr Cole." She glided forward and kissed him on both cheeks before she did the same to me.

"Miss Hart. So wonderful to have you both here. I have everything arranged precisely as you asked." She gave me a look that suggested it absolutely mattered who I was. Not as Abbie Hart, the singer, but as a welcome, cherished guest.

No wonder people liked to come here. Pun intended.

"Thank you, Desdemona." Tully kissed her cheeks in return.

I hesitated before I did the same. Her skin was smooth and cool under my lips, soft compared to kissing any of the guys.

"Please, come through." She gestured toward the door she'd come out of with hands coated in gold rings and dripping with diamonds. There must be money to be made in owning a place like this.

What was I saying? If there was a golden rule in this life, it was that sex sells.

His hand still on the small of my back, Tully guided me through the doorway and into a small but opulent room with a view over the Swan River.

I was so busy gaping at the wide, four poster bed and silver covered tray that sat on the top of the table beside it, that I didn't notice Desdemona leave until the door closed behind us.

"This is next level all right," I said in awe.

The floor was a dark hardwood, no doubt easy to clean, but expensive.

Even the curtains hanging on the windows looked like they cost more than a pretty penny.

"Is that wallpaper on the ceiling?" It looked like marble with gold veining running through it.

"Yes, and jets in the bath." Tully gestured.

My gaze followed where he pointed and I did a double take.

"I didn't even see that." Which was bizarre since it was the biggest, longest, widest clawfoot tub I ever saw. The sides were painted a glossy black while the tub itself was a glistening white. Steam rose off water inside the tub, which was decorated with a sprinkle of rose petals.

"This feels like the honeymoon I never had." I shook my head in amazement. "You asked for all of this?"

"Everything," he said. "She has a room which is completely black and no light can get inside. It heightens all the rest of your senses. It's incredible, but I thought maybe for your first time here, I'd ease you into it."

"I appreciate that," I said. Even trusting him the way I did, to be in complete darkness sounded freaky. That was definitely something I'd have to work up to.

"Now remember, you're in charge of this," he said. "I'm here to guide you and help you enjoy the experience, but you get to say when something is too much or too little. Okay?"

I nodded. "Okay. Where do we start?" I was hoping he had some ideas, because I could easily get overwhelmed right now. Just imagining what was on the tray, under the cover, made my mind race.

"Why don't we start by sitting down?" He waved toward the bed. "Let me try a few things and see what you like. And if you need to tap out, just say the word."

"Any word?" I asked. "Or, like, cucumber or something?"

He grinned. "Cucumber works. If you need or want me to stop, just say that, okay?"

"All right," I agreed. I sat down on the edge and watched as he picked up a red, silk blindfold off the table beside the tray.

"Can I put this on you?" he asked.

I hesitated for a short while.

Did I trust him enough to let him do things to me I couldn't see?

Yeah, yeah I did. More than that, the idea got my heart racing.

I sat around to face away from him and said, "Yes please."

He slipped the smooth fabric over my eyes and fastened it in place. "Any time you want to take that off, go ahead. You're in control of that too."

I pulled out a section of hair where it was caught up in the fabric and nodded.

"Okay. I'm good for now." I couldn't see, but the fabric wasn't so thick that I was completely devoid of all light. "Thank you for being sweet."

"I was going to say the same to you," he said. "Now, I'm going to put something to your lips, but it won't be anything horrible. All right?"

"I trust you," I said.

"Good," he said. "Here's the first thing."

I heard the rattle of the cover lifting off the tray and he pressed something cool to my lips. I breathed in the delicious scent of strawberry. One of my favourite foods.

I slid my tongue against it, felt the rough skin of the fruit, tasted the flavour for a moment before I took a bite.

"Yum." I couldn't remember eating a tastier one. It could have just been picked, it was so fresh.

"Yes, you are," he agreed. He waited until I opened my mouth wider before popping the rest of the strawberry into my mouth.

I chewed and swallowed, then waited. "That was a good start. What else you got?"

He chuckled. "That's my girl. Let's try…" He rattled around before he lightly pressed something hard against my lips.

I breathed in the smell. It didn't take long to identify what it was.

"Mmmm, chocolate." I licked it eagerly. And kept licking and nibbling when it became evident he wasn't going to pop it into my mouth. I ate right down to the tips of his fingers and licked those as well. After a moment, he popped one into my mouth and let me suck.

"You're even tastier than strawberries and chocolate," I said.

"You too." The next thing he pressed against my mouth were his lips, but the kiss he gave was soft and brief. "Can I take off your dress?" he asked.

At this point, I was pretty sure there wasn't anything he could do to me I wouldn't like. What can I say, I'm easily won over by strawberries and chocolate.

Not to mention smoking hot rock gods like Tully.

"Please." I turned around again so he could work the zip down and tug the straps of my shoulders. The fabric slid against my skin down to my waist before he took my hand and encouraged me to stand. When my dress fell in a pool at my feet, I stepped out of it and shoved it aside with my toe.

"Black lace, my favourite," he remarked.

"Oh, it is?" I filed that in the back of my mind for future reference.

Asher and Zeke liked my white lace bras and panties, although I think they preferred me without any underwear. The feeling was mutual.

"Okay, let's try something different," he said.

I listened for the sound of him rattling around, but it didn't come. Nothing touched my lips. For a while, I started to think he wasn't doing anything.

"What—" Then I felt a light touch on my cheek, down my neck to my throat.

The edge of a feather.

I shivered slightly. "That tickles."

He paused the moment I spoke. "Do you want me to stop?"

"No," I said quickly. "It's not a bad tickle."

"Okay, great." He continued to run it lightly over my neck and down my chest.

For some reason, that slight touch was incredibly erotic. It was soft and gentle and made my skin tingle all over.

He slid the feather down between my breasts and over my stomach. He ran it back up and over one nipple, barely touching through the fabric of my bra.

I groaned softly. This might be the longest, slowest tease ever, and it was going to drive me completely wild. I loved every moment of it.

He passed the feather over the other nipple and back down across my stomach, over the side of my thigh and down one leg. He brought it up the inside of my thigh which I opened eagerly, my body already begging for more.

When I wanted him to touch my pussy, he moved in the opposite direction.

"Let's try something different," he mused. "Hmmm. Ahhh." He must have put the feather away, because the next time he touched my mouth, it was with something so cold it made me jump slightly.

"Is that okay?" he asked.

"Yeah," I said immediately. "I wasn't expecting ice." The sudden increase in sensation wasn't unpleasant, just different.

"Great." He pressed the cube to my lips and let me lick before he slid it down my cheek and across my throat. It left behind an ache that I wanted to feel all over.

He didn't disappoint. He let the cube slide down my chest and over my nipple.

If it wasn't hard before, it was after the shock of the cold over my sensitive nub. It left the fabric of my bra wet and freezing against my skin.

"I never knew ice could feel so good," I whispered.

"It's surprising what you can feel when you can't see and you don't make expectations," he said. "Everything is…"

"More?" I suggested.

"Yes, more," he agreed. The ice cube must have all but melted before he passed it over my opposite nipple, leaving that bra cup drenched as well.

I shivered, but it was with need, not with cold.

"I see why you like this," I said. "Pun not intended."

He laughed softly and said, "Stick out your tongue." When I did, he put the last small chip of ice on my tongue.

It melted away in a second or two, leaving a drop of cold water, which I swallowed.

"Let's try something else," he said. "Lie down on your stomach."

I did, with my hands out to either side of my face. I thought he was going to use the feather again, but when he touched me it felt more substantial.

"Is that—"

"It's a flogger," he said. "I'll start gently."

"I trust you," I said again.

I felt the brush of multiple strands of butter soft leather swipe over the back of my wrist. I turned my hand to let it run smoothly over the underside of my fingers and the pads of my fingertips.

He ran it slowly and gently up my arm, over my elbow to my shoulder. From there, he traced lines slowly up and down my back and over my ass.

I shivered as every touch increased my arousal. We'd barely done anything and I was as turned on as hell. And still mostly dressed. I was definitely a convert to Tully's sensation play. It was next level and then some.

"Can I unhook your bra?" he asked.

"Please." I wasn't sure if I was agreeing or begging for more. Maybe both. My whole body was on fire in the best possible way.

He released the hooks and the fabric sprang apart.

"Your skin is so beautiful." I felt the brush of his lips on my back before he worked his way up to my shoulders. The bed moved as he sat up and started to trace lines up and down from the back of my neck to the top of my panties with the flogger.

"Mmm, Tully. Can you do that a little harder?" I said breathlessly.

"Absolutely I can," he agreed. He brought the flogger down on the skin of my lower back hard enough to leave a slight sting.

The jolt of heat that went all the way through my body was insane.

Holy shit. Somehow he knew just the right amount of pressure to use.

"Is that all right?" he asked.

"Mmm, more than all right," I said. "Can you do that again? Please."

"Of course."

And he did, three or four more times, before I had to say, "Harder, please."

The stinging slap of the leather against my skin was absolute perfection. If foreplay was an art, then he was an artist.

"Oh God, yes, that." I moaned. "Again, please."

He brought it down several more times, before he stopped. "Your skin is the most beautiful shade of pink. Let's try something else, shall we?"

"Yes, yes, anything," I said. I didn't even care at that point, as long as he did *something* to me.

"Can I take off your panties?" he asked.

"Yes please," I said immediately. I lifted my hips to let him hook his fingers into the waistband. He slid them down my legs and off my feet.

As much as anything else he was doing to me, I loved that he stopped to check back with me at every step. His middle name might be consent.

For a trained assassin, he was the master of respect. I adored him all the more for it.

I listened carefully, trying to figure out what he'd do next. I was tempted to peek, but the anticipation was half the excitement.

"I'm going to let you feel this first," he said. "Turn your hand over so your palm is upward. Please."

Because he asked so nicely, and because I wanted to, I turned my hand over.

He ran something firmer, but still smooth, over my skin. Something round, with a flat surface. Curious, I brought over my other hand and felt three flaps of leather which were attached to a handle.

"A paddle?" I guessed.

"Yes," he said. "And because you guessed right, I'm going to use it on you. If that's all right?"

"I'll be disappointed if you don't." Honestly, I couldn't fucking wait. My ass was singing out for his attention. The rest of me wasn't far behind.

"I don't want to disappoint you." Like he did with a feather and the flogger, he ran the paddle lightly over my skin first, touching me all over before he gave me a slight slap on the palm of my hand.

The sections of paddle cracked against each other. The sound and touch was like lightning shooting through me. I was so wet from it, I was drenched.

"I'm going to use this on your ass now," he said. "I'm going to make you nice and pink there too." The bed moved as he shuffled down.

"Come here." He put a hand in mine and guided me up onto all fours. He slipped my still damp bra off the rest of the way. "Hold on to the bedpost."

He pressed my palm against the cool timber until I curled the fingers of both hands around it.

I stuck out my ass and scrunched up my face in anticipation of the pain, but the sting was only slightly more intense than on my hand.

"Again, please." I didn't ask for him to do it harder, not yet. The slap of the paddle was so different to the flogger, it was a sensation in itself.

Two, three more times he slapped the paddle down on my bare skin. Never in exactly the same place. Each time sent a spectacular burst of pain and desire through me. I was so hot I was about ready to hump the bed post.

"Tully," I said with what little voice I could muster. "I want you. Please."

"Loveliness, I want you too." He must have tossed the paddle onto the tray because it landed with a clatter.

He knelt beside me and cupped my ass with his hands. Slowly and deliberately, he slid his calloused fingers around my cheeks and up my back. When he reached my sides, he slipped his hands underneath me, over my stomach and up under my breasts.

I wanted to see him, but at the same time I only wanted to feel him touch me. For now, I left the blindfold in place.

He slid his hands up between my breasts and up to my face. He traced circles around the still fading bruises on my cheek before he kissed my mouth.

He tasted lightly of beer and garlic from the dinner we shared. His upper lip and chin were rough with a few days' worth of growth of stubble. His mouth, so wide and generous, felt like he might devour me.

I'd let him.

He drew me away from the bedpost and onto my back beside him.

My hands free of the bedpost, I let my hands wander over him. At some point during all of this, he'd shed his clothes. It almost didn't seem fair that I couldn't see him naked, but what I felt was pretty fucking impressive.

His body was firm and hard, ripples of muscle, slanted here and there with scars and dips where his skin moulded over his bones.

"You feel amazing," I said between luscious, deep kisses.

"No, you," he said. He broke off from my mouth and kissed down the side of my jaw to my throat. From there, he slowly worked his way down to my breasts.

Both of them were aching to be touched. By the time he slid his tongue over my nipple, my whole body was ready to scream.

Instead, I huffed a breath out through my nose and ran my fingernails over his back.

"You can do that harder if you like," he said between licks. "Leave some scratch marks."

While he mercilessly licked and sucked my nipples, I did just that, digging my nails into his skin until he groaned with pleasure.

Eventually, and I sensed with reluctance, he kissed and licked his way further down my body. He teased my belly button with the tip of his tongue and made me giggle.

"That tickles," I protested, but not too hard.

He chuckled and moved down until his stubble grazed the inside of my thighs.

I shivered with delicious anticipation.

Anticipation he drew out as long as he could, by kissing his way down to my knees and back up the other thigh.

"You are such a tease," I complained.

"I like to take my time," he said unapologetically. Still, he gently bent my knee and, lighter than a feather, lapped the tip of his tongue over the hood of my clit.

I didn't hesitate to say, "Harder, please."

"Yes ma'am." He lapped firmer now, his tongue deliberate and skilled. He played me as well as he played any of his guitars, with care and attention, obviously watching for my reactions so he knew what I liked.

I liked it all, especially when he slipped a couple of firm, rough fingers inside me.

"You're wetter than the bath," he said.

"I bet I am," I said. I was so fucking aroused I could barely think straight. "I'm going to come."

"Please do." He went on working me until a peak of pleasure rushed over me.

I curled my fingers into the bedcovers and bucked against his mouth. The orgasm was hard and fast, with the promise of only being the first of many.

He waited until I came down before he slid his fingers out of me. The bed moved and I found something else pressed against my lips. His fingers, slick with my juices.

"How does this taste?" When I opened my mouth, he slipped them inside and let me suck. The taste of his skin and my arousal was delicious.

"If I could bottle it, I would make a fortune," I said around his fingertips. When he slipped them back out, I added, "I want you inside me. Please"

"Gladly," he said. His voice was rough with desire. He rolled me over on my side so I was facing him, and drew one of my legs over his hip.

I felt his erection against my thigh before he pressed the tip into the entrance of my pussy. He stayed like that for at least a minute or two.

"I want to enjoy every second of this," he whispered. "You're so fucking worth the wait."

"So are you," I said.

Just as I started to think he was going to stay like that forever, he slid in deeper and let out a soft groan.

Again he went still for a minute or two before he started to move with slow, intense strokes. There was nothing frantic or hurried about his movements. He slid all the way to his balls, then all the way back to his tip, drawing out each thrust.

"You feel incredible." He filled me to the brim with his cock. He must have had a piercing, I felt something smooth nudge my g-spot with each thrust.

"You don't feel so bad yourself." I couldn't take it anymore. "Can you take this off, please?" I needed to see him, to watch his hard body move as he fucked me.

"Of course."

The blindfold slipped off my eyes and I blinked at the sudden light and his soft smile.

Just as I suspected, his body was all muscles, tattoos and scars.

Holy shit, he was hot.

"You're beautiful," I told him.

"No, you." He grunted and his breath quivered. "I'm going to come. Can I come inside your gorgeous body?"

"Oh, fuck, yes please." I was on the edge again myself before he asked. Afterward, I was absolutely out-of-my-mind aroused.

He thrust a little faster now and slipped his hand down between us to rub my clit. A few strokes was all it took to have me quivering and shattered on the end of his fingers and cock.

As if me coming drew his orgasm out of him, Tully came too, grunting and bucking against me, balls grinding, prolonging the pleasure for us both.

Finally we fell in a tangle of arms, legs and sweat. I lay there panting until my head cleared and I caught my breath.

"That was... Wow." I exhaled long and low.

"Just the beginning," he said. "The bath should still be warm enough. Let me clean you up."

CHAPTER
SEVEN

ABBIE

WHAT THE FUCK?" I stared at the photo on the screen.

I was a little sore and tired from the night before, so I'd left Tully to sleep and had a quick shower before getting dressed in a tee and track pants. A lazy start to the day called for casual clothes.

While the kettle heated up for a much-needed coffee, I picked up my phone to scroll through social media.

The first thing I saw, after a picture of someone's cat, was a photo of the guys in the restaurant last night. They looked like they had a good time. They were smiling and laughing with a group of other people. No one I recognised.

I smiled in response to their infectious smiles. Even in candid photos, they were hot and charismatic. And mine.

I scrolled on down the feed and froze.

"What the—"

In the next photo, Penn was sitting with a woman on his lap.

Okay, that was cool. We weren't together like I was with Zeke, Asher and Tully. He could do what he wanted, with whomever he wanted, whenever he wanted.

Then why the fuck did it bother me so much?

All right, I admit it, I enlarged the photo for a better look at her. Who was she?

Probably a random fan of the band. From the look on her face, she was having the time of her life. Penn looked indifferent, but he wasn't pushing her off.

Whatever, come on, Abbie. Let it go. He's made it clear he's not interested in you. Why shouldn't he hook up with her?

I knew the answer to that. Right or wrong, I was drawn to the guy. I wanted him, even now. Fuck, I was jealous.

I needed to get a grip.

I pinched the screen back to the normal size and went on scrolling.

I froze again.

What the absolute mother-loving fuck?

The next photo on my feed was one of all of the guys. They sat at a table in the restaurant, empty plates in front of them. Landon and Channing had their arms looped around each other. Penn had the same woman on his lap.

Asher and Zeke each had a woman on their laps.

My heart stopped.

Like the woman on Penn's lap, these two looked like they were having a shit ton of fun. Each had an arm around the guys' shoulders, their cheeks pressed to theirs, and were smiling at the camera.

The guys were grinning like they were out on a date with their girlfriends.

"What the fuck?" I said under my breath.

"What is it?" Tully was standing near the hotel phone, looking at the room service menu. I hadn't even noticed him get out of bed.

If I wasn't so floored, I would have taken the time to appreciate how beautifully naked he was.

Instead, I rose from the chair I was perched on and walked over to show him my phone.

His eyebrows rose. "Oh." For a while that seemed to be all he could say. Then finally, "I'm sure there's a perfectly good explanation."

"I'm sure there is," I said wryly. "Like when I'm not around, they do shit like this?" They hadn't even tried to hide it. They knew the camera was on them.

"Abbie—" Tully put a hand on my arm. "Do me a favour and don't jump to conclusions until we've spoken to them. If this shit is how it looks, then we'll deal with it."

"Are you going to kill them for me?" I was joking.

Mostly.

Ish.

"Maybe after the tour." Evidently, he wasn't ruling it out either.

Okay, I didn't want them dead and he was right, there might be a perfectly reasonable explanation for it, but the photos still made me incredibly uncomfortable. How would they feel if I was sitting in a strange guy's lap, smiling at the camera? As jealous as I felt right now, wouldn't they?

"I was going to order us breakfast, but would you prefer to go down and eat in the restaurant with them?" he asked gently.

It was completely unfair that I was standing in a hotel room in Perth with a gloriously gorgeous, naked rock god who paddled my ass last night, and all I could think of was a bunch of stupid photos. I should be enjoying my time here with him.

"We'll get lots of other chances," he said as though he read my mind. He drew me into his arms and slowly kissed my mouth.

"When you put it that way," I slipped my arms around his neck, "maybe we could go back to bed instead? We don't have to be at the soundcheck for a while. There's plenty of time to fit in breakfast somewhere in there."

My irritation didn't completely melt away, but I wasn't going to ruin this time between us with what might be jealousy over nothing. If there was something to it, I'd fucking deal with it later.

"I know better than to argue with a beautiful woman." Tully pushed my track pants down until they dropped to the floor. My panties went next, while I pulled off my shirt and bra that I'd only worn for about five minutes.

Oh well, it was good while it lasted.

"When did you get so enlightened?" I asked.

He cupped my ass, then slid his hands down lower to hoist me up until my legs wrapped around his waist. He carried me over to the bed and lowered me down. He lay down beside me before grabbing me and rolling me so I was full length on top of him.

He grinned up at me. "When I realised not arguing was more likely to lead to you lying on top of me just like this."

"Oh." I kissed his wide mouth. "You have it all figured out." I kissed him again.

"You better believe I do," he said. "It was all part of my nefarious plan."

"Nefarious?" I echoed. "I don't know, but I think it might be too early in the day, and we haven't had enough caffeine, for a word like that. What does that even mean?"

He chuckled. "I'm not exactly sure, but it probably applies to me. It sounded like a good fit."

"Speaking of a good fit..." I reached between us and curled my hand around his already erect cock.

My fingers found the warm metal of what I now knew was a reverse Prince Albert piercing, and slotted in under the barbell.

He explained he got it to make himself suffer for killing a man for money, but it felt so good inside me. That might be wrong on some level, but I couldn't bring myself to care right now.

Just the thought of it was enough to make me fucking wet.

As soon as he was fully hard, I placed my hands on his chest and lowered my pussy down onto his cock. With a little manoeuvring, his piercing massaged by g-spot. My clit slapped against the base of his stomach.

"Why did you get the reverse Prince Albert not the Prince Albert?" I asked, my eyes half closed.

He smiled at me and reached up to run his hands lightly over my breasts.

"Because this works better for face-to-face. I like to look at you. To know you feel good. And I get to see your gorgeous breasts. It seemed like all the winning to me."

"Me too." I rode him slowly. How funny that something he did as punishment to himself brought a ton of pleasure to me. I tried not to think about that in a way, a man died for this. If Tully said he deserved it, I believed him.

And the sex was really, really good.

I closed my eyes fully, and like I did the night before, surrendered to sensation and stopped thinking too much about things that didn't matter right now. The only thing that mattered was here and now, this moment, our two bodies sliding together, the delicious friction created between us.

"You are the most incredible woman," he said so softly I almost missed hearing him say it.

"You're incredible yourself," I whispered back. I thought I was satisfied last night, enough to keep me for a while, but I was quickly hurtling towards a beautiful abyss where I would happily stay forever if I could.

My hands curled and I raked my nails lightly over his chest. The marks I left there now would match the ones on his back.

I wanted to cling to him forever, to make this moment last, but I couldn't hold back the orgasm that rushed over me. It made my blood thunder through my body like a tsunami of pleasure with a few bolts of lightning and some fireworks thrown in for good measure.

I threw back my head and cried towards the ceiling.

As if the sound pushed him over the edge, Tully came, thrusting harder and harder into me, his breath a series of ragged grunts. His hands gripped my breasts to the point of exquisite pain. It drew my orgasm out longer, until I felt like my body might be completely sucked dry of every drop of pleasure.

Only when it was done was I able to start to catch my breath, a little bit of reality came crashing back in.

I was going to have to deal with the other guys and those photos.

CHAPTER
EIGHT

ABBIE

I DIDN'T NEED a mirror to know my expression was grim when I stepped into the hotel room the other guys were sharing.

Tully followed me in, a hand on my shoulder for reassurance.

"I was wondering when you two would appear," Asher said lightly. "Did you have a nice time?" He didn't even look slightly guilty.

Should I be more worried than I was, or less?

"Yes, it was lovely," I said vaguely. "How about you guys?" If they did something to piss me off, I hoped they'd admit to it now.

This was their chance, before I asked about the photos.

"It was about the usual," Zeke said. "Dinner and a few drinks. Nothing exciting." He also didn't look guilty. He got up from the chair he was sitting in and pushed his phone into his pocket.

Considering their *usual* seemed to involve a different groupie every night, his words weren't encouraging. Maybe they were so desensitised to it that they didn't see anything wrong with it.

"Nothing exciting, huh?" Tully stepped out from behind me and crossed his arms over his chest.

"No new heads," Landon said.

"Thank fuck," Penn muttered.

That was something, I suppose. We had all survived the night.

"Are you okay, love?" Asher asked. "You look a little pale. Did Tully go too hard?" He looked worried, but at the same time, like he was trying not to smile.

"No, Tully was fine," I said absently. "More than fine," I added when I realised I might have made him sound inadequate. "Like I said, it was lovely."

Zeke frowned and looked from Tully to me and back again. "Okay, what's going on? Did you two get married or something?"

"Oh, hell no," I said immediately. I was never going to do that again with anyone.

At least, I couldn't *imagine* doing it again. Not even with any of these guys. Relationships were so much more than a piece of paper. I didn't need that to know I was loved.

But—was I loved?

"We saw some photos of you guys online," Tully said.

Every single face stared at us with a blank, confused look.

It was Asher who broke the silence with, "Penn, have you been posting dick pics online again?"

Penn snorted. "If I posted pics of my cock online, they would break the internet with my awesomeness." After a moment he added, "That would be a no."

"We figured," Asher said.

"What photos are you talking about, sweetheart?" Zeke asked me.

I cocked my head at him, but he seemed genuinely confused. That or he was a good actor. What line had he spun for the woman on his lap?

I pulled out my phone and switched on the screen. I found the last photo and turned my phone around to show him.

He leaned forward and peered at it. His eyebrows twitched, but that was the only sign of any kind of emotion.

"Oh, that." He was still completely unworried.

"Yes, that." I tilted the screen so all the guys could take a look.

Penn seemed the most interested. "See, I don't even need to share photos of my cock. I look pretty fucking good right there." He gestured towards my phone, palm upward.

"That's a good angle for you," Asher agreed.

I lowered my hand. "Really? That's all you have to say about it? What about the fact there are women sitting on your laps, their hands all over you?"

They all frowned at me. Did they really not understand why I might be pissed off? Apparently they didn't. Was I not being clear or did they not give a shit?

"Right," I said finally. I tucked my phone into my pocket. "Of course. It's no big deal. You met some women and hooked up like you've done, what? A thousand times before? No big deal."

Only, it *was* a big deal. I felt like they'd stabbed me through the heart and twisted the knife. It wasn't even a nice, quiet assassination while I slept. It was yet another, very public act, and it was humiliating. It dredged up a bunch of old—okay not that old—heartbreak.

Those feelings were more raw than I expected.

Now confronted by them, I realised I hadn't put them behind me as well as I thought. I felt like I was starting to unravel, just when I thought my life was back on track.

I should have known I couldn't put all the shit of my past behind me. Whatever happened and wherever I went, I kept making stupid fucking decisions. Was trusting these guys yet another one?

Right now my brain was topsy-turvy and I wanted to throw up.

Asher laughed.

Laughed.

I swung my face around and glared at him.

None of this was okay. I was angry and he thought it was funny. What the fuck? Maybe I didn't know him at all.

"What's so funny?" I demanded. "I thought you cared about me." Fuck, now I was going to cry in front of them. I blinked back tears that threatened to slide down my face.

Fucking hell.

"We didn't hook up with any of them." It was Zeke who responded. "You have no idea who they are?"

"Should I?" I asked. Demanded.

"I don't have a clue," Tully said.

"Ohhh, I get it," Asher drawled. "No, it's definitely *not* what you think. Those women, they're Cameo Orchid. They just signed with White Wolf Records. They're doing a small tour and happened to be in town the same time as us. Jackson introduced us and suggested we take some photos as publicity for them."

He made it all sound perfectly reasonable.

"Jackson suggested they sit on your laps?" My voice sounded colder than I intended, but his words barely made a dent in my emotions..

"No. That was their idea," Asher said lightly. "We…" He exchanged glances with Zeke. "We didn't think there was any harm in it."

"We would have told you, but you were busy with Tully," Zeke said, as if that magically made everything all right. As if it was okay to make this Tully's and my fault.

Zeke looked at me intently. "Like Asher said, it wasn't a big deal. It was just a couple of photos for publicity. Jackson took the photos. I'm sure he'd show you the rest if you want to have a look. They'll show you nothing went on."

"Did they know it was just for publicity?" I asked. "This… Cameo Orchid? Because they seemed awfully comfortable."

I sounded like a jealous bitch, but it went deeper than that. I believed them when they said nothing happened, but there was more to it. Something apparently none of them considered.

"Jazz tried to touch my cock," Penn said. He shrugged like it was an everyday occurrence. Maybe it was.

Zeke and Asher exchanged confused glances again.

"Like we said, it was their idea," Zeke said. "The whole thing was over faster than Penn getting himself off."

Penn flipped him the bird. "I'm not that quick, asshole."

"But the photos were," Asher said. "I promise you, that was all there was. Just a couple of publicity photos."

"Photos designed to make the public think you guys are with these women," I said. "Photos designed to generate gossip. Photos designed to boost their popularity because people think they each managed to snag a member of Wolf Venom, even if it's just for a night."

I watched their faces as the penny started to drop. They should all know by now how I felt about using fake relationships to make and sell a person's image.

"I can see how it might be construed that way," Zeke said carefully. "That wasn't my intention."

"No, but it was probably theirs," I agreed. "But you guys went along with it. And so did Jackson. He of all people should know better."

They all fucking should. Hot tears prickled the corners of my eyes.

"To be fair to Jackson, his job is to sell all of us," Zeke said reasonably. "Sometimes that means doing shit like this."

"Are you okay with that?" I asked. "Would you be okay with it if Jackson told you to marry one of them, just for publicity?"

Zeke looked at me in shock. "Fuck no. There's a big difference between that and having someone sit on your lap."

"Is there?" The expression on his face made me wonder if I was overreacting, but after the way I was used, I didn't want it to happen to anyone else, the guys, or another band.

"You're still presenting a fake relationship to the public," I said. "Those photos are very... I don't know. It looks like you're dating them." I twisted the knife into my own heart by saying that out loud.

Zeke stepped towards me and put out his hand, but I moved away. I was too pissed to let him touch me.

"Abbie—" He lowered his hand and sighed in frustration. "Sweetheart, you know what this business is like. Most of what the public sees is fake."

I knew that, I really did, but I didn't have to like it.

"Is it any different when you take a selfie with someone?" Zeke reasoned. "Don't you make it look like you're friends?"

"No, I don't," I said. "I certainly don't sit on anyone's laps. Not if it's someone I'm not in a relationship with."

"So you're jealous they were sitting on our laps and you weren't?" Penn asked. He shook his head and sneered.

"That's beside the point," I said.

"Is it?" He crossed his arms over his chest. "I think that's the whole point. You thought you had those two pussy whipped," he waved his fingers towards Asher and Zeke, "and you can't handle one little publicity shot with another woman. How are you going to handle it when they have photos taken with backing singers? You know they have photos taken with fans, don't you?"

"Of course I do," I spluttered. "That's beside the point—"

"It's exactly the point," he said evenly. "Our lives don't revolve around you twenty-four hours a day, seven days a week. And you *hate* that." He took a step towards me. "And you know what else you hate? You hate the fact you didn't realise what Vance did to you was a publicity stunt. You automatically want to assume every woman is as clueless as you. But they weren't. They knew exactly what was going on. And you know what? They enjoyed it, and so did we. *All of us.*"

I gaped. This was nasty, even for him.

I looked him right in the eyes and said, "Fuck you."

Through a haze of tears I turned and yanked open the hotel room door.

"Abbie—" One of the guys called out after me. I didn't know who and I didn't care right now.

I let the door bang shut behind me and headed down the stairs and away from the hotel.

CHAPTER
NINE

TULLY

"FUCKING HELL, PENN," Zeke growled at the keyboardist.

I glared daggers at the man. Did he really need to be such an asshole?

Penn shrugged. "What about that wasn't true?"

"The part where you made it sound like we were fucking them," Asher growled.

"We were innocent bystanders," Landon pointed out.

Channing nodded his agreement.

"It was fucking innocent," Zeke said. He ran a hand over his hair. "But I'm starting to wish we'd said no to doing it."

"Why?" Penn scoffed. "Because you're as pussy whipped as I said you were? Come off it, dude. It was no big deal until she made it a big deal. It's still not a big deal. It was one little fucking photo. We weren't rolling around naked in mud. If we were, it still wouldn't be a big deal. Not everything is Abbie's business."

"When are you going to admit you've fallen as hard for her as the rest of us?" I asked softly. "We all know it but you have to keep being a motherfucker and pretending you hate her guts."

He glared at me. "Has it ever crossed your mind that I *do* hate her guts, Tull?"

"No," I replied. "But it's crossed my mind she might hate yours if you keep behaving like a shithead. I'm going after her."

Without waiting for a response from him, I grabbed the door handle and jerked it open.

"I'm going with you," Asher said.

"Me too." Zeke was right behind us. "You three stay here in case she comes back. If she does, let us know."

Penn grunted something.

I suspected he had no intention of coming with us anyway. That was fine by me. He'd done enough damage.

"Will do," Landon said. "Keep in touch with us. I'm scared for her with a killer out there. What if they get to her next?"

"They won't," Channing said firmly. "She'll be fine. They'll find her." He gave Landon a hug and a quick kiss on the mouth.

I let the door swing shut behind us and hurried towards the elevator. Of course, it was on the ground floor so we had to press the button and wait for it to come back up to us.

"It might be quicker to take the stairs," Asher pointed out when the elevator was on the floor below ours.

"Too late now." Zeke shrugged. A couple of seconds later, a ping echoed through the corridor and the doors slid open.

We stepped inside and Asher turned to face me as the doors slid shut.

"Are you pissed off at us too, Tull?" he asked. "It seemed like a good idea at the time."

I shrugged. "It is what it is. If I was there, I would have posed with the rest of you. When Abbie calms down, she'll realise she would have done the same thing."

"Maybe." Asher looked uncertain. "But it wouldn't have happened at all if Abbie was there. We would have stood, a group of musos, hanging out together."

"Abbie was right," Zeke said slowly. "People will assume shit. That includes Reuben, and the killer."

"Unless they're the same person," Asher pointed out.

"Yes, unless Reuben hired the killer," Zeke agreed. "Either way, they could go after Cameo Orchid to get at the label or at us, or think they're getting rid of another of Abbie's enemies. Now was a stupid fucking time to get chummy with anyone." He looked furious with himself.

"Anyone could go to the White Wolf Records website to see who else they've signed," I pointed out. "If they wanted to go after the label, they don't need a photo."

If the killer wasn't after the label then yeah, the guys potentially made the other band a target.

"Can we blame Jackson?" Asher asked lightly.

"Only partially," Zeke said. "Mostly it was us not thinking, and getting caught up in the moment. We've done shit like that a thousand times before, but never when so much was at stake."

"Is this where you suggest leaving the band to keep us all safe?" Asher asked. "Because you know we're not letting you leave, right Tully?"

"Right," I agreed. "We're all in this together. And fuck knows we can look after ourselves." We all had the skills to kill if we had to.

"Yeah, we can," Asher agreed. "But I've never been more tempted to hire you to take out Penn."

"I've never been so tempted to let you hire me," I said, only half joking.

"No one is taking a hit out on Penn," Zeke said. After a moment of expectant silence, he added, "If anyone is going to organise it, it will be me."

We all gave brief laughs. None of us would ever act on that, we just shared a dark, sometimes macabre sense of humour.

The elevator pinged and the doors opened on the ground floor.

I looked around the lobby, but saw no sign of Abbie.

The people behind the front desk had their eyes down on the computers. Those sitting in the café to the side of the lobby sipped their breakfast coffee without giving us more than a passing glance. A couple looked slightly disapproving at our torn jeans and faded T-shirts, not to mention the abundant tattoos we all had on display.

Evidently they thought the hotel was too fancy for scruffy rock stars.

Penn probably would have flipped them off and told them he had more money than they did, but I just walked past like I belonged there.

Fuck them, I was as entitled to be there as they were.

Asher muttered something about entitled assholes, as we stepped out the front doors when they slid open for us.

It was another beautiful day in Perth. The sky was a striking blue and the air was warm. Summer was only a handful of weeks away. Tonight's concert was in an open roofed arena, and this was the perfect weather for it.

If we found Abbie in time to get there. A public whipping would be the least of our trouble if we missed it.

"I can't see her anywhere." Zeke stopped and turned a slow circle. "She couldn't have gotten too far."

I scanned the street around us, but saw no sign of the beautiful blond.

"She had her phone with her, let's try her on that," I said.

"Yes. Good idea." Zeke pulled out his phone and tapped at the screen. He put it to his ear and waited.

And waited.

"It's gone to voicemail. I guess she doesn't want to talk to us yet." He ended the call and tapped at the screen again. "I'll send her a text. She'll know we're out here looking for her."

"If she looks at it," Asher said.

"She'll look at it when she's ready," I said.

"Maybe you should send her one," Asher said. "She's not pissed off at you."

"Or try calling," Zeke suggested.

I pulled out my phone and tried her number. It rang a few times but then went to voicemail.

"We're worried about you. Call me back." I ended the call and sent the same message via text. I watched until my phone said it was sent, then tucked it away in my pocket.

"Should we split up and look?" Asher asked.

Zeke shook his head. "I'm starting to get a bad feeling about this and I don't want anyone off by themselves."

"Same here." My spine tingled uncomfortably. All my senses were on high alert. I was trained to be observant, to take in every potential threat or observer that might cause me trouble. I leaned on that now.

"No one in the lobby seemed concerned," I said slowly. "There's no other way out without going via the front desk or the garage. The elevator came from the ground floor, so she didn't go through the garage."

Zeke nodded as he followed my reasoning. "When she came out of the elevator, she must have been walking, so no one paid attention to her."

"If she was running, the people in the lobby would still be reacting," Asher said.

"Exactly," I said. "So she got out here slowly, but then quickly disappeared out of sight. How does that happen?"

"A number of ways," Zeke said. "None of them good." He pulled out his phone. "Luckily I put a tracker on her phone, in case shit like this happened."

"Babe, you could have said that when we first got out here," Asher said.

"I just remembered," Zeke admitted. He squinted at his screen, then pointed down the street. "She's this way."

We followed him and his phone, but I kept all of my senses open. Would there come a day when I could completely relax and forget about my training? We were on tour, we should be enjoying ourselves, not worrying about threats and heads in boxes.

I wanted to agree with Channing's assumption the killer wouldn't get to Abbie, but I wasn't so sure. They seemed to be getting more and more brazen. Taking Abbie right off the street might be their next step.

If that was the case, I would hunt them down and make them pay, and I wouldn't regret a second of it. I would make the motherfucker scream, not in a good way.

"Are you sure this is the right direction?" Asher asked. "Also, when did you get a chance to put a tracker on her phone?"

Zeke glanced up and grinned. "Back when she was staying in my place. After what happened with Jonah, I wanted to keep an eye on her. I would have put a tracker on her, but it's difficult to do without the person knowing about it."

Asher blinked at him a couple of times. "Where is it?"

"Where is what?" Zeke cocked his head and frowned.

"The tracker," Asher insisted. "Did you put one on me?" His hands hovered by his sides like he was ready to pat himself down to find it.

Zeke grinned. "Maybe I did, maybe I didn't."

While Asher stared at Zeke with wide eyes, I shook my head.

"You'd set off airport security if you had a tracker inside you," I said. "If he has a tracker on the rest of us, it's in our phones."

"Zeke?" Asher asked.

"I neither confirm nor deny," Zeke said. "This way. She's not far." He nodded in the direction of a small park maybe a hundred metres away.

It made sense for her to be there, clearing her thoughts. It was the kind of place I'd go too.

I squinted and scanned the area, but couldn't see any sign of her.

"She might be sitting under a tree," Asher suggested.

But she wasn't. We checked around every tree and even behind some bushes as we got closer to the tracker signal.

"It's just ahead," Zeke gestured. "Right… there."

A park bench sat under the shade of a tall gumtree. In the centre of the seat lay a phone.

In case there was any doubt, I pulled out my phone and pressed Abbie's number.

On the bench, the phone started to vibrate and play the start of one of our songs. Abbie's ringtone.

"That's hers all right," Asher said softly. He crept forward and picked up the phone as though he expected it to explode.

Honestly, I wouldn't have been surprised if it had. But it didn't.

Asher tapped the screen. "Missed messages and calls from us, but that's it. No numbers I don't recognise. Her phone doesn't seem to be damaged. It's like she put it down and walked off without it."

Zeke shook his head. "She wouldn't do that. She wouldn't risk anyone finding it and her personal photos."

I turned around and scanned the area. "Then where the fuck is she?"

CHAPTER
TEN

ABBIE

I WOKE SLOWLY, with a pounding headache and crusty, dry eyes.

My mind was groggy and slow, but I acknowledged two things.

First, there was something over my eyes, like a blindfold or a scarf. Secondly, my wrists and ankles were bound.

It didn't feel like the Kim Jelly, and I did—was it still just last night? I had no idea how much time had passed. It didn't feel like long, but it could have been days. Or longer. Had I missed any concerts?

Hell, why was that the first thing that popped into my head? What about the fact I was tied up by fuck knows who, who might not let me live for much longer?

That should worry me a shitload more than work.

"She's awake," a male voice said.

That gave me two more pieces of information. A man was involved and he wasn't alone. Unless he was talking to himself. That was confirmed a moment later when another voice spoke.

"So she is. I told you I didn't give her too much."

Too much what?

Memories came crawling back to me slowly, unpleasantly.

I walked out of the hotel like nothing was wrong. I didn't want to draw attention to myself. At the same time, I was trying not to cry.

Maybe I was overreacting about the photos, but Penn didn't need to be a prick about it. He certainly didn't need to imply I was a complete idiot because I didn't know what Vance planned.

I was naive and in love, yeah, but not stupid. I saw the red flags, but I ignored every one of them. I wanted to believe he loved me too. There was nothing wrong with having faith in people.

Was there?

If Penn thought there was, then he could fuck off.

Once out on the street, I turned and walked in no particular direction. I found a small park and sat down on the bench. A guy came and sat beside me.

Memories came crashing back in, faster and more vivid now.

Hunter Brantley smiled at me. "Hey. Parker and I missed you."

I blinked at him in surprise. "What the fuck are you doing here?" The last time I saw Zeke's youngest, twin brothers, they dropped me off outside his house after they took me to speak to Reuben. At gunpoint. They were the last people I expected to see today. The last I wanted to see, except Penn.

"Shouldn't you be in school?" I asked.

"We're on holidays," Hunter said. "We thought we'd pop over to WA and say hi."

I didn't believe a single word of that. Still I gave him a fake smile and said, "Hi. I should be going."

The flicker of his eyes was the only warning I had that anyone was behind me. Before I could move, something clamped over my mouth. Cold, rough fabric, saturated with something that smelled medicinal and made my head spin.

"Not too much, Parker," Hunter said. "We don't want her asleep for too long."

Asleep? What the fuck?

In a matter of seconds, my eyes got heavy. I didn't know anything else until I woke up here.

"What do you want?" My voice was groggy but at least I wasn't gagged. Yet.

"Maybe we just want your company," Parker suggested. His voice was slightly deeper than Hunter's. That was the only way I could tell them apart.

"You could have asked." I struggled to sit up, but my head spun.

"Where's the fun in that?" Hunter asked cheerfully. He slid his hand up the inside of my thigh.

I shuddered and tried to pull away. Even if I wasn't half drugged, I wasn't strong enough to fight off both of them if they decided to rape me.

"Are you the ones killing people?" I asked. "Jonah. Vance." Those were the ones I knew the evil twins would know about. If they didn't know about the others, I wasn't going to tell them.

"I don't know, did we kill anyone Parker?" Hunter asked

"Recently?" Parker asked. "It's possible, but not Jonah."

"I don't think we killed Vance either, did we?" Hunter asked.

"No, I don't think so," Parker agreed. "Should we have?"

"It doesn't sound like it matters," Hunter said. "I mean, if he's dead already, then we don't need to do it."

"Good point," Parker said. "Plus Reuben doesn't like it if we kill people he doesn't tell us to kill."

"Did he tell you to kill me?" I asked. If they raped and killed me, they would have Zeke to answer to. And Asher and Tully at least. Maybe Landon and Channing too. Penn would probably find it funny. Asshole.

"Not yet," Parker said. "He sent us with a warning. He doesn't think Zeke or you took him seriously."

Hunter's fingers ghosted across the gusset of my panties. "He also wants to remind Zeke that he can reach him wherever he goes."

"We totally took him seriously." I was trying hard not to freak out. It wasn't the first time I'd been touched without my consent, but it was the most intimate. It was one thing to have my ass grabbed, but another to only have a thin sliver of fabric between Hunter's fingers and my pussy.

"I told him what Reuben said. You know what Zeke is like. He's not going to let me or anyone else dictate what he does."

"How hard did you try?" Hunter slid his fingers back the other way.

I swallowed and tried not to cry or give in to fear. "I don't know what you want me to say. I passed on the message. I can't make him leave Wolf Venom. The band is his life."

"Is that right?" A hand, I assumed it was Parker's, stroked over the side of my breast. "You must not be as close as we thought you were. What lengths would he go to, to keep you safe?"

I blinked away tears, glad now for the blindfold that stopped them from seeing them.

"Would he give up the band to save your life?" Hunter asked. His fingers stroked back the other way again.

"I don't know," I admitted. "He cares about me." I didn't mention that the last time I spoke to Zeke, I was angry at all of the guys except Tully. If the twins suspected we had any kind of fight, then my life might not be worth anything. I suspected they wouldn't kill me until they'd followed through with their implied threat of forcing themselves on me.

This day kept on getting better and fucking better, didn't it?

"You might need to impress upon him that he needs to make that choice," Hunter said. "You see how easy it was to get to you. How helpless you are right now. How vulnerable. Right now, Parker and I could do whatever we wanted to you and you would be powerless to stop us. You know that, right?"

"Yes." My voice came out in a squeak. I sounded like a terrified mouse.

Honestly, that was more or less accurate.

"I know that." Did I beg them not to, or did I remind them what their big brother would do to them if they harmed me? I didn't know if Zeke would give up the band, even for me, but I knew he would kick their asses into next year. He might even be tempted to let Tully use his skills on them. Or better yet, lock them in a room with Penn and his bullshit attitude.

Fingers lifted up the corner of the blindfold, before it was peeled off my face.

I blinked against the sudden glare. I lay in what looked like a hotel room, on a narrow bed. Judging by the way the sun was slanted in through the window, it was late afternoon. If it was still the same day, then I hadn't missed the concert yet.

I would like nothing more than to get there on time, alive and unraped.

Hunter smiled at me then took his hand out from under my skirt. "As much as we would like to have more fun with you, we don't have time. Besides, that will give you something to look forward to when we meet again. If Zeke hasn't listened by then."

"That's something to look forward to," I said sarcastically. My mind was a little clearer now, and relieved that apparently I wasn't going to be raped today. Or murdered.

"It really is." Parker gripped my nipple between his thumb and forefinger and squeezed.

I winced.

Hunter moved so his face was right in front of mine, close enough for his breath to brush my cheek.

"We are reasonable, you know," he said as though that was actually true. "Reuben doesn't expect Zeke to quit the band in the middle of the tour. All he has to do is assure our big brother that he'll come back to the family when it's over. Otherwise, we will find you again. Next time, we'll make sure we have longer to play with you. A few days maybe."

The idea made me want to bring up my breakfast. And last night's dinner.

"What would your girlfriend think of that?" I asked.

Hunter froze in surprise. He forced a smile onto his face, obviously trying to cover the fact I'd caught him off guard. "What girlfriend would that be?"

I wasn't sure if I should step in any deeper or back the fuck off right now, but I doubted he was going to let it go until I told him what I knew.

"Lila Bell," I said.

According to Asher's brother Dane, the Brantley twins were sleeping with her. From what Dane said, Reuben would be pissed if he knew. Zeke wrestled with the idea of telling him. Judging by Hunter's reaction, he hadn't, and neither had anyone else. He was probably working under the illusion no one knew.

Surprise, asshole. Only, how fucked was I for springing it on him?

Hunter's eyes flicked to Parker. He looked more than slightly alarmed. That sent a shiver of fear through me. This could either be a bargaining chip, or my death warrant.

"It's interesting you know that," Parker said slowly. He moved into view and sat down beside me.

"Does Reuben know?" I asked. Fuck it, I'd gone this far, I might as well wade right on in. When neither of them answered, I continued. "Would you prefer he not know? Because Zeke knows. He might be persuaded to keep his mouth shut."

"It's not that simple." Hunter looked disconcerted for the first time since he'd taken my blindfold off. "We're only here doing what Reuben told us to do."

"Kidnap me and threatened me with rape?" I said. "Your brother is charming. Not."

Hunter shrugged. "Whatever it takes to get his way."

"What will he do with you if he hears you're fucking Lila?" I asked.

They exchanged glances again. "We'd prefer he didn't know about it just yet," Parker said.

"In return for what?" I wanted them to promise to leave me, Zeke and the rest of the guys alone if we kept our mouths shut, but that didn't seem to be in their power to give. If Reuben sent them somewhere, they would go, or risk whatever punishment he would give them if they refused. I suspected that wouldn't be pretty. Not that I gave a shit about that, but it was what it was.

"We'll go back to Reuben and tell him you're working on Zeke," Hunter said. "That's all we can offer."

"How about you promise not to rape me, no matter what Reuben asks you to do," I said. "We can always pretend you did." Was I really having this conversation? Yes, for fuck sake I was. Self preservation was important to me.

Hunter sighed like he was giving up his left arm. "Fine, we promise. But I can't promise Reuben won't send somebody else."

"Noted," I said. "Now you can tell me how long I've been here and if I've missed the concert?"

"Only a couple of hours," Parker said. "I guess we could drop you off at the venue before we fly back to Sydney."

How fucking big of them. At least I believed them when they made their promise.

Of course, that didn't mean they wouldn't kill me.

CHAPTER ELEVEN

TULLY

"WHAT THE FUCK, DUDE?" I muttered under my breath. "We shouldn't be here."

"I know, but we have to," Zeke said, every bit as frustrated as I was. "The show must go fucking on."

I opened my mouth to respond, but bit back my anger. It was nothing we hadn't said over and over the last few hours. Abbie was out there and we were supposed to pretend everything was fine and get on with the concert?

Things weren't fine.

Things were fucked the fuck fucking up.

"If it wasn't for Penn and his big, fucking mouth." Asher glared daggers at Penn, who rolled his eyes in response.

"I didn't make the silly bitch walk out," the keyboardist retorted.

I put a hand on Asher's arm before he threw himself at Penn and punched his lights out.

Honestly, it stopped me from doing the same thing.

"Jackson is out there doing what he can to find her," Landon said. "Along with everyone the tour can spare."

"We should be out there," Landon said sulkily. "If it was any one of us, we would be."

"Landon is right," Asher said. "If one of us was missing, the rest of us would be out there looking." He glanced at Penn like he was thinking he might not bother if the keyboardist went missing.

Penn flipped him off. "Chances are, she'll come crawling back any minute now, and all of this worry was for nothing. She probably put down her phone and then fucking forgot when she put it. She's been out there all this time looking for it."

I considered the possibility she put her phone down and walked off without realising, but if that was the case, she would have returned to the hotel hours ago. Or made her way here, to the stadium.

It wasn't far from the hotel... if she was capable of walking here.

At this point, the only thing that made sense was the one thing none of us wanted to think about.

Someone took her. The only, and preferable, alternative was that she was so pissed off at all of us, she deliberately stayed away. I knew what happened brought back memories for her, but I didn't think she was so furious she would hide for hours, or miss the concert.

I was about to lower my hand from Asher's arm, but I slipped it over his shoulders instead.

"She'll be okay," I said firmly. "She's strong and tough. The world has thrown a shit load of things at her and it hasn't broken her. She was angry, but she'll get over it."

He looked miserable, but he nodded. "I wish we hadn't agreed to that stupid publicity shit. If we hadn't done that, she would be here, getting ready to go on stage." He glanced towards the hydraulics for the steps which led up to the stage.

They were currently closed while Blazing Violet performed. The support act had just started, so there was still time for Abbie to appear.

I sent a plea to the universe to make it happen. We hadn't waited millions of years to meet, only to have it end so quickly.

"No offence, dude, but I wish you hadn't too. Or at least told her or me what the fuck was going on. But it's done now and can't be undone. We have to move on from it." Which would only be possible after Abbie returned to us.

I had to believe it was a when and not an if.

"I'm coming to the conclusion the rest of them can't be left unsupervised without you, Tull," Penn said dryly.

"No shit," I said. "I'm away from you guys one night and all hell breaks loose."

"The moral of the story is, don't go off by yourself," Penn said.

"Fuck that." The night Abbie and I shared was one I would never forget. I planned on a repeat performance as soon as we could find a time and place.

After all, she wasn't pissed off at me. Although, she would be if I admitted I would have done the same thing the other guys did. And honestly, I would tell her. I hated keeping secrets from people I cared about. If it meant she punched me in the cock, then so be it.

Better yet, she could save it until we were alone and paddle my ass as hard as she wanted. Okay, first of all, I didn't need to be alone for that, and second of all, I would enjoy it. It might make her feel better though. As far as I was concerned, everybody won.

I paced from the hydraulic stairs to the door of the green room and back again.

While I did that, I ran through the events of this morning through my head. What could we have done differently? We could have used the tracker sooner. We could have gagged Penn. I could have kept her in bed for a few more hours until she was too exhausted to be angry.

Okay, I wouldn't get away with the last one. I managed to distract her for a little while, but she had to deal with those photos at some point. Maybe I should have tied her up and gone to yell at the guys before she could?

Everything seemed to be one long *maybe if...*which at the end of the day changed absolutely nothing. Abbie wasn't here and we were going to have to go onstage and explain her absence. Or not explain and hope the audience didn't throw things at us.

Either way, I wasn't looking forward to performing tonight.

"I'm going to call Jackson," Zeke said impatiently. "He must know something by now."

I didn't bother to correct him. We all knew if Jackson found her, he would have called one of us. Whatever, if it made Zeke feel better, there was no harm in trying.

He moved away from the stairs, to a quieter part of the backstage area and put the phone to his ear.

It was clear he didn't like what he heard. He looked like he was going to turn and walk out of the stadium before our set even began.

I walked over to him as he mashed his thumb against the screen to end the call and shoved his phone forcefully into the back of his jeans.

"Still nothing?" I asked.

"Not a thing," he growled. "It seems like no one has seen her. It's like she dropped off the face of the fucking earth."

That did nothing to settle my anxiety for the woman. If the audience wouldn't notice, I'd leave the stadium and go looking for her. I was sorely tempted. Being here seemed all kinds of wrong. The woman we all cared about was fuck knows where and we were supposed to go out there and pretend we were having the time of our lives.

Surely concerts were cancelled for lesser reasons?

I scrubbed my face with my hand and shook my head. "This is bullshit. Blazing Violet will be finished soon. What the fuck are we supposed to do?"

"Abbie," Asher said.

"Well of course we'd all like to do Abbie—"

"No, Abbie," Asher insisted. He gestured behind me.

I turned around to see her hurrying up the corridor. She looked pale and tired, but in one, beautiful, glorious piece.

We all started toward her, but I was the first one to reach her, put my arms around her and pick her up off her feet. "Where the fuck have you been?"

She gave a little squeal and I set her down. "It's a long story. I'm sorry I'm late."

"Late?" Asher echoed. "You've been missing for hours and we've been worried sick, and you're concerned about being late?" He all but shoved me aside and gave her a firm hug.

"Like I said, it's a long story." She hugged him back. "I'll tell you about it later. It sounds like it's almost my turn to go on."

"It is," Zeke agreed. He had his phone to his ear again. "Yes, she turned up. She's here at the stadium. No, she's fine." He listened for a moment, then shook his head. "No, we don't know where she's been, but you should get your ass here. Yep, bye."

He gave her a hug and said, "Jackson and a bunch of others were out there looking for you. Are you all right?"

"I'm fine," she said lightly.

She didn't seem fine to me, but I suspected that was all we were going to get out of her for now.

"You worried the shit out of me." Zeke pressed his mouth to hers in a hard, heated kiss.

"She worried the shit out of all of us." I eyed Penn. If he said anything stupid now, I might do something I'd regret. Like push him off the stage in front of fifty thousand people. Or grab one of Asher's drumsticks and shove it up his ass.

Whatever it was, I'd probably have to get in line to do it.

"Abbie!" Landon and Channing came bounding down the corridor from the green room like a pair of golden retrievers. When Zeke stepped back, they both threw their arms around her.

She hugged them both back. "I'm sorry for scaring you and I'm sorry for overreacting." She, too, eyed Penn as though expecting him to say something shitty.

For once, he had the sense to keep his mouth shut.

I still might shove him off the stage.

"This is Blazing Violet's last song," Zeke said. "Are you really up to going out there?" He put his hands on her shoulders and leaned her back to look her in the face.

"Yeah, I'm fine," she said. "If I'm not going to let a little can in the face stop me, then I'm not going to let being late stop me either. I'll be okay. I promise."

"Promise never to run off like that again," Zeke insisted. "There's a killer out there. Did you forget that?" The only time he had that soft look on his face was when he looked at Asher. Clearly his feelings for both of them ran deep.

She gave him a watery smile. "For a couple of minutes, I did. Look, I can't explain it now. After the concert I will tell you everything. I swear."

I knew I wasn't the only one getting the vibe that something bad happened to her. I also knew she wasn't going to tell us until she was ready. Whatever it was, she wasn't going to let it get in the way of tonight's performance. Did that mean it was only something minor that didn't matter, or something so bad it would distract all of us?

Either way, I was going to have half my mind on her and the other half on the concert. I didn't know when she had become more important to me than music, but she had.

I was one hundred percent here for it.

CHAPTER
TWELVE
ABBIE

"I'M GOING to kill those mother fucking pricks," Zeke snarled. "They fucking took you in broad daylight and threatened you?"

"Yeah." That and more. I didn't want to tell him the evil twins got touchy with me. I managed a quick shower after they dropped me off at the hotel, but my skin still crawled. Thinking about the way they touched me was bad enough. Talking about it...

At some point, maybe I'd be ready to share more details. For now, I kept it vague.

I had a feeling the guys knew what I wasn't telling them anyway.

"For what it's worth, I threatened them back," I said. "It would seem Reuben still doesn't know about their relationship with Lila Bell. And they'd like it to stay that way. They agreed to give us some breathing space in return for us keeping our mouths shut."

"You blackmailed the Brantley twins?" Jully seemed impressed.

Asher groaned. "It's not gonna take them very long to realise where you got that information from."

I glanced at him regretfully. "Dane. I didn't mean to bring your brother into it. I freaked out and spoke without thinking."

It wasn't until an hour or two later I realised what I'd said and the trouble my big mouth might have caused.

Asher spread his hands out to either side, palms upward. "Dane can take care of himself. I should tell him they know. Although, they won't go after him now. If they did, Reuben would want to know why. I'm sure he'll find some way to turn all of this to his advantage. Dane is nothing if not an opportunist."

I rubbed my wrists where the restraints left bruises. "They said they didn't kill any of the victims. I have to say I believed them. They'd brag about it, wouldn't they?"

"Yeah," Zeke agreed. "That doesn't mean Reuben didn't send someone else. He has a phonebook of assassins to call on."

He glanced toward Tully. "I know it doesn't look like a professional did it, but that might be what he wants us to think. Fuck only knows what goes through his head."

Tully conceded the point with a nod. "It's possible the kills look rough on purpose."

"What do you mean rough?" Channing asked. He and Landon were sitting side-by-side on the couch, sipping beer and eating pizza.

I only managed a slice or two before my stomach rebelled. Whatever the twins drugged me with was still affecting my system. Or my nerves were. Either way, the food wasn't sitting well.

"A professional would use a more precise incision to remove the—" Tully started.

I interrupted him. "Do we have to talk about that now? Some of you are eating and, personally, I'm trying to hold down what I already have." I grimaced and swallowed hard.

"Yeah, sorry." Tully picked up his beer from the table in front of him and moved over to sit next to me on the end of the bed. "No more gross stuff for today."

When he placed an arm around me, I nestled against him. "Thank you."

My eyes went over to Penn, who sat in the chair in the corner, quietly sipping beer. He hadn't said a word for the last couple of hours.

If I didn't know better, I'd think he felt bad for the things he said. Not because he didn't mean them, but because of what happened after. It wasn't entirely his fault, but fucked if I was going to tell him that. I was too tired to be pissed off at him, but I might resume being angry at him later.

"Speaking of gross stuff," Zeke started, "you were right about those photos. They were supposed to introduce Cameo Orchid to new fans, but that's wasn't the way to do it. I, for one, promise shit like that won't happen again."

The other guys muttered their agreement.

I managed a faint smile in response. "It better not," I growled, more playful than firm, or angry.

The whole thing with the photo seemed like such a small deal now. It was just a photo for publicity. At the end of the day, the music industry was a business like any other. Crap like this was all too common. I needed to put it in the, 'shit happens,' box and move on.

"I can't believe you went out on stage and sang after what they did," Asher said. "Everyone would have understood if you'd been too freaked out to perform."

He gave me a soft look that conveyed so much emotion. He was a big, badass, muscular rock god on the outside, but a soft, sweet, squishy marshmallow on the inside. I adored him for it.

I shrugged. "I guess I'm a badass after all. Besides, the audience wouldn't have understood."

That was another act of pretence. That everything was absolutely fine in my world. That was exactly why I didn't tell the guys what happened before they went out on stage. Zeke's reaction said it all. He would have been too busy being angry and wanting to rip his brothers' heads off to go out and have a good time. As it was, he held back for the first song or two before he found his groove.

I knew he was worried about me, but all I would have done was make it worse.

"We would have told them you were sick," Zeke said reasonably. "It happens all the time. Last-minute food poisoning or laryngitis. No one would question either of those."

"Unless she started speaking," Asher pointed out.

Zeke punched him lightly on the arm. "You know what I mean, dickhead. We tell them whatever. What are they going to do? Tell us we're lying? They won't do shit."

"Food poisoning would have been plausible, given the way I'm feeling, Whatever they gave me..." I shook my head and grimaced.

"Should we take you to the hospital?" Tully looked worried. "If they gave you something nasty, it might have a lasting impact."

I waved him off. "I'm fine. Nothing a good night's sleep wouldn't fix." I hoped, because doctors asked questions and I didn't want to have to give them any answers. Bruises on my wrists and ankles would be difficult to explain.

Not to mention the ones on my ass from Tully's paddle.

"You said they were flying back to Sydney?" Zeke asked.

"That's what they said," I agreed. Who knew if it was true? They weren't exactly fine, upstanding citizens.

"I'll look into it and see," he said. "I want to make sure that's where they actually went. Those two are like a pair of snakes, slithering around and popping up when they're not wanted. Which is most of the fucking time. If we weren't leaving the country in a couple of days, I'd follow them and tear them both a new one."

"I'd go with you," Asher said.

"Me too," Tully agreed.

"And us," Landon said.

Channing nodded in agreement. Not that he needed to. Wherever Landon went, he went.

I wondered if they ever disagreed about anything. They must, but I'd never heard it. Not yet anyway.

My gaze returned to Penn.

He looked back at me, something dark in his eyes. "I'm always up for ripping the heads off little motherfuckers," he growled. "Kidnapping helpless women is a dog act. They deserve to have their balls served to them on a plate."

I wasn't sure how I felt about being referred to as helpless but I couldn't argue with the rest of it.

"Yeah, they do," Zeke said. "At some point I'm going to have to deal with them. They need to back the fuck off. I'm done with this bullshit. Furthermore," he looked at me firmly, "if you ever go off alone like that again, it won't just be Tully paddling your ass. We can't keep you safe if you do things like that."

I sighed. "I know. Although, a girl should be able to walk around by herself without getting kidnapped." Since they already did it to me twice, I had to agree that not being alone was a good idea.

"Yes, you should," he said. "But no going off by yourself, at least until we know it's safe out there. We need to figure out who is killing people, and get all my brothers to fuck off. Even after that…"

"I'm going to have one of you following me around for the rest of my life?" I asked. I could think of worse ways to spend my time, but it was going to get really old for them fast. Wasn't it?

"You want the answer to that?" Zeke rubbed a hand over the back of his head.

He seemed like he was worried I wanted clarification that he was prepared to make a lifetime commitment.

I wasn't ready for that, not yet. We had plenty of time.

"The answer is yes," Asher said with certainty. "Maybe I'll quit the band and become your bodyguard." He looked like he was actually considering it.

"That might be a bit extreme," I said.

"No shit," Penn muttered. "We can multitask."

"We?" Asher swivelled around to face him.

Penn grunted. "She's not going away anytime soon, is she? If I don't help in some way, it will piss you guys off."

"So you will do it so you don't piss us off," Tully said slowly. "Is that the only reason?"

Every eye in the room was on Penn now.

He narrowed his eyes and looked like an angry, cornered animal. "Has anyone told you guys peer pressure is lame?"

"He's right," Zeke said. "He'll admit it when he's ready."

Penn rolled his eyes toward the ceiling. "Give it a fucking rest."

"Only when you—" Asher started.

Penn interrupted him by picking up an olive off his pizza and flicking it at Asher. It hit the drummer on the cheek and bounced off his face.

"What the fuck?" Asher glared at him. "Why do people keep throwing food at me?"

"Because you deserve it." Penn threw a chunk of pineapple in his direction.

Asher caught it and ate it. He grimaced. "Shit, I forgot I hate pineapple."

We all laughed, including him.

"You guys suck," he said with a grin. He stuck out his tongue with distaste.

"That's what you like about us," Zeke said. "We suck, and taste better than pineapple."

"That's what I like about you and Abbie," Asher agreed. "The rest of them, not so much. I'm a one man and woman guy."

Zeke leaned over to give Asher a kiss so hot I forgot how tired I was.

These guys, they knew how to get me going without trying. The whole day was pushed out of my head. All I could think about now was watching them, and the way Tully felt with his arm around me.

"Get a room," Penn said.

"This is our room," Asher said. "If you don't want to watch, feel free to go somewhere else." To punctuate his words, he wound his arms around Zeke's neck and pulled him closer, until the singer was almost lying on top of him on the other bed.

"Fucking hell," Penn muttered. "I need more beer." He stood and grabbed another bottle from the fridge, but didn't leave.

"I guess that means he wants to watch," Tully said.

"I guess so." I slid my arms around Tully's neck and drew him to me.

"You don't mind an audience?" Landon asked. "Because I'd like to stay too, if that's okay?"

"Me too," Channing agreed.

"Fine by me," I said.

Tully didn't say anything, but judging by the way he pushed me back on the bed gently and laid his weight full-length on top of me, he didn't object either.

Zeke and Asher were busy tearing off each other's clothes. I wasn't sure if they even heard. Presumably, on some level, they were aware of the other guys' presence in the room.

I caught a glimpse of Channing and Landon kissing on the couch and almost felt sorry for Penn, who sat by himself. At least he had his hand. Hell, if he wanted to join in, he'd be welcome. Did he realise that?

As Tully and I started to remove each other's clothes, I forgot to worry about it. All I knew was the way the air touched my skin when Tully peeled off my skirt and blouse.

I closed my eyes and let myself slip back into the place I was in last night, where all I did was feel, smell and taste.

Thankfully, Tully didn't suggest putting the blindfold on me again. Either it didn't occur to him or he thought it might freak me out after what the evil twins did. Ruining that for me was further confirmation they were evil.

"Can I take off your bra and panties?" Tully whispered in my ear. "Do you mind the other guys seeing you?"

"No," I said without thinking. "I mean, yes. You can take them off, I don't mind." I opened my eyes to see him smile before I closed them again.

I wanted them to see me. All of me. I felt less vulnerable naked with these six guys than I did fully dressed around the twins, or even onstage. And a whole lot sexier.

I rolled over onto my stomach so he could unhook my bra, then rolled back so he could slide it off. Then my panties.

"Holy shit," someone muttered. It sounded like Penn.

Knowing he was watching made me wetter than the Murray River during a downpour. Added to that was the sounds of the other guys making out and my senses were going wild.

Asher groaned.

I opened my eyes and glanced over. I was glad I did.

Zeke was propped on one elbow, his mouth around Asher's cock. He looked over at me and smiled around his delicious mouthful.

I smiled back. I knew he didn't want to rush things, being new to having sex with another guy and all. Going down on Asher was a huge step for him and I was here to see it.

And it was fucking hot.

I glanced over to the couch where Landon and Channing were lying top to tail, cocks in each other's mouths.

Holy hotness.

"There seems to be a trend here," I said to Tully as he slipped off his T-shirt.

"I noticed that." He dropped his shirt on the floor.

"I'd hate to be off trend." I sat up and pushed him back before lying beside him and undoing his jeans. "Can I take off the rest of your clothes?"

He laced his hands behind his head, the picture of a confident rock god. "You absolutely can."

Did he have any idea how sexy he was?

"Thank you," I said graciously. I slid down his jeans and smiled at his boxers, which were decorated with smiley face emojis. Very badass. They soon joined my clothes on the floor.

I curled my hand around the base of his cock and worked my fingers up and down, making him rock hard and throbbing hot. I closed my eyes again and massaged his balls until a groan washed from him. I hooked my hand over his slit to feel his pre-cum before I tasted it with the tip of my tongue.

Delicious.

Before I could lower my mouth onto him, he swivelled around and pulled me over to straddle his face. He blew a warm breath onto my pussy.

"Now here's one hell of a view," he said happily.

"It looks pretty good from here too." I shivered with delight before lowering my mouth onto his cock and starting to suck.

He gripped my hips with his fingers and traced slow, tantalising circles around my clit and into my folds. The harder he lapped, the harder I sucked.

The whole world disappeared, leaving only the taste of him and the way he filled my mouth, the wet sounds of sucking and groans from all around the room. Both mine and from all the other guys.

I opened my eyes and glanced over to Penn. It was worth it to see the concentration on his face, and the way he was looking at me. We locked eyes on each other and, as pissed off as I still was with him, I couldn't help myself. I came, rolling my hips and grinding my pussy against Tully's mouth.

Penn, being the fucker he was, grinned, clearly taking credit for my orgasm.

Yeah, okay, whatever. I was quickly too busy with Tully coming, and keeping rhythm with him.

He gasped, "Can I come in your mouth?"

"Mmmhmm, I said in agreement, my mouth too full for words. Fuller still when he came, hot juices flooding my throat.

My eyes still on Penn, I swallowed down every drop.

His eyes widened and he came, bucking into his hand and spilling pearly cum over his fingers.

I slid my mouth off Tully's cock and grinned. Now it was my turn to take credit for his orgasm.

Penn made a face at me, but at least he didn't flip me off. Although, he was kinda busy pulling his track pants back into place before he headed to the bathroom to wash his hand.

He couldn't deny I did it for him.

The feeling was mutual. One of these days...

CHAPTER
THIRTEEN

ABBIE

"I THOUGHT YOU MIGHT NEED THIS." Zeke reached into his suitcase and pulled out something.

"How did you have my phone?" I took it from him and looked it over. It didn't have any damage, as far as I could see. Thank fuck for that. My bank account was still not healthy enough to afford a new phone. Honestly, every dollar the label gave me so far had gone on outstanding bills.

I don't mean outstanding in the good way. I came painfully close to having to declare bankruptcy. If it wasn't for Levi Jones, I would have been screwed.

"We found it on a bench in the park." Zeke said. "I presume that was when you bumped into my dear brothers." Apparently a night of fucking and sleep hadn't dimmed his anger.

"Yes, it was." I tried to suppress a shudder but failed. Every time I thought about yesterday, my stomach twisted and my whole body wanted to freeze up. I guessed this was why Zeke wanted me to learn how to use a gun. If I froze with a weapon in my hand, things wouldn't end well. An assailant might take it and use it on me.

"Can you guys teach me self-defence?" I asked. "Realistically, you can't watch me twenty-four hours a day, seven days a week."

"Yes, we can. Even if we have to take turns having a shower with you." He smiled.

"What a chore," I said ironically. "Am I still allowed to go to the toilet by myself?"

"I want to say no, but I have a feeling you would punch me in the face if I did." He leaned his upper body back as if he was actually scared of that possibility.

"I wouldn't punch you in the face," I told him. "I'd hurt my hand. I can't rule out throwing things at you though."

He chuckled. "Maybe we shouldn't teach you self-defence. You might use it against me." He raised his arm in front of his face.

"I think you're confusing defence with offence," I said. "I wouldn't mind learning how to throw a few kicks and punches. It's got to be better than receiving them."

He put his arms around me and drew me to him until my face rested against his chest. "If I have it my way, no one will throw punches, or anything else, at you. Not physically or verbally. They sure as fuck won't be drugging you and dragging you away again."

"I too have a preference for me not being drugged and dragged away," I said. "Being that vulnerable is..." I shook my head. "It was scary as hell." They could have done literally anything to me, and I would have been powerless to stop them.

A tiny voice in the back of my mind asked if maybe they did something while I was asleep. I silenced that fucker. If they had, I'd be sore and sticky when I woke, and I was neither.

He stroked my hair. "Did..." He started hesitantly. "Did they do anything other than what you've told me already?" He pulled back and looked me in the eyes. Worry lived in his, laced with that still-simmering fury.

I knew what he was asking, but I was scared to put it into words. My tongue darted over my lips.

"They touched me a little bit," I said finally. "Nothing that went too far but—"

"Fuck," Zeke growled. "I will rip off their nuts and shove them down their throats."

"As much as I'd like to see that, I made them promise not to...you know, rape me, if we didn't tell Reuben about Lila Bell." I couldn't meet his gaze now. Couldn't deal with his anger. My own emotions were overwhelming enough.

"How the *hell* did you have that conversation?" he barked.

I hesitated. "They implied they would force themselves on me the next time they came for me, if you don't listen to what Reuben wants."

If I thought Zeke was angry before, it was nothing compared to now. His face turned red. I wouldn't have been surprised to see steam pouring out of his ears.

I actually flinched.

"They threatened to rape you if I don't do what Reuben says?" His tone would have been terrifying if it was directed at me.

I had no doubt if Hunter and Parker were in front of him right now, he would literally kill them. Reuben too.

"Yeah, but now they won't, because you'll tell Reuben about Lila. They're so shit scared about him finding out, we have them by the balls, so to speak." My tone was lighter than I felt. It was all very well until the day Reuben found out and we lost our leverage. What would happen then? Presumably all bets would be off.

"Those little pricks," Zeke growled. "If I'd known they would grow up to be monsters, I would have drowned them in the bath when they were babies."

I put a hand on his cheek, felt the roughness of his stubble under my fingertips.

"You never would have done that," I said. "You're not a monster, you just have some nasty relatives. Who we will deal with, because we are big, badass rock gods."

He looked surprised but managed a faint smile. "That's the first time I've heard you refer to yourself as a rock god."

I shrugged. "Yeah, well, I'm more of a rock princess, but close enough."

"You're a female alpha wolf," he said. "Complete with the teeth to rip the throat out of your enemies."

"I don't know about that, but I like the sound of it," I said. "Abbie the alpha wolf."

"Mate to Zeke, also the alpha wolf." He pulled me back to him and nuzzled his face into my hair. "And the rest of the crazy wolf pack. We're all ready to tear out the throats of your enemies. I'll start with my brothers."

"Do you think Hunter and Parker would be different if it wasn't for Reuben's influence?" I asked.

"Would they not be dickheads if they were left to think for themselves? I have no idea," he admitted. "I'm sure they'd find some other shit to get into. If they get involved with the Bell family, then they'll have a whole different set of influences. Worse ones than Reuben, if that's possible."

I didn't much like the sound of that.

I leaned against him and listened to the comforting beat of his heart for a couple of minutes. "How did you know where to find my phone?"

He stiffened.

I pulled back and looked up at him. "Zeke?"

His expression made me think it was more than just a lucky guess.

"What did you do?" Whatever it was, it had him looking guilty as shit. For some reason, my mind went straight to thinking maybe he was in on the kidnapping with his brothers.

Yeah, okay, that was stupid, but that was where my mind went. I actually started to feel everything crumbling down around me.

He must have seen that on my face, because he quickly said, "I put a tracker on your phone."

"Oh." I couldn't decide if that was better, worse, or just as bad. Honestly, it took a full minute to process what he said.

"Wait a minute, you put a fucking tracker on my phone? Without my knowledge or consent? In what world is it okay to put a tracker on your girl-friend's phone and not mention it?"

"In the world where there's a motherfucking murderer and a mobster after us both," he said calm and reasonable. "And we have no idea if they are the same person or two different people. I told you I would do whatever I had to do to keep you safe. This was one thing I could do that should have fucking helped, but it fucking didn't. I failed to protect you. I will not fail at that again. If I have to give up the band, if I have to give up everything, I will protect the woman I love."

"Love?" I echoed. Was that just a word he threw out there in the heat of the moment?

He bent to touch his forehead to mine. "Yes, love. I love you, Abbie."

My heart raced faster than one of those high speed trains in Japan. Tears sprang to my eyes, then slid down my cheeks.

He brushed them away with his thumb. "I'm sorry, I didn't mean to upset you." My response seemed to have him genuinely confused.

I shook my head slightly. "You didn't upset me. I love you too, Zeke Brant-ley. Even with your crazy family and all the shit that's gone on. I don't regret a moment I've spent with you. From the very second I saw you in that club." That felt like years ago now. Decades. A lifetime.

He breathed a sigh of relief. "That's good, because it would have been as awkward as fuck if you said you hate my guts or something."

I slapped him lightly on the chest and laughed. "I could never hate your guts."

"Even when strange women sit on my lap for publicity photos?" He looked tentative and unsure if he should have brought that up or not.

"Even then," I said. "I can be pissed off once in a while, that doesn't mean I would stop loving you. I'm sure you'll find plenty to get pissed off at me about."

"Never," he said firmly. "Worried, anxious, nervous, but never angry or pissed off. Unless you start snoring really loud. Or say Violet is a better lead singer than I am. Or tell me all the guys have bigger cocks than I do."

I shook my head at him and laughed. "I have no control over whether or not I snore, but I would never say the rest of it. Even if it was true."

He raised an eyebrow.

"Which it's not," I said to put him out of his misery.

He wiped the back of his hand across his brow. "Phew. You had me worried for a moment there. I mean, not really; I know I am pretty fucking amazing and have a massive cock."

"It matches your massive ego," I teased.

"My ego and my cock are a match made in heaven," he said. "Just like you and I." He kissed me lightly.

I kissed him back and then asked, "Do I have to worry about having a tracker anywhere else? There's not one on me somewhere is there?" I started to pat myself down as if I would find one that way.

He chuckled. "No, just your phone. Now you mention it, I should put one in your watch. And one of your earrings." He cocked his head and looked at my ears. "Anything you would have to take out to go through airport security, or that they wouldn't worry about because it's already metal."

"Don't you dare," I growled. "It's bad enough you put one on my phone. I don't need you tracing me every second of every day." I lightly rested a hand on his chest. "I appreciate you wanting to take care of me, but that would be excessive. Okay?" Not to mention what might happen if the tracker was hacked. The last thing I needed was anyone else in his family knowing where I was and what I was doing. Or the killer. Or the press, for that matter. Rather than keep me safe, it might make me a target.

Hard pass.

"Do you have a tracker in your phone?" His hesitation to respond told me everything I needed to know. "Maybe you should. What happens if you go missing?"

"Anyone who tried anything with me would have a very short life expectancy," he said. "But if it'll make you feel better, I'll put one in my phone. And all the other guys' too."

"I'm not sure if it would make me feel better, but if you think it will keep us all safer, then do it," I said. If it was good enough for me, then it was good enough for everyone else.

"I think I hear the guys back with breakfast," Zeke said.

"It's about time." I was actually starting to get hungry. For food.

CHAPTER
FOURTEEN
ABBIE

"HOLY SHIT," Violet's eyes were huge. "Jackson said you had some trouble with Zeke's brothers. Something about you being kidnapped?" She looked as though she wouldn't believe it until she heard it from me.

She drew me a little apart from the guys. Zeke looked like he was about to argue, but I waved him back. What was going to happen here, in full view of everyone?

He nodded, but pointed to his eyes, then my face. He was watching closely. Got it.

I blew him a kiss and followed Violet. Evidently, knowledge of Zeke's family went beyond the band and the manager. Who else knew about them? It was starting to feel like the worst kept secret in Australia. An exaggeration, no doubt.

Maybe.

"So, is it true?" she pressed. She looked very much like she wanted me to deny it.

I shrugged. "Something like that, yeah. I'm okay though. It was no big deal."

She narrowed her eyes at me sceptically. "No big deal? *Right*, because people get kidnapped every day."

It was starting to feel that way, yes.

Hopefully they weren't planning to make a habit of it. There were better ways to spend my day than being drugged and tied up.

Like being tied up and spanked.

Before I could answer, one of the tour staff hurried past, carrying a large box.

I stepped over closer to the wall to get out of their way. I couldn't help eyeing the box as he carried it down the corridor toward the door. Chances were, it contained something completely innocent, like empty water bottles.

I shook my head. I was getting paranoid. There were probably no body parts in that box. Part of me wanted to chase the guy down and check.

That wouldn't look suspicious as fuck would it?

Since it would, I cleared my throat, leaned back against the wall and tried to look as casual as I could.

"Lucky for me, they just wanted to talk," I said evenly. "They just have a... a slightly heavy-handed way of going about it."

That was an exaggeration. For all I knew, Reuben told them to talk to me, and they decided on the method themselves. Since they were both the evil twin, they'd gone with sneaking up behind me and drugging me.

Whatever shit they'd used to knock me out seemed to be out of my system now. Hopefully without leaving any lasting damage. If it did, I might join the guys in tracking down the twins to feed their own balls to them.

Hell, I might do that anyway.

"Just a little, from what Jackson said," Violet agreed. "What the fuck happened? You're always surrounded by six hulking rock stars. Did they jump you while you were in the toilet or something?"

I sighed. Since she apparently wasn't going to let it go, I pushed myself off the wall and waved towards a side room. It was out of sight of any of the guys, but I should be safe in there with Violet. In the unlikely event she tried something, I only had to shout and they would come running.

Just in case, I left the door ajar.

The room looked like an office of some kind, with a couple of desks on either wall. I sat on one of them and crossed my legs. I told her about the photo and how I got angry with the guys and stormed off. I expected her to laugh or think the way Penn had, that I overreacted.

Instead, she nodded her understanding. "I've met most of Cameo Orchid. They're lovely, but they would one hundred percent jump the guys' bones, given half a chance. Those photos for sure have that vibe. As for the guys... Until you came along, they would have totally gone there. Without a second thought. But you know what?" She reached out and put a hand on my arm. "Next time they piss you off, come and talk to me. We can have a good, old-fashioned bitch session about them. With optional ice cream."

I smiled. "Bitch sessions are one of my top three favourite kinds of sessions."

She grinned and together we said, "After sex sessions and jam sessions." We both fell into laughter.

"See?" she said once she had regained her composure. "It's good to have another woman around. We're surrounded by so much testosterone, it's easy to forget we have options. For the record, I'm not complaining about all that testosterone, but variety is the spice of life."

"So they say," I agreed. "It's just...I'm not used to having female friends."

Candy, the producer, and I got along really well. And now Violet and I, but I wasn't used to confiding in another woman. Or... much of anyone really. I used to tell Vance everything and look where that got me.

"You better start getting used to it," Violet said. "Because you're stuck with me for the next couple of months." She popped out her hip and planted her fist on it, as though daring me to contradict her.

After a moment, she relaxed her pose. "Don't get me wrong, we don't have to be friends and you don't have to tell me anything. But I like you and I think sometimes it's good to have a break from all those guys. You know? I know I need a break from mine. Especially Blaise." She rolled her eyes towards the ceiling.

"He seems like a handful," I said.

She snorted a laugh. "He certainly is that. In more ways than one, I'm guessing. I wouldn't know, since we haven't gone there, if you know what I mean?"

"Yeah, I know what you mean." I guessed that about them. They seem to have the same kind of relationship Penn and I have; antagonistic but with a hint of lust. Okay, more than a hint, but we still wanted to strangle each other more than we wanted to fuck each other.

For now.

"We should go out for a drink sometime," she suggested. "If the guys will let you out of their sight for long enough."

I laughed bitterly. "I'd love to go out for a drink, but they'd probably surround us like circling wagons, to make sure we're safe."

"As long as they don't interfere, then I'm down for that." She sat on the other desk. "You've been through some shit, haven't you?"

"That's an understatement." I sighed. "I seem to be a magnet for it. Maybe I was a total asshole in a past life. I mean, that would explain it, wouldn't it?"

"Nah, I can't imagine you being an asshole, even in a past life." She waved her hand in a gesture of dismissal. "In my experience, it all comes down to jealousy."

"That was what Tully said." I placed my hands to either side of me on the desktop and leaned back slightly.

"Tully can be a wise dude when he wants to be," she said. "People see successful women and love to tear us down. I don't only mean stale, pale males. Some women are just as bad. Worse. Especially if they think we're after their man or some shit."

"Like me being angry over those photos?" Looking back, I felt shitty about the whole thing and the way I reacted. Not just because of the kidnapping, but because I didn't want to be that kind of woman. The one who tries to pussy-whip men.

She tilted her head. "You were pissed off at the guys, not the girls. Right? I bet it never occurred to you to try to tear them down or go after them."

"No, it didn't," I admitted. "When the guys said it was the women who suggested sitting on their laps, I was still pissed off at the guys for doing it."

"Why was that?" Violet asked curiously. "Why not be angry at the girls for suggesting it?"

I thought about that for a moment. "I don't know. Is it arrogant as shit to say I didn't see them as a threat? If the guys did anything, it would be them betraying our relationship, not those women. I mean, if it wasn't them, it would have been someone else."

"Plenty of girls would blame the other woman for seducing their man," Violet said.

I snorted. "That's such bullshit. You can't seduce someone unless they want to be seduced."

Violet snapped her fingers loud enough to make me jump. "Exactly. You should hang out with the Orchid girls sometime. They're sweet and super talented, but naïve as fuck. They could use some big sisters like us. Girls who have been around and have seen enough to know the pitfalls of this industry. Mind you, they made the right choice signing with White Wolf Records. They have plenty of us looking out for them."

"I wish I had us a year or two ago," I said with a sigh. "It would have been nice to have someone kick my ass in the right direction. And save me from making stupid mistakes like marrying Vance."

"Would a kick have helped?" Violet tilted her head so her purple ponytail swung out behind her.

"What do you mean?" I pushed myself back up straight and crossed my arms.

"I mean, you were in love with him, weren't you?" she asked. "Would you have listened if anyone told you he was full of shit?" She gave me a look like she expected an honest answer.

I wanted to give her one.

It took me a couple of moments to respond with, "Probably not. I was head over heels for him. Ass over tits. I had doubts, I'd be lying if I said I didn't, but I ignored myself. Looking back, it seems so obvious."

I blew out a breath, frustrated with past me. "I talked about us moving in together but he always changed the subject. He was more interested in talking about singing a duet, or making an album together."

"Career stuff?" she said.

"Exactly," I agreed. "He never wanted to discuss us or a future together. When he talked about eloping, I thought it was spontaneous and romantic, and that somehow he got past his fear of commitment or some shit. I even suggested the timing was tricky because he had an album dropping a couple of weeks later."

I shook my head and laughed bitterly. "Even saying this out loud, I feel so stupid."

"Hey." She slipped off the desk and moved to sit next to me. "Not stupid, just naïve and in love."

"I guess so." I shrugged. "The sex was pretty awful anyway. He was all about his own satisfaction." At least he didn't take his time with it. The guys were a huge leap from that. A different planet.

"Now why does that not surprise me?" Violet said dryly. "He sounds like a grade A prick to me. I wouldn't wish what happened to him on anyone, but I don't feel too sorry for him either."

"Neither do I," I admitted. "I would have been happy if someone slashed his tires or threw a rock through one of his windows. That would have been enough. But I'm not going to mourn his death. I'm not going to celebrate it either," I added quickly.

"Of course not," she said. "It takes a special kind of asshole to find pleasure in stuff like that. Someone like Zeke's brothers."

"How do you know about them?" I asked carefully. I had no idea how much she knew. I had to assume it wasn't much until she told me otherwise.

"My brother told me," she explained. When I looked questioningly at her, she added, "He's my stepbrother really. Levi Jones. His father is married to my mother."

She gave me a guarded look and I could tell exactly what she was thinking.

"That's cool," I said lightly. "I know you got signed to the label for your talent and not because you're related."

She relaxed visibly. "See, I knew you were awesome." She gave me a quick hug.

"Hell yeah I am," I said, mostly joking. I have heard her sing, she is incredible. If anyone suggested Levi signed her because they were related, they could answer to me, and my guys.

CHAPTER
FIFTEEN
TULLY

"I'M NOT ASKING you to do anything, just meet with me." My father's tone was insistent. When wasn't not?

I sighed, and resisted the urge to throw my phone through the nearest window.

Xavier Lane was nothing if not persistent. He'd flown all the way from the other side of the country to see me, whether I liked it or not.

"Dad." I didn't remember when I started calling my adopted parents Mum and Dad, it just happened at some point along the way. I never took their last name, they hadn't asked me to, but they were my parents in every way that counted.

Including my privilege to rebel against them.

"We're flying out to Singapore in the morning," I said. Dad tried to pin me down for the last couple of days, including calling me when we were looking for Abbie.

I suspected that wasn't a coincidence. Dad was tight with Reuben. If Zeke's brother told him he sent Hunter and Parker after Abbie, Dad might have seen it as an opportunity to get my attention while I was distracted.

He of all people should know I wasn't easily distracted.

"Then you're free tonight," he said. "I know you don't have a concert."

That was information anyone could get with a quick Internet search. Evidently he assumed it meant I didn't have plans.

Okay, I didn't, not really, but I wanted to enjoy our last night in Australia before we left for Asia.

Not to mention, it was a rare night off. Could I get Abbie and I into Desdemona's again at this short notice?

"Maybe you can tell me what this is about," I said reasonably. "Over the phone." That didn't seem like too much to ask. He was busy, I was busy. We could chat quickly and get back to all the things.

"If I could do that, I would have called you from Sydney," he pointed out. "What I need to talk to you about, I need to do in person."

Fortunately for him, he couldn't see me give him an epic eye roll. Whatever he wanted could probably be done by email, but he wouldn't get his point across as well as he would while looking me in the eyes. That meant it was something important to him. As opposed to important to me. Our agendas were rarely the same these days. Were they ever? I guessed they were when I was young enough to still seek his approval. Those days were long gone, but not forgotten.

"If this is anything to do with me quitting the band and coming back to—" I started.

"Tully, you've made your feelings about that clear," he said evenly.

And yet, here he was, wanting to see me in person. It didn't take a genius to figure out he was up to something. Like most people, he always had an angle.

"You're not going to take me out are you?" I'd love to suggest I was joking, but if Reuben asked him to do it and paid him well enough, he'd at least consider it. In some ways, he was as bad as the evil twins, but Reuben's motives would have to match his. He was a minion, not a lackey.

He chuckled. "Only out to dinner. My treat."

Okay, if I didn't suspect something was up before, I certainly did now. He never offered to pay for our meals. Or to be more specific, he was always happy to let me pay. I didn't mind, I had more money than I knew what to do with, but for him to offer sent up a shit ton of red flags.

"I can meet you for drinks," I said finally. "Before dinner. I already have plans for dinner and after dinner."

I'd have to think quickly if he asked me what they were, because I was lying through my teeth. Don't get me wrong, I loved the man and was grateful for all he did for me, but like Zeke, that life was behind me. If that meant turning my back on my adoptive family, then so be it.

"If that's all my son can give me, then that's what I'll take," he said, sounding testy. "It shouldn't take too long anyway."

It probably shouldn't, but that didn't mean he wouldn't drag it out as long as he could. He was never shy in reminding me he took me in when I was a kid.

I was surprised we got through a five-minute phone call without him mentioning it.

"Okay great." I gave him the name of a bar a few streets away. We could have had drinks in the hotel bar, but for some reason I didn't want him knowing where we were staying. That was silly, I knew. If Reuben knew where to find us, my father would.

And we both knew it.

He confirmed that a moment later when he said, "Okay, that's only a short walk for us both."

I realised he had the advantage, because I had no idea where he was staying.

Why did everything between us feel like a chess game? Move a piece, manoeuvre it into position, anticipate your opponent's next move, wait to strike.

Half the time, I was waiting for him to say checkmate.

Whatever, as long as he didn't try to take my queen.

I wondered what he knew about Abbie. I wasn't going to tell him much of anything, not until I heard what he had to say, and knew it wasn't anything bad.

For all I knew, it could be something totally innocent. Maybe he came all this way to ask me to teach him to play the guitar.

Okay, I didn't believe that either.

"You want me to swing by your hotel and pick you up?" I asked casually. "I know Perth better than you do." And then I would know where he was staying.

Of course, he saw right through the suggestion. "No, that's all right, I'll meet you at the bar. Don't be late."

"When am I ever late?" I asked.

"There's a first time for everything, Tully. We'll all be late some day." He laughed.

I didn't. In spite of his assurances, it still felt like a veiled threat.

"I'll see you at seven," I said.

"Make it six," he said. "I'm an old man, I don't want to be out too late past my bedtime."

"You're not an old man," I assured him. "You're barely out of the egg." He loved fishing for compliments. It was his favourite hobby.

"Hundred year old egg," he said with a laugh.

This kind of silly talk made it feel like we were father and son, at least more than the rest of the conversation had. We always got along pretty well, but on his terms.

As long as they didn't interfere with my music career, or my other relationships, then I'd accommodate him.

I had a feeling whatever he wanted to discuss in person would overstep by a long way.

"I thought I could smell something nasty," I joked.

He snorted. "Thanks, Tull, love you too."

I chuckled. "I know you do, I'm awesome."

"You're certainly my favourite adopted son," he said.

"I know I don't need to point this out, but I'm your only adopted son," I said.

"Huh, you're right. How about that? I'm sure you'd still be my favourite even if I had a dozen," he assured me.

"Sure," I dragged the word out slowly. "It's easy to say that when you don't."

"When did you get so cynical?" he asked.

When my mother was murdered and my father went off the rails, I thought.

Out loud, I said, "I was born cynical. I think it's in my DNA or something."

"Something like that," he agreed. "I'll see you in a few hours."

"Yeah, see you in a bit." I ended the call and put down my phone as Zeke stepped into the room, dripping with sweat. I looked past him, but he was alone.

"Abbie is with the others," he said.

I nodded slowly. "Good." I already couldn't remember a time when I wasn't looking out for and worrying about her. The moment I met her I was fully invested in everything about her. She was easily the most incredible, beautiful and sweet person I ever met.

I was happy to wait as long as it took for her to be ready to be invested in me as well. That wait was one thousand percent worth it. The memory of smacking her ass with a paddle until it was red, then fucking her until we both screamed, was seared into my memory like a brand. The way she'd taken to the blindfold, and let me touch and feed her, was arousing as hell. Nothing, no one, ever came close.

Honestly, there was nothing about her that wasn't arousing and compelling. The way she looked, the way she spoke, sang, smiled and laughed; I felt like I'd known her for a thousand lifetimes the moment she walked into the studio on that first day. I had no doubt, not even a drop, that we would be together.

Fate said so, and who was I to argue with fate?

Yeah, I was falling for her hard.

"You okay?" Zeke crouched beside his suitcase and opened it. He pulled out some fresh clothes and put them aside. He must have just come from the hotel gym, or a run around the city.

I should have done either of those myself, but a song idea sprang to mind and I was busy scribbling down chords and lyrics until my father called.

"My father is in town." I told him about the phone call and my suspicion that he was up to something.

He slammed his hand against the floor. "That's it. We're buying an island

and dropping out of civilisation. I'm done with these motherfuckers." He sighed through his nose and stood. "If only it was that easy."

"Yeah. Wherever we go, they would find us." Unless it was somewhere really, really remote, and I doubted we would give up streaming movies just to keep our families from hassling us.

Priorities.

Zeke pulled off his sweat-drenched shirt and tossed it aside.

I wasn't into guys, but I couldn't forget seeing him and Asher together. I wasn't blind, they were both good-looking guys, and watching them kiss and fuck was as hot as hell.

Me touching Abbie, Abbie touching me...

I could get used to sessions like that. Even Penn, who had only gotten himself off, wasn't complaining about it.

It was a new experience for us, but one I was certain we would do again.

And again.

And again.

Everything about it felt normal and natural, and amazing. Although, there had to be a better environment for an orgy than a small hotel room.

I filed that in the back of my mind under things to think about when the tour was over.

"Are you going to meet with him?" Zeke asked.

"If I don't, he'll come here," I said. "I'm not ready for him to meet Abbie yet."

"If my family hasn't scared her off, your family won't," Zeke pointed out. He looked like he was barely holding back a smile.

"That's true," I agreed. "I'm almost certain my father won't kidnap her."

"Almost certain isn't certain," Zeke pointed out.

"That's what I'm worried about," I said. "Something about all of this is off."

"And by off you mean— What?" Zeke asked. He looked like he'd caught my unease.

"I don't know," I admitted. "It might be good, old fashioned paranoia." After a moment, I added, "And then, maybe it's not." My father obviously had some ulterior motive. The question was, was it innocent, or guilty as fuck?

Zeke looked frustrated but he nodded. "We'll be on high alert either way. They can reach us anywhere in the world, but the moment we leave Australia, it'll be that much more difficult for them. They'll have international authorities to contend with."

We both knew there were ways around authorities anywhere on the planet, but potentially, coming after us would take them longer and cost them more money.

No, if they were going to do anything, it was more likely to happen here in Perth than anywhere else in the world.

Whatever they had in mind, they only had hours to do it.

"I should send Asher with you," Zeke said. He didn't look as though he liked that idea any more than I did.

I considered it for about half a second, then shook my head. "I can handle myself. If I turn up with Asher, Dad will know we're onto him. Besides, you might need him here."

"Yeah," Zeke agreed. "But I have an idea."

CHAPTER
SIXTEEN

TULLY

I WAS RIGHT ON TIME, but my father was already waiting for me. He had that look on his face like he was *slightly* annoyed because I was *slightly* late.

Since I wasn't, I ignored his expression and smiled.

"Hey," I started over and gave him a quick bro hug.

He glanced down at my outfit and made no effort to hide his disapproval. "You're looking... *well*."

What did he expect? A three-piece suit? That wasn't gonna happen.

Instead, I wore my usual rock star uniform: jeans with holes in the knees, a faded Wolf Venom T-shirt, leather jacket and leather boots.

Personally, I thought I looked pretty fucking good.

Wasn't it a father's job to disapprove of what his son wore while in his mid-twenties anyway? I made a mental note to get myself a dinosaur costume to wear next time. He'd enjoy disapproving of that.

"Sorry, if I knew you were in town I would have gone out and bought a ball gown," I joked.

"Four hours' notice should be plenty to find the perfect dress." He smiled and waved towards a table in the back. "Maybe something bright yellow."

"Nah, yellow's not my colour." I slipped into the stool opposite him. "Maybe bright pink or dark red."

Yeah, right. If I was going to wear a ball gown it would be black. Since I would look absolutely ridiculous in it, I might as well be slick at the same time.

"Would you like something to drink?" he asked.

"I'll get it," I said. It wasn't that I didn't trust him to slip something into my drink...

Okay, maybe that was it, to some extent, but I didn't mind buying the old guy a beer or two.

He looked at me like he thought I was going to slip something into *his* drink, but he nodded. "You know what I like."

"Fast cars, good food and a successful business deal," I said with a grin.

An obedient son might not go astray either.

I slipped off my stool and headed to the bar. After a brief chat with the young woman behind the bar, who obviously recognised me, I grabbed us both a beer and sat his in front of him.

"I think she likes you," he nodded his thanks, then jerked his head toward the bar. "She hadn't stopped looking this way."

"Are you playing matchmaker now?" I sat back down and took a sip. "So, you want to talk to me about something? Other than my love life."

I didn't see any point in dragging this out any longer than necessary. If we could clear the air between us, maybe we could have a civil conversation like father and son.

"I have a business proposal for you," he said. Apparently he caught the same 'let's get this over with' vibe.

"Yeah?" I said casually. I was sure I wasn't interested, but I'd do him the courtesy of hearing him out before I told him to fuck off. "I'm all ears."

Usually that would have provoked a joking reply from him, such as only being able to see two ears. This time, he just smiled faintly and sipped his own beer.

"I know you're not going to go back to the work you were trained to do," he said carefully. He was clearly mindful we sat in a public place.

Of course, people would notice if he stood up in his stool and shouted, "Hey, my adopted son is a trained assassin. How about that? Anyone need someone killed for them?"

There was a time and place for that and this was not it.

"Nope," I said simply and firmly. "I appreciate the skills my training gave me, but I'm not that person." I couldn't kill people for money. I didn't want to kill people for any reason.

"I understand." He wasn't happy about it, but that was his problem and he knew it. "I have something else in mind."

That had me immediately on guard. He never mentioned an alternative before. I couldn't guess what he had in mind.

"Yes?" I said carefully. "I'm listening. I can't make any guarantees about how I'll respond, but I'm listening."

The sides of his mouth drew back in displeasure, but he nodded. "You may have noticed I'm not getting any younger. I might not be a hundred year old egg, but I'm starting to feel like one." He almost smiled.

"You're not that old." For the first time, I worried about the direction this conversation was going. Was he saying his time was limited or something like that? I was wary of his intentions at times, but I still loved the man. I didn't want to lose him.

"No, but I want to slow down at some point," he said. "And I want to hand my business dealings over to someone I can trust."

I blinked. Okay, I hadn't seen that coming.

"Wait, you want to hand your business over to me someday?" That had my head spinning. Parts of the Lang Corporation were actually legal. If I could strip off the stuff that wasn't, I might actually have a viable enterprise on my hands.

"Who else?" he asked easily. "As far as I'm concerned, you're my son. You're smart, competent and compassionate." He said the last word like it left a bad taste in his mouth. "Why would I not want you to work with me?"

"I can think of a few reasons," I said. "For one thing, if you sell off everything, you'll have a shitload of money to retire on. I thought that was your plan?"

"It was, until I realised I spent my lifetime building something and don't want to sell it off to any old person." He took a gulp of beer.

"Sell it off to any young person then," I said, half joking. I didn't need his money. I didn't need to work another day for the rest of my life if I didn't want to.

On the other hand, running his business might give me something to do other than sit around and practice guitar, or sip cocktails on the beach.

Although, he could have a comfortable retirement and spend his own time drinking cocktails on the beach. Surely that was more fun than handing everything over to me?

"I don't want to sell it off to anyone." He rested his elbows on the table. "I want it to keep running. I'd like to see you run it and then hand it down to your children someday."

My children? Now there was an interesting concept if I ever heard one. I wasn't sure how I'd even begin to explain that to him.

Abbie might not want children, and with five other guys in the equation, I might never have one that was biologically mine. Of course, any child she had I'd think of as mine. If there was anything my adopted parents taught me, it was that biology isn't everything. A person can be a parent even if they aren't related by blood. Any child shared between the seven of us would certainly have an interesting life.

They'd never be short on love or money.

Idly, I wondered how long it would take them to learn that if their mother or one of their fathers said no to something, they could keep asking father after father until someone said yes.

Or they would go straight to Asher. If anyone said yes to them doing something they shouldn't, it would be him.

"So, what do you think?" Dad asked. "I haven't heard a 'no fucking way' yet."

I snorted softly and smiled. For some reason, hearing him swear was funny. Maybe because he was so straight laced and uptight most of the time.

"I haven't ruled it in or out," I said finally. "There's a lot to consider. I'm not done with the band yet. I don't know when I will be. I know you'd want me to learn the ropes before you hand over the reins to me. That could take a year or two."

He seemed pleased I was actually considering it. "We have time. I don't plan to step away for another ten or twenty years."

I nodded and sipped my beer in silent contemplation for a minute or two.

"What's the rush then?" I asked him. "Why fly all the way out here for this? You could have asked me at Christmas or at Mum's birthday." I always tried to get home for those, his birthday as well. I had to play the dutiful son once in a while.

He glanced at his watch.

A tingle passed up and down my spine. There was definitely something going on here. But what was it?

He looked back up. "I want to hand part of the business over to you as soon as possible. If only in name for now. The legal stuff takes time and I didn't want to wait to get started on it."

"What part of the business?" I asked carefully. I wasn't interested in the part that involved training and hiring assassins, and making sure they got paid. Or the money laundering.

"Believe it or not, I bought a record label not long ago. I thought you might be interested in having a say in how it's run." He swallowed another gulp of beer.

I stared at him. He'd surprised me so much, a small shove might have knocked me off the stool.

"You bought a record label?" If I was all ears for anything, it would be this.

"Which one?" I asked eagerly. I didn't try to hide the fact my interest was piqued. I hadn't thought about running a label, but now he mentioned it, it might be exciting. I'd learnt a lot from Levi about how to do it right.

"Onyx Riot Records," he said.

My jaw dropped open slightly. Abbie's old label. That couldn't possibly be a coincidence. Not in a million years.

"I didn't know it was sold," I said carefully. I didn't keep up with that part of the industry, but if only for Abbie's involvement, I was surprised I didn't know. Did she?

Dad shrugged. "Apparently they've had some shady business dealings and the police and tax office were looking into them. A lot of their acts left when their contracts ended and they were going under. I picked it up for a song, so to speak."

I chuckled. "Good one."

"I thought so," he said smugly. "So, are you interested? You can pick executives to run it until you're ready to take over, but essentially it would be your baby. I'd be a silent partner, but I'm sure you could make me a lot of money."

"I'm sure I could," I agreed. "Can I have some time to think about it?"

"Of course, but why do you need time? I thought this would be exactly your thing?" He cocked his head at me and looked irritated, like he was holding the hoop and expecting me to jump straight through.

"It is," I agreed. "Like you said, though, a lot of the acts left. The label's reputation isn't stellar right now." That was what Pietro Rossi got for screwing Abbie over. It seemed she wasn't the only one the label pissed off. "It would be a lot of hard work to build it back up to something reputable and profitable."

"If anyone can do it, it's you," he said. "Give it ten years and it will be the biggest, best label on the planet. Bands will be lining up down the street to sign with you."

"To be fair, bands line up down the street to sign with *anyone*," I said dryly.

Could I resist the opportunity to search out new talent and give them the same chances we had? Who wouldn't want to give back like that?

"They would do it even more for you." He glanced at his watch again, then sat back on his stool.

I had the distinct feeling whatever he brought me here for, he kept me just long enough.

Was it just long enough for Zeke to do what he planned?

CHAPTER
SEVENTEEN

ABBIE

"EVERYONE, get all your things together. We're getting the fuck out of here," Zeke said. His tone was calm, but with a heavy undercurrent of urgency.

"What the hell?" Colin stood with his shirt in his hand. Naked from the waist up, he was a wall of muscle like the rest of the guys. Muscle and tattoos, and hair damp from the shower. "We're supposed to be going out to dinner."

"Yeah, well, change of plans." Zeke grabbed his suitcase and nodded to me to get mine.

"What's happening?" Channing asked. He didn't look scared, none of them did, but Zeke's urgency was contagious.

Asher and Landon were already stuffing T-shirts into their suitcases and closing them.

"Maybe nothing," Zeke said. "Maybe something. In the event that it is in fact something, we're getting out of here."

"Tully just left," I pointed out. Something about talking to his adopted father. Whatever it was, he hadn't seemed happy about it.

"Exactly," Zeke said. "He suspects something is going to go down, so we're not gonna be here if that happens."

I opened the door to the adjoining room where my suitcase was. "Why would they make sure Tully wasn't here?"

Zeke followed me and started to shove Tully's things into his case. "Tully has a specific skill set. They won't want him here if they come after us. Don't worry," he flashed me a smile, "the rest of us have skills of our own. We'll be fine."

"But having Tully here would help us?" I asked. What the hell did he think might happen that we'd need an assassin for?

"It would help," he agreed. He hesitated and looked up at me. "I know Tull seems all sweet and zen and shit on the outside, but trust me when I say you don't want him pissed off at you. Mostly because you would never see him coming." He went back to packing up Tully's things.

"I don't know if I should be scared or find that hot," I said reflectively. "Maybe both."

Zeke chuckled. "Whatever you do, don't panic. They think we don't know what they're planning and that they'll catch us by surprise, but they won't. If I was really worried, I'd ditch our suitcases and shit, and run. I don't think that's necessary. We just need to relocate for the night, or fly out to Singapore if we can get a flight tonight. They'll turn up here to find us gone."

He sounded so certain, it went a long way to calming my nerves. The deep, lingering kiss he gave me once he finished packing Tully's stuff helped too.

"Trust me," he said softly, his fingers tangled in my hair.

"I do," I told him. "I love you."

"I love you too. Now let's get the hell out of here." He gave me a last kiss and reluctantly slipped his hands from me.

He grabbed the handle to my suitcase in one hand and Tully's in the other and hauled them through the door into the other room.

"Everyone stay here. I'm going to tell Blazing Violet to get out too. If something happens we don't want them to be collateral damage."

"Got it, babe," Asher told him. "Be careful."

"Always." Zeke kissed him, then ducked out the door and closed behind him.

Asher gestured for us all to move our suitcases to one side of the door, where we could grab them quickly.

"This is bullshit," Penn said. He pulled on his shirt, but his usual scowl was in place. "Can't we enjoy one night of peace without everything going to shit?"

"Apparently not," Landon said. "At least life isn't boring." He hooked an arm around Channing's waist and leaned against him.

"Yeah," Channing agreed. "If it was boring, you would complain about it."

"I fucking wouldn't—" Penn started.

"Maybe now isn't a good time to fight with each other," I suggested.

A sliver of fear crawled down my spine like a spider. If we were going to get out of this in one piece, we needed to be united and quiet.

"Abbie is right," Asher said. "Save the fighting for later, when we have some mud for you to roll around in."

The mental image of Penn rolling around naked in mud was almost enough to settle my fear. It was certainly enough to distract me for a couple of moments.

What were the chances that would happen in real life? Slim, I was guessing, but a girl could dream. Or at least fantasise.

The door knob rattled, making me jump.

"Let me in," Zeke's voice came from the other side.

Asher opened the door slightly and peered out. "How can we be sure it's really you?" he asked teasingly.

"Ha, fucking ha," Zeke said sarcastically. He shoved the door the rest of the way open and stepped inside.

Jackson was on his heels. "Are you sure they're coming for us?" He looked concerned but not scared.

I wondered what skills the band's manager had. For all I knew, he was a sniper or an accomplished getaway driver. Or had a black belt in some martial art. Or was really good at baking cakes.

What? When I'm anxious, I think about food.

"I'm not sure of anything," Zeke said. "Tully said his father was cagey as fuck on the phone, and this is a long way to come to be cagey. I'd rather be safe than sorry. The sooner we get out of the country, the better."

Jackson nodded, but didn't question Zeke's reasoning. "I found us a little hole in the wall place we can stay for the night. The kind where no one asks questions."

"Sounds like my kind of place," Asher said with a grin.

"Since when did you stay anywhere less than five stars?" Penn asked him.

"Plenty of times," Asher said. "Remember some of those fleabag places we stayed when we were first starting out?"

"I try not to," Penn said. "Some of those places were shitholes. I don't know how it's legal to ask people to pay money to stay in dumps like that."

"Who says it's legal?" Asher asked.

"Asher has a point," Landon said. He looked at me and added, "We did some dubious things back then."

"Just back then?" I teased.

He grinned. "She knows us too well already."

"Right." Zeke fixed us with a serious look. "Let's go."

He opened the door as Violet and her guys trudged up the corridor dragging their suitcases behind them.

"Just in time," Asher said.

"Better than coming late," Blaise said. "What the fuck is going on?"

"I'll explain everything when we get out of here," Zeke said. "You four take the elevator down. Jackson, you, Penn, Channing and Landon, go across to the other side of the hotel and take the stairs down there. Asher, Abbie and I will take the stairs down here, on this side of the hotel."

Everyone nodded and headed off where they were told. No one, not even Penn, argued.

At the same time, no one was rushing. We looked like we were casually leaving the hotel, nothing more.

Except—if we were casually leaving, we would all take the elevator down together. Wouldn't we?

Hell, if anyone asked, we could always say we needed the exercise. The guys didn't get as buff as they were without working at it. That included taking extra steps whenever possible.

Okay, that usually meant taking the steps up and not down, but close enough. Hopefully no one would ask.

I glanced over my shoulder as we headed for the stairs.

Penn looked back at me. For once, he didn't glare at me like something he might scrape off the bottom of his shoe. He gave me a nod, then turned and disappeared around the bend with the other guys.

I didn't know quite what to make of that, but then Asher ushered me to the door that led to the stairs, and Zeke took my suitcase.

"It'll be quieter if we carry them," Zeke explained. "And since you apparently carry bricks in yours, I'll help you out." He flashed me a grin.

I huffed and pretended to sulk. "Not bricks. Just several pairs of heels and a bunch of makeup."

"No clothes?" Asher grinned. "I knew you were my kind of girl."

"Mine too," Zeke agreed. "I can't wait to see you walking around just in heels."

"Ha ha," I said sarcastically. "Unfortunately for you two, there are clothes in there. Fortunately, you might convince me to just wear heels, if you ask nicely."

"Shhh." Zeke stopped walking so suddenly I almost walked past him.

I caught myself at the last moment and turned to face him. He seemed to be listening carefully for something.

I listened too, but couldn't hear anything. I mouthed, "What is it?"

He shook his head. "I can't hear anything now," he whispered. "Let's walk as quietly as we can. No more talking."

Asher and I both nodded.

I put a hand on the rail for support, and pulled off my shoes. I'd move silently without them clicking on the concrete steps as I went.

We made our way down to the next landing in almost absolute silence. It was so quiet I heard my heart racing.

My mind was doing the exact same thing.

Zeke said Reuben didn't want him dead, because he wanted him to return to the family. What did that mean for the rest of us? I realised I assumed up until now that Reuben was involved, but what if he wasn't? What if this had something to do with the killer?

Hell, it might be some ploy by the press to flush us out so they could humiliate us in some way.

Okay, that was far-fetched, but I wasn't ruling out anything just yet. Not until I knew exactly what, if anything, we were up against.

It was possible Tully's father just wanted a chat and we were doing nothing more than jumping at shadows.

Honestly, I'd prefer to jump at shadows than be caught out if there was some plot against us.

Noise came from outside the door of the next landing.

We paused for a moment, but it was nothing more than music and people talking. I'd hate to be in a room near whoever that was. They weren't even playing anything by Wolf Venom, Blazing Violet or me.

Sad.

Zeke nodded at us to keep going. If he was straining carrying the two heavy suitcases, he gave no sign of it. He probably lifted more weight at the gym on a daily basis. He wasn't even sweating yet.

If it was me, my arms probably would have fallen off by now.

We crept past the door and down the next set of stairs.

I glanced over the railing. We had three more floors to go before we were out of the hotel. I hoped the others were okay. With any luck, Penn wasn't being an asshole and giving anyone an excuse to push him down the stairs.

I'd feel better when we were all together.

We crept past the last three landings and made our way to the door which should lead right outside. It would be locked from the other side, but being a fire escape, we should be able to let ourselves out.

Should being the key word here.

We reached the bottom and Asher put a hand on the crossbar. The door opened with only a squeak of protest.

Thank fuck.

That relief was short-lived.

Two familiar, identical faces greeted us.

"Going somewhere?" Hunter Brantley asked.

CHAPTER
EIGHTEEN
ABBIE

PARKER GRINNED AT ME. "Long time no see."

"What the fuck do you want?" Zeke snapped. He looked like he was ready to grab them by their hair and smash their heads together.

I wasn't sure I would try to stop him.

"Hey Asher," Parker said. "I haven't seen you for ages. How have you been?"

Asher shrugged. "Fine, thanks. You?"

Parker shrugged back. "Not bad. Keeping busy, you know how it is."

"Yeah, I do," Asher agreed. "I'd kinda like to know what the fuck you're doing here too. I mean, if you don't mind me asking."

"Would you believe we're here to help?" Hunter asked.

Zeke barked a laugh right in his face. "Not for a second, no."

"Ouch." Hunter turned to Parker and said, "That's not very nice. Is it Parker?"

"It really isn't," Parker said. "But we're actually legit. We were on the way to the airport when Reuben told us to turn around."

"Reuben told you to help us?" Zeke said in disbelief. "Why?"

"Tully's adopted father, Xavier Lang, has been dealing with the Fiorellis. Reuben thinks he's going to make a move on you to prove his loyalty," Hunter said. "And before you ask, no, it has nothing to do with the Bells. Lila knows nothing about it."

"Sure she doesn't," Zeke said. He shrugged. "We can take care of ourselves. You guys can piss off."

Parker pressed a hand to his chest, over his heart. "You hit me right here, bro. Fortunately for you, I don't follow your orders. Reuben said to help you and that's what we're going to do. That starts with getting out of here."

"It should start with being less predictable," Hunter said. "We figured out exactly where you'd come out. And when. And exactly with who."

Parker stared at him. "We did, too, didn't we? Fuck yeah. Go us." They shared a high-five.

"You're my brothers," Zeke said dryly. "You should have some idea how I think. Just like I have some idea how you think."

"Lucky you," I said sarcastically. To the evil twins I said, "Are we really supposed to trust you?"

"We're very trustworthy," Hunter said. "We said we would help you and we will. We said we wouldn't rape you, so relax."

Zeke growled low in the back of his throat. "If you little pricks touch her, I will rip off all four of your heads, one after the other."

"That's not very nice," Parker remarked.

"It really isn't," Hunter agreed.

Zeke leaned towards them. "Then keep your motherfucking hands to yourselves. I won't warn you again."

"I'd like to point out I would help him rip off your heads if you touch her," Asher said, his tone much nicer than his words.

"So will I," I said darkly.

"So will we," Landon said as he and the other four guys stepped around the side of the building towards us.

Channing nodded in agreement.

Penn looked at the twins like he would prefer to bash their heads together and save the time ripping off any body parts.

I had to admire his train of thought if that was what he was thinking. It would be a lot quicker and easier.

"Oh look, they're multiplying," Parker said, looking completely unruffled.

Only Hunter laughed at his remark. "We should get out of here. I can't guarantee we won't be outnumbered. I don't know about any of you, but I'd prefer not to have that happen."

"I prefer that too," Parker said. "This way." He waved towards the street.

"Are we supposed to trust them?" I asked Zeke. Who knew what was waiting for us if we followed them? Just because there was a ring of truth to what the twins said didn't mean it was all true. It made sense that Tully's father would draw him away, out of trouble if someone was going after Zeke and the rest of us. Apart from that, it might all be crap.

"No," Zeke said. "But we were headed that way anyway. If they want to tag along, they can. But they can tag along in front of us, where I can keep an eye on them."

"The brotherly love is touching," Hunter said ironically.

"You fuckers kidnapped Abbie twice and you think I should trust you?

Fuck that." Zeke gave them a withering look and picked up the suitcases before nodding at the twins to walk ahead of us.

"Only because we were ordered to," Parker said as if that made everything all right.

"If you were ordered to suck your brother's cock, would you do it?" Penn asked.

Asher responded with a choking laugh. "Good question."

"Which brother?" Hunter asked.

Penn stopped for a moment to stare at him. "Does it even matter?" He started walking again, shaking his head to himself while he muttered something about sick fucks.

Hunter shrugged. "I guess not."

He didn't answer the question, which was probably just as well. I didn't think anyone wanted to know. If he would do that, then who knows what else he would do?

We stepped towards the street which seemed darker than usual. A couple of streetlights were out near the front of the hotel. Were they like that last night?

"Everyone play it cool," Zeke said. "We're just leaving the hotel to go somewhere else."

"I'm always cool," Asher said. He was probably as on edge as I was, but he didn't look it. Neither did Zeke. In fact, all of the guys except Penn looked calm. Penn looked as agitated as always.

I doubted he knew the meaning of the word relax.

"Yeah, Asher is almost as cool as me," Landon said. "And I'm almost as cool as Channing."

"Ah, that's sweet," Channing said. "But you're much cooler than I am."

"Can we have this conversation when we're not tiptoeing through the streets of Perth?" Jackson asked.

"Yeah, what Jackson said," Zeke muttered. "Only, we're not tiptoeing. We're just walking along, minding our own business. Maybe waiting for a car to take us to the airport or some shit. Okay?"

"Wouldn't that make talking about who is the coolest fit into this scenario?" Asher asked. "For the record, it's me."

"I've always thought so," Hunter said. "Drums are definitely the coolest of all the instruments."

Asher turned his face towards him. "You really think so? Wait, I still hate you for what you did to Abbie." After a moment he added, "But you're right, they are the coolest."

"That's such bullshit," Penn said. "What's cool about smashing sticks against drums?" He rolled his eyes, but his tone was more joking than I had ever heard from him before. Presumably the guys razzed each other out a lot about having the best instrument. That was an argument they could have until the end of time and never have a resolution. They would always think their instrument was the biggest and best. Like their cocks.

"Only everything," Asher said. In the same tone of voice, he added, "Zeke."

"I see them," he said.

Landon stepped up beside me. "Don't look," he said softly. "Keep your eyes ahead, otherwise they'll know they've been noticed."

"Who is it?" I whispered. Because nothing says 'subtle' like a loud whisper.

"Dunno," Landon said. "I'm not looking either." He had one hand on his suitcase and slipped the other into mine. He gave me a reassuring squeeze, then kept hold of my hand. It felt as natural as holding any of the other guys' hands.

"Shouldn't there be a car waiting?" Zeke asked Jackson. He sounded like the perfect, spoilt rock star.

"You should know by now that I'm good, but I can't perform miracles," Jackson snapped. He was also perfectly in his role as the hassled manager. "Let me call them."

"You do that," Zeke told him. He stopped at the edge of the road and put the suitcases down.

"It's so hard to get good help these days," Asher said.

"Depends how much you pay them," Parker said. "If you pay people well enough, you'd be surprised the things they will do for you."

"Like kidnapping?" I gave him a dirty look.

"And sucking off your brother's cock," Penn said. The keyboardist looked disgusted.

"We never said we would do that," Hunter said.

"You didn't say you wouldn't," Asher said. "Getting closer."

"Yep," Zeke agreed. They were both looking roughly over my shoulder, behind me. That wasn't disconcerting at all.

"Can you dance?" Landon asked.

I gave him a funny look. "Dance? I mean, I have some moves onstage."

"No, I mean like waltz." He left his suitcase where it was and put his hand on my waist. While I was still as confused as hell, he twirled me around, then swept me off to the side.

"What—"

I barely got the word out when Zeke was scooping up one of the suitcases and hurling it right where I was standing a moment earlier.

I hadn't seen the man coming up behind me, but I saw him now, as the case struck him right in the stomach. He staggered back, holding his torso and grunting in pain.

That would be why Zeke wanted us to bring our suitcases. I thought they might slow us down. It hadn't occurred to me he might use them as a weapon. Why would it? This whole crazy life was new to me.

"Fuck yeah." Parker punched the air. "That was epic, bro."

Zeke didn't look so impressed. "Friend of yours?"

He and Asher stepped towards the man who looked to be in a lot of pain. Of course, Zeke had thrown *my* suitcase at him. All those heels were bound to do some damage.

Fuck yeah.

"No one I know," Hunter said.

"Me neither," Parker agreed.

Zeke and Asher grabbed the man by his upper arms and hauled him up so we could all see his face.

"Does he look familiar to anyone?" Zeke asked. He looked around at us all.

I shook my head. "I've never seen him before, that I remember." I was half expecting it to be the guy who threw the can at me, but it wasn't. It would make sense if he was paid to do that to piss me off or get to Zeke, but I suspected he was just some random asshole. This guy on the other hand...

"Who hired you?" Zeke asked insistently. He shook the guy so violently I was surprised I didn't hear his bones rattle. As it was, Asher barely hung on to his other arm.

"Fuck off," the man grunted. "I was just minding my own business."

"So this isn't a gun in your pocket?" Asher asked.

While Zeke held the man still, Asher dug into his pocket and pulled out a small handgun.

"What do you know, it *is* a gun." He smiled and put it to the man's temple. "It's been so long since I've used a gun, my finger is getting twitchy." He could have been talking about the weather or the colour of his favourite T-shirt.

I should not have found what Asher was doing hot, but I did. He smiled, but the expression in his eyes was pure violence. I had no doubt he would kill the man to protect the rest of us. And the rest of us would help him bury the body.

"People will notice if you kill me out here," the man said.

Asher looked thoughtful. "That's true. That doesn't mean we can't kill you somewhere else." The sound of him cocking the gun echoed through the street. "On the other hand, I'm impatient."

"How about you don't kill him and he tells us how many people he's working with?" Zeke said. He sounded perfectly reasonable.

"I can work with that," Asher agreed. He poked the gun harder into the man's temple. "You know the question."

"Enough," the man growled. "You'll all be dealt with."

"Wrong answer, motherfucker," Asher said. "Try again."

"Fuck off." The man closed his eyes and braced himself.

Asher shrugged. "Thanks for bringing a gun with a silencer."

He pulled the trigger.

CHAPTER
NINETEEN
TULLY

"WHAT DID you really bring me here for?" I asked.

We'd spent enough time on pleasantries. Now Xavier needed to tell me the truth.

"A man can't give his son a record label?" Dad asked. He toyed with his empty beer glass as though he intended to use it as a weapon. We both knew he'd have to be faster than me if he did.

"It's a done deal, by the way," he added. "I've already had Onyx Riot Records transferred into your name. You're welcome."

"Why?" I kept a loose grip on my glass to match my posture. Most people would be fooled, but I knew he wouldn't. He knew I was ready to act in the blink of an eye if I had to.

Hopefully him knowing that would make it unnecessary. I was younger, stronger and faster than him. And I had a feeling I had a fuck ton more at stake.

"Cut the crap. We both know you brought me here as a distraction."

He looked unruffled at the accusation. "And yet you came. Why would you do that if you were concerned about my motives?"

"Because if you're up to something and it involves my band, I know they can take care of themselves," I said easily. "What I don't know is why you'd be up to anything. You've been supportive up until now."

More than Zeke's family. More than a lot of families who preferred their children to chase solid careers, not dreams. Music was a tough industry. Most people didn't make it. It made sense for parents to want their kids to have a stable life and always know where their next meal is coming from.

"I am supportive of you," he said. "That's why you're here. But I have other interests as well, and those interests sometimes clash with yours."

"Meaning?" I wished he would just get to the point.

He took both hands off his glass and leaned forward to place his elbows on the table. "Meaning I'm doing business with a new partner here in WA. Very lucrative business. So lucrative, one record label was a virtual drop in the ocean."

"Congratulations," I said carefully. There was a chance this new business venture was above board, so maybe this was a good thing and, like he said, he just wanted to give me something nice.

"Thank you," he said. "We'll all be a lot better off after this."

"After what?" I asked. "Can you stop talking in riddles and tell me what the fuck is going on?"

"The first rule of business is to get people to trust you," he said reasonably. "When you started out, you had to prove to your fans you could be consistent, right? And versatile. Otherwise, they don't know what they're getting and they won't bother with you. It's the same with any industry, creative or otherwise."

"Trust is an important commodity," I agreed. "In families as well as in business." That was my not subtle way of telling him he needed to be careful not to lose my trust.

"That's true," he agreed. "Sometimes you have to be ruthless to prove your trust to the other party."

"So you're here in Perth for a hostile takeover?" I asked. Those were an accepted part of business, even though they pissed people off at times.

He smiled slightly. "You could say that. My new business partner has a rival he'd like to put out of business."

That was nothing new either. Plenty of businesses wanted to push their rivals out of the marketplace. Destroy the competition and form a monopoly. It was a practice I wasn't interested in pursuing if I took over his business some day.

"What has that got to do with me?" I asked.

His long hesitation sent goosebumps all over my body.

"Dad?"

"His rival is Reuben Brantley. Dante Fiorelli doesn't only want to put him out of business, he wants to take them all out." He shrugged.

My blood went cold. The Fiorellis. I should have guessed it was something like that. They were bound to make a move at some point.

"All of them?" I echoed. Being right that something was going down gave me absolutely no satisfaction. What did was the knowledge Zeke would have gotten everyone out by now.

"You know Zeke wants nothing to do with his brother, right?"

"The apple never falls far from the tree," Xavier said. "Either way, the decision wasn't mine. I'm doing what I have to do to look after our interests."

"*Your* interests," I corrected him. "I don't want anything to do with anyone who would want to kill Zeke Brantley." The rest of the family, maybe, but not Zeke.

"You're not seeing the bigger picture," Xavier said patiently, like I was an eight-year-old again. "He's collateral damage. We stand to become extremely wealthy from this business deal. I'm not asking you to stop doing your music thing, just don't stand in my way on this."

My hand tightened on my glass. "You want me to sit by and let you kill my friend? Because of money? Are you out of your fucking mind?"

"He's just one person," Xavier said. He looked like he was running out of patience now. "I'll deal with the rest of them over on the east coast. When that's done—"

I picked up the glass and slammed it down on the table so hard it shattered. "Will you listen to yourself? You think you can kill one of my best friends and my life is just gonna keep going on as normal?!"

"There is no reason why it can't," he said. "The band is still—"

"Not the band without its lead singer," I snarled. "Not the same without our friend as a part of it. More than a friend, he's a brother to me. All of them are more family to me then you have ever been."

I was vaguely aware of shards of glass in my fingers, and blood starting to drip onto the table. Shallow grazes. Nothing that would stop me from playing, but I made my point.

His eyes flashed with anger. "After all I did for you, this is how you repay me? I've let you live your life and play around at being a guitarist, even after all the training your mother and I put you through."

"Training I didn't ask for," I hissed. "Training I was never suited to."

He responded to that with a chilling laugh. "You're perfectly suited to it. You just don't want to admit it. It's in your DNA. In your blood. Someday you'll admit that to yourself. When you do—"

"I will never admit that, because it's not true," I said, colder.

I could have been sitting across the table from a complete stranger. One who apparently had a hard time separating murder from money. One who seemed to have put his conscience aside. If he ever had one.

He sat perfectly still and looked at me across the table top. "Isn't it? Wouldn't you kill me right now if you had the chance? If you thought it would save your friend?" He lifted his chin in challenge.

I thought about it, and on some level, he was right.

But he was also wrong.

"In defence of my family, I would do anything," I said. "But I'm not going to kill you in cold blood. I'm not like you. Just like Zeke isn't like his family. Just like Asher isn't like his. Just like— okay, Penn is as uptight as his family. But the rest of us are our own people. I know you tried to mould me in your own image or whatever shit it is they say, but I'm not you or my father or my mother."

I referred to my biological parents now. How would I have turned out if they were still around? I might well have become the man Xavier accused me of being, but I hoped not.

I wanted to be so much better than my dark past, or my family's dark past.

"I will tell you this." I pulled out a couple of pieces of glass from my fingers and pressed my thumb against a deeper gash. "If you come after me or anyone else in the band, or anyone related to or close to the band, I will act in defence against you. And anyone you send after us."

"It's too late for that," he said. "By now, Zeke is dead. My people had orders not to let anyone stand in their way. *Anyone.*"

Chills went through me again. "Meaning if I hadn't come here tonight..." Who the absolute fuck was this man? I had no idea who he was. Maybe I never had.

"I knew you would," he said. "There was never any risk."

"There was a risk," I said. "I had plans. I could have said no. Then who would you have left your business interests to? You would have made all that extra money, and for what?"

"Like you said before, I could have a comfortable retirement," he said easily. "I would prefer to hand things over to you but whatever happens, happens."

"Who wouldn't want a business built on the blood of his best friend?" I asked sarcastically. "You can shove it up your ass. And your fucking record label. I don't want your bribe."

"That's still a done deal," he said evenly. "Either way this goes down, it's in your name. It's yours to do whatever you want with. Or sell it. I don't care."

I wanted to tell him to screw himself and the label, but I knew the label would have employees and, if he dumped this on me, I would have to do something sooner or later.

When I calmed down, which might take quite a while after this conversation.

I could so easily pick up one of the bigger pieces of glass and cut his throat with it. Right here, right now. I might not feel bad about doing it.

Okay, he might be slightly right about who I really was. The difference was, though, I wouldn't act on my feelings of suppressed violence. Not unless I had to. That depended on him.

"This is where I tell you I never want to see you again," I said coldly.

I doubted he'd shed a tear if I was dead now, at the hands of whoever he sent after Zeke. I wouldn't shed a tear for him if he stepped out the door and was hit by a car. I might cry for the driver.

Fuck, I actually thought I loved the man. Right now all I had for him was disgust and anger.

"You'll change your mind when you realise how much I've done for you," he said. "How rich our family will be."

"There's more to life than money." It was easy for me to say, I had lots of it, but it didn't make me who I was. My music was more important to me than my bank account balance. Getting up on stage and making people happy meant everything to me. Doing it with people I loved was everything. The best, most important thing I could be doing with my existence.

"That's true," he said. "The one thing more important in life than money is power. The more money you have, the more power you can buy. With power, you can make real change. Think about that for a while." He rose from his stool. "Don't forget to call your mother for her birthday." Just like that his personality snapped back to the warm man he'd pretended to be all these years.

How did I not see through it sooner?

I didn't answer him. I turned and walked away.

My real family needed me.

CHAPTER
TWENTY

ABBIE

"FUCK, I hate having brains on myself," Asher complained. He flicked at the front of his shirt for the hundredth time.

"Get changed then," Zeke said. "People are going to ask questions if they see you like that."

They talked so calmly, as if Asher hadn't blown a man's brains out a couple of minutes before.

Meanwhile, I was still trembling. Landon hadn't let go of my hand. Or I hadn't let go of his. I wasn't sure I could. The feel of his calloused skin in mine was the only thing keeping me from losing my shit right now.

Asher killed a man. Right in front of us. He hadn't even blinked. None of them had. No one but me. I was still trying to keep myself from vomiting.

Zeke caught the man and lowered him to the ground, while Asher wiped the gun with his shirt. When it was clean of his fingerprints, he shoved it into the man's pocket.

"We'll take care of this." Hunter and Parker lifted the man between themselves and carried him away like he was their drunk friend.

"You trust them to get rid of that?" Penn asked. He looked disgusted, as usual. It was impossible to tell what he thought about this whole thing.

Zeke shrugged. "Worst case scenario, someone sees them with a dead body. Not our problem. Our problem is keeping an eye out for more trouble. We need to find Violet and the others."

I almost forgot about the other band. Thank fuck they hadn't seen what I saw.

"Why do they call it a silencer?" I asked. There was nothing silent about it.

Muffled, but still loud. The traffic roaring past the hotel must have covered the sound, because no one came running.

Unless they were hiding.

Fuck.

"They don't sound like they do in the movies do they?" Landon asked. "The movies get a shitload of things wrong. Especially that."

"Yeah." A man was dead and we were talking about movies? This was all sorts of wrong.

The worst part was, I didn't feel bad for the man Asher killed. He would have killed one of us and I doubt he would have lost any sleep over it. Witnessing it was horrifying, but I was already halfway to accepting it.

We stopped for a minute while Asher changed his shirt and shoved the dirty one into a rubbish bin.

With any luck, the bin would be emptied before they found the dead body. If they found it. If there was anything these guys and their families were good at, it was disposing of corpses.

I guessed it went with the territory.

"You okay?" Landon asked me. "You look rattled."

"I'm getting used to seeing death," I said. "But a killing that close up is a new thing for me. Are you not rattled?"

"I've seen all sorts of shit," he said. "That was relatively clean."

"Said the guy who didn't get brains on him." Asher pulled his clean shirt over his head and tugged down the hem.

"You were the one who grabbed the gun," Zeke said. "You can have a shower at the airport." Apparently he wasn't too worried about blood and brains, because he stepped over to give Asher a quick kiss on the mouth.

"Count on it." Asher kissed him back. "Maybe you and Abbie can join me." He deepened the kiss and ground his groin against Zeke's.

Trust him to be horny after killing a man.

"We should focus on getting the fuck out of here." Zeke reluctantly pulled away and adjusted his pants.

Asher sighed. "I hate cockblockers." He grabbed his suitcase and we headed to the front of the hotel where it was better lit.

"There you lot are." Violet stood with her guys outside of the hotel. "I thought you must have left without us."

"Nah, we got a little sidetracked," Asher said lightly.

"There's a taxi," Zeke said. "Violet, you and the guys take that and go to the airport. Jackson, go with them. See if you can organise an earlier flight, and make sure the rest of the crew are okay. We'll be right behind you."

I thought Jackson might argue, but after a moment he nodded.

"Abbie?" he asked.

"She stays with us," Zeke said firmly. "Don't worry, we will get the next taxi. We'll be a couple of minutes behind you at the most."

Jackson's mouth was tight, but he gripped his suitcase and waved for the other band to head for the taxi in front of him. "Stay safe."

"You too," Zeke said.

We all kept watch while they climbed in. I don't think anyone breathed until the taxi pulled away into the traffic. I certainly didn't.

"Now would be a really good time for another taxi," Asher said.

"We could call for one?" I said. Figures there was never one around when you needed one the most. Unless you were at the airport. There was never a shortage of them there. That wasn't helpful, since we had to get there first.

Zeke pulled out his phone and tapped at the screen. "Looks like it's going to be at least ten minutes. Keep your eyes out for any trouble. That first guy was sloppy. Another one might not be."

We formed a loose circle, back-to-back to cover every possible angle.

I faced the road, to keep an eye out for the taxi. I knew what to look for with one of those. With an attacker, they could look like anyone. They didn't exactly walk around with a big sign on their forehead saying, 'I've come to get you.'

Of course not, that would be way too convenient. Jerks.

The longer we waited, the more sweat gathered on my palms and under my arms. Landon didn't complain about holding my sweaty hand, but it couldn't have been comfortable. I was glad he didn't let go. I was about ready to run into the traffic, pull over the first car and tap on the window to insist they take us out of here.

Since that shit didn't go down well in movies, then I assumed it wouldn't go down very well in real life either. With my luck, I'd probably get *run* down.

"Hey," Asher moved to stand beside me. "I'm sorry you had to see that. You know that shit doesn't happen very often, right? I usually don't go around killing people."

"I know," I said quickly. "It was him or us. I just—"

"Seeing someone shot in front of your eyes isn't nice?" he suggested.

"Not nice is an understatement." I looked at him intently, searching his face in the glow of the streetlights. I realised how little I knew him. How little I knew any of them. I mean, if I had to guess, I would have thought Zeke was the one most likely to kill someone. Seeing Asher do it sent my mind into a spin.

"I'll understand if you don't want anything to do with me," he said softly. "If seeing that side of me is too confronting."

"It's not like that at all," I said quickly. "What you did…it doesn't change how I feel. I need to get my head around it, that's all." After a moment, I was forced to admit, "It…it was kinda hot."

"But people coming after us isn't?" he guessed.

"It really isn't." I nodded. "I can't think of anything less hot."

"Not even Penny in his underwear?" Asher grinned.

"Me in my underwear is hot," Penn growled. "Almost as hot as me out of my underwear."

Now there was a mental image to make my panties wet. Fuck, with everything that was going on, these guys could still make me hot as hell. Wasn't there a law about that or something? If not, there should be.

Oh, right, the guys would break it anyway.

"That's true," Asher agreed. A fraction of a second later, he added, "Zeke, are you seeing what I'm seeing?"

"Yep," Zeke said. "Taxi is three minutes out." He tucked his phone away and crossed his arms like he was impatient, but unaware of anything out of place around us.

"What are you looking at?" I managed to keep myself from glancing around wildly. So far, all I saw was traffic gliding past. It was starting to thin as it got later in the night.

"There's a few people, I count three," Asher said. "Right now, they look like tourists, but they look cagey as fuck to me. It's a matter of knowing what to watch out for."

"Right." Was that a skill I would learn with time? Hell, was it one I wanted to learn? I didn't want to think nights like this would become normal. At some point, I wanted a regular life, without looking over my shoulder for people with guns or drugs, ready to shoot me or threaten me or any of the guys.

"Dude with a cat T-shirt," Penn said.

"That makes four," Zeke said.

I spotted a car with a taxi sign on its roof as it slid around a corner. "I don't know if it's ours, but a taxi is coming."

"Get ready with your suitcases," Zeke said.

I wasn't sure if he meant to get ready to get into the taxi, or throw them, but he had the handles of his and mine in either hand. Every muscle in his body looked poised and ready.

"Girl with black jeans," Channing said. "She looks harmless, but I used to date a girl who looked like that so…"

"Always be suspicious of anyone who looks like your ex," Asher agreed.

"I would definitely be suspicious of anyone who looked like any of your exes," Penn said. "Mine too, come to think of it."

"We both had dubious taste in the past," Asher said. "Lucky that's in the past."

I made a note to ask about that later. Although, I doubted their exes were as horrible as mine. That was a pretty high fucking bar.

The taxi started to slow and came to a stop at the curb right in front of us.

"Thank fuck," I muttered. I went to open the door.

"Wait," Zeke said. He trotted around to the driver's side and leaned in to talk to the driver. After a tense minute or two of waiting, he straightened up and nodded. "Okay, get in."

"Quickly," Landon told me. He opened the door and pushed me inside, while Channing put their suitcases in the back of the car.

The guys hurried to do the same with the rest of the suitcases and Asher slid in on the other side of me. Penn sat by himself in the third row of the long SUV and Zeke climbed in beside the driver.

"What was that about?" I whispered to Asher. Could he tell if the driver was dubious by just talking to him?

"Zeke was watching to see what our would-be assailants would do," Asher whispered. "My guess is they melted back into the shadows when we started to get into the taxi. This is much too public of a place for them to attack us. The taxi has security cameras all over it and a radio to call for help faster than we could grab out a phone."

"Does that mean we're safe?" I asked.

"Not until after wheels up," Asher said reluctantly. "We can breathe a sigh of relief when we're in the air."

That wasn't what I wanted to hear, but at least he was honest. The question was, where was Tully?

CHAPTER
TWENTY-ONE

TULLY

I DIDN'T BOTHER to check the hotel room, they would have been long gone by the time I got there.

Instead, I dropped from a trot to a walk half a block from the hotel and moved silently through the shadows.

This, right here, was one of the reasons I preferred black. Also, it looked good on me.

Part of my training involved learning to keep myself from being seen. And if I was seen, to keep myself from being noticed. Okay it was difficult to avoid being noticed when people knew who I was just by looking at me, but before I was famous, I was good at blending in amongst the crowd.

Now, I had to be content with blending in amongst the shadows.

All of my instincts told me danger was right in front of me. Almost close enough to smell. To taste. To hear.

Unfortunately, night vision goggles weren't standard issue uniform for rock stars. I made a note to discuss that with Jackson and Zeke. We could start a new trend.

Okay, probably not. I should stop distracting myself with useless thoughts. I shouldn't have had that beer with Xavier. I should have stayed with the band and Abbie. They should be at the airport by now, at least on their way there.

A shuffle up ahead was faint, but unmistakable.

I stopped mid-step.

"This fucker is heavy," a voice said.

I frowned. I knew that voice. And if he was here—

"Maybe you need to lift more weights," said the other twin.

Yep, there he was. What the fuck were the Brantley twins doing still in

Perth? And who were they carrying? My heart skipped a couple of beats. My mind raced ahead.

Was it Abbie or one of the guys? If it was, this was the evil twins last night breathing. They wouldn't hurt a hair on any other members of my family.

I started forward slowly, focusing on the sound of their voices and movement. They didn't seem to be trying to hide their presence. Or if they were, they weren't doing it very well. Both of them knew better than to be that sloppy. They must be feeling confident.

That was cause for concern.

I made out two shapes in the dark. No, three. One was lying on the ground at their feet. Who was that?

"I need to learn that move," one of the twins said.

I thought it was Parker.

"You already know how to shoot someone in the head," Hunter said.

Parker chuckled. "I meant the suitcase. The way Zeke threw the suitcase at this asshole was pretty fucking epic, don't you think?"

Hunter scoffed. "I could do that. Easy. Probably better than Zeke too."

"No offence, bro, but Zeke is taller and stronger than us. He could probably throw us better than you could throw a suitcase." Parker sounded admiring.

I frowned. What did all of this mean? Had the Brantley twins got wind of what my father and Dante Fiorelli were cooking up and decided to team up? That made a twisted amount of sense. Reuben was an asshole, but he didn't want his brother dead. And Zeke didn't want to get dead. If he had to work with his brothers to achieve that, he might.

"I didn't know Asher had it in him to shoot someone in the head like that," Parker added. "His big brother would be proud of him."

That wouldn't be good news for Asher. Wait. Did he say Asher shot someone in the head? Was that who was lying on the ground? There were a couple of ways to find out, but one included waiting, and the other meant confronting the twins right now.

Since I wasn't afraid to take them both on by myself, I stepped out of the shadows as though I hadn't been standing there listening. In fact, I might have swaggered like I was out for a stroll.

"Evening," I said casually. I chuckled as one of the twins jumped in fright.

"Fucking hell," Parker said. "Where did you spring from?"

"Here and there," I said lightly. "What's happening?" Apart from them looking suspicious as shit. I took a half a second to glance down. I didn't know the man. Presumably the hole in his head was from Asher, if what the twins said was true.

"Apart from trying to save our brother from your father?" Hunter asked. "No, that's about it." Judging from the tone of his voice, he was wondering if I was in on it with my father.

"My father, as you call him," I said slowly, "has been telling me about how he's no longer aligned with your brother. Reuben that is." I knew they knew that, but I added it anyway.

Before they could jump to any conclusions, I added, "I told him my loyalty is with Zeke, not him. I don't give a fuck who he's in bed with, whether it's Reuben or Fiorelli. Frankly, anyone who comes after my friends is my enemy."

Even if that meant I had to work with shitheads like the twins.

"Anyone who comes after our brother is our enemy," Hunter said. "I guess that makes us friends." He crouched to pull something out of the dead man's pocket. In the dim light, I recognised a gun.

I snorted a laugh. "That's a stretch. Where is Zeke? And the others?" Was Abbie okay?

I held my hand up before they could answer. There it was again, the scuffle of footsteps.

"There were others with him?" I whispered.

"Without a doubt," Hunter whispered back.

"Then you should know, they weren't just after Zeke. They'll kill any Brantley they find." After what they did to Abbie, I should probably slip away and leave them to their fate, but if Zeke worked with them, maybe they were redeemable.

Okay, that was the second big stretch of the last five minutes, but any trouble between them and whoever was coming would give me a chance to get further away.

"Well, that's not very nice," Parker said. "For the record, the others went to the airport. We decided to take care of this asshole to give them time to get out of the country."

"We need to get out of the state," Hunter said.

"We all need to get out of here," I agreed.

Before we could take a step, the light from a phone shone on us all.

I blinked against the sudden glare.

"Look, a two for one," said the voice behind the phone. A man around the same age as me, I guessed.

"Three," said another voice. "The boss said if his son gets in the way it's too bad."

"Tully." Hunter threw me the dead man's gun and pulled out one of his own.

I caught it and ducked out of the light. I raised the gun and aimed it at the man who held the phone. I squeezed the trigger.

"Shit!" The phone dropped to the ground and the light went out. The man clutched his arm.

There, that was better. It was hard to get a kill shot with the light in my eyes.

Without it—

I squeezed the trigger again and the man dropped.

"Shit, dude," Parker said. "That was epic."

"Yeah." I ducked down into the shadows. There were at least another two of them and no doubt they were armed. "We should go."

I listened, trying to discern exactly where the other assailants were. When the first shot rang out, I heard a shuffle of feet as they'd retreated. I wasn't sure exactly how far. No more than a metre or two. Three at the most.

"Going sounds like a plan," Hunter agreed. He ducked as a shot rang out. It hit the wall right where he had been standing. Good to see he was smart enough to know speaking would make him a target.

I reached out with my foot and kicked the phone in the direction I guessed the attackers went. Footsteps moved in response.

I hated guesswork, even educated guesswork, but I raised the gun and took the shot.

Judging by the grunt and a moment later, a thud, my third bullet found its mark. How many did I have left? I couldn't be sure, but that last attacker would have a fair idea where I was right now.

I slipped out of the shadows and moved as swiftly and silently as I could to the other side of the alley.

A shot rang out, striking the wall where my head was a second ago.

Not today asshole, I thought.

I raised the gun to fire back, but one of the twins got a shot off first.

The attacker let out a howl of pain and rage. Not a kill shot then. Enough to distract the man.

"Let's go," I hissed.

I turned and moved towards the entrance of the alley, mindful there might be other attackers at this end too.

I paused a few metres from the entrance.

Someone was there. At least one. They weren't moving but I almost heard them breathing or thinking. Something.

Put it down to well-trained instincts if you want, but I knew.

I put out a hand to stop the twins and hoped they would see it and whoever was waiting didn't see me. I heard the smallest sound of surprise from one of them, but they stopped. I should have known Zeke's brothers would be as good at this shit as he was.

Alone, I started forward again. I kept every sense open wide. Especially the one that told me my life depended on me being careful. Xavier had written me off, but I wasn't done yet.

My finger lightly on the trigger, I kept the gun aimed forward, letting my instincts point it, and me in the right direction.

There were two people there, waiting. One just inside the alley, to the left. The other maybe two metres away, to their right.

I visualised the way they stood and waited, guns in their hands. I pictured their posture, the way they held their heads. They would be listening, the way I was. But they wouldn't have had my training. There was being quiet and careful, and then there were the skills of an assassin.

The two couldn't compare.

The question was, how many bullets were left in the gun? If any. If it was none and I tried using it, I was screwed. If it was one, I could take out one of the enemies, but then I'd have to contend with the other one. If it was two, piece of cake.

The problem was, I couldn't guess. Guessing got you killed.

I stopped and tucked the gun into my back pocket. Yeah, I know, don't put the gun in your pants, but I had nowhere else to put it.

I dropped down low and kept moving forward. My first target—the person on the right. The one on the left was already inside the alley. They would be easier to pin down once I took out the first one.

I circled slowly around until I was behind the person on the right. Another man, judging by their size and shape. They still faced the alley, waiting for us to appear.

You're out of luck, fucker, I thought.

I surged forward, hooked an arm around his neck and the other over his mouth. With the right amount of pressure, I was able to wrench his head to the side, twisting and breaking his spine. His death was almost silent. The only sound was the scuffle of his feet on the ground.

I lowered him down as the other would-be attacker turned.

His face was caught in the light of a distant window. I saw his mouth form an O of surprise and the fear in his eyes. The glint of the gun in his hand as he raised it towards me.

"Tully—"

I struck Xavier with an uppercut he taught me, the heel of my palm smashing into the bottom of his jaw. His head snapped back so hard he only had time to make a terrified gurgle.

"Thanks for the training," I said as he started to fall.

I grabbed him but I had no remorse as I lowered the body of my adopted father to the ground.

CHAPTER
TWENTY-TWO

ABBIE

"WE'RE on the flight out in ninety minutes," Zeke said as he slipped into the chair beside me. "We have thirty minutes to check in our bags and go through airport security into the lounge area." He rubbed a hand over his forehead and sighed heavily.

I felt as tired as he looked. "I can't wait to get out of here. Perth was one of my favourite places to visit, but now..." I couldn't get out of the city fast enough.

"Yeah." He tucked an arm around me and settled me so my temple rested against his chest. "At least no heads turned up without their bodies."

I let out a choking half laugh. "Just bodies with their heads." I glanced over to where Asher sat, talking in a low voice to Landon. I couldn't hear what they were saying, but they both looked as cheerful and light-hearted as ever.

Anyone watching them wouldn't suspect a thing.

Asher must have sensed me looking, because he turned toward me and grinned.

Did he really have to be so fucking hot?

Yes, yes he did. I still couldn't believe he cared about me as much as I cared about him. I was nothing special, just Abbie Hart, the singer who went through some rough times but managed to come out the other end more or less intact.

But here I was, sitting in Perth airport, having watched one of my boyfriends kill a man, after another threw a suitcase to disarm him. Tully was fuck knows where, and everyone else was acting like it was just another day in Wolf Venom.

A sensible person would run for the hills. All I could do right now was worry about the band's lead guitarist, and count my blessings I met the guys.

"At least we know who did it this time," Zeke said. "No mysterious stalker."

"Just a mysterious drummer." I smiled back at Asher.

Zeke's chest rumbled as he laughed. "You think Asher is mysterious?"

I looked up at him. "Not as mysterious as you."

The smile he gave me was both heart and panty melting. Fuck, these guys were going to be the absolute end of me.

"I'm not mysterious," he said. "I'm just a regular guy who is in love with you. And I kinda sing okay."

"I love you too," I said warmly. "You sing amazing but there's much more to you than that. Every day I find out new things about you. Just in the last couple of hours, I found out you throw suitcases. You didn't even break it."

"You're welcome." He leaned forward to kiss my nose. "Every day I learn new things about you too. I look forward to a lifetime of finding things out."

My heart fluttered at the idea of a lifetime with him. That sounded just about perfect.

"I want that too," I said softly. After a couple of minutes of silence, I broke it by saying, "How long do we have?"

He rolled his hips to the side so he could pull out his phone and check the screen. "Twenty minutes." He put his phone away and looked towards the entrance to the airport. "I don't want to leave without—"

"Tully," Channing said.

"Exactly," Zeke agreed.

"No." Channing stood up and waved. "Tully!"

I rose and looked in the direction he pointed.

Sure enough, Tully was weaving his way through the crowds.

He looked terrible. He was as hot as hell, as always, but his clothes were rumpled and his eyes looked haunted.

I trotted a few steps to close the gap between us, and threw my arms around him. He embraced me so tight I thought he might never let go.

"Are you all right?" The question was rhetorical. He was clearly not all right.

"Nope," he said softly in my ear. "But I will be. Thank you."

"What for?" I asked.

"Being you." He kissed me on the mouth, tasting my lips with his tongue, before he drew back and offered a faint smile.

He kept one arm over my shoulders and glanced past me. "You clowns better have brought my suitcase." He sounded like himself again, although the hardness in his eyes was unchanged.

All of the guys exchanged glances.

"Did anyone think to bring Tully's suitcase?" Asher asked. He scratched the side of his head. "I mean, I guess you can buy stuff in Singapore. Or in one of the shops in the lounge before you leave."

Tully sighed.

Asher grinned. "Just kidding. Of course we brought yours. We don't leave anyone behind and that includes dragging their shit along with us."

Tully shrugged. "I would have shared your stuff with you. We're about the same size aren't we?" He tilted his head as though sizing Asher up.

"Nah," Asher said lightly. "My underpants are way bigger. They have to be."

"Dream on," Penn said. He was the only one still sitting in his chair. He gave Tully a nod, then went back to scrolling through his phone.

"Jealousy is a curse, Penny," Asher told him.

Penn ignored him.

"Hey," Zeke greeted Tully. "It's good to see you in one piece." He gave the lead guitarist a bro hug. "What took you so long?" His tone was light but what he was asking was obvious.

"Tidying up some loose ends," Tully said. "Your brothers say hello by the way. We helped each other out a bit. They needed to clean up some more, and then they're headed back to Sydney. They're satisfied most of the loose ends are tied up for now."

He closed his eyes and let out a long breath through his nose. "Xavier Lang won't be a problem anymore."

"Fucking hell," Zeke said softly. "Are you sure?"

"I handled it myself," Tully said.

I frowned. "Is that…"

Tully nodded. "My adoptive father. It was him or me."

That explained the haunted look in his eyes.

"Oh, my god," I whispered. "Tully…" He killed his adoptive father? How was he keeping it together? I would be a complete mess.

He squeezed my shoulders. "He came after my family and didn't care if I was collateral damage. It is what it is. Now, don't we have a plane to catch?"

"Yes we do." Zeke clapped him on the shoulder. "We have ten minutes to check in. Let's get going. Everyone keep your eyes open. There might be another loose end or two out there."

We hurried to grab the handles of our suitcases and drag them towards the check-in counter. Fortunately, at this time of night, there wasn't much of a queue. We only had to wait behind a couple of other people before, one by one, we passed our suitcases through and had a tag with our destination woven through each of the handles.

With Tully on one side of me and Zeke on the other, I stepped through airport security without a ping. Presumably no one put a tracker on me.

Yet.

We walked through to the lounge and made our way down to gate sixteen. It was so quiet, we managed to get seats together, but away from everyone else.

While we waited to board, Tully told us about his conversation with Xavier and altercation with the assailants and the Brantley twins.

"How far behind us do you think they'll be?" Asher asked.

"Hunter and Parker?" Zeke asked. "I'd like to say they'll be on their way back to Sydney by morning, but honestly... Probably the flight behind ours."

"Is there any chance they'll keep protecting you?" I asked.

He shrugged. "If they're told to, they will. If they're told to fuck with us, then that's what they'll do. With any luck, Dante Fiorelli will keep them distracted for a while longer. I like it better when they're on our side."

"Yeah, I didn't want to have to kill them," Tully said. "There's been enough killing tonight."

"More than enough," Landon agreed. "Any more of it and Channing and I are going to start feeling left out."

"I don't think killing is something you need to join in on," I said dryly.

"I'd prefer not to," Landon said. He was leaving something unsaid, but I decided not to ask what it was. Another time maybe. The last few hours were overwhelming enough without learning some dark secret from the blue haired bassist too.

"Did it cross your mind I might be feeling left out too?" Penn asked. He frowned at Landon.

Landon scratched his chin. "Did you want to take part?"

"Not particularly, no," Penn said. He went back to looking at his phone.

Landon and Channing shared a look and shrugged.

"There you are," Jackson said as he and the other band appeared from another part of the lounge. They were carrying boxes of food and trays of paper coffee cups. "I figured you'd be hungry."

"I could eat," Asher said.

"Now you mention it, I'm starving," Channing said.

I wasn't particularly hungry after what I saw and what Tully told me, but I needed to eat. We all missed dinner and it was nearly eleven o'clock at night.

Jackson and Blaise handed out boxes of burgers and cups of coffee.

I would gratefully drink the coffee at least. Thank fuck it existed.

Once I opened the cardboard container with my burger inside, I realised I was hungry after all. The smell hit my nose and my stomach rumbled.

Asher raised his cup towards Jackson to toast him. "Best manager ever. Who else would remember to feed us?"

"Every manager," Jackson said dryly. "I wouldn't be good at my job if I let the label's star act starve to death.

"You wouldn't be very good at your job if *you* starved to death," Violet pointed out.

"That too," he said around a mouthful of burger. "Are we good?"

"For now," Zeke agreed. "I'll feel better when we're in the air. Until then, play it cool but keep your eyes open." He bit into his burger like he hadn't eaten for days.

To him, it probably felt like he hadn't. He was a big guy with a healthy appetite. He burned it all off onstage, so he could afford to eat whatever he wanted.

Maybe I should be more energetic. I could eat more donuts.

Jackson nodded, then turned to Tully. "All good with you?"

"Good enough," Tully agreed. "Better for having this." He nodded towards his dinner. "I might have a bottle or two of wine when we get to Singapore."

"I'm in," Asher said. "But make mine beer."

"We could all use a night out," Zeke said. "One that ends better than this night out did."

"What could be better than sitting in an airport eating hamburgers?" Landon asked. "Surrounded by my brothers, sister and Abbie. We made it this far."

"I'll drink to that." I toasted him with my coffee cup.

"I need something stronger than coffee," Penn grumbled.

"Don't we all," Tully said. "As long as it's not stronger than alcohol."

While Penn gave him a dark look, I gave Tully one of surprise. That was the first time anyone alluded to Penn's past since that article Zeke stopped me from reading out loud when we first met in the studio.

"No one is having anything stronger than alcohol," Jackson said firmly. "Eat up, we'll be boarding soon."

While I finished my burger, I watched Penn. He looked more pissed off than usual. And something else.

He looked troubled.

CHAPTER
TWENTY-THREE
ABBIE

"I CAN'T HELP NOTICING we haven't upgraded to private jets yet," Asher said as we were waiting in line to board the plane.

"Are you kidding?" I was feeling a lot better, having eaten. "Still no king-sized bed? How is that even legal?"

Considering everything I saw tonight, having a plane without a big bed was the most logical thing to have happened. That included those burgers. I wasn't sure anyone should be eating shit like that. It couldn't be good for us. Hell, I could say the same about coffee and alcohol, but life was too short to deprive yourself too much. Right?

"You're all shockingly deprived," Jackson said ironically.

"You said depraved wrong," Asher grinned.

"That too," Jackson agreed. "I'm not sure if it counts if you're proud of it."

"Of course it does," Asher said. "Admit it, that's one of the things you love the most about us."

"Yeah, it has nothing to do with how much money we make for him in the label," Landon said with no hint of resentment.

"Nothing at all," Asher agreed. "Our awesomeness might also play a part."

"It certainly isn't your modesty," Jackson told him. He showed the flight attendant his phone with his boarding pass on it, and was waved ahead of us.

Rather than following Violet and her band onto the plane, he stood and waited for us. He didn't bother to hide his concern. His eyes were glued on the space behind us, watching for trouble.

Every so often, I looked over my shoulder, waiting for someone to jump out at us. Or hand me a box containing a head. Or throw a can at me or even just an insult.

The flight staff did nothing more than glance at me and my boarding pass before they waved me forward. For the most part, their eyes were on the guys.

"Great show last night," one of them said. She was a gorgeous brunette, with legs for days and perfect makeup.

There I was, dressed in a knee length skirt and a singlet top, my hair wound up into a messy bun. They probably assumed I was a tour staff, or one of the guys' sisters. Either way, I felt frumpy and plain next to this woman.

"Thanks." Asher grinned at her. "We had a lot of fun. Perth is always amazing. The label is forever saying, *come on, you guys don't want to play there, it's so far away from everything else.* But we always insist, right Zeke?"

"Fuck yeah," Zeke agreed. He also gave the woman a warm smile. "It's awesome over here. I wish we could spend more time."

"I wish you could too," she said in a flirtatious voice that made me want to punch her in the face. "I'd be happy to show you around next time you *come.*"

"That would be great," Asher said. He elbowed Zeke. "You hear that, babe?"

For the first time, the flight attendant looked uncertain. She clearly hadn't expected that from two big, muscular guys with a reputation for being with a different woman every night.

"I did," Zeke said. He seemed to be enjoying himself all of a sudden. He draped an arm over Asher's shoulder. And then, for good measure, he draped one over mine.

I was starting to feel sorry for the flight attendant, who didn't know where to look now.

"We should get on board," Zeke said. "Wouldn't want to delay the flight."

The attendant shook her head. "Um, Yes, right. We wouldn't want that." She looked at me like I was from another planet. Her eyes widened further when Tully stepped to the other side of me and took my hand.

I just smiled at her and shrugged. Somehow, the guys managed to make me feel beautiful, even when I was looking scruffy as shit. It was just another one of their many, many charms.

I managed to ignore the whispers of both flight attendants as we stepped away into the tunnel and headed into the plane.

"You guys are shit stirrers," Jackson said. "You know that, right?"

"What?" Zeke asked. "She was flirting with my boyfriend in front of my girlfriend. What was I supposed to do? Weren't you the one who said there's been enough violence tonight?"

"That was me," Landon said.

Zeke nodded slowly. "So it was. My bad."

"I had to step in, because Abbie is my girlfriend too," Tully said. He smiled at me with his beautiful, wide mouth and squeezed my hand.

That was the first time he called me that. I liked the way it sounded. It seemed now I officially had three hot boyfriends. Maybe it should have felt more complicated, but it didn't. It felt right, natural and incredible. I wouldn't change a thing about it.

"Of course you did," Penn said. "None of you can help yourselves."

"It's not my fault if I'm irresistible," I told him.

He snorted. "You said irritating wrong."

"How much longer are you going to be an insufferable asshole?" I asked him.

"How does until the end of time sound?" he retorted.

"About accurate," I replied. "Maybe you should try not being a dickhead once in a while. You might surprise yourself by enjoying it."

"I did try it once," he said. "Worst thirty seconds of my life."

"I'm surprised you lasted that long," Asher said.

Penn flipped him off.

I laughed and stepped through the door and onto the plane. My heart was racing like crazy. A lot of it was the burning desire to get the fuck out of the country, but a good percentage of it was because, even with nasty words, the banter with Penn made me wet as hell.

We made our way to the back of the plane. I felt like I was getting on the bus to go to high school. Of course then I always sat at the front. But I wished I was one of those kids who dared to sit at the back and get up to whatever they did back there. Not that I necessarily wanted to be bad, but the kids up the back seemed to have a freedom the rest of us didn't.

It was all an illusion, I know that now, but back then it seemed like they had all the fun.

Now it was me having all the fun. Me and my amazing, sexy guys.

Tully, Asher, Zeke and I sat in a row of four seats. Penn, Landon and Channing sat across the aisle from us. Jackson, Violet and her men sat directly in front. That arrangement worked perfectly when Zeke threw a blanket over us both and snuck his hand up my skirt.

Only if anyone came down the back of the plane to use the toilet would they suspect what was going on. Hopefully everyone went before they boarded the plane.

Zeke parted my thighs gently with his fingers and teased my panties aside. He stroked his fingertips over the front of my pussy before delving down lower to my clit and folds.

He leaned in to whisper, "You're so wet."

"You're so hard." I slipped my hand down onto his cock. He felt like a rock under his jeans.

"Need some help there?" Asher asked from the other side of Zeke. He slipped his hands under the blanket and undid the front of Zeke's pants.

"I could use some help." Zeke lifted his hips to help pull them down far enough to free his erection.

While Asher traced circles around his tip with his fingers, I worked mine down lower to massage his balls. At the same time, I tucked up my knee so Zeke could slip his fingers inside me.

On the other side of me, Tully palmed my nipples through the fabric of my shirt, and guided my other hand to his already bare cock which was hidden by another blanket.

It wasn't easy, but I managed to coordinate my movements so my hands were sliding up and down both guys at the same time. Judging by the way the blanket in front of Asher rose and fell, Zeke was doing the same to him.

We all fell still and looked as innocent as we could as an attendant checked on us and made sure the overhead baggage lockers were all closed, ready for takeoff.

Something was ready for takeoff all right. Several somethings. All of them hot and hungry.

The attendant, not the one who flirted with the guys, gave us all a look like she knew we were up to something, but moved on. She probably saw a million crazy things while on the job. This might be tame in comparison. At least we weren't going to get drunk and violent.

Drunk maybe. Violent no. At least, I hoped not.

She moved back to the front of the plane as the aircraft started to taxi towards the runway.

"Almost made it," Asher said.

"That was quick," Zeke said teasingly. "I know I have mad skills, but I didn't realise I was that good."

Asher laughed, low and husky with desire. "Yes you do, and you are, but I'm not that quick. I'll leave that to Penn."

"Fuck off," Penn said from the other side of the plane. Apparently he was listening in to the conversation.

I glanced over to see him with a blanket over his lap. Evidently he was doing more than just listening. Remembering him watching us the other night made me even hotter. I was one lucky girl.

Asher might not be that quick, but I was. It only took a dozen or two strokes of Zeke's fingers on my G spot, while the heel of his hand rubbed my clit, and Tully rolling my nipples between his thumb and finger, for me to come.

I bit my lip to keep from screaming, because that might have resulted in the plane being turned around and us being kicked off.

We hadn't come this far to have me risk us by having an orgasm. That would definitely be the worst orgasm ever.

Even after I came, Zeke and Tully kept working me until the pressure started to build again.

Underneath me, the plane rumbled and started to pick up speed. As it did, my hand picked up speed as well. Both guys rolled their hips and thrust into my fingers, their breathing quiet but ragged.

I couldn't help feeling powerful and sexy with both of their cocks in my hands. I enjoyed making them feel good and the fact they all wanted me was even hotter. A girl could certainly get used to this. Maybe with a king-size bed next time.

Although, we were making do pretty well.

The engine roared. The front wheels of the plane lifted off the ground. A second later, the back wheels followed.

A second after that, I came again at the same time Zeke and Tully came in my hands. My stomach dropped with the momentum of the plane at the same time my orgasm rose. It was a strange sensation, but not unpleasant. It was heightened by the feeling of warm, pearly cum on my fingers.

Asher was only a couple of moments behind the other guys, just as the sound of the wheels tucking up into the plane echoed through the cabin.

"We fucking made it," Zeke said with relief.

"We made it fucking," Tully said with a grin.

We all laughed and sagged together under our blankets. All I wanted to do now was curl up and sleep until we arrived in Singapore.

And hope like fuck the trouble didn't follow us all the way there.

CHAPTER
TWENTY-FOUR

ABBIE

"I NEVER THOUGHT I'd be glad to be away from Australia," I said.

Our suitcases even made it all the way here with us.

Bonus.

Maybe things would start to turn around from now on. We could all use a bit of good luck and relaxation for a change. And by relax, I mean focus on the tour.

There was nothing relaxing about it, really, but we all loved performing, so it never felt like a chore. Well, unless people were throwing cans at us.

"Same here." Tully slipped his hand into mine as we walked through Changi airport.

This must be the cleanest airport in the world. It was certainly right up there at the top. I felt dirty walking through it, like I should have washed before I came somewhere so clean and tidy.

Thank fuck it wasn't too far to the hotel where I could have a shower.

"I know we shouldn't rest completely, but I feel like I can breathe now," Asher said.

"At least until the next flight," Zeke said. He nodded towards a board which showed the next ten or fifteen flights which would land. It didn't show another one from Perth, but it wouldn't be long. No one doubted Hunter and Parker would be on board.

"I'm starting to feel like we're on that show where they travel around the world and teams race each other," Landon said. "We got on the first flight out of Perth, but sooner or later they'll catch up with us at some kind of challenge. With any luck, it'll be a singing or dancing one, not eating gross food." He made a face in disgust.

"I wish that was all it was," Tully said. He looked tired, and his usual smile and good humour were nowhere to be seen.

Killing your father was something anyone would take time to bounce back from. Even though they weren't related by blood, I knew Tully loved the man. Things must have been extreme for him to do what he did.

So far, he hadn't gone into much detail. I hoped at some point he would open up to me about what really happened.

"We all do," Zeke said. "Let's pretend for a while we're just rock stars on a world tour."

"I can pretend that," Asher said.

"Of course you can," Penn said. "You've been pretending to be a rock star for years."

Asher turned and stuck his tongue out at Penn. "You're just jealous of my good looks."

Penn snorted.

"I'm sorry to interrupt your charming conversation," I said, "but I need to use the ladies room."

They all hesitated.

"I can go in by myself," I told them. "I'll only be two or three minutes. Promise."

Zeke reluctantly nodded. "We'll be right outside. If you need anything, just shout."

"Anything at all." Asher grinned.

I patted the drummer on the cheek and slipped into the women's toilet. As tempting as his offer was, I felt messy. I wanted to shower before I got intimate with any of them again.

I hurried past the basins and into the area that held the cubicles.

I didn't pay much attention to anyone else who was in there with me, I just locked the door behind me and did what I needed to do.

As I reached to undo the latch, heavy footsteps stopped outside the door.

My first instinct was to freeze. I reminded myself the guys were outside. Close enough to hear me if I screamed for help. Assuming I could actually do that in time.

The footsteps paused for maybe half a minute, then walked on.

You're just being paranoid, I told myself. After everything that happened, a little bit of paranoia was understandable. Just because we got out of Perth, didn't mean everything was suddenly perfectly safe.

I decided to play it cool but keep my eyes and ears open. I stepped out of the cubicle and walked over to the sink to wash my hands.

I jumped as someone appeared behind me in the mirror.

"Abbie?"

I stared at his reflection, eyes wide.

What the fuck?

I knew the man who stood behind me. The former owner of Onyx Riot Records and, very briefly, my lover.

"Pete? What the hell are you doing here?"

———

Thanks for reading! The story continues in Saving Abbie books 4-6

ALSO BY MAGGIE ALABASTER

Pucking Hardened Hearts

Dusk Bay Demons

Puck Drop

Breakaway

Power Play

Brutal Academy

Book 1 Heartless

Book 2 Cruel

Book 3 Vengeful

Court of Blood and Binding

Book 1 Song of Scent and Magic

Book 2 Crown of Mist and Heat

Book 3 Sword of Balm and Shadow

Book 4 Whisper of Frost and Flame

Dark Masque

Book 1 Bait

Book 2 Prey

Book 3 Trap

Novella A Very Dark Masque Christmas

Saving Abbie

Book 1 Pitch

Book 2 Pound

Book 3 Session

Book 4 Muse

Book 5 Rhythm

Book 6 Encore

Novella Venomous

Saving Abbie books 1-4

Saving Abbie books 4-6 + Venomous

Ruthless Claws

Book 1 Ivory

Book 2 Crimson

Book 3 Elodie

Harmony's Magic
Book 1 Summoned by Fire
Book 2 Summoned by Fate
Book 3 Summoned by Desire

Shifter's Vault
Book 1 Discarded
Book 2 Deceived
Book 3 Disgraced

My Alien Mates
Book 1 Star Warriors
Book 2 Star Defenders
Book 3 Star Protectors

Academy of Modern Magic
Book 1 Digital Magic
Book 2 Virtual Magic
Book 3 Logical Magic
Complete Collection

Summer's Harem
Book 1: Shimmer
Book 2: Glimmer
Book 3: Flicker
Complete collection

Short reads
Taken by the Snowmen
Jingle All the Way

Also by Maggie Alabaster and Erin Yoshikawa
Caught by the Tide
Book 1–Pursued by Shadows
Book 2 Pursued by Darkness
Book 3 Pursued by Monsters

ABOUT THE AUTHOR

Maggie Alabaster writes reverse harem romance.

She lives in NSW, Australia with one spouse, two daughters, one dog, and countless birds.

Shop direct from Maggie! Store

Sign up for Maggie's newsletter! Sign Up!

Join Maggie's reader group! Join here!

Follow Maggie on Bookbub! Click here to follow me!

Check out Maggie's website- www.maggiealabaster.com